SWEET VENOM OF TIME

THE FORBIDDEN SAGA OF AMIR & ELIZABETH

BLADE OF SHADOWS
BOOK SIX

SARA SAMUELS

BLADE OF SHADOWS

BOOK 6

Sweet Venom of Time

SARA SAMUELS

FAMILY

LAZARUS
AMARA
JOHN JAMES
JACK JAMES
THEADORA
MATHIAS
CORA
RAUL
ALINA
ANGELO
SCARLETT
BALTHAZAR
TRISTAN
BLADE
OF
SHADOWS

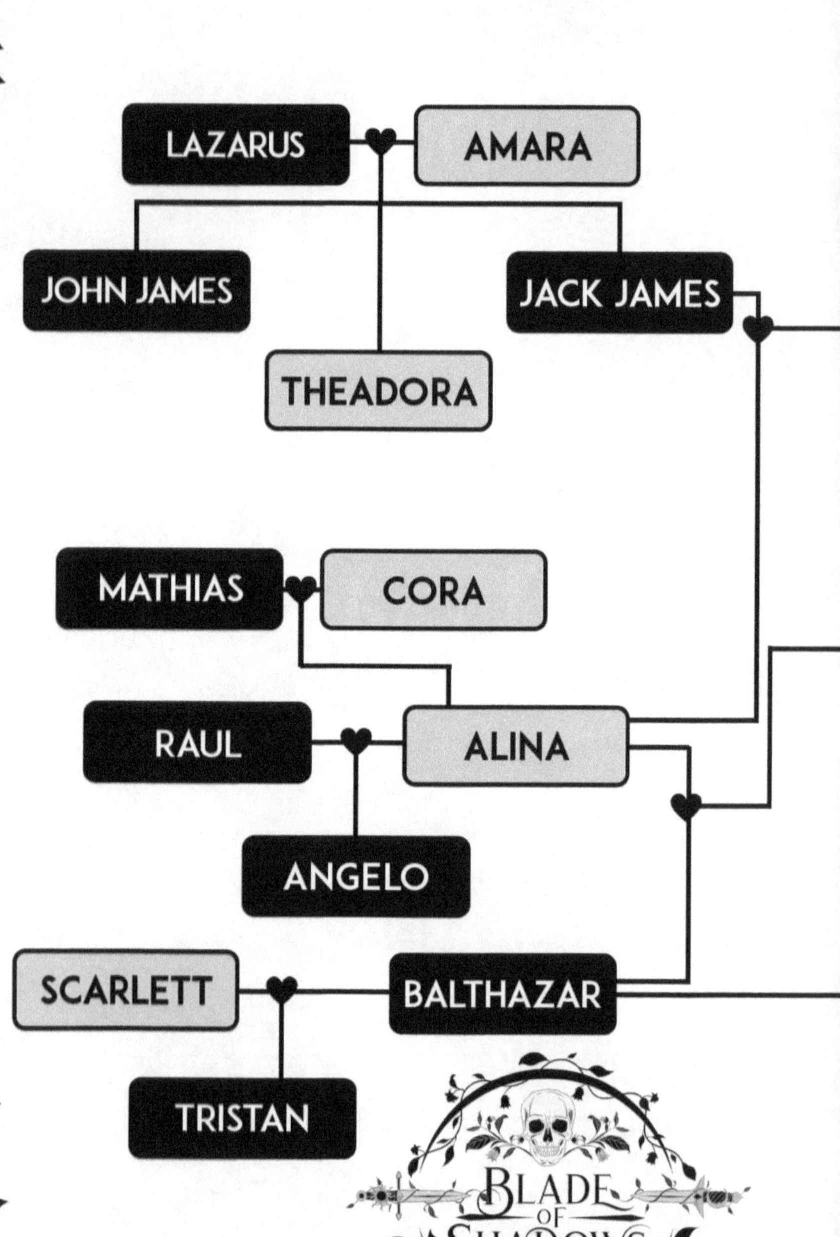

TREE

ELIZABETH
AMIR
REYNA
OLIVIA
ROMAN
ROSIE
LUNA
EMILY
MARCELLIOUS
LEO
ZARA
ASTRID
MEYA
REVNA
TOVE
FREYA

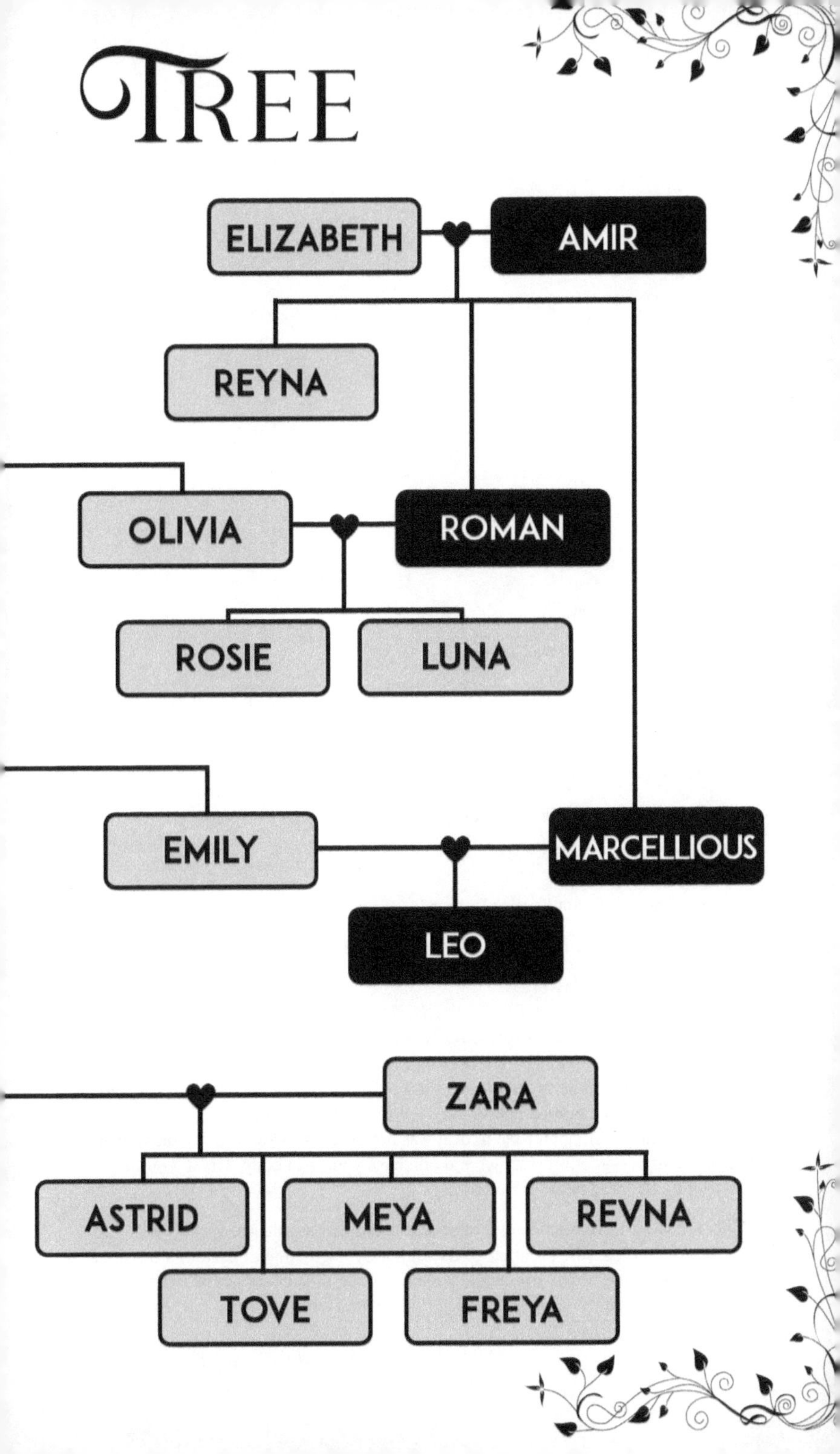

Sweet Venom of Time

Book 6 in the Blade of Shadows series

Published by Sara Samuels

Denver, CO 80237

First Edition

Copyright © 2025 by Sara Samuels

All rights reserved.

Cover image copyright Krafigs Design

Editing and Proofing by Charity Chimni

Formatting Storytelling Press

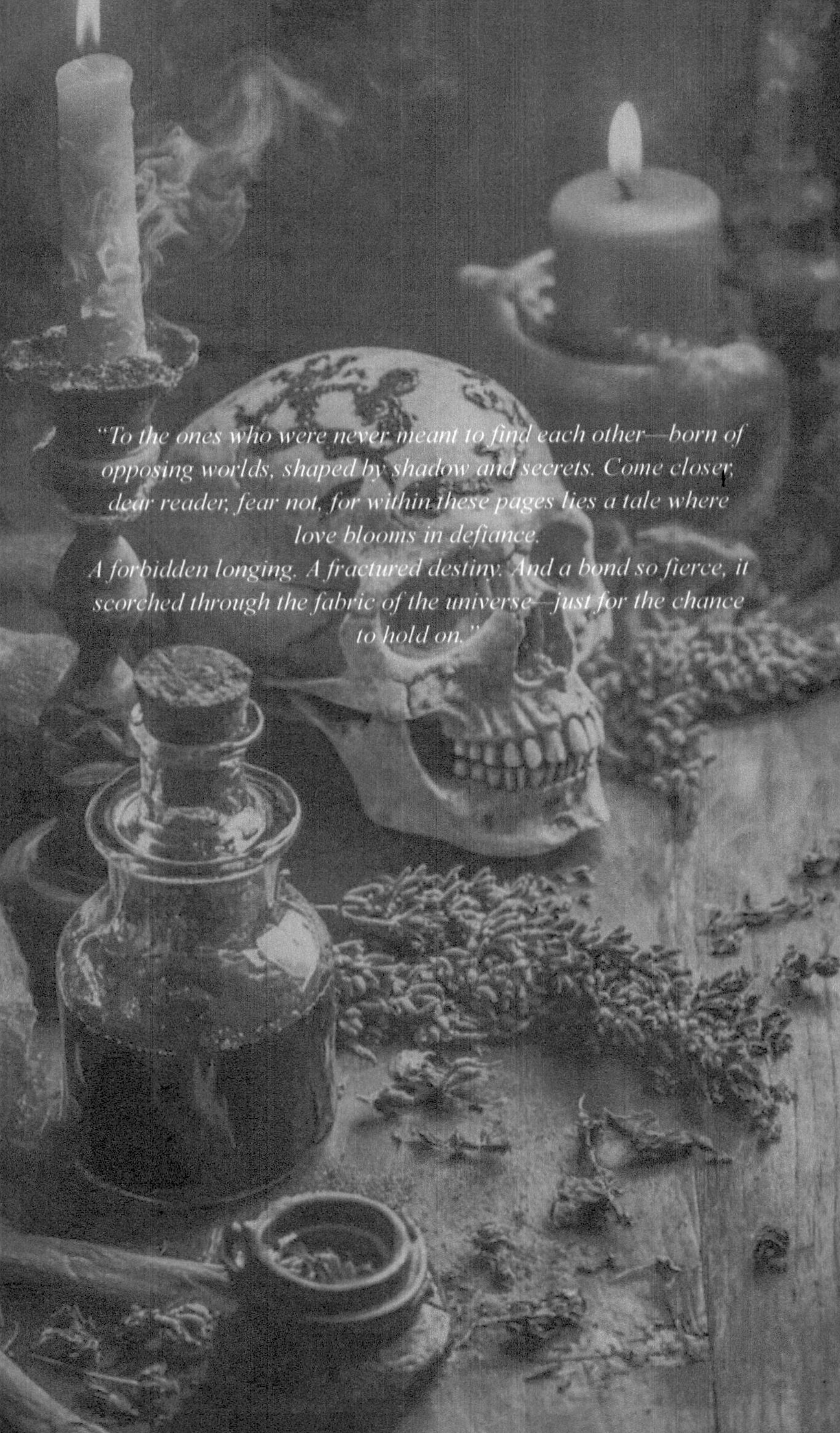

"To the ones who were never meant to find each other—born of opposing worlds, shaped by shadow and secrets. Come closer, dear reader, fear not, for within these pages lies a tale where love blooms in defiance.
A forbidden longing. A fractured destiny. And a bond so fierce, it scorched through the fabric of the universe—just for the chance to hold on."

AUTHOR NOTE

Dear Reader,

Thank you for returning to the shadows.

This story is unlike the others. It is the beginning before the beginning—the forbidden tale of Roman and Marcellious' parents, and the love that defied everything—fate, blood, and the Timehunters' wrath.

Here, you will finally hear Amir Hassan's voice—the very Darkness you met in Book 5—unraveling his past, his secrets, and the woman who changed everything. She was the daughter of a ruthless Timehunter… and she carried secrets of her own.

This book is best read after Book 5, when Amir first steps out of the shadows. Now, you will walk beside him into fate, deception, and chaos.

This story is the behind-the-scenes tale before Roman and Marcellious were born—the one that reveals who played a part in their eventual separation, how two doomed lovers found one another, and the hidden truths that will twist your understanding of everything you thought you knew.

With all my love and twisted devotion,

Sara

CHAPTER 1

AMIR

FRANCE 1761

Beneath the cloak of night, the rhythmic pounding of hooves against the hardened earth echoed like a haunting melody in my mind. The world had become a shadow-draped tapestry—fields lying dormant, villages silent, their shapes fading into the gloom. My men had gathered quickly, and beside me rode my steadfast companion, Moon Lee. We charged forward with unwavering determination, our hearts united by a single purpose—the utter annihilation of our enemy—the Timehunters.

Since I had razed Mathias' school of darkness and cast aside the vile demon Balthazar, I had become the blade of Lazarus' will—his wrath given human form. My men and I were more than exiles of Solaris; we were executioners, hunting Timehunters with the cold precision of a storm, wiping their taint from history.

We had been relentless. We had scorched the Timehunter society of the Polish Lithuanian Commonwealth, dismantled their stronghold in the Russian Empire, and shattered their influence in the Habsburg Monarchy. The Kingdom of Prussia had fallen at our hands; its Eastern Realm societies were ruined, and every trace of their corruption was purged brutally.

Now, our sights were set upon France.

"France is next," I declared, my voice cutting through the

night like the edge of a blade. My men, their silhouettes merging with the darkness, nodded in silent agreement.

Ahead, the city lights of Paris shimmered like stars scattered across the earth, a beacon of civilization and power. Gone were the days of the modest Parisi settlement and the subdued Lutetia of Rome's conquest. Now, it was a city reborn, the crowning jewel of the Age of Enlightenment, where philosophers and scientists sculpted the world with ideas as intricate as the opulent architecture that clawed toward the heavens.

Yet beneath that splendor lurked the rot of unchecked ambition—narrow streets choked with refuse, the air thick with the stench of unwashed bodies and festering waste. Overcrowded tenements pressed against the city's gilded heart, a stark reminder that enlightenment did not banish squalor, only masked it. And within this paradox, hidden among the grand avenues and labyrinthine alleyways, lay our quarry—the Timehunters of France.

"Le Manoir de la Rivière, 14 Rue des Cygnes, Île Saint-Louis." The address was carved into my memory, another mark in a long ledger of doomed sanctuaries. Île Saint-Louis, a bastion of affluence amidst the city's decay, harbored the festering core of Timehunter influence. The grand townhouses lining its quiet streets stood as monuments to their wealth, their facades gleaming with self-importance, oblivious to the ruin we carried in our wake.

"Prepare yourselves," I commanded, my voice low but tinged with finality. Another society would fall tonight. Another stain on the world would be wiped clean.

We moved like shadows, slipping through the silent streets, the hush of our advance mirroring the tension thrumming in my veins. The moon, a sliver of silver in the void, cast just enough light to glint off the steel at our sides. I pulled the mask over my face with muscle memory—The Black Wraith made flesh. This was more than mere cloth. It was bone. Vengeance sculpted into a grin.

The surface was a dead white, fractured with fine cracks like veins of old rage. Each line told a story—every failure, every betrayal etched into its design. The eye sockets were deep, hollow voids that swallowed light and mercy alike. No reflection, no soul—just silence.

The nasal bridge was narrow and cruel, and the cheekbones jutted out like knives. The jaw, hinged and hidden, moved if I needed it to—but mostly, I didn't. I let the mask speak for me. And when I did open it, the sound that came through wasn't a voice anymore. It was a ghost. A weapon.

The grin—always there, and cruel—was the final insult. Jagged teeth curled upward in a frozen sneer, as if daring the world to try and soften me.

It wasn't just a disguise.

It was who I became when the man inside wasn't enough.

With the mask on, there was no Amir. No doubt. No mercy.

To the Timehunters, I was not just a man. I was an omen—a harbinger of reckoning.

Only the Wraith.

The monster they whispered about in firelit corners.

The shadow they prayed never turned its gaze their way.

And tonight…

They would remember why.

Le Manoir de la Rivière loomed before us; its grandeur muted beneath the velvet shroud of night. Its towering facade, statuesque and imposing, should have pulsed with life—the hum of conversation, the distant strains of music, the flicker of candlelit debauchery behind gilded windows. But tonight, there was only silence. No light. No revelry. Just the hollow stillness of something unnatural.

"Something is wrong." The words slipped from my lips, barely a whisper—yet they fractured the quiet with chilling finality.

We dismounted, every movement measured, every breath controlled. The mist creeping in from the Seine curled around our steeds, shrouding them in eerie stillness. The absence of movement—the lack of servants, of watchful eyes behind drawn curtains—unnerved the most hardened among us. The manor should have been alive with the murmurs of a clandestine gathering. Instead, it stood cold and waiting, like a beast already feasted.

The air itself seemed to tighten around us.

Something was waiting inside.

And it knew we were coming.

I approached the manor's entrance, my fingers resting lightly on the hilt of my weapon, senses honed to the quiet language of deceit. Each step carried anticipation, unspoken dread. Had we been expected? Or had some other fate already claimed the souls within this accursed place?

The Timehunters never shied away from their excesses. Their feasts of flesh and indulgence were not mere revelry but a declaration of dominance—a grotesque display of power, a celebration of the lives they twisted and discarded. And yet, where the air should have thrummed with drunken laughter and debauched moans, there was only silence—a void where their wickedness should have flourished.

"Stay alert." The command left my lips like tempered steel, threading through my men, binding us with our purpose. We had come to purge. But first, we would unearth the truth lurking behind the manor's silent facade.

Our gazes met in fleeting exchanges, unease settling over us. The hush was oppressive, broken only by the muted clink of weapons and the distant echo of our boots against the uneven cobblestone. At the manor's grand entrance, I lifted the lion-head knocker, its cold brass biting against my skin. The heavy door shuddered as I let it fall—a single, resonant thud.

The door swung open with a slow, reluctant squeal.

And what lay beyond was not revelry but torment.

From within came sounds not of whispered pleasures but of suffering. Groans of anguish seeped through the darkness, chilling my blood.

We moved forward, steps cautious, the air thickening with something unseen—something wrong. The scent of rot and a deeper, hidden malevolence clung to the walls, weaving into the air. Ahead the ballroom doors stood, their gilded edges gleaming in the dim light. I put my palm against them, pushing just enough to part the gap, enough to see.

And what I revealed turned my blood to ice.

Bodies lay strewn across the marbled floor, not in the careless abandon of excess but in the convulsions of agony. Flesh blistered and peeled, dissolving like wax held too close to a flame, pooling into mangled remnants of what had once been dancers and courtiers.

"Stay here." The order was barely a whisper, yet it carried the force of command. My men did not protest.

Alone, I stepped through the threshold.

The stench of decay rushed to meet me, coating my throat with the taste of something vile. My boots met the floor with a sickening stick, the residue of ruined flesh grasping at the soles.

What had once been a chamber of opulence was now a grotesque tapestry of suffering. Boils marred faces frozen in expressions of unholy agony, their eyes wide with silent screams. Limbs twisted at unnatural angles like their very bones had turned against them. And through it all, the air pulsed with a sound that made my skin crawl—the rasping, wet gasps of the dying, each breath a futile plea for salvation that would never come.

I stood amidst the carnage; my heart hardened against compassion, yet my mind reeled. This was my duty—my purpose—to be the blade that severed the plague of the Time-hunters from existence. But someone, or something, had already claimed that finality before me.

Who else possessed the knowledge of such devastation? Who else harbored the will to execute it?

"Who has done this?" My voice, muffled beneath the Black Wraith's mask, was a whisper of bewilderment. "Who has usurped my role as harbinger?" There was no pride in the question, only the cold realization that my vendetta had grown more complicated. The path of vengeance had veered into unfamiliar shadows.

Stepping carefully over the misshapen remains of the Time-hunters—flesh sloughed from bone, limbs frozen in nightmarish contortions—I moved toward one of the dying, slumped against the wall. His breath rattled, and each rise and fall of his chest was a battle against the inevitable.

I knelt beside him, my gaze locking onto his pain-clouded eyes.

"Who did this?" The demand left my lips in a controlled murmur despite the chaos around us.

The dying man's lips cracked apart, a whisper like brittle parchment escaping.

"A vat… of smoke," he croaked. "Nobody saw… It filled the room, and then… darkness. The poison was—"

His head lolled. Silence swallowed the rest. He would speak no more.

A jolt of something primal shot through me—terror, nausea, a dread that curled through my veins. The macabre distortions, the bodies dissolving like wax under a flame… I knew this work. This was no earthly poison.

This was something far worse.

The only place I had seen alchemy of such unnatural malevolence was Solaris.

A shiver coiled down my spine—not from fear but understanding. Someone else possessed knowledge of those ancient mysteries. Someone else had brought that power into this world.

But who?

"Amir?" The voice of one of my men interrupted my thoughts, laced with quiet tension.

I exhaled slowly, my fists clenching at my sides. The hunt had just changed.

Turning, I found them framed in the doorway, black garb stark against the dim light, their expressions taut with trepidation. Their loyalty was unwavering, yet they could sense the wrongness of what lay before us. One of them staggered forward, dropped to his knees, and retched. When he had emptied his gut, he wiped his mouth with the back of his hand, cheeks flushed with both revulsion and shame.

I cast him a fleeting look of sympathy before addressing the five of them.

"Do you want the good news or the bad?"

A beat of silence. Then one of them answered. "The good."

I nodded. "The good news is that someone took care of our job for us." The words felt hollow as I spoke them, my mind churning with questions that had no answers. "The bad news is we don't know who did this."

My gaze shifted past them, just in time to catch a flicker of movement in the hallway—a shadow, clad in black garb eerily identical to mine, a mask that mirrored my own.

A phantom. A reflection. Or another harbinger of doom.

"Get out of here." My command came swiftly, clipped. I gestured toward the macabre ruin before us. "Burn it. End their suffering. I will return."

They hesitated only for a breath, then moved to obey. Their masks slipped into place, the faceless executioners they had been trained to be. The scent of oil and smoke permeated the air as they set to work while I stepped away from the dying embers of our mission and toward something far more dangerous.

The hunt was not over. It had merely veered into unknown terrain.

I pursued the enigmatic figure down the dimly lit corridor, my boots whispering against the polished marble. The manor's grandeur loomed around us, a mockery of civility against the darkness we both carried—me, the hunter of shadows, him, a phantom clad in the same guise.

Then, without breaking stride, he moved. A hand emerged from his cloak, swiftly uncapping a vial. He flung its contents behind him, and in an instant, a rolling, choking vapor polluted the air.

The moment it touched my lungs, I knew.

Poison. The kind only known in Solaris.

It seared like fire, scorching through my veins, setting every muscle ablaze. I staggered, doubling over as my body rebelled against itself—bones twisting, muscles coiling like serpents beneath my skin.

When I looked up, my quarry had vanished, swallowed by the darkness we both wielded.

The only proof he had ever been there was the lingering black cloud curling in the space where he had stood.

And the agony that was tearing me apart from the inside.

"Can't… breathe…" The words scraped from my throat, raw and ragged, as I clawed at the stone floor. My limbs warped, grotesquely reshaped, betraying their human form. Every nerve blistered, and every muscle rebelled.

Then, from somewhere beyond my spiraling senses, a voice bellowed—

"Pasha Hassan!"

My men. They had fulfilled my command and torched the manor and its wretched inhabitants to the ground. Now, they had returned to find their master undone.

"Can't… breathe…" I grated again as they came closer, their faces blurring into a shifting haze of shadow and firelight. Every word felt like a battle waged against the poison devouring me from within. "This has no cure… Made on Solaris."

No cure. Only death.

They wasted no time. Strong hands gripped me, dragging me from the ruins of that cursed place. The cool night air hit my sweltering skin, but it was a hollow relief against the torment searing through my veins.

"Get him to Lazarus immediately! We return to Anatolia at once!" The urgency in their voices was ironclad, an order carried by desperation.

Through the haze, through the writhing agony, one thought prevailed, sharp and insidious—

Who was this man?

And how did he possess a poison that should not exist outside Solaris?

CHAPTER 2
AMIR

I clung to the rough fabric of the tunic before me, my gnarled fingers digging into the coarse fibers as the horse's persistent gait jostled us forward. The pain had become a living thing inside me, a parasite coiled around my bones, contorting my limbs into warped echoes of their former strength. Sweat slicked my brow from exertion and the searing agony that pulsed with every movement. The opium meant to grant me mercy had only dragged me deeper into a fevered abyss, fueling tremors and visions that blurred the line between reality and nightmare.

The road to Anatolia stretched endlessly ahead, an unforgiving expanse between my torment and the fragile promise of refuge. My body—once a vessel of war, of command—had betrayed me, leaving my mind to drift between the shadowed borders of consciousness and oblivion.

"When can we time travel?" The words escaped from my lips, raw and strained, a fleeting spark of lucidity emerging from the fog of suffering.

"Soon, Pasha Hassan. The full moon is in two days. You must hang on," came the reply.

Moon Lee. A warrior of the Sioux tribe. My closest friend. He had fought beside me in our mission to eradicate the Time-hunters, his unwavering loyalty as steadfast as the walls of

Solaris before its fall. Now, he was my anchor, his back a pillar of strength against my failing body, carrying me forward as the darkness threatened to consume me.

We moved swiftly, yet not fast enough to outrun the perpetual onslaught of my torment.

"We're seeking healers along the way. No one has any remedies," Moon Lee said, the helplessness in his tone mirroring the despair coiling within me.

"No more opium," I hissed, each word a battle, each syllable a fresh wound. "It doesn't help. Nothing helps." Speaking was agony, each breath dragging through me like shards of glass, my resolve crumbling like ancient ruins beneath the siege of my affliction.

"Has the full moon come yet?" The question scraped from my throat, as torturous as the air charring my lungs.

"In two days, Amir. Two days. Hang on, my friend."

Moon Lee's voice softened, but desperation threaded through it. "Don't leave this world just yet," he pleaded. "I couldn't bear to lose you. It would be like losing a part of myself."

He attempted to lighten the moment with a joke, but reality crushed it before it could take form. Yet in the darkest hour, he was a constant—a lighthouse in the storm, guiding me through the violent waves of my suffering. His words, his sheer will, were a force against the creeping oblivion, a tether pulling me back from the abyss.

I focused on the rhythmic cadence of the horse's hooves, the beat offering a fragile semblance of stability. But this was a double-edged sword, each step a reminder of the miles yet to cover and the unknown that awaited beneath the looming specter of the full moon.

At last, moonlight pierced through the canopy above, silver beams slashing through the darkness, casting elongated shadows that danced along the ground. My men laid me down with a gentleness that belied their warrior hands, their faces etched with silent concern.

Each breath was torture. Each movement sent fire through

my veins. Bone and sinew rebelled, a grotesque war waged within my flesh.

Then, Moon Lee's voice rose—not the voice of a man, but something ancient, something vast. His words thundered through the night, carrying forgotten power as he chanted the sacred verses that bound time and reality.

The cool bite of steel kissed my palm, potent enough to anchor me in reality—if only for a breath—before surrendering me to the abyss. The air shimmered, rippling as if torn apart by an unseen force. With each utterance from Moon Lee's lips, my body contorted, shedding its broken form. I became something else—something unbound—a vessel of pure energy, ready to slip through the fabric of time itself.

And then, the sweet void of time travel took me once more.

A voice—my own, distant and raw—broke the silence as I resurfaced.

"Someone did my job in France," I complained, the words heavy, fractured, flickering like the last embers of a dying fire.

Lazarus stood above me, his towering authority reassuring and foreboding, a sentinel of shadow and stone. The underground palace loomed around us, its ancient walls breathing with the wisdom of forgotten ages. Beyond him, the vast Anatolian sky stretched endless and blue.

"Save your strength," he commanded, his voice a low rumble that seemed to vibrate through the earth itself. "The more you speak, the more energy you waste. It won't help you."

His hands hovered over me, sweeping across my ruined form with the adept knowledge of a man who had mastered fate. Yet his expression darkened.

"I've examined you as you fought to regain consciousness," he admitted. "The poison in your system is beyond my reach. It blocks my healing power."

The words struck harder than the pain. The one who could bend destiny, who had defied death, was powerless against the toxin that coursed through my veins.

Orders rang out. Shadows moved. Strong hands lifted me

again, the world tilting as the darkness at the edges of my vision finally closed in.

I surrendered to it.

And I knew no more.

Awareness crept back into my senses like a reluctant dawn. The earth was unyielding beneath me, my skin prickled with the slithering touch of serpents—cold, indifferent scales tracing the contours of my prone form.

Naked and vulnerable, I lay within the cavernous belly of stone, surrounded by a writhing, hissing congregation.

The air was dense with the musty scent of old rock and the acrid stench of reptiles. Beneath it lingered something fouler— the faint, unmistakable bite of decay. Death had marked this place, a grim reminder of my mortality.

The cavern walls were jagged, dust clinging to them like remnants of a forgotten time, shimmering in the torchlight. Snakes of varying sizes and colors coalesced in endless motion, their cold scales glinting like scattered jewels. Beady, malicious eyes watched me, forked tongues flicking as they coiled and writhed in eerie harmony.

"What are you doing?" My voice scraped against my throat, barely more than a whisper. My gaze locked onto Lazarus, standing motionless above me.

"This is an Inland Taipan," he explained with steady hands as he cradled the serpent. The stark, creamy yellow, white-speckled patterns of its underbelly were like ghostly imprints of something long forgotten. Its fangs lay bared, glistening with lethal promise.

"That snake's venom will kill me," I said, a sudden jolt of panic slicing through me for the first time in what felt like eons.

"No," Lazarus countered, his voice full of resignation. "The venom won't kill you. Not truly. Only three things can destroy the darkness within you—the Blade of Shadows, Belladonna poison if it lingers long enough in your veins, or the Noctyss flower. This venom?"

He exhaled slowly, watching me with an unreadable gaze.

"This will keep you alive."

Before I could muster a protest, Lazarus drove the serpent's fangs into my thigh.

An inferno erupted, the venom searing through me like liquid fire. A raw, unbidden scream tore from my throat—a sound I barely recognized as my own. The agony was overwhelming, obliterating thought, obliterating self. My body convulsed violently as it surged through my veins, a raging river of torment dragging me under.

It swallowed me whole.

When I clawed my way back to the surface of consciousness, the world was slow to take shape. My breath came in ragged gasps, the echoes of my screams still clinging to the cavern's cold air.

The snake dangled limply from Lazarus' grasp, its deathly task complete. With a flick of his wrist, he cast the carcass aside, and it landed with a soft, unceremonious thud against the stone floor.

The slithering mass that had constricted around me had finally withdrawn, retreating into the shadows. Yet their cold, scaly touch lingered like an unwelcome memory, sending shivers through my exhausted frame. With trembling hands, I brushed at my skin as if I could rid myself of the phantom sensation of their coils.

Weakness weighed heavy on my limbs, but beneath the exhaustion, something else stirred. A shift. A quiet, insidious pain that whispered not of destruction—but of restoration. The twisted sinews of my body began to unravel, the broken jigsaw of my bones slowly realigning. I could feel it happening, the venom forcing my form back together, piece by agonizing piece.

Lazarus snapped his fingers, the crack of it echoing through the cavern like a command.

From nowhere, several figures emerged. Clad in black robes, their faces veiled beneath Tagelmust-like coverings, they moved like specters—silent, knowing. Yet, I did not need to see their faces to recognize them.

They were my brothers in arms.

We had fought side by side for centuries, our bonds forged in blood, sweat, and sacrifice. Each scar we bore was a testament to our trials together, a symbol of unending loyalty.

"Carry him into the healing chamber," Lazarus commanded, his gaze never leaving mine. Then, turning to another, he added, "And bring me those subjects deemed worthless and beyond redemption."

Strong hands lifted me from the cold stone, their grip firm yet reverent. My body, still weak but no longer overridden by agony, felt weightless in their grasp.

The corridor ahead stretched endlessly, a tunnel bathed in the glow of torches. Their flames licked at the walls, casting elongated shadows that mimicked ghosts of the past. The black-robed men carried me with solemn strength, their footsteps a steady cadence in the hush of the underground. The chill seeped into my skin, a welcome reprieve from the feverish torment that had racked me moments before.

At last, we reached an ancient door, its wood groaning in protest as they pushed it open.

Inside, a dimly lit chamber unfurled before me, the air thick with incense and the timeworn scent of stone. Candlelight revealed a space of quiet opulence—silken tapestries hanging like whispers of forgotten tales, marble basins filled with scented water, and, in the center, a feather-stuffed mattress draped in fine silks that shimmered like the twilight sky over Anatolia.

They laid me down with the care of men who had carried the wounded before, the horror of war still etched into their souls. My head sank into the pillow, and for the first time in what felt like an eternity, I allowed myself the novelty of rest.

I closed my eyes, surrendering to the dimness, knowing the battles ahead would not allow such mercy again.

But the peace did not last.

The clank of chains. The scuffle of struggle. The ragged breath of men who knew they would not leave this room alive.

My eyes snapped open.

They stood before me—bound, shackled, terror apparent in every line of their faces. Their eyes darted wildly, searching for salvation in a place where none existed.

"You must feast, Amir," Lazarus' voice echoed through the suffocating tension, each syllable a decree that left no room for defiance. "Kill these men and restore yourself. Breathe in their essence. Let their souls be recycled into your body."

"Can't," I rasped, my throat raw, my body nothing more than a husk clinging to the last threads of life. "Too weak."

Lazarus did not hesitate.

Steel flashed, quick and merciless. A blade dragged across the throat of the first prisoner.

The scream that followed was full of terror, vibrating through my bones. Blood erupted in a violent arc, splattering against the dark stones in a monstrous bloom of crimson.

Lazarus leaned in, gripping the dying man's head, angling it toward me as the body convulsed, the final remnants of life spilling out.

And then, I saw it—

A wisp of ethereal energy untangled from the man's fontanelle, writhing as if seeking release. It shimmered, translucent and spectral, a soul severed from its mortal vessel.

Instinct took over.

I inhaled quickly.

The essence rushed into me, a searing, electric force filling my hollowed veins like life's first breath.

More followed. More souls, shackled and dragged before me; their life forces offered up to mend what had been broken.

With each one, strength seeped back into my limbs. Sinew knitted. Bone realigned. Flesh and spirit wove themselves whole once more. Slowly, my body remembered its former might, the fog of pain and poison thinning from my mind.

The ritual was macabre—a dance with death teetering on the edge of the abyss. Yet, it anchored me to life.

By the time the last essence seeped into my being, I was no longer at death's door. Not fully restored, but far from the fragile husk I had been—power thrummed beneath my skin, a continual hum like embers waiting to catch flame.

With the last of my newfound strength, I pushed myself upright. My legs held firm, no longer betraying me with their weakness.

The black-robed men who had borne witness to my gruesome revival moved with practiced efficiency, dressing me in fresh garments before guiding me from the chamber of horrors. Through arched doorways, we stepped into another world.

A private dining chamber, intimate yet regal.

The walls, whittled from warm stone, cradled the glow of iron sconces. At the room's center, a heavy wooden table gleamed beneath candlelight, its polished surface reflecting the golden hues of the flames. Two chairs with high backs stood at either end, waiting.

Tapestries adorned the walls, their weavings rich with the echoes of ancient hunts and long-forgotten battles. Above, the ceiling curved gently, painted with a night sky so deep and exquisitely detailed that the stars within it seemed to flicker with real, celestial light.

A plate of food awaited me—roasted meats, their aroma rich and inviting, fresh bread, still steaming from the oven, an assortment of cheeses, and figs dripping with honey. A feast fit for a king. Or perhaps, for a man who had clawed his way back from the brink of death.

I sat, my body still frail but my hunger ravenous. With each bite, I tied myself further to this realm as if it could cement my place among the living. Across from me, Lazarus watched in silence, his ageless gaze betraying nothing. He was patient—an eternal observer, a man who had seen the rise and fall of empires and understood the fragile balance between power and ruin.

I was no mortal but something beyond—imbued with the same dark power that coursed through him, bound to an existence that defied time. We were not truly immortal, only cursed with a lifespan that stretched across centuries, aging so slowly that the world seemed to wither around us. And yet, beings like us were not immune to the slow decay of existence, forever teetering on the brink of destruction.

I had proven that not long ago.

Course after course was placed before me, and I devoured each one with a fervor that surprised myself. Every mouthful was a silent victory, a reclamation of strength that now pulsed through my veins once more.

When I could eat no more, when my stomach begged for respite, I leaned back in my chair and nodded. The silent figures lingering at the room's edges moved like shadows, clearing the remnants of the meal with swift, skillful efficacy. The quiet clink of metal against porcelain was the only sound as they vanished into the periphery, leaving nothing behind but the faint scent of wine and spice.

Silence settled over the chamber, starkly contrasting the violence that had led me here.

Lazarus remained across from me, unmoving. Fingers steepled, gaze intent. Expectant.

Waiting.

"Thank you," I said, my voice rough from disuse. "For... everything."

Gratitude did not come quickly to a man such as myself. But Lazarus had pulled me from the brink, from the clutches of something far worse than death.

He inclined his head in acknowledgment, the gesture deliberate. "It is not often one gets to cheat death so brazenly, Amir. You carry a heavy burden—a warrior's heart and a destiny unfulfilled."

His words struck true. I felt my duty settle over me once more, as real as the pain that had racked my body. There was still much to be done—societies to dismantle, vengeance to be wrought.

I was Amir Hassan, the man who had walked through fire and shadow and emerged unbroken.

"Tell me what comes next," I said, my commitment hardening like steel tempered in the forge. "For I am ready to face whatever darkness this path holds."

Lazarus smiled then—a slow, knowing curve of his lips, an omen of secrets yet to unfold, of battles yet to be waged.

I leaned back into the cushioned chair, my fingers tracing the fine silks beneath me as I gathered my thoughts.

"Tell me everything. How did this happen?" Lazarus asked, his voice low—demanding answers.

The memories crashed over me like an obstinate tide, inescapable.

"When we arrived at Le Manoir de la Rivière, it was chaos," I began, the images still seared into my mind. "People lay paralyzed, their bodies contorted in agony. Their faces... marred with red boils, grotesque and swollen." I swallowed hard, bile rising in my throat. "Their limbs were twisted beyond recognition—far worse than what I endured. I've never seen anything so gruesome."

Lazarus' expression darkened, his gaze clouding as if he were staring into some distant horror only he could see.

"The poison is from Solaris," he murmured, almost to himself. "The noxious flower that creates it only grows there."

A frown creased my brow. "I know. But how is it here?"

"That," Lazarus said, his gaze narrowing with focus, "is what we must find out." His fingers worked absentmindedly along his jaw, tracing the tension there. "Whoever has the flower holds a weapon unlike any other. My power vanished when it was near me, so I had to use the snake to heal you."

His eyes lifted toward the ceiling, calculating.

"If they had the full-strength flower, you would not be here now. The one who created this poison isn't skilled enough to wield its true power."

A thought flickered through my mind, and I voiced it aloud. "Maybe it was Mathias and Salvatore who created the poison."

Lazarus shook his head slowly. "No. It's someone else. Someone who despises the Timehunters. Someone cast out, perhaps. A quest for revenge?"

He leaned forward, his hands clasped together, his expression grave. "We need to find out how they got it. The flower is eternal—someone knows where it is. And whoever holds it must have found it somewhere. That place is near one of the four portals to Solaris."

His voice dropped, weighted with certainty. "No one knows where those portals are. But if we find the flower, we find the portal."

His words settled between us like an unsolved riddle, a puzzle with pieces scattered across realms and time itself. I nodded, our next endeavor giving us purpose.

The hunt for the flower was no mere quest—it was a chance to strike at the heart of those who dared wield the toxic bloom of Solaris for their perverse ends.

Silence stretched between us teeming with the gravity of Lazarus' revelations. I shifted slightly in my chair, the newly healed muscle fibers in my thigh throbbing in protest.

"But that quest will take time," Lazarus said at last. "I must consider our next move. For now, your strength has returned—and your mission remains unchanged. You must continue your pursuit of the Timehunter societies."

I nodded. "Who's next?" My voice was steadier than I felt.

Lazarus' gaze darkened, a predator's gleam flickering in his eyes. "The English society," he said, his tone full of contempt. "They have become monstrous in their methods. They skinned Timebornes and Timebounds alive. Tortured them. Took their vile pleasures from their suffering before granting them death."

His voice was ice and fury, each word spat like venom.

"And now, Amir, you will be the weapon that ends them."

A surge of revulsion twisted in my gut, my jaw tightening. "Sick fucks," I muttered, my hands clenching into fists.

"Indeed," Lazarus said, his tone heavy with disgust. "They were once masters of alchemy. But now? Now, they are the worst of the worst. The depraved. You must go to England."

"England…" I echoed, the name leaving a bitter taste on my tongue. "How will I kill them?"

"Infiltration," Lazarus replied. "You can't simply walk in and expect to succeed. You must become one of them first."

He hesitated for a moment before continuing, his expression dark with amusement. "They sent us a letter. They believe we are the Timehunter society of Anatolia. Thomas Alexander has asked for our aid—to help destroy the masked man decimating Timehunter societies."

I stilled.

Lazarus' lips curled slightly. "They fear England will be next. They want to ally with you, Amir—to kill the Black Wraith."

A laugh escaped me before I could stop it—low, dark, edged with something almost feral. Across the table, Lazarus let out a chuckle of his own.

The irony was too rich.

Me. Amir Hassan. Tasked with hunting the Black Wraith.

The very legend I had created.

Lazarus' gaze locked onto mine, cold and calculating. "Moon Lee will not be joining you this time. I have sent him back home to be with his people. You will have your other men."

His tone left no room for protest.

He stepped closer, his voice resolute. "They believe Anatolia is a ruthless Timehunter society. They've asked for our help and are eager to ally. You will go as Lord Amir Hassan. Infiltrate. Gain their trust. Find a tactic with your men to destroy their society. It's a perfect plan. Accept their invitation. You're the hooded figure—play the game, don't break your cover. Destroy them and move on."

"Understood. Destroy and move on," I echoed the words, a mantra that had become second nature.

Lazarus' lips curled slightly. "Remember, the English society is closely tied to Mathias and Salvatore. Mathias believes you are dead. He thinks the fire at his school killed you." There was an edge of satisfaction in his voice.

I rose to my feet, the power from my rebirth still thrumming in my veins, a gift wrenched from agony and venom. "I won't let you down," I said, my voice a low growl, filled with certainty.

As I turned to leave, I remained oblivious to the unseen threads of fate tightening around me.

England would be more than just another battleground.

In its shadowed heart, something far more dangerous than any enemy awaited—something that would change everything.

CHAPTER 3

ELIZABETH

I traced the intricate carvings on my mahogany bedpost, following each swirl and whirl as they twisted into delicate points. My fingers lingered on the cool wood before I pushed myself up from the sea of silk sheets that had become a veil for my sorrow. Morning light filtered through the sheer drapes, casting a soft glow on the ornate wallpaper adorned with golden fleur-de-lis. My bedroom was a sanctuary of luxury within our vast estate, yet no opulence could thaw the bitter chill of desolation that clung to me.

My gaze drifted to the vacant chairs by the small table near the fireplace. Just weeks ago, laughter and jest had filled those seats—my brothers, so full of life, their voices carrying through the room. Now, silence reigned, broken only by the occasional crackle of the fire my maid had lit to chase away the dampness of an English morning. They had gone to a party, an evening of revelry and indulgence—and it had become their end. Poison, the staff had whispered when they thought no one was listening. But who? Why? The unanswered questions festered against my ribs like iron shackles.

Memories swarmed me; each one was a ghost haunting the corners of my room, offering fleeting solace from the crushing isolation that threatened to smother me.

And then there was Father. His silence had become a barren

echo in the wake of my brothers' deaths, a reminder that his love had never been mine to claim. They had been his heirs, his champions, the pride of our family's enigmatic Timehunter legacy—a legacy that felt more like a curse than an honor. But his withdrawal had begun long before their demise, back when Mother still lingered between this world and the next. Her final days were seared into my soul—the image of her struggling for breath as consumption ravaged her body, her frail hand trembling in mine.

They had all slipped away one by one, leaving me adrift in the vast, suffocating emptiness of what remained.

When I was barely a teen, my mother had been confined to her bed, swallowed by the sterile white linens that seemed to mock the vibrancy she once possessed. I remembered clutching her hand, feeling the frailty of her bones beneath my fingers, listening to the labored gasps that fought against the oppressive silence of the room. I would read to her, my voice soothed, a feeble attempt to soothe the rattling cough that marked the slow, merciless advance of her disease. Her sky-blue eyes—so much like my own—dimmed with each passing day until, at last, they closed forever.

Her death was the first fracture, the first jagged crack splintering through our family. My father and brothers withdrew into themselves, into the dangerous allure of their secretive society, leaving me alone to navigate the ruins of what we once were. To them, I became a porcelain doll—too fragile, too breakable to be exposed to the world they thrived in. And yet, that very world had annihilated them, too, leaving me the sole survivor of our shattered home.

Exhaling a sigh that carried my loneliness, I rose and crossed the room, pressing my forehead against the cool windowpane. Beyond the glass, the gardens lay still beneath the early morning light, dew clinging to the petals of the roses my mother had once adored. Their delicate beauty stood in cruel contrast to the decay that had taken root in my life, a reminder of what we had lost, of the warmth that had once filled these halls before the shadows crept in. Now, I faced those shadows alone, wrapped in mourning, my dress as black as the grief that had taken up residence in my chest.

The silence in my chamber was a living thing, a specter that coiled around me, suffocating in its constancy. The room's grandeur—with its heavy drapes, gilded mirrors, and towering bookshelves—offered no comfort. Instead, it was a cage, a lavish prison filled with echoes of a past that no longer existed.

I spent hours by the fireplace, watching the flames twist and flicker, their restless dance casting ghostly silhouettes along the walls. The portraits of my ancestors loomed above me, their painted eyes cold and impassive, as though evaluating my worth —judging my right to carry on the family name. But what legacy remained now, beyond tragedy and death?

My father's words from the day of my brothers' funeral echoed in my mind, a wound that refused to heal. "You're worth-less to me now." The cruelty in his voice more damaging than the words. I had gone to him, seeking solace in the wake of our shared loss, but he had turned away, leaving me to drown in my grief alone.

When my bedroom walls loomed too close, I wandered through the gardens, seeking refuge among the vibrant colors of the flowers. Here, amidst the roses my mother had once adored, the world felt softer, less suffocating. But no amount of beauty could change what had been taken from me. I had been raised to be seen, not heard—a rule that had left me voiceless when I needed to scream, to rage against the unfairness of it all.

A soft knock at the door pulled me from my reverie.

"Come in," I whispered, my voice barely louder than the rustle of the silk curtains swaying in the breeze.

Mary entered, her movements as graceful and quiet as the deer that roamed the woods beyond the estate. She offered me a small smile—a touch of warmth against the cold that had settled deep in my bones.

"Let's have you at the vanity, Lady Elizabeth," she said gently, guiding me toward the ornate mirror. The glass reflected my hollowed expression, a pale ghost of the girl I used to be.

Mary's brush glided through my hair in slow, rhythmic

strokes, the soothing motion a fragile balm against the ache in my chest.

"How are you coping?" Her voice was soft, laced with the kind of genuine concern that no one else dared to offer.

A lump formed in my throat, and the words spilled forth before I could stop myself.

"Mary, without your voice to keep me sane, this silence might just kill me."

My desperation startled me. I had spent so long concealing my grief behind layers of decorum, yet here I was, unraveling at the mere kindness of a friend.

"Don't be silly," Mary chided, though there was nothing dismissive in her tone. Her eyes held a quiet strength, a tenderness that wrapped around me like a shield against the storm. "You are strong. And capable. You would survive."

But survival was not the same as living.

A protest welled inside me, a tide of despair I could no longer hold back. Clutching at my chest, I tried to quell the ache that grew more piercing with each passing day. "How can you say that?" I murmured, my reflection in the mirror, a ghostly echo of the girl I once was. "Survival feels like a punishment without them… without anyone."

Mary paused, her hands settling gently on my shoulders, grounding me in the present. Our eyes met in the mirror, hers filled with something close to sorrow. "Lady Elizabeth, you mustn't think such things," she whispered. "You've weathered storms before. You'll get through this one too."

Her faith in me was a lifeline thrown into the turbulent seas of my grief. Yet, as she spoke those words of encouragement, I couldn't shake the feeling that this storm might be the one to pull me under.

A resounding rap at the door disturbed the fragile quiet between us.

Still weaving through my hair in tender strokes, Mary's fingers stilled abruptly. I felt the shift in her—how, in the space of a breath, she became once more the silent, efficient maid. The warmth in her gaze retreated behind an invisible barrier, leaving only the polished composure expected of her.

"Come in," I called, though the quiver in my voice betrayed the sudden apprehension curling in my gut.

The door swung open with a force that sent the air shuddering. My father's tall, rigid figure loomed in the doorway, his presence filling the room, though he did not cross the threshold.

His gaze found mine, piercing and imperious, holding me captive momentarily before he spoke.

"My study, Elizabeth. At once."

And then he was gone, the door left ajar in his wake, his footsteps echoing down the corridor like the toll of a distant bell. For a moment, his words hung heavy in the air, thick with foreboding.

Yet something stirred within me—an ember of hope flickering in the depths of my grief. It was absurd, foolish even, but the mere act of being summoned and acknowledged ignited a spark of excitement in my hollow chest.

"He wants to speak to me!" The words slipped past my lips before I could catch them, the realization a sudden, dizzying thing.

Mary, ever composed, resumed her task with quiet efficiency, her fingers deftly gathering my golden strands into a semblance of order. "Go on, Lady Elizabeth," she urged, her voice hushed. "Don't keep him waiting."

I rose, my legs trembling as if they, too, sensed the gravity of this moment. With a final glance at my reflection—a pale specter staring back at me—I turned away from Mary, my sole confidante in this silent world, and stepped beyond the hold of my sanctuary.

The hall stretched ahead, long and shadowed, each step a measured beat against the polished floor. By the time I stood at my father's study, my excitement had dwindled, smothered by uncertainty.

The chill struck me when I crossed the doorway, seeping into my bones like an unwelcome guest. The room was an expanse of dark wood and looming bookshelves, where sunlight seemed reluctant to linger, its pallid rays barely reaching the cold stone floor.

My father sat at the massive mahogany desk, an immovable figure surrounded by scattered parchments and weighty tomes. The quill in his hand moved quickly, its brittle scrape the only sound in the suffocating silence.

I stood there, waiting.

Waiting to be acknowledged.

Waiting to understand why, after all this time, he had finally summoned me.

He did not look up when he spoke. His voice was as cold and unfeeling as a winter night.

"You have been betrothed to Lord Winston. You will be married in two months."

The words struck like a physical blow, stealing the air from my lungs. I staggered back as if burned, my pulse thundering in my ears.

"No." The protest escaped before I could think, raw and breathless. "He's three times my age—if not more! He's vile. Cruel. A monster."

My voice quivered with disbelief, with fury, with the sheer injustice of it all.

At last, my father looked up, and a slow, measured exhale left his lips as though my refusal was nothing more than an inconvenience.

"What nonsense is this?" he asked, his brow arching in disdain. "You speak as though your desires matter. Your life, your choices—they are mine to command."

The words were more than I could bear.

"Father, please!" The dam of my composure broke, and I fell to my knees, hands clasped together, trembling. "Don't make me do this. Don't bind me to a man like him. I will wither. I will die."

"Silence!" The word exploded from him like cannon fire, invading the fragile space between us. And for the first time in what felt like an eternity, he looked at me—really looked at me.

His eyes, as unforgiving as the winter sea, bore into mine with an intensity that turned my blood to ice.

"I won't hear another word." His voice was a hammer striking the final nails into the coffin of my fate. "Your brothers —my heirs—are dead. Killed. My legacy, the English Time-hunter society, has no rightful successor. And a woman cannot manage a Timehunter society. A woman is for the household, for the family. You will marry Winston, and I will pass my title to him. You will obey. You will satisfy his every whim."

His decree reverberated through the room, a death knell ringing in my ears. It settled over me, heavy and suffocating, wrapping around my ribs like iron chains.

I couldn't breathe.

I stood frozen, ensnared by the icy tendrils of my father's will, bound tighter than any corset.

My shoulders shook as I stood and took a step forward, arms wrapped tightly around myself like armor against the ache. "Please, Father," I whispered, my voice barely carrying across the vast, unbridgeable distance between us. "Ever since Mother died, you've been so distant. You shut me out. I need warmth, and you give me silence."

"Stop it at once." His retort came without mercy, cleaving the air between us. "This groveling is beneath you."

The finality in his tone left no room for argument.

There was no room for hope—no room for me.

As if summoned by my despair, the door groaned open, its hinges wailing in protest. And then he entered.

Lord Winston.

My breath caught, my pulse hammering against my ribs as my gaze locked onto the man who would soon hold dominion over my fate. Time had ravaged him cruelly, his skin sagging in loose folds like melted wax, each crease and wrinkle whittled deep by the passing years.

His eyes, cloaked in the milky haze of cataracts, carried an eerie, sightless quality—yet they saw me. Pinned me. The spectral glaze over them did nothing to dull their unnerving effect, as though they could strip away flesh and peer straight into my soul.

A sneer curled his withered lips, the cracked skin splitting at the motion, revealing the remnants of what had once been teeth —now jagged, yellowed, and gnarled like ancient tombstones crumbling in an abandoned graveyard. His nose, long and hooked, cast a daunting shadow over his twisted mouth, completing the grotesque profile of a man who seemed more phantom than flesh.

And his hair—what little remained—formed a greasy halo around his liver-spotted scalp, wispy white strands clinging stubbornly as if defying the inevitability of time. Tufts jutted from his ears and nostrils, lending him an unsettling wildness, a monstrous parody of life that sent a shiver racing down my spine.

I fought to keep my composure, to swallow the revulsion building in my throat.

I was to belong to this…

This wretched husk of a man.

And no one—not even the father who had cast me aside— would save me.

Lord Winston raised a trembling hand to adjust the brocade jacket draped over his stooped shoulders as if the act could summon back a dignity long since lost. His fingers, gnarled and knotted like the roots of an ancient, dying tree, twitched with palsy's tremors, making the simple movement seem Herculean. The veins that webbed his hands stood out starkly, blue rivers in the pale parchment of his skin. Each blackened fingernail curled unnaturally over its fingertip, clicking softly against the fabric of his coat like brittle talons.

He shuffled forward, his steps slow, laborious, as if dragging unseen chains. His spine, curved into a permanent question mark, seemed to ask how much longer he could bear the burden of existence. His limbs bent at odd angles, his joints stiff and uncooperative, giving him the unsettling appearance of a marionette barely held together by fraying strings.

Revulsion and pity warred within me.

Once, perhaps, he had been a man who commanded attention, a figure of authority whose arrival alone was enough to silence a room. But now, no finery could mask the truth—he was little more than a hollow shell, a dying relic of a past gilded in wealth and power. The extravagant velvet of his coat, the lace at his throat, and the glint of polished brass buttons could not disguise the decay. His attire, meant to signal status and strength, only whispered of ruin, of the inexorable decline that came for all men, regardless of title or fortune.

I watched, transfixed by the tragedy unfolding before me.

A decayed nobleman swathed in the remnants of his former glory. A ghost haunting the world that had long since moved on without him.

And soon, I was to be bound to that ghost.

Condemned to wither beside him, trapped in his shadow, my life razed by the same emptiness that had hollowed him out.

The thought sent a tremor through me, a silent scream building in my chest.

But there was no one left to hear it.

Lord Winston moved suddenly, a lurching, unnatural motion, as though some unseen puppeteer had yanked his strings. His decayed features twisted into something vilely eager, a parody of joy stretching across his withered face.

"Oh, my dear Lady Alexander. What a surprise! I didn't know you were here," he crooned, his voice thin and rasping, like dead leaves scraping against stone.

Before I could recoil, his icy, skeletal fingers clamped around mine. My skin crawled beneath his touch as he dragged my hand to his parched lips, pressing them against my flesh in a mockery of affection. His chill seeped into my bones, a sensation so wrong and revolting that my body reacted before my mind could catch up.

I ripped my hand away, nausea burning my stomach.

His eyes widened, surprise flickering across his sallow features—just for a moment. Then the confusion melted into something darker, something more insidious.

"You'll learn to love me," he murmured with certainty. "I can't wait for the two months to fly by."

The words echoed hollowly in my ears, warping as panic surged inside me. My head shook back and forth in silent rebellion, like a weathervane caught in an errant gust.

No.

This could not be happening.

His gaze hardened, locking onto me.

"Make no mistake, dear one," he said, his tone now cold steel. "We are to be married. I have paid your father greatly for this transaction to take place."

A transaction.

That was all I was—a purchase, a bartered possession.

"And if you're not obedient—if you do not comply with my every request—when we are married, I will punish you."

The room seemed to shrink around me.

He leaned in, his cracked lips curling into a sneer. "And if you dare to defy me," he whispered, his breath rancid, "I will make sure your father hears about it… and he will punish you more severely."

A slow, sick smile spread across his face as if savoring the taste of his threat.

My blood ran cold.

The words lingered in the air, a vile, choking force that coiled around me like invisible shackles. A shiver raced down my spine as realization set in—this was not simply an arrangement or an unfortunate match. This was a sentence. A slow, drawn-out execution where my only choices were submission or suffering.

"Give us a moment," my father's voice tore through the tension, as impassive as ever.

Lord Winston gave a curt nod before shuffling out of the room, his retreating footsteps dragging like the pull of an undertow. But his absence did nothing to ease the pressure crushing my chest.

I was alone. Alone with the man who should have protected

me—who should have been my shield. Instead, he towered over me like a tyrant.

"You are behaving most unbecomingly!" my father barked, advancing on me. His face was a tempest, eyes alight with the fury of a storm barely held at bay. "Do you know how many strings I had to pull to make this betrothal happen?"

His words struck like a slap, though his hand had yet to fall.

"Maybe that's a sign it shouldn't happen!" I snapped, the rebuttal bursting free before I could stop it.

The air crackled with my rebellion. My heart pounded against my ribs as my pleas poured forth, desperate and fragmented, trying—begging—to reach any remaining part of him that might still be my father.

His expression darkened, rage boiling over, turning his face crimson. The vein in his temple pulsed like a warning drum.

"You are not allowed to go against your parents," he thundered, rising to his full, imposing height. His hand lifted in a threatening arc—

I flinched, my breath catching in my throat.

But I didn't wait to feel the sting of his wrath.

A surge of adrenaline took hold, and I ran before thought could catch up to action.

I tore from the study, my skirts tangling around my legs as I stumbled into the hallway, my heart hammering against my ribs. A flicker of movement—Lord Winston's surprised visage— flashed before me as I darted past him without so much as a glance. His reaction mattered little to me now.

My mind pulsed with four harrowing truths, each one a nail driven deeper into my coffin—

My brothers were murdered.

My mother died.

My father was cruel.

And I was to be wed to a despicable man.

The corridors that had once been my childhood sanctuary now felt like the walls of a prison, each ornate frame, each flickering candle, another bar in my gilded cage. The air closed in around me with every breathless step.

My flight was blind, fueled by desperation rather than direction. The world blurred in streaks of gilt and shadow, my pulse roaring louder than the muffled thud of my slippers on the carpet.

Then—impact.

The turn came too quickly, my momentum unchecked, and I crashed into something—or someone—solid. A shockwave of force jolted through me, sending my fragile composure fracturing like bone.

Strong hands seized my shoulders, steadying me. But unlike my father's grip or Lord Winston's clammy grasp, these hands were warm, gentle.

"Oh, forgive me," I gasped, my voice thin, a whisper of lace torn by thorns. "I should watch where I'm going."

I dared to look up.

And my eyes locked onto a gaze that stopped the frantic beat of my heart.

He stood before me like an ancient statue given breath, his swarthy complexion and chiseled features starkly contrasting the opulence of the estate's gilded corridor. Shadows played across the sculpted lines of his face, his dark hair framing a severe and compelling countenance. Strength radiated from him—not just in the defined sinew of his muscular form, but in the silent authority that clung to him, the unmistakable air of a man who had seen distant battles and sworn unspoken oaths.

A breath of tempest air in a suffocating room.

"Who are—" My words faltered, failing me as my mind struggled to reconcile this sudden encounter with the nightmare surrounding me.

He did not speak.

Instead, he watched me, those deep, inscrutable eyes assessing, weighing something unseen. In them, I caught a whisper of danger that did not belong to this world of silk and submission.

Then—footsteps.

Heavy. Murderous. Each tread a drumbeat of impending doom.

My father.

Panic surged in my chest. Flustered, I wrenched myself from the stranger's grip, though his touch lingered on my skin like an unspoken promise. I could not afford to linger—not with the specter of my father's wrath looming ever closer.

"Elizabeth, come back here!"

The command cracked through the corridor like a whip. My pulse leaped.

I stole one last glance at the enigmatic man who had momentarily anchored me in the storm, memorizing the dark intensity of his gaze—the quiet power coiled beneath his stillness.

And then I ran.

I gathered the remnants of my skirts and fled, leaving behind the fleeting possibility of sanctuary for the certainty of my cursed haven. My lonely existence had gone from awful to horrible in an hour, and I knew, deep in my marrow, that it could only get worse from here.

My only hope was escape.

But as I hurried through the labyrinth of my prison, something new blossomed within me. A glimmer of hope, fragile but insistent.

The stranger.

Our collision—a moment as swift as a heartbeat—burned in my mind, refusing to fade. His eyes had spoken of untold secrets, of something beyond this life I was shackled to. A daring escape? A chance at freedom?

Or had I only imagined it?

Fate, I knew, was not so kind.

And yet... for the first time in years, I dared to believe it might see me.

CHAPTER 4

AMIR

s I approached the estate of Thomas Alexander—the infamous Timehunter—an eerie sensation crept up my spine.

The stone steps before me, vast and inexorable, rose from the earth like a monument to his power. Pale limestone slabs, expertly curated and smoothed, bore the marks of time's relentless touch—rain-softened edges and faint weathering that whispered of age and endurance. Yet they remained strong, unmoving, an unspoken warning that those who ascended did so at his will.

My footsteps echoed as I climbed, the sound swallowed by the towering facade looming overhead. The steps were shallow, almost leisurely in their design, as though meant for men who never hurried—least of all, to escape.

Wrought-iron railings flanked me, cold beneath my fingertips. Their patterns—twisting acanthus leaves and cruel, spiraling thorns—spoke of elegance and danger as if the very metal had been shaped to mirror the man who ruled within. Here, wealth was not a mere display, but a weapon for all to see.

The doorway at the summit of the steps loomed, framed by stone pillars and encased in dark, timeworn wood. Every carving that adorned it—symbols of victory, strength, dominion— offered no comfort, only a promise of the disturbed mind that had ordered them into existence. Above, the triangular pediment jutted forward, an unspoken sneer, as though the house itself watched and judged all who dared approach.

Lanterns flickered at either side of the entrance, their dim, ghostly light casting uneasy shadows along the facade. They swayed like restless sentinels, their glow barely piercing the oppressive air, yet they made the stone seem alive—a house that breathed, watched, and knew.

The massive oak door was before me, a silent guardian, its polished surface a deep, almost bloody-red. The lion's head knocker—impossibly lifelike—stared at me with piercing eyes, its expression frozen in a perpetual snarl. The beast's gaze was almost predacious, a silent warning to those who dared disturb the house's master.

I hesitated, my fingers twitching at my side.

Beneath the grandeur, beneath the masterful craftsmanship, this entrance reeked of calculated cruelty. Every detail had been chosen with purpose. This was not merely a home; it was a statement, a fortress of power belonging to a man who understood dominance.

Drawing a slow breath, I squared my shoulders. My hands smoothed over my waistcoat, adjusting the folds with meticulous attention before fussing with the crisp knot of my cravat. Appearances were everything in Georgian London. To slip, even for a moment, was to invite ruin.

But I had not come to slip.

I had come to deceive.

Lord Hassan of Anatolia. The title sat upon my shoulders like a suit of armor, impenetrable, forged in careful study and endless preparation. My disguise was flawless and calculated down to the finest detail. And yet—beneath the layers of silk and civility—my heart drummed a constant war beat.

One wrong move.

I grasped the lion's head knocker, its weight solid in my grip. The brass was warm where my fingers touched, polished smooth by years of use. I lifted it, inhaled, and let it fall.

The sound rang through the morning air, brisk and commanding.

It was not merely a knock—a summons, an announcement of arrival. A declaration of the attention I sought.

And now, there was no turning back.

The door creaked open with a slow, eerie groan, revealing a comely young maid standing on the threshold. Her long, dark hair was neatly tied back with a red ribbon, a stark contrast against her pale skin. She was delicate, almost doll-like, yet there was something measured in her demeanor—something practiced.

"How may I be of assistance?" she asked, her voice smooth and melodic, like a gentle stream flowing over polished stones. She spoke slowly, carefully, every syllable rolling off her tongue with a refined elegance that felt cultivated rather than natural. It was the voice of someone who had spent years perfecting her speech to match the upper class—an artifice carefully constructed.

"I am here at the request of Lord Alexander. I am Lord Amir Hassan of Anatolia," I said, offering a polite bow.

The maid inclined her head, her expression unreadable. "Of course," she murmured, her voice as cool as frost. "You are expected, my lord. Do come in."

I stepped across the threshold of Thomas Alexander's estate, and an icy sensation swept through me—one that had little to do with the damp English air.

The grandeur I had anticipated was there, but it was not welcoming. It was cold, calculated. The air was loaded unspoken history, as if the walls held their breath, waiting.

The maid led me through a foyer where the furniture stood rigid, draped in heavy, lightless fabrics that seemed to drink in the dim light. The portraits lining the walls eyed me with the same disdain their subjects might have in life, their gazes hollow and condemning.

Joy had long been banished from this house.

A mausoleum of wealth remained—a place where shadows

clung to the corners, where whispers of loss and lamentation settled like dust on forgotten relics.

And I had just walked into its depths.

The corners of the room were steeped in darkness, untouched by the weak slivers of sunlight that struggled through the tall windows. The dim glow barely reached the polished floors. For a fleeting moment, I half-expected to find a coffin at the heart of this mausoleum masquerading as a home, surrounded by silent mourners paying tribute to the long-departed.

Instead, there was only the emptiness—an oppressive void that seemed to mirror the cruelty for which Thomas Alexander was known.

The maid's footsteps echoed through the hush as she led me up a sweeping staircase. Beneath us, the carpet was threadbare, starkly contrasting the grandeur that had once thrived here. This house had known better days, but time, like its master, had stripped it of warmth, leaving only the skeletal remains of its former splendor.

A voice rang out from beyond the halls—imperious and laced with impatience.

The maid stilled, her posture shifting with quiet caution. Her expression remained unreadable when she turned to me; her rehearsed politeness was impeccable yet absent of warmth.

"I apologize; I've been summoned elsewhere. Lord Alexander will see you shortly," she said, her tone clipped, impersonal. "Please proceed to the end of the hall and turn left. Lord Alexander's study is the last door on the right."

A single, shallow nod.

Then she was gone, disappearing down a dim corridor without another word.

Silence enveloped me once more.

Now, I was alone.

I followed her instructions, my fingers grazing the cold banister as I ascended, each step drawing me deeper into the lair of the Timehunter who had bludgeoned his name into history with blood and ruin. Merciless and calculated, Thomas Alexander had orchestrated the downfall of so many Timebornes and Timebounds. My fallen comrades. Their ghosts walked with me now, silent phantoms against my spine, reminding me why I had come.

For justice.

For vengeance.

The air was heavy with the scent of aged wood and something bitter—something old and resentful that clung to the very bones of this house.

I had barely taken a few strides down the dimly lit corridor when something—someone—collided with me.

She stumbled against my chest, her nearness a jarring warmth against the cold I had wrapped myself in. My hands shot out instinctively, gripping her shoulders, steadying the fine-boned frame that trembled beneath my touch.

"Forgive me, I should watch where I'm going," she whispered, her voice as delicate as porcelain, yet beneath it ran a current of quiet strength.

And then she looked up.

Eyes the color of a forgotten sky—wide, searching, brimming with a silent plea—locked onto mine.

We were different.

I was cloaked in shadows and deception.

She was a beacon of light trapped within the gloom of this house.

For a moment, I forgot where I stood. I forgot the mission, the vengeance, the name I carried.

"Who are—"

Her voice faltered, the words collapsing on her tongue. I didn't answer. I didn't have to. Silence spoke louder. I studied her—the confusion in her eyes, the slight parting of her lips, the way her breath hitched like she was already bracing for a blow. There was no mask on her. No pretense. Just raw, unfiltered fear.

She met my gaze, and for a split second, I knew she saw it— the danger coiled in me like a serpent beneath still waters. But also, something else. Not mercy. Not comfort. Just... awareness. Recognition. Like she understood I wasn't from this world of silk and protocol either. And maybe, I wasn't her enemy.

Then—footsteps.

Deliberate. Heavy. I knew that rhythm before she reacted. That arrogant, malicious cadence that turned every corridor into a battlefield. Her father was coming.

She stiffened in my arms. Her panic struck me before she moved, radiating off her like a rising fever. She tore herself from my grasp, but her wrist lingered in my palm a second too long. I felt the tremor, the way her pulse jolted beneath my touch. Her breath hitched, caught in her throat like it feared making a sound. My fingers stayed suspended in the space she left behind—open, empty. A promise I hadn't made. A warning I hadn't voiced.

"Elizabeth, come back here!"

His voice cracked through the air like a gunshot. She flinched violently, her entire frame going rigid, spine snapping to attention like a soldier summoned to heel. Trained. Conditioned. It wasn't discipline—it was fear etched into her bones.

And then—she ran.

She darted like a deer beneath the jaws of a lion, pale skirts trailing behind her like smoke fleeing fire. The hallway swallowed her, but the echo of her flight lingered—soft footfalls, the whisper of fabric, the faint scent of rosewater.

She was gone in seconds.

But the icy aftermath she left behind didn't fade. It settled in my chest like a bad omen.

I took a step forward, instinct urging me to follow—to ensure her safety or perhaps to quiet the inexplicable concern stirring in my chest—when the heavy thud of approaching footsteps shattered my focus.

I turned abruptly, coming face to face with him.

Lord Thomas Alexander.

His arrival cast a pall of dread over the corridor.

My eyes narrowed, a silent snarl curling beneath my carefully composed expression. So, this was the man I had come to destroy.

Alexander looked like he had been sculpted from stone—but not in a way that inspired awe. His face, weathered and deeply lined, bore no traces of noble hardship, no echoes of sacrifice or valor. The creases around his mouth and eyes didn't speak of battles fought with honor—they spoke of cruelty. Of blood spilled without remorse.

I didn't need to know the stories.

I could feel the malice emanating from his very skin.

Whatever personal losses Alexander had endured, he had let them twist him, shaping him into something monstrous. Something beyond redemption.

And now, I stood before him.

A wolf in a borrowed name.

And he had no idea that I had come to bury him.

His long, dark hair fell past his shoulders in an untamed mass, tied carelessly at the nape of his neck. It might have lent another man the air of a battle-hardened warrior, but on Alexander, it only deepened the unease he exuded. I imagined it coming loose in the heat of combat, framing that cruel face in wild, unbound strands—a beast unleashed.

But his hair was the least of it.

It was his eyes that spoke the most.

Icy-blue. Glacial and bitter. Yet utterly devoid of warmth. There was no grief in them, no hint of mourning for his slain sons, no lingering sorrow for the lives he had crushed beneath his heel.

Only rage.

A seething, unflinching rage.

The kind that didn't just ignite in moments of fury but thrived in destruction. The kind that fed on suffering.

Thomas Alexander wasn't a man who fought for honor, nor did he kill out of duty.

He fought because he relished it.

"Lord Hassan?" His voice broke through the silence, crisp and edged with something unreadable. He extended his hand.

"Yes," I replied, gripping it firmly. "I am pleased to make your acquaintance."

The pressure between us was a silent battle. His jaw

clenched, his expression a mask of cold civility, but I could feel the violence barely contained beneath it.

This was not silent strength—this was a killer's patience.

I recognized it. The way a wolf watches its dinner, waiting for the perfect moment to strike.

Alexander moved with planned grace; his every step was calculated. He wasn't just a man who commanded soldiers—he commanded fear. And he reveled in it.

His noble attire was nothing more than a well-crafted disguise. Beneath the pristine lines of his vest and fold of his shirt lurked a man who thrived on violence—not a warrior forged by hardship, but a pillager who wore civility like armor. I could see him on a battlefield—not for honor, but for the thrill. His coat flaring behind him, steel carving through flesh without hesitation. No bloodied straps or battered scars marked his legacy. He didn't need them. His power was in the cruelty masked behind polish.

His clothes bore no stains of war, yet they reeked of it.

Not burden. Not memory.

Triumph.

Time had hardened Lord Alexander, but not how it should have. There was no wisdom etched into the lines of his face, no quiet strength learned from suffering. Only bitterness. Cruelty. A mask of hardened hatred had consumed whatever he once was, leaving behind nothing but a man who thrived on the misery of others.

Alexander's resolve had not been forged by hardship—it had been sharpened by the desire to inflict it.

I felt no respect as I stared at him—no grudging acknowledgment of strength, no recognition of a fellow warrior.

Only revulsion.

Lord Alexander wore his cruelty like a second skin, and the longer our hands remained clasped, the more it felt like holding a blade by the edge. I released him, the gesture brittle and brief —enough for appearances, nothing more. Whatever goodwill his title implied, I felt none of it. Nothing good could come from this man.

"I see you've encountered my daughter," he said at last. His tone was cold, indifferent, as if she were little more than an afterthought.

His lips curled into something that barely passed for a smile as he offered a perfunctory apology. "I must apologize, Lord Hassan. My daughter has no manners. Forgive her rude behavior."

There was no concern in his voice. No fatherly irritation or disappointment. Nothing.

His eyes flicked past me, scanning the corridor where she had fled. And when he finally looked at me, his gaze was like a frozen abyss.

Empty. Inescapable.

"Please, join me in my study."

A command disguised as an invitation.

With one last glance toward the young woman's path, I acquiesced, falling into step beside him. His stride was assured, purposeful—but it couldn't hide the malicious air that clung to him.

Much like the faint scent of tobacco that lingered in the air.

So did the promise of something worse to come.

As I entered his study, a guttural disgust clawed up my throat.

Standing in the center of the room was a man whose reputation for cruelty was second only to Alexander himself. The sight of him—the vile, corpulent figure surveying his surroundings with the self-satisfied air of a man who owned everything he touched—ignited a slow, smoldering wrath in my chest.

"Meet Lord Phineas Winston," Alexander announced, a glint of something unreadable in his cold gaze. "This is my second in line."

Winston.

The name alone was enough to curdle my blood.

Swathed in layers of velvet and lace, the old brute looked more like an overindulged peacock than a man of power. But beneath the pretense of finery, his gluttonous appetite for dominance seeped through, coiling in the way he stood, in the smug curve of his lips, in the possessive way his beady eyes flicked toward me.

"Charmed," I bit out, my voice a careful blend of civility and restraint.

Across the room, Alexander poured the brandy, the rich amber liquid swirling in crystal glasses. I took the offered drink, though the company of Lord Winston soured any appeal it might have held.

"Please forgive Elizabeth's earlier behavior," Alexander continued, his words smoothed with feigned apology. "There is no excuse for such behavior. She is to be betrothed to Lord Winston, and I believe the reality of it… took her by surprise."

His words settled into the space between us, packed with unspoken transactions.

My grip tightened around the cool glass as realization dawned.

The reason for the young woman's fear, her frantic escape, and the silent plea in her pale-blue eyes became painfully clear.

Elizabeth.

The ethereal creature who had collided with me, a fleeting breath of light in this decaying house, was to be bound to this twisted ruin of a man.

It was an abomination of a match.

A cage for a bird meant to soar.

And yet, to the men in this room, it was nothing more than a profitable arrangement.

"To a fruitful union between Elizabeth and Lord Winston," Alexander declared, lifting his glass into the dim light. The crystal caught the glow of the lanterns, casting fractured reflections onto the walls—like the horrid future they had decided for her.

I raised my glass in reluctant mimicry, the brandy's rich aroma doing nothing to mask my disgust. With each sip, I committed her name to memory—Elizabeth.

A beacon of purity, bound to be sullied by this unholy union.

After a moment steeped in false pleasantries, Alexander exhaled heavily, lowering himself to the imposing mahogany desk that dominated the room. He gestured toward two chairs, their ornate carvings more a testament to excess than taste.

"Please, have a seat, gentlemen," he instructed.

I complied, lowering myself into the heavy chair. The wood groaned beneath me, a quiet protest to the unfolding conversation.

Alexander steepled his fingers, his gaze assessing. He was a man who calculated his every move, and this—this—was his opening gambit.

"Lord Hassan, your reputation precedes you." His tone was almost indulgent, as if he were drawing me into some elaborate game he believed himself destined to win. "The Anatolia Time-hunters are renowned for their prowess. It is a great honor to host one of such esteemed standing."

"The honor is mine," I returned smoothly, allowing my words to carry the right measure of civility. Play the role. Become the mask.

A pause.

Then, with methodical ease, I added, "I heard about the tragedy of your sons. My condolences."

The words passed my lips like silk, effortless and empty. In the recesses of my mind, however, there was no grief, no sympathy.

Those sons had been cut from the same cloth as their father —ruthless raiders, men who had spent their lives wielding power like a bludgeon. They had met the fate they had earned.

Alexander nodded stiffly, the briefest flicker of something passing over his features before vanishing entirely. "Thank you," he said, but there was no sorrow, no grief—only the hollow response of a man who understood loss not as pain but as incon-venience.

"Their loss is deeply felt."

"Indeed," I acknowledged, keeping my voice even.

Inside, my thoughts moved like pieces across a board, arranging themselves for the next play.

The game had begun.

And I would play my part to perfection.

Alexander's gaze darkened, his voice laced with venom as cold as his frostbitten soul.

"It was the Black Wraith who killed them. That masked scourge."

A shiver coursed through him—fear, rage, or perhaps anticipation. Then, with a sudden burst of fury, he slammed his fist onto the desk, making his crystal glass rattle in protest.

"That man must be caught and tortured. We will make an example of his death."

His voice rose like a gathering storm, each syllable charged with wrath. "His men are decimating our Timehunter societies. He released a foul poison and burned the place to the ground."

I lifted the brandy to my lips, allowing its warmth to coat my throat, buying myself a moment to consider my response. Careful. Calculated.

"Why do you think it's just one person?" I asked, letting my words hang like an unwelcome guest. "In our society, we operate in teams."

Alexander's jaw tightened. "It has to be him," he insisted, as stubborn as the ancient oaks lining his estate.

I tilted my head slightly, feigning intrigue. "A serial killer craves notoriety. He wouldn't change his stripes. This is the first we've heard of a poison being used. I'd wager it was someone different."

A test. A flick of the blade, seeing how deep I could injure, before he noticed the wound.

"Nonsense," Alexander scoffed, waving a dismissive hand. "The Black Wraith is the culprit. He has been known to experiment in his killings."

Experiment.

Has he?

A slow smirk threatened to curl at the edge of my lips. I stifled it with another sip of brandy, the irony almost too rich to swallow.

Because I knew his every move.

Because I was the Black Wraith.

Alexander's eyes simmered with conviction, blind to the

irony before him. "Your Anatolia society is strong," he continued, shifting gears, sensing an opportunity. "We can help each other. My friend, Lord Francis, says you have different methods."

I leaned back slightly, letting the firelight flicker against my composed expression.

Lifting the brandy to my lips, I took one final sip—the liquid fire searing away any lingering taste of complicity.

"You have my partnership," I declared, each syllable as brittle as the winter air beyond these walls.

No sooner had the false allegiance left my tongue than Lord Winston stirred beside me, laboriously heaving himself upright. His voice, meant to be a hushed whisper for Alexander alone, carried through the room like an ill-timed proclamation.

"We should ask Mathias before consulting with the legendary Timehunters of Anatolia. We shouldn't be allying with them without Mathias' approval."

The room tensed.

Alexander's response came like a thunderclap, a bellow of sorrow and rage so sudden it sent a jolt through the air.

"Where was Mathias when the tragedy happened?"

His face contorted, grief twisting his chiseled features into something raw and unnatural. "He didn't save any of them! I had to leave the festivities. And when I returned—" His voice broke, his hands clenched into fists at his sides.

"Everyone was dead."

Then, as if it had grown unbearable, he threw back his head and howled—a guttural cry, full of anguish and something more dangerous—something unhinged.

"My sons were among the dead."

The cry echoed through the study, rattling the empty glass in my hand.

For a moment, no one spoke.

Then, with a shuddering breath, Alexander collected himself, though his wild, fevered eyes remained.

He turned to Winston, his gaze ablaze with something far more than grief—conviction.

"No, Lord Winston. The best thing is to join forces with Anatolia."

A smile ghosted his lips, but it was not a smile of warmth. It was the smirk of a man who had made up his mind and decided how history would be written.

"Mathias will be happy."

I studied him carefully, my expression unshifting.

Desperation had its claws in him.

And desperation forged alliances that reason never would.

At that moment, I knew—this was a battlefield, and the true war had just begun.

I would have to tread carefully, for the path before me was treacherous.

And I intended to survive it.

"Indeed, Lord Winston, the Black Wraith must be ensnared," I said smoothly, my voice calm amidst the storm brewing in this room. Every word was a move on the board, a carefully placed piece in a high-stakes game. "However, I suspect there is more to this shadow than meets the eye—a secondary player, perhaps."

Alexander leaned forward, his eyes narrowing with interest.

"And how, pray tell, might we unearth this mysterious accomplice?"

I allowed a calculated pause, feigning deep contemplation while ensuring my next words steered the conversation.

"By baiting a trap grand enough to draw them both from hiding," I proposed, masking my revulsion beneath a facade of eagerness. "A masquerade. A lavish affair where none can resist the allure of obscurity."

Something dangerous crossed Alexander's face, his earlier grief momentarily forgotten, replaced by the glint of intrigue.

"Brilliant, Lord Hassan!" he exclaimed, the burden of his sorrow cast aside like a discarded cloak.

I stiffened at the title. It was not mine. It had never been mine.

"Please, call me Amir," I corrected, my voice firm but

controlled. That borrowed name was a shackle, an illusion I had forged—but I would not let it define me.

Alexander inclined his head, his lips curling slightly as he let my name roll over his tongue. "Very well, Amir."

He savored it. It was as if, at that moment, he believed he had won some silent battle between us.

"We shall announce Elizabeth's engagement at the soirée," he added, his tone brimming with satisfaction.

Something churned inside me.

The thought of her bound to another—to Winston—sent a slow, rumbling revulsion curling through my chest. But I buried it, forced my hands to remain still, my expression unreadable.

"Yes," I murmured, my voice betraying nothing. "The Black Wraith would not pass up such an occasion."

Across the room, Winston's rheumy eyes gleamed with something repulsive—anticipation, desire, victory.

"We'll extend invitations to every society," he crooned, his lips parting in something akin to glee.

And in that moment, I saw it for what it was.

This was not just a game to them.

This was a hunt.

And I was standing in the center of the snare, waiting for the jaws to snap shut.

But they had made one fatal mistake.

They believed they were the predators.

They had yet to realize—

So was I.

Alexander, ever the master of pretense, slid down from the edge of the desk with the ease of a man who believed himself untouchable. He crossed the short space between us, his heavy hand landing on my shoulder—meant to feel welcoming but laced with possession.

"Amir, I am overjoyed that you're here," he declared with satisfaction. "I insist you stay as my guest."

I resisted the urge to recoil. The idea of remaining within these walls, steeped in their machinations, was insufferable.

"Thank you, but no," I declined smoothly, unwilling to let

them draw me deeper into their world of cold stone and colder hearts.

Alexander's smile did not falter, but I caught the flicker of something else beneath it—an irritation he was too controlled to voice.

"Then at least grace us with your company at dinner tomorrow," he urged, his determination as tireless as a wolf scenting fresh blood. "The betrothal announcement will be made. And then we will follow up with a grand announcement at the soiree."

I hesitated for the briefest moment before inclining my head.

"Very well."

The words left my lips like a sentence passed.

As I turned to leave, retreating into the solitude of my thoughts, the image of her lingered—porcelain skin, soft blue eyes gleaming with untold sorrow, a fleeting moment of fragility colliding into me in the dim corridor.

Elizabeth.

A woman about to be sealed into a fate worse than death.

One question gnawed at the edges of my mind, refusing to be silenced.

How could I stop it?

CHAPTER 5

ELIZABETH

The afternoon sun painted the chamber in gold, its warmth spilling through the tall windows and casting long, shifting shadows that danced across the walls. Tapestries lined the room, intricate depictions of a fiery phoenix rising from the ashes—an omen or a cruel jest?

For a moment, I lay still, allowing the sun's gentle heat to kiss my cheek, a fleeting comfort before the catastrophe of the evening ahead soured the sweetness outside my window.

As I rose, my toes curled into the rugs, their plush weave a poor consolation for the cold settling deep in my chest.

Today was not an ordinary day.

It was the night of my father's announcement.

The first public declaration of my betrothal to Lord Winston.

This should have been a joyous occasion, an event worthy of celebration. Had my intended been anyone but a tyrant. Instead, it felt like a sentence, one inked in blood long before I could protest.

I moved toward the window, my fingers grazing the cool glass. From below, the scent of roses drifted in—lush, untamed, free—a painful contrast to the gilded prison closing around me.

The reflection staring back at me was not my own.

It was the face of a girl I no longer recognized—pale, wistful, framed by wheat-gold hair and sky-blue eyes that once held dreams. Now, they held only resignation.

"Lady Elizabeth, please," Mary's gentle voice pulled me back from the edge of my thoughts.

She stood at my bedside, fussing over the gown laid across the silk sheets—a Robe à la Française, exquisite in its craftsmanship. The delicate brocade shimmered in the sunlight, floral embroidery twining like ivy over satin and silk—a gown fit for a queen.

And yet, as I stared at it, all I saw was armor.

Each stitch, each delicate fold, a chain in the shackles I was to wear.

"Mary, must we?" I whispered, my voice barely more than a breath.

She stilled.

But Mary understood.

Mary always did.

Mary was more than just my maid.

She was my closest confidante. My best friend. In many ways, she was the sister I never had.

We had grown up within the same walls, breathed the same air, and lived parallel lives divided only by status. Though she served me in name, her loyalty was never born of duty—it was something deeper, unspoken yet steadfast. Mary knew me in ways no one else did. She saw my fears before I spoke them and understood my hopes when I dared not voice them.

And now, she was the only tether keeping me from drowning.

"Stay strong, Lady Elizabeth," she murmured, her hands deft as she guided me into the gown.

The bodice was drawn tight, each pull of the laces a slow, painstaking theft of my breath. The fabric molded to my frame like a second skin, and yet it felt nothing like my own. With every tug, I felt the constriction of my fate wrapping around my ribs like iron bands.

We moved on to the stomacher—the ornamental panel meant

to complete the illusion. A masterpiece of embroidery, pearls, and gemstones, each detail fastidiously crafted, each gleaming facet a cruel mockery of the facade I was expected to present to the world.

Mary pinned it carefully, ensuring every embellishment caught the light. The gown shone brilliantly.

I did not.

"Look at you," she whispered, and despite the sorrow in her eyes, there was pride in her voice. "Fitting of a lady about to change the world."

If only that change were mine to command.

The gown. The room. This house—a gilded cage built to contain me.

I wanted to scream. To tear it all away, to strip myself bare and run until the memory of Lord Winston's grotesque sneer faded into nothingness.

But I did not.

I stood—silent. Still. A statue scored by years of obedience, sculpted by fear.

The rebellion in my heart clawed at the walls of my ribcage, but it did not reach my lips.

"Thank you, Mary," I murmured, though the words felt distant, hollow.

My reflection stared back in the mirror—a perfect portrait of aristocratic grace, poised and untouchable. A mask so finely crafted that, for a fleeting moment, I almost believed it.

Almost.

The rustle of silk and the whisper of linen filled the chamber as Mary hoisted the wide skirts of my gown, fluffing the layers of petticoats beneath. The panniers at my hips extended the fabric outward in exaggerated opulence, their rigid whalebone structure dictating my movements, trapping me in a frame of false grandeur.

I was meant to glide. To move like a vision of elegance, to be admired and envied.

Instead, I felt enslaved.

I watched the shadow of my reflection shift against the

polished glass—a ghostly silhouette of excess and expectation shaped by fashion's cruel hand.

"Steady now," Mary soothed, her fingers deftly arranging the fabric, ensuring the voluminous shape remained flawless. The layers of starched petticoats whispered against one another, a rustling symphony of control, a counterpoint to the rising drumbeat of my heart.

They gave my form exaggerated fullness—a testament to wealth, to status.

To a life that was not my own.

"Your hair next," Mary announced, guiding me to the dressing table where silver brushes and powder pots lay in perfect, unerring order.

With ease she twisted and pinned my wheat-blond locks into an intricate updo. My hair, once free and loose in the gardens of my youth, was now sculpted into an elaborate crown, dusted with fine white powder until it resembled a confection, delicate and untouchable.

Fit for a queen.

Or a prisoner.

I sighed as Mary threaded ribbons through my curls, their soft hues blending seamlessly with the fabric of my gown. Feathers were nestled into the arrangement, bobbing with every subtle tilt of my head. Finally, she placed a lace cap—as delicate as a spider's web—atop the intricate construction, its edges kissing my forehead like a ghost of a blessing.

My father had insisted on the final embellishments—tiny pearls and glinting jewels woven throughout the elaborate updo. A nod to the opulence demanded for tonight's charade. A final reminder that I was to be seen, admired, and owned.

"Almost done," Mary whispered, returning to assess her work.

Our eyes met in the mirror, and for a moment, words were unnecessary. She knew what this night meant. She knew what it would take from me.

And yet, she had adorned me for the occasion as though

dressing a sister for her wedding day—with tenderness and quiet sorrow.

"Thank you," I said, though the words rang hollow. "It's perfect."

Mary's lips curved into a bittersweet smile as her hands came to rest gently on my shoulders. "You look beautiful, Lady Elizabeth. Truly."

She spoke the words like a blessing.

Beauty might soften the edges of the night ahead.

I swallowed, my fingers ghosting over the smooth fabric of my gown. "Beauty can be a curse."

My reflection stared back—pristine, untouchable, a vision sculpted to perfection.

This was my armor. My powdered curls, my jeweled cage. A gown wide enough to conceal my trembling knees.

But beneath it all, the spirit that longed to soar stirred, restless and yearning.

Tonight, I would wear the mask they had given me.

But one day… I would escape.

Mary fastened the clasp of the pearl necklace around my neck, the cool touch of each smooth orb sending a shiver down my spine. They rested against my skin, deceptively light yet unbearably heavy. Each pearl was a perfect sphere of iridescence, a fragment of ocean-born beauty—shining, flawless, and confined.

Much like I was expected to be.

"Your mother's," Mary reminded me softly, her fingers lingering on the final pearl as if willing strength into it.

I nodded, my throat tight. The familiar necklace was a whisper of my mother's touch, a relic of love long since buried.

Matching earrings dangled from my ears—delicate pearls nestled atop drops of diamond, catching the candlelight. Their fractured brilliance scattered prisms across the chamber walls. The bracelet at my wrist, a slender chain of glittering stones, clasped tightly—too tightly. A mocking mirror of my fate.

"Time for your shoes," Mary murmured, breaking through my reverie.

She held them up, and I swallowed hard.

Silk heels, the color of blushing dawn. Their surfaces were as smooth as still water, untouched, unblemished. The ornate buckles caught the light, sparkling with cruel elegance, while soft bows sat atop each one—innocent adornments for a march to the gallows.

I reached for them slowly, my fingers brushing the silk.

This was it.

Step by step, I was being bound, polished, and offered.

Slipping into the shoes, I felt the shift—not just in height, but in expectation. These were not shoes meant for running through fields or escaping into the woods. They were crafted for poised steps across polished floors, for standing tall when all you wanted to do was crumble.

"Beautiful, Lady Elizabeth. Just beautiful," Mary gushed.

"Thank you," I whispered, taking a tentative step.

The shoes carried me forward with a refinement that belied the storm beneath my skin. Each click against the floorboards reminded me of the role I must play and the expected performance. Tonight, I would move with grace, even if every step led me closer to a future I dreaded with every fiber of my being.

My fingers found the fan, and with a delicate flick of my wrist, I unfolded it—a flourish practiced, perfected, deceiving.

The painted silk spread before me, revealing a pastoral scene of delicate beauty—idyllic, serene, a lie.

The knot of dread coiled tighter in my chest as I traced the soft edges of the painted landscape—a world untouched by duty, expectation, or the cold grip of inevitability.

The lace-edged leaves rustled softly in the still air, whispering secrets against the silence of my chamber.

I set the fan fluttering, each motion rehearsed—a performance crafted to mislead.

Like a caged bird pretending its clipped wings had never known the sky.

With every delicate wave of the fan, I summoned a coolness the evening air refused to grant, willing it to soothe the heat blooming across my cheeks. But this fan was more than an accessory.

It was a shield.

A fragile barrier to conceal the quiver of my lips, to hide the tremor of fear threading its way through me, threatening to unravel all at once.

"Your gloves, my lady."

Mary's voice pulled me back from the precipice of my thoughts. She presented them with reverence, their silk fabric gleaming under the candlelight—an understated elegance, soft yet inescapable.

I slid my arms into their long, encasing embrace, feeling the fabric tighten over my skin like a second layer of flesh, smooth and deceptive.

The gloves stretched past my elbows, a seamless extension of the gown's creamy hue. They were paradoxical—shielding yet exposing, concealing yet proclaiming. A whisper of status, wealth, and quiet power stitched into every seam.

I folded one hand over the other, the fan resting lightly between my fingers as the silk whispered secrets only the wearer could hear—secrets of restraint, of silent suffering, of a woman adorned for admiration but never for freedom.

With gloved hands and a fluttering fan, I became the perfect portrait of poise and nobility.

Yet beneath the fine fabric and gilded expectations, my heart still raged, beating a furious rhythm against the constraints of silk and circumstance.

"Let's have a look at you, Lady Elizabeth," Mary's gentle voice coaxed me to turn.

I spun, my movements slow, cautious. The heavy skirts cascaded around me in shimmering waves, pooling at my feet like the petals of an opulent flower caught in an unforgiving breeze. For a fleeting moment, I was anchored only by Mary's touch—a lifeline against the undertow of satin and duty.

She peered at me through the looking glass, her soft smile holding something deeper than mere admiration. She could see me—not just the polished surface, but the turmoil roiling beneath it.

"You look beautiful," she murmured, eyes searching mine with quiet understanding.

"Thank you, Mary," I replied, though the words felt like a fragile whisper, barely carrying my gratitude.

I found something rare within these stifling walls in her friendship—a semblance of solace. She was merely a maid to others, but to me, she was more. A confidante. A sister in spirit. The one soul who might understand the storm churning beneath my poised exterior.

"Try not to worry so much," Mary said, smoothing a stray curl with a motherly tenderness. "This night will pass, as all nights do. And I'll be there in every thought."

I held her gaze in the mirror, gripping those words like a talisman.

She meant them as comfort, but they only brushed against the raw, exposed edges of my anxiety.

Tonight, I was to be paraded before a room full of watchful eyes, offered to a man I loathed. That truth crushed me, stealing the breath from my lungs and leaving me dizzy with dread. But it was not only the fear of the evening that unsettled me—it was him.

The stranger.

The man whose arrival had upturned the monotony of my suffering, igniting a fire within me that no sense of duty could extinguish.

I remembered the collision in the hallway, the jolt of impact as his hands found my arms, the startling intimacy of his grip —steadying, strong. The memory was still imprinted on my skin.

And his eyes—gods help me, his eyes—had burned with something wild, untamed.

A glint of wilderness in a world that demanded order.

The mere recollection sent my pulse racing.

His attire had been an anomaly among the meticulously curated wealth of my father's estate; the styling of his coat was unfamiliar, his self otherworldly in a place built on rigid decorum. He was not one of us.

A traveler, perhaps. A man accustomed to lands beyond the reach of our noble circles. There had been something in how he carried himself, a quiet defiance in the set of his shoulders—as though he belonged to a world far greater than the gilded cage I inhabited.

And then there had been his smile.

Oh, that smile—a mere flicker, gone before I could grasp its meaning. But it had changed something.

A fleeting curve of his lips, yet it had unraveled me.

"Lady Elizabeth?"

Mary's voice pulled me back to the present, laced with quiet concern.

"Forgive me," I murmured, smoothing the front panel of my gown as if I could press away the lingering thoughts that refused to leave me. "I was… somewhere else."

Mary tilted her head, eyes twinkling with knowing mischief. "Somewhere, or with someone?"

I hesitated for the briefest moment before conceding, "Perhaps both."

Her lips curved into a conspiratorial smile as she leaned closer. "Whoever he is," she whispered, her voice as light as a feather against the charged air between us, "he has certainly made an impression."

Heat bloomed across my cheeks, betraying me before I could form a proper defense. "It's foolishness," I admitted, though they felt like a lie as I spoke the words.

Because no matter how much I tried to dismiss it, I knew.

I would carry that moment with me for as long as breath filled my lungs—the unexpected thrill of contact, the firm grip that had steadied more than just my body.

And as I vanished down the corridor, he left behind more than just a fleeting memory.

He left behind questions.

And a longing for answers I feared I would never receive.

Nestled within my chamber's silk and brocade confines, I

felt like a ship adrift, my thoughts unmoored, wafting ceaselessly toward him—toward the stranger whose touch had set my world alight.

He became something more in my mind's eye with each passing moment. A wanderer. An adventurer. A man who had braved the tempests of distant oceans and stood with quiet confidence in foreign courts, his stories as plentiful as the stars.

The clock ticked, marking the march of time, yet I remained ensnared in the past. I traced the memory of our collision, the firm pressure of his hands against my shoulders, the fleeting charge that had passed between us.

I closed my eyes—and there he was.

A ghostly aura lingered in the quiet of my room, half-formed from shadows and whispers, compelling in ways I could scarcely articulate.

My heart, once so disciplined and so accustomed to the restrained pace of expectation, now beat with its own will.

It fluttered as the lace brushed against my skin, mistaking it for his touch.

It soared at the rustle of leaves beyond my window, imagining it the sound of his return.

I chastised myself for such fancies—what sense was there in yearning for a specter, for a phantom who existed only within the hazy realm of chance?

And yet…

As the gloaming cast its velvety curtain across the sky, I allowed myself the indulgence of dreams where our paths might cross again.

In the grandeur of a ballroom, our hands might find one another, our steps aligning in a dance as old as time itself.

Across the throng of reception, our gazes might meet—a look laden with secrets and silent promises.

Our voices might mingle beneath the moon's gentle glow, soft as the summer breeze that kissed the roses below my window.

And just for a moment, I let myself believe.

The infatuation nestled within me—a clandestine spark, flickering in the darkness, threatening to ignite the air I breathed.

It was irrational—a fantasy spun from a single, stolen moment.

An ember in the otherwise cold hearth of my existence.

Yet it warmed me, as the reality of my betrothal loomed like an execution. Lord Winston. The very name sent shards of ice through my veins, unnerving me to the marrow.

"Off you go," Mary murmured, tucking an errant strand of hair into place.

My feet carried me forward with hesitant grace, each step down the grand staircase a silent plea for courage. The balusters blurred into a maze of intricate carvings, the sweeping arc of polished wood guiding and entangling me.

This house, this world—a gilded prison.

And at the foot of the stairs, time stilled.

As if the world itself had paused, holding its breath.

He stood there.

The stranger.

The man who had haunted my thoughts, slipping unbidden into my waking reveries. He had stepped through the open door of my father's estate as if willed into existence by my longing, as if fate had drawn him back to me.

Dark. Handsome.

His being filled the space like smoke—intoxicating, inescapable.

Our eyes locked, and in that instant, a tempest raged between us—silent but undeniable.

Was there recognition in his gaze? A torrid understanding?

Or was it merely the hopeful whisper of my heart, desperate to believe that destiny had not been so cruel?

"Elizabeth."

My father's voice decimated the silence, splintering the moment.

I turned, finding him standing there—his frame rigid, his attire as ostentatious as ever, crowned by one of those stark white wigs that seemed an affront to fashion itself.

I reached the last step just as he beckoned me forward, his voice steeped in importance. "I'd like you to meet our guest, Lord Amir Hassan of Anatolia. Lord Hassan, I present my daughter, Lady Elizabeth Alexander."

Lord Hassan.

The name curled through the air, unfamiliar yet his.

With a poise I scarcely felt, I approached the man who had unknowingly kindled such turmoil within me.

He took my gloved hand, and a jolt shot through me when his lips brushed the back of it—like the first flash of lightning splitting an oppressive sky.

The contact was fleeting, yet it left an imprint, a quiet claiming of space between us. His grip was gentle but firm, the warmth of his skin stark against the cool propriety demanded of us both.

His dark eyes held mine, secure and unreadable, but I swore I saw that same unspoken recognition within them. The same awareness had lingered between us since that first, unguarded collision in the corridor.

I was ensnared.

Trapped in an invisible web of longing, restraint, propriety, and something far more dangerous.

"Please forgive me for my outburst the other day," I stammered, my voice a breathless whisper of decorum.

"No need to apologize."

Lord Hassan's voice was relief, smooth and silken, his accent curling around each word like smoke.

Deep. Rich. Laced with something elusive, something that hinted at lands beyond the horizon. There was a melody in his cadence, a quiet strength woven through his tone as if his words carried the warmth of sun-soaked deserts and the mystery of faraway kingdoms.

Something about him felt untouched by the rigid world I knew.

"I was the intruder in your household," he continued, his gaze never wavering from mine. "I am the one who should take responsibility."

A pause.

Something unreadable passed through his dark eyes—sorrow? Regret?—before his voice softened.

"Please accept my condolences for the loss of your brothers. If there's anything I can do to soothe your sorrow..."

The words struck me unexpectedly, like an arrow loosed in the dead of night.

But before I could respond—before I could fully absorb his unexpected kindness—my father's voice bombarded the moment, shattering the fragile thread between us.

"Lord Hassan is from distant Anatolia. He is here to do business with our society."

The words hung in the air, overflowing with meaning.

Business. Our society.

My gaze hardened.

Dread crept down my spine, dousing the flicker of warmth that had so briefly thawed the ice of my existence.

How could he—this enigmatic stranger who had ignited such a tumult within me—wish to aid in my father's shadowed dealings?

"The journey from Anatolia to England must have been long, Lord Hassan. It likely took you several months," I said, my voice carefully controlled, masking the storm within.

"Fortune smiled kindly upon us," Lord Hassan replied, his composure unshaken by the miles he had traversed. "The trip was without incident. And now, I'm happy to be here. Thank you, Lord Alexander, for the invitation to celebrate your lovely daughter's betrothal to Lord Winston."

The word betrothal crashed into me, and the blood seemed to drain from my body, leaving me weightless and raw.

A tightness coiled around my ribs, my breath hitching—a quiet, involuntary gasp. The sound barely escaped me, but I felt it—a small, invisible betrayal.

I forced a smile, one that did not reach my eyes.

Then, before anyone could notice the fracture in my composure, I turned quickly, my skirts rustling in a swift, desperate retreat.

The library.

Its towering shelves and the scent of old parchment offered sanctuary. A place where time stood still, where I could breathe without expectations pressing down upon me.

I placed my palm against the cool mahogany bookcase, grounding myself as I willed my heart to still its frantic pace.

Lord Hassan—this man who had stirred something dangerous within me—was he merely another piece in my father's grand design?

Was he a fantasy come to life, an illusion of something freer, something unattainable?

Or was he just like the rest?

A man entangled in my father's intrigue.

A man I could never trust.

And yet…

Why did I long to?

As I watched, hidden among the shadows of knowledge and history, I felt my own trembling heart.

The man of my dreams was in my father's foyer, yet dream and reality seemed locked in battle, warring within me.

My mind raced, caught between fear and an inexplicable longing.

How could I reconcile the two?

How could I blindly follow a heart that led me straight into the arms of a man who aided my father in his dark and treacherous schemes?

How could I dream of such things when I was already bound to Lord Winston?

The very thought made my spirit turn to stone.

At precisely a quarter until six, I was summoned to dinner.

The grand dining hall of my father's estate was a monument to wealth and austerity—where excess and severity sat side by side like uneasy companions.

The mahogany table stretched before me, its polished surface gleaming under the golden glow of the chandeliers, reflecting a world that felt increasingly distant.

Servants moved in a quiet ballet, their appearance a whisper against the opulent hush. Plates were set down with proficient elegance, each brimming with delicacies meant to impress.

Roasted quail, fragrant with rosemary, lay in perfect rows. Oysters, still glistening from the sea, rested in their half-shells like stolen pearls. Glazed vegetables, vibrant against the stark china, added an illusion of warmth to the cold world around me.

Yet none of it touched me.

I perched at the edge of my seat, a rigid spectator to the feast. The aroma of decadence filled the air, but it only deepened the nausea curling in my stomach.

Beside me, Lord Winston's bloated hand lunged forward, thick fingers closing around a drumstick with the graceless hunger of a man who had never known restraint. His meaty knuckles scraped against the delicate china, the jarring sound sending a shiver up my spine.

I swallowed hard, forcing myself to look away.

Across from me sat Lord Hassan, his authority an undeniable force amidst the sea of powdered wigs and perfumed excess.

Unlike the other men, he bore no such pretense, whose artificial halos of white powder framed their ruddy faces in a parody of nobility.

His dark hair was slicked back, a mark of refinement. The neatly trimmed beard framed his jaw, highlighting the sculpted meticulousness of his features, and every time I dared steal a glance at him, the butterflies in my stomach pirouetted more fervently.

What was this?

This unfamiliar feeling—this quiet, simmering pull—toward a man who should have meant nothing to me?

Surrounded by pomp and circumstance, I felt like an intruder in my home.

The cloying scent of perfumed hair powder and the musk of ambition permeated the air. My father's associates—all members of his enigmatic society—exchanged nods and knowing glances, their conversation a private code I had never been permitted to translate.

Around me, the only women present were those who served. Their eyes remained downcast; their movements practiced and silent, their existence an extension of duty.

"Elizabeth."

My father's voice tore through my thoughts—brisk, commanding, inescapable.

"Yes, Father?"

His stare seared through me, intense and unrelenting—a gaze filled with unspoken threats and expectations woven into every glance.

A silent warning.

A reminder of my place.

And yet, despite the silent command that held me prisoner, I felt it again.

That magnetic pull toward the man across from me.

Toward Lord Hassan.

The one existence in the room who felt as if he saw me.

And I longed to be seen for the first time in my life.

I closed my eyes briefly, willing this night to dissolve into nothingness. But when I opened them, the nightmare remained.

My father was positioned at the head of the table, his glass raised high. The candlelight glinted off the crystal, casting fractured reflections against the towering walls.

"I am so glad you are all here," he announced, his voice a proclamation, a decree that bound me tighter to my fate. "Tonight, we celebrate the union of two great families and strengthen our society."

My heart pounded, its rhythm a warning drumbeat in my chest.

"Lord Winston is an esteemed member of our society who has brought us to our current glory." My father's voice rang with conviction. "Would you like to say a few words, Lord Winston?"

All eyes turned to the man who would be my husband.

But mine remained fixed on Lord Hassan.

Something was unnerving in the stillness that settled over his features. His expression remained impassive, composed, yet I felt the storm beneath his exterior—the subtle tension in his jaw, the unreadable depth in his dark eyes.

Was he truly one of them?

Or was there something more to this enigmatic visitor from Anatolia?

The scrape of a chair against the polished floor jolted me back.

With a creaking of bones that seemed to reverberate through the grand dining hall, Lord Winston heaved himself to his feet.

The flickering candlelight only accentuated his monstrosity —the waxy pallor of his skin, the folds of flesh around his neck, and the way his bloated fingers trembled slightly as he placed them against the table for support.

His voice slithered through the air, full of unctuous pride.

"It is indeed an honor to be betrothed to Lady Alexander," he declared, his tone dripping with self-importance.

The words left his lips like a sentence passed, a claim stamped upon me.

And then—

"I have no doubt our union shall be most fruitful, and you shall bear the next heir for our society."

The air in my lungs turned to ice.

The words hung there, wrapping around my throat like a noose.

Every gaze in the room bore into me, waiting. Watching.

But I could not move.

I could not breathe.

I averted my eyes, a shudder rippling through me as I met the grotesque spectacle of Lord Winston. His gaze held the mottled gleam of a half-eaten feast, glistening with something that sent revulsion crawling over my skin. Greasy strands of hair escaped the confines of his powdered wig in rebellious wisps, and flecks of the evening's repast clung grimly between the yellowed nubs that masqueraded as teeth.

A smear of something—pheasant, perhaps, or the remains of a tarte tatin—adorned his cheek like a vile emblem of gluttony.

The scent that wafted from him was a miasma of decay.

I fought the violent urge to recoil.

"Here's to the lovely couple!" someone bellowed, raising their glass high.

The chorus of agreements that followed rang through the chamber like a funeral dirge to my hopes.

My hand trembled as I lifted my glass, but I could not meet Lord Hassan's gaze.

Earlier, he had set butterflies loose in my stomach.

Now, only loathing lingered, curling around my ribs like an iron vice.

I wished—prayed—for the earth to open beneath me and swallow me whole.

With a graceless thud, Winston's ponderous form collapsed back into his chair, jostling the table and nearly toppling into my lap.

Instinctively, my hands shot out to steady him, and my fingers brushed against his coat's damp, clammy fabric.

I recoiled, horrified, but only once he was upright did I snatch my hands back, my stomach twisting violently.

I grabbed my napkin and scrubbed at my skin as though I could wipe away the sensation of his touch.

But no amount of silk and friction could erase the taint of his filth.

A sudden shift swept through the room.

My father cleared his throat.

The low hum of conversation halted, his voice shattered the silence, crisp and unyielding.

"Gentlemen," he began, his eyes dark with solemnity, "the Black Wraith has become a serious threat to our society and cause."

A ripple of murmurs surged through the assembly, a tide of unease.

From down the table, my father's gaze slid to where Lord Hassan sat, composed and silent.

Their eyes met.

A nod passed between them—so brief and subtle—that I almost doubted I had seen it.

Yet it spoke volumes.

What pact lay between them?

"He has destroyed important leaders in our society, as well as the societies themselves," my father continued, his voice steeped in venom. "The Black Wraith's ruthless and barbaric actions have reduced our influence, eliminating our strongest allies across Europe. The French society has fallen. And my sons—" He spat the words, a snarl curling from his lips. "My sons were slaughtered by his hand."

A hush settled over the room.

"He becomes bolder with each passing day," my father said, his fists clenching at his sides. "And now, it seems, he—or perhaps an accomplice—employs a poison so deadly it melts flesh from bone."

A chorus of horror swept through the chamber, gasps and muttered curses breaking the charged silence.

Fear.

Outrage.

The perfect storm of emotions, coiling and twisting, ready to consume.

And yet...

From the corner of my eye, I watched Lord Hassan.

Still. Silent.

His expression did not change, yet something about him shifted, an imperceptible tightening in his posture, a flicker in his gaze that sent my mind reeling.

Was it calculation? Restraint?

Or something far more dangerous?

My pulse pounded in my ears as I tried to assemble the pieces of this sinister puzzle—

To understand what game was truly being played—

And what role Lord Hassan held in its unfolding design.

"The Black Wraith is a coward," Lord Winston declared with contempt.

My fingers gripped the edge of the table, knuckles whitening.

I could almost smell the putrid stench of his breath as he leaned forward, savoring his cruelty.

"He lurks in the shadows, a marauder waiting to strike from the darkness," he said, his words dripping with a perverse pleasure. "But we will not let him escape. When we finally apprehend him, he will pay dearly for his heinous crimes."

A slow, oily grin spread across his bloated face.

"We will make him reveal his powerful alchemy recipe through brute force and relentless torture—no matter the cost."

Torture him?

A fierce, primal crack echoed through me, breaking past the corset's tight laces and society's strangling grip.

Was my father truly involved in the business of torture?

A fire roared to life within me, an indignation that no longer fit within the confines of my silence.

My chair scraped loudly against the floor as I rose.

The clinking of cutlery ceased.

A stunned silence fell.

All eyes turned to the anomaly in their midst—a woman standing when she should not.

"What if this masked man isn't a villain?"

The words left me before I could stop them, trembling yet defiant, breaking through the stillness.

"Is it possible that he's trying to reveal the flaws in our methods? Perhaps he sees societal issues and wants to create change by showing us the truth."

A beat of silence.

And then, as if a conductor had lifted his baton—

Laughter erupted.

Harsh.

Mocking.

Cruel.

It tore through the room, a symphony of ridicule that burned my skin, stripping me bare before their amusement.

But across the table, one man did not laugh.

Lord Hassan's face remained unreadable, his dark eyes locked onto mine.

Silent. Inscrutable.

Briefly, something passed between us—something unspoken that sent a shiver down my spine.

"Good gods, Elizabeth," my father snarled.

The laughter ceased at once.

His gaze burned through me, devoid of warmth, devoid of anything but cold, absolute authority.

"What tales have you been filling your mind with?"

His voice was deceptively calm—too calm. The kind of calm that preceded a storm.

"Where could you have possibly conjured up such a ludicrous notion? Have you been reading treasonous literature, hmm?"

The sneer curled my father's lips as he leaned forward.

"Books of seditious libel?"

His snort reverberated through the hall, a sound not unlike an enraged bull, nostrils flaring, braced to charge.

Heat seared my cheeks, the blood pounding in my ears as though trying to drown out their scorn.

"I don't read treasonous books, Father," I muttered, the words barely audible above the low rumble of their continued mirth. "I'm a good and honorable woman."

The declaration tasted bitter on my tongue; an admission meant to pacify rather than convince.

My father waved dismissively, already turning back to his loyal cohorts. "Leave the serious matters to the men. You've been reading too much tomfoolery."

And just like that—

The laughter rose again.

It was a physical force, pushing me back, shoving me down into my seat.

Slowly, I lowered myself.

Each burst of laughter, each smirk exchanged across the table, was a lash against my armor.

I felt small. Foolish.

A flickering flame, snuffed out by their ridicule.

But beneath the shame, beneath the trembling—

Something remained.

A whisper of anger.

A smoldering ember that refused to die.

It curled around my ribs, whispering of justice and change—a whisper I could not, would not, ignore.

Then—

Silence.

A heavy, oppressive hush descended upon the room.

And then, Lord Winston's voice—

Dripping with venom, slow and measured, slashing through the stillness like the tip of a dagger pointed against my throat.

"And what insight could you possibly offer, my delicate flower?"

He drawled the words, savoring them, letting them fester in the air between us.

"You flutter in ignorance while we brave souls wage battles beyond your feeble comprehension."

The sneer in his voice was meant to wound.

Meant to humiliate.

Meant to remind me of my place.

"I... I... I know enough to imagine change might be in order," I managed, though as the words left my lips, they felt fragile.

Truthfully, I knew little of my father's dealings—only the whispers behind locked doors, the veiled warnings in Mary's hushed tones, and the fear that coiled in my stomach when my brothers left and never returned.

My father's chair crashed with violence that sent a shudder down my spine.

Then—

A thunderous slam.

His palm struck the polished wood, the force rattling the crystalware, the chandeliers quivering in their chains.

I flinched, shrinking back, my heart hammering against my ribs.

Regret sank its teeth into me.

"Elizabeth, that's enough!" My father's voice cracked like a whip, raw with barely restrained fury.

His eyes blazed—not with concern or patience, but with something far colder.

"Stay out of this and let the men handle these important matters," he spat. "The Black Wraith is no noble saint, after all."

He swept his arm out, a theatrical gesture toward the men gathered before him, their expressions ranging from bemused to annoyed.

"Your insolence is not only unwelcome but laughable. Know your place!"

His words struck like a physical blow, stripping away any illusion of agency I might have possessed.

Across the table, Lord Hassan did not move.

A silent observer. A shadow carved from the darkness.

For a moment, I dared to meet his gaze.

Searching.

For what, I did not know—an ally, an ounce of understanding, a thread of insolence stitched into his unreadable expression.

But his silence was a wall I could not breach.

And perhaps I was foolish to have thought otherwise.

Slowly, I lowered my gaze.

But the final blow did not come from Lord Hassan's silence.

It came from the brutal, undeniable truth—

My father saw me as nothing.

A pawn on his chessboard of power.

No voice.

No worth beyond the marriage that would secure his ambitions.

I stood, every muscle trembling, my voice barely a whisper.

"Forgive me, Father... will you excuse me? I need some fresh air."

No response.

No acknowledgment.

The plea fell into nothingness, swallowed by the clinking of glasses and the murmur of conspiratorial voices weaving their dark plots.

As if I had never spoken at all.

And that was when I knew—

I was not just powerless in this room.

I was invisible.

Leaving behind the dining room, I slipped through the ornate French doors at the end of the grand hallway. The crisp night air kissed my cheeks, cool and bracing against the heat of my humiliation.

Tears welled in my eyes, unshed, filled with everything I could not say.

The scent of roses clung to the air, their sweetness almost mocking.

I reached out, tracing a finger along the velvet petals, but the softness did nothing to ease my bitterness. I had been in the garden longer than I realized—the sky had shifted, shadows stretching across the stone path, unnoticed. I was caught in a maze of thorns and regrets, my life closing around me like the vines coiled along the iron trellises.

"I need to find a way to escape before it's too late."

The words slipped past my lips, a whisper lost to the night.

A sliver of hope flickered, fragile against the fortress of my father's plans.

But fear and uncertainty gnawed at the edges of my resolve —how? When? Who could I trust?

And then—

Footsteps.

Leisurely. Unhurried.

Drawing closer.

I froze, my breath catching in my throat.

Whoever it was—

They weren't supposed to be here.

The garden had been empty moments ago.

I turned slowly, the shadows shifting around me.

"Lady Elizabeth," a voice murmured from the darkness. Low. Smooth. Dangerous.

A shiver ran down my spine.
Because it wasn't just any voice.
It was his.

CHAPTER 6
AMIR

I remained seated, my posture rigid as the heavy oak door shut with a resounding thud, sealing Elizabeth's departure from the dining room.

Thomas Alexander's domain was cold—the cold that seeped into your bones and never left.

Just like the man himself.

The others resumed their banter, oblivious to the injustice that had played out before them. Elizabeth's humiliation was a trivial spectacle to them, a woman's place reaffirmed with laughter and condescension.

But I couldn't shake the image of her retreating.

The slight quiver in her frame.

The way her breath had hitched, just for a moment, before she forced herself to remain composed.

Her father viewed her as chattel, an asset to be bartered and controlled—a tool to strengthen his empire.

But Elizabeth… she was an anomaly.

A spark flickering against the wind of tradition, against a world that sought to smother her into submission.

That spark should not have mattered to me.

And yet—

It did.

I had strict orders—do not get involved.

But watching her stand, her voice trembling yet resolute in the face of ridicule had stirred something within me.

A dangerous, unwelcome feeling.

How arduous it must have been to dare to speak against the tide in a room where her words were meant to be dust beneath their boots.

My chest tightened with a foreign instinct—an urge I had no right to feel.

Protect her.

Shield her.

It was an impulse that should have died the moment it was born.

This was not my battle.

This was not why I was here.

I was The Black Wraith—a specter, a shadow, a force of reckoning, not a man who tangled himself in sympathy.

Detachment was my armor.

My survival.

And yet—

Here I was.

Watching.

Waiting.

Knowing that, despite every warning in my mind, despite the danger of my growing awareness of her—

I was already too close.

"Lord Hassan, do you fancy another glass?"

The sneering voice interrupted my thoughts. One of the men, his smirk curled with amusement.

My spine straightened. Across the table, Thomas Alexander's glacial gaze scrutinized me, assessing, calculating.

"Thank you, but no," I replied evenly, masking the tumult inside me.

It took every ounce of discipline to remain composed, to silence the clamor in my mind, to smother the reckless pull of something that should not exist within me.

I waged a war in the quiet of my skull.

Each rational thought clashed against the unbidden empathy that had taken root.

And deeper still—

Something altogether forbidden.

Desire.

It was a sickness festering beneath my skin, growing stronger with each stolen glance, each unspoken moment between us.

Lady Elizabeth had awakened an avalanche within me—one of lust, of longing, of something far more dangerous than my mission itself.

I could not afford distractions.

I was a weapon, an instrument of vengeance, honed and sharpened for a singular purpose.

My resolve, once impenetrable, splintered beneath her gaze.

Her anguish was an ache I wanted to soothe.

Her beauty—an opium I wanted to devour.

And my desires were savage.

A primal hunger coiled in my gut.

I yearned—

To ravage her.

To consume every inch of her, to unearth the fire hidden under her delicate frame, to leave her trembling and breathless beneath me.

To ruin her in the most exquisite way imaginable.

But I was a man who existed in the shadows.

And she was a woman drowning in chains.

As the dinner continued around me—a theater of hollow civilities—I made an inward vow.

A silent oath that transcended orders, duty, and the carefully constructed walls of my mission.

I would protect Elizabeth.

Regardless of the cost.

Regardless of the chaos it would invite.

I could not stand idly by while she suffered, while men like her father and that creature she was promised to continued to tighten the noose around her.

With every clink of silverware against fine china, I reminded myself of the dangerous game I was now playing.

I was The Black Wraith, bound by shadows and secrecy.

But perhaps, in the darkness I inhabited, there existed a sliver of light—one that could, in some small way, illuminate the path for a soul as undeserving of cruelty as Lady Elizabeth Alexander.

I surveyed the room from my vantage point, noting each man's carefully arranged mask of civility.

At the head of the table, Thomas Alexander sat with an air of cold calculation, the strings of power wrapped around his fingers like a master puppeteer.

In contrast, Lord Winston's facade of nobility barely concealed the rot festering beneath.

I watched him. Studied him.

And in doing so, I felt it.

The cruelty simmering beneath his skin.

The perverse enjoyment he derived from the power he wielded over Elizabeth, from the knowledge that she would soon be his possession.

An icy sensation ran down my spine, despite myself.

And a thought crept into my mind—unbidden, undeniable.

He is more of a monster than I am.

The dinner concluded with Alexander rising from his seat, his movements crisp and deliberate—a signal for us to retire to the smoking room.

A transition from one chamber of power to the next.

From the grandeur of the dining hall to the heady warmth of a room where men held power as if it were their birthright.

I stepped inside, the massive stone fireplace commanding my attention, flames crackling, casting elongated shadows along the paneled walls.

A fire meant to warm—but here, it only made the room feel smaller, more suffocating.

Cigars were passed around—symbols of status, camaraderie, and unspoken alliances forged in smoke and ambition.

I accepted one out of necessity, rolling it between my fingers, but my mind was elsewhere.

Somewhere beyond this room.

Somewhere in the moonlit garden, a woman was alone—trapped in a life she did not choose.

And for the first time in my life, I questioned what was stronger—

My duty.

Or my desire to burn this world to the ground for her.

One by one, tapers caught fire, dipping into the roaring hearth, igniting the cigars in their hands.

Flames flickered, reflected in the cold glint of their eyes.

Men lounged in overstuffed armchairs, exhaling smoke like a dragon's breath, the haze thickening around us, distorting, softening the brutal nature of the company I kept.

The scent of tobacco curled through the room, rich and intoxicating, masking the stench of power, corruption, and quiet cruelty.

Laughter rumbled low, conversations laced with conspiratorial whispers. Deals were forged beneath the guise of leisure, empires secured between the exhale of smoke and the clink of crystal glasses.

Yet none of it could distract me.

Not from her.

Elizabeth's face hovered in my thoughts—grace and boldness entwined, her blue eyes carrying her suffocating reality.

And now, she haunted me.

After what could be considered appropriate discourse, I moved to stand.

"Thank you for this lovely evening, but I must be off," I announced to Lord Alexander, my voice tempered, unwavering—though inside, everything churned.

The room quieted just slightly, enough for his gaze to settle on me.

For the flicker of surprise to cross his features—so fleeting it might have been imagined.

Then, just as quickly, it was gone.

Masked beneath the cold veneer of a man who wielded control like a weapon.

"Please, stay." His voice was smooth, casual—a well-played move in a game where every word carried intent. He gestured toward the grand staircase beyond the door. "We have lovely accommodations upstairs."

A calculated offer.

A leash disguised as hospitality.

"No, thank you." My refusal was firm, my intent unshaken.

"I appreciate your generosity, but I have secured lodging elsewhere. However, I will return tomorrow to discuss our plan more."

The words were carefully chosen, maintaining the delicate facade of a guest—when, in truth, I was anything but.

A silent beat stretched between us.

Then, with a curt nod, I excused myself, stepping away from the smoky sanctuary and its denizens lost in their revelry.

The fresh air of the foyer met me, a welcome reprieve from the chamber of cigars and secrets.

Then—

A flicker of white.

Through the ornate window, her silhouette was unmistakable.

Elizabeth.

Wandering through the garden, her figure ghostlike beneath the moon's silver glow.

She moved like someone untethered, lost in a world that no longer belonged to her.

A prisoner without chains.

My chest tightened.

How I yearned—to have shielded her from the indignity she had suffered, to have been her advocate amidst the throng of wolves.

But I had stood in silence.

And that silence seared through me.

With a final glance at the window—now clouded by the shifting shadows of the night—I made an impulsive decision.

She needed someone.

And despite every instinct screaming for caution, despite my purpose pressing against me like an iron chain—

I committed to be that person.

Stepping across the threshold, the crisp night air bit against my skin.

I welcomed it.

I welcomed its clarity and a cold reminder of the world outside those walls.

My footsteps were quiet against the stone path, each step carrying me further from the manor's oppressive grasp.

And yet—

The more I walked, the louder my mind rebelled.

The conflict within me reignited a battle of duty and something else.

Something dangerous.

Something that whispered in the voice of a woman who had been alone in a room full of men who had already decided her fate.

"I am here for one reason," I muttered as if saying it aloud would reinforce my purpose.

As if the words would anchor me back to the mission that had once been everything.

But logic was overruled by the sight of her—

Standing alone beneath the moonlight, Elizabeth's sorrow was woven into every delicate line of her frame.

"Damn it all," I cursed softly, dismissing my orders, dismissing my restraint.

What harm could an offer of solace do?

But as I approached, doubt shadowed my steps.

I was no savior.

I was a monster born of darkness, a man who had built his legacy on destruction.

I had no business offering comfort.

Mortals wept. They suffered. Their lives were fleeting, their sorrows as insignificant as whispers lost to the wind.

And yet—

Elizabeth.

She was different.

A beacon of innocence in a world that had long since turned cruel. A testament to the last vestiges of goodness that men like me had long since forsaken.

And I—who lurked in the shadows, who dealt only in death and despair—felt the uncharacteristic urge to protect that light.

The very notion was foolish.

I should have walked away.

Lazarus had warned me not to get involved. His words echoed in my mind, his power looming over me now like an unseen specter.

"Stay detached, Amir. It is the only way to survive."

He had spoken not as a friend but as a Shadow Lord—his voice laced with centuries of knowledge drawn from a past littered with mistakes I had no intention of repeating.

Nevertheless, I found myself here.

"Am I going to do this?" I muttered into the night, expecting no answer but the rustling of leaves and the distant hoot of a vigilant owl.

No turning back.

The die was cast.

And my feet carried me onward—toward the unsuspecting angel ahead.

The night held a chill that felt at odds with the warm glow spilling from the manor's windows.

I moved silently through the garden, my steps sure, practiced—nothing but a shadow among shadows.

And yet, Elizabeth's silhouette merged with them as if she belonged to the night just as much as I did.

Then—

A sound.

Soft. Fragile.

A sob broke the silence.

My resolve flickering like the flame of a candle in a draft.

I had spent a lifetime detached from the sorrows of the living.

But her grief—

It rooted me to the spot.

And for the first time in longer than I could remember—

I felt something.

Something I had no right to feel.

Something that would change everything.

"Lady Alexander."

My voice barely rose above a whisper, yet she stiffened—a doe alerted to a being in the dark.

She glanced up, her eyes wide and glassy in the faint light.

"Who's there?"

Her words trembled, as delicate as leaves on the verge of falling.

"Don't be alarmed. It's me—Lord Hassan."

I took a cautious step forward, though I knew my appearance was a trespass. I was breaking the rules I had lived by for centuries, stepping onto sacred ground.

"I'm not here to hurt you."

The words felt hollow, even to my ears.

Because I was a man who hurt.

A man who destroyed.

She wiped her cheeks with the back of her hand, straightening her spine—her gaze locking onto mine with an intensity that belied her fragile exterior.

"If you're not here to ridicule or hurt me, then why are you here?"

Her voice was firm despite the remnants of sorrow clinging to her like morning mist.

"You have seen how little regard I am to be given."

The bitterness in her tone struck something deep within me.

They had sought to break her. To render her voiceless.

And yet—

She still stood.

I took another step closer, drawn into her orbit against my better judgment.

"I beg to differ."

Something passed across her face—doubt, curiosity, something more.

"May I ask why you're out here?"

The quiver in her voice did not escape me—nor did her effort to conceal it.

"I couldn't leave without saying something."

The admission hung between us, heavy, laden with meaning I dared not explore.

Her lips parted, the faintest hitch in her breath betraying a moment of hesitation.

"To address the earlier spectacle at my expense?" she asked at last, her words laced with a bitterness that suited her ill.

Her pain whittled new edges into her beauty, turning something delicate into something dangerous.

I remained silent, offering only a gesture toward the stone bench nestled among the roses.

She hesitated.

Then, with a wary grace, she moved to sit, her posture rigid, her frame coiled with unspoken distrust.

I joined her—but kept a respectful distance, acutely aware of the space between us.

The space where doubt could linger.

Where uncertainty could breathe.

Where logic whispered that I should not be here.

Sitting beside her, the world narrowed to just the two of us—

A weeping angel.

A silent monster.

Each hiding behind our masks.

And in that moment, I realized—

Perhaps I was not the only one cloaked in shadows.

The evening air curled between us, cool and weightless, carrying the faint scent of roses and regret.

I studied her silhouette against the moonlit garden, the soft tremor in her shoulders betraying the tears she refused to shed.

"What you did was brave," I said at last, my voice low, careful.

"Speaking out among those men."

A bitter chuckle slipped past her lips—cold enough to rival the frost creeping over the grass beneath our feet.

"Brave?" she echoed, her laughter hollow, chiseled from something achingly raw.

"I was stupid."

She turned her gaze to me then, her eyes gleaming with an emotion I could not yet name.

"I should have kept my mouth shut."

Her voice dropped to a whisper, years of expectation in each syllable.

"I should know my place."

The sarcasm dripped like acid from her tongue.

But beneath it—

Beneath the anger, beneath the bitterness, beneath the quiet resignation—

It was a flicker of something else.

Something wild.

Something undone.

And against every warning in my mind—

I wanted to set it free.

"You weren't stupid," I said softly, my voice barely above a whisper. "You spoke the truth, when no one else dared to. That takes courage."

Her eyes—a serene summer sky—now blazed with something untamed, something undeniable.

"What good did it do?" she asked, her voice breaking like glass.

"They laughed at me. They treated me like I was nothing."

Then—

Her gaze locked onto mine, the blue depths searching, demanding.

"And you… you said nothing."

I swallowed hard, her disappointment rending through me—cleaner, deeper than any weapon ever could.

"I couldn't," I admitted, my voice quieter than intended.

It wasn't the answer she wanted.

It wasn't the answer she deserved.

"There are… things you don't know, Elizabeth."

She shook her head, frustration rising.

"You're just like them, Lord Hassan. Just like my father and Lord Winston."

Her voice trembled—but it wasn't from fear.

It was anger.

"You stayed silent while they humiliated me."

A pause.

A breath.

And then—

"Why didn't you stand up for me if you thought I was right?"

The words hit harder than I expected.

She had every right to ask.

And I had no right to answer.

Because if she knew the truth—

If she knew who I was, what I had come here to do—

Her hatred for her father and Winston would be nothing compared to the loathing she would feel for me.

I tore my gaze away, staring into the darkened garden, searching for an answer in the cold night air.

"It's complicated," I murmured.

It was a hollow excuse.

A lie wrapped in half-truths.

"I didn't want you to get hurt."

But the words tasted bitter on my tongue.

Because the truth was—

If I stayed in her orbit much longer…

I would be the one to hurt her most of all.

Elizabeth let out a shaky breath, her hands trembling as she clutched the edge of the bench as if anchoring herself against a fate closing in around her.

"I don't want to marry him," she whispered.

It was so soft that I almost didn't hear it.

"I can't marry Lord Winston."

Her voice was raw, splintered at the edges—helpless and defiant all at once.

"He's old, cruel… I feel so trapped."

The words tore at something inside me, something I had long thought dead and buried.

I knew exactly the kind of man Winston was.

And the thought of Elizabeth bound to him, suffering beneath his vile hands—

A future stolen, a light snuffed out—

It was unthinkable.

Inside, my turmoil raged as fierce as any storm.

Intervening would be reckless.

It would threaten everything.

But to do nothing?

To leave her to that fate?

I would be no better than the monsters I hunted.

"Elizabeth."

Her name escaped me as a whisper, heavy with the weight of a war I had yet to win.

She turned to me, her gaze pleading—desperate—but it was not mercy she sought.

It was freedom.

"He is not worthy to stand in your shadow," I said, my voice low, and firm—a vow I had no right to make.

"Let alone claim your hand."

And just like that—

The moment shifted.

A silent promise.

A dangerous truth.

An unspoken declaration hanging between us, like the last breath before a fall.

Because I knew, as surely as I knew my name—

I would not let her be his.

The garden around us lay silent, save for the rustling leaves, whispering secrets in the dark—a fitting audience for this clandestine meeting between two souls caught in a web far more elaborate than we could have imagined.

"Listen to me, Elizabeth," I implored, my voice deep and stable, though my pulse was anything but.

I leaned in, close enough to catch the faint trace of roses on her skin.

"You don't have to marry him."

Her breath hitched, her eyes widening. Moonlight caught in their depths, reflecting something new.

A flicker of hope.

"And what way is that?" she whispered with disbelief. "Running away? To where?"

Her voice trembled—not with fear, but with a raw, acerbic desperation.

"The thought of facing my father's wrath, of being cast out into a world that would see me as nothing—" she swallowed hard, her fingers twisting together. "It makes bile rise in my throat. I would have nothing. No one. My entire existence would crumble to dust before my eyes."

Her pain sank into me like a dagger buried deep.

She was trapped.

And I—of all people—knew what it meant to be caged by duty.

I reached into the inner pocket of my jacket, fingers brushing against the embossed card I had prepared for such unforeseen circumstances.

The exit I had never planned to offer.

"You wouldn't be alone," I said, drawing out the card—a simple thing, yet weighted with meaning far greater than ink and paper could convey.

Lord Amir Hassan.

The name was not mine, but the only one she could know.

I extended it toward her, and our fingers brushed.

A current, unexpected and undeniable, licked up my spine.

Her lips parted—barely, a soft inhale that sent heat rushing through me.

Sparks danced between us.

And my body responded—viscerally, ruthlessly.

It was alien to me, this sensation.

But in that instant, I knew.

I wanted her.

Not as a pawn in this war.

Not as a woman in distress.

I wanted Elizabeth Alexander.

Completely.

Wholly.

In every way, a man could claim a woman.

And gods help me—

I would have her.

"If you ever feel unsafe," I said, releasing the parchment into her safekeeping. "Or if you need to get away… this is where I'll be. My townhouse. You'll be safe there."

Elizabeth's fingers curled around the card, gripping it like a lifeline.

A long silence stretched between us before she spoke, her voice soft, trembling slightly with vulnerability.

"Why are you helping me?"

Her question was raw, stripped bare.

"Why do you care?"

I hesitated.

Because I shouldn't.

Because I couldn't.

But the words left me before I could stop them.

"Because you shouldn't be treated this way."

My voice was steady, but inside, a war raged.

"And because you deserve better than this."

It was the truth. And it came from a place of honor I had long feared was dead within me.

I forced aside the heat coiling in my blood, the pull of something far more dangerous than desire.

She studied me in the dim glow of moonlight, her gaze searching, weighing me with a scrutiny that made my chest tighten.

And then, finally—

"Thank you."

A whisper, yet deafening.

"I don't know what I'll do."

She bit her lip, hesitating, before tilting her head slightly. Her eyes on mine was like a thread binding us together.

"I take my words back," she murmured. "You're not like them."

A pause.

"You might think you are, but you're not."

The words struck harder than they should have.

Because she didn't know.

She didn't know.

I was worse.

Far, far worse.

A monster wrapped in a man's skin.

And yet—

I wanted to believe her.

Rising to my feet, I felt the pull of our strange connection, a force unseen yet undeniable. The gravity of it crushing my chest, threatening to crack something open inside me.

I had no right to her trust.

No right to this moment.

But I took it anyway.

"Stay safe, Lady Alexander."

Her name left my lips in a whisper, a ghost of something I did not deserve.

Gently, I lifted her hand to my mouth, my lips barely grazing the silk of her glove.

A fleeting promise.

A sin waiting to be committed.

As I released her hand and stepped back, the tremor coursing through me unsettled me.

Because in that moment—

I knew.

I had just made a choice.

A choice that would change everything.

A choice that could save us both—

Or doom us completely.

CHAPTER 7
ELIZABETH

My fingers worked methodically, pinching off the withered blooms of my mother's roses—as if I could discard my worries just as easily.

Petal by petal, they fell, a soft rain of decay littering the soil beneath my feet.

Their lingering perfume could not mask the stench of despair that clung to me since that night—

Since that disastrous betrothal dinner.

With each dying flower I cast away, it felt as if a part of my soul fluttered to the ground alongside it, crushed beneath the inevitability.

I was amidst a splendor of color and life, yet inside—

I was a garden wilting in drought.

My hands moved from one rose bush to another, deadheading the spent flowers, coaxing life where it no longer wished to remain.

But there was no delaying the death sentence that loomed over me.

No removing the rot of fate.

I was to be chained to Lord Winston—

A monster draped in gentleman's clothing.

The thought sent a shudder up my spine, as cold as the shadow stretched across the garden walls.

And yet—

Despite the dread sinking into my heart, my thoughts drifted where they should not go.

To him.

To Lord Hassan.

His image was etched behind my eyelids, an unwelcome specter in the depths of my mind.

Those dark, piercing eyes—

Seeing through me.

Understanding, and yet unfathomable.

He had come to the garden that night, and he was an unexpected solace in my world of chaos.

And then—

He had given me his address.

A single slip of paper now burned into my memory.

I chastised myself for entertaining thoughts of him.

No good could come from such dangerous daydreams.

And yet—

They persisted.

Fantasies wove through my mind like vines curling around trellises, twisting tighter—

Pulling me in.

Offering a fleeting escape from the grim reality that awaited me.

With a deep sigh, I let my gaze drift from the delicate petals to the far end of the garden, where shadows slithered between the hedges.

It was there that my father's associates had gathered after the betrothal dinner—

Their laughter, grating against the stillness of the night, had reminded me of carrion crows coming to roost.

I had never met most of them before that evening, yet—

They had all carried an air of familiarity.

As if they already knew who I was.

As if they already knew the role I was to play in their macabre theatre.

They had circled my father like vultures, their heads bowed together in urgent and secretive conversation.

I had not needed to hear their words to know.

It had been the way they stood—hunched, conspiring—that sent a chill through me.

The way their backs remained turned, indifferent to my existence.

Their murmurs, too low to catch, had coiled through the air like serpents sliding through grass.

I had told myself it was horrid to think of my father's guests as scavengers, as beasts drawn to the scent of something rotting.

Even so—

The unease in my gut had clenched too tightly to ignore.

A rustling sound snapped me from my reverie.

I turned, straightening.

From between two towering yews, my father emerged.

His gaze found mine, and without preamble, he spoke—

"Elizabeth, you are summoned for tea at Lord Winston's estate."

My stomach plummeted.

The word summoned lodged in my throat like a stone.

"Now?" I asked, feigning a calm I did not feel.

"Immediately," he replied.

Emotionless. Cold.

An executioner announcing a sentence.

I nodded—a hollow gesture of obedience.

And then I turned, moving toward the only sanctuary left to me.

My chamber.

Mary was already waiting, an array of garments across my bed.

She did not ask why.

She did not have to.

She merely began.

Fastening buttons. Tightening stays and smoothing lace.

Layer by layer, she built the cage I was expected to wear.

Layer by layer, she prepared me for the lion's den.

And all I could do was stand there—

And let it happen.

First came the stays, laced tight enough to ensure an elegant posture. My ribs compressed, and my breath shortened, but I did not complain.

Then came the hooped petticoat, the framework beneath the gown—a silhouette not of my choosing, a shape not my own.

Mary selected a gown of robin's-egg-blue silk, the fabric as cool as water against my skin. Delicate cream-colored flowers embroidered across the bodice—so soft, so lovely, so at odds with the terror coiling inside me.

Over this, she draped a matching Caraco jacket, the lace-trimmed sleeves brushing against my wrists with every move, as gentle as a caress, as choking as a chain.

I was being adorned like a gift to be unwrapped.

My hair was gathered, woven with ribbons that matched my dress, twisted into curls, and piled high atop my head—

A lady's hairstyle.

Mary secured the final touch—a pair of soft kid gloves, sliding them over my fingers as though she could shield me from what lay ahead.

I could not help but feel like a doll being prepared for a child's play.

A child's game—

Where I had no say.

"Lady Elizabeth, you look most becoming," Mary said, stepping back to admire her handiwork, offering me a small, comforting smile.

I tried to return it.

I failed.

Because all the finery in the world—

The silk. The lace. The ribbons.

It could not mask the foreboding that clung to me like a second skin.

None of it could stifle—

The silent scream that echoed within my chest.

"Thank you, Mary," I whispered, though my thoughts had already strayed far from the reflection in the looking glass.

They drifted—unbidden, unstoppable—

To him.

To Lord Hassan.

To the man whose stoic countenance and resolute gaze had marked my mind.

He was a puzzle. A man ensnared in my father's web, yet somehow... different.

Uncorrupted.

Untouched by the decay that lurked in the folds of power and privilege.

And that difference—

It called to me.

A beacon in the encroaching night.

The carriage wheels crunched over the gravel, a discordant lullaby against the silence of the journey.

A breeze whispered through a small crack in the window, carrying with it a scent that sent ice curling down my spine—

Faint. Rotting. A breath of putrefaction on the wind.

The manor loomed ahead.

Its grandeur was long lost to time and neglect.

Ivy clawed at crumbling stone walls, clinging like desperate fingers to a ruin that refused to let go of the past.

The gardens, once vibrant, were now a tangle of withered blooms and thorny brambles.

A corpse of a house.

And inside it—

My fate awaited.

"I'm with you. I'll be there. Don't worry," Mary murmured beside me, her voice a soft reassurance against my fears.

Her hand found mine—

A comforting squeeze.

A reminder that I was not alone—
Even if the walls of this house had already begun to close in.
We alighted from the carriage.
The silence of the great house swallowed our footsteps whole.
And as we crossed the threshold—
The doors closed behind us with the finality of a tomb.
The parlor was a dying room.

Once, it might have been grand—its faded opulence whispered of wealth long past—but now, it felt hollow, rotting from the inside out.

And at its center—
Lord Winston.
A corpse draped in velvet and arrogance.

His pallid skin stretched thin over his skull, waxy and unnatural, as though death had already begun to claim him in slow, unhurried increments.

And his eyes—
Milky. Vacant. Orbs of malice, fixing upon me with hunger, made my stomach turn.

A slow, shuddering breath left my lips, and I forced my feet forward.

His gaze clung to me like filth, something I could feel but never scrub away.

Every step was a silent war between duty and the primal instinct to flee.

I sat.

The ancient chair beneath me sighed with dust, exhaling remnants of time long lost.

Across from me, he watched.

Mary positioned herself discreetly against the wall, a silent lifeline I dared not grasp.

Her sympathy was a small comfort, but it could not penetrate the layer of dread throttling me.

Because this was real.

This was happening.

And the screams in my mind—

They were deafening.

The clock struck, its pendulum swinging in time with my dwindling freedom.

Tick.

Tick.

Tick.

And all I could do was sit there—

Trapped.

Caged.

Awaiting my fate in a house that had already begun to bury me alive.

The delicate clink of porcelain broke through the silence as the butler placed the tea service before us.

The cups were chipped.

The glaze was cracked.

A reflection of this house, the man who sat across from me, and the rot that festered beneath wealth and power.

Lord Winston poured with an exaggerated flourish, his fingers trembling slightly, betraying the illusion of control he desperately clung to.

I took the cup he offered; its once-vibrant pattern now faded to ghosts of its former glory.

And so, I sat—nodding, feigning interest, listening to the droning hum of his hollow words, trying to drown in the monotony of civilized discourse.

Until his voice cut through the air like a rusted blade—

And I wished I had never listened at all.

"It won't be long, Lady Alexander. Soon my cock will fill you up and produce my heirs."

The teacup clattered in my grip.

My mind refused to process the words for a moment—just a moment.

But then they settled.

They seeped in.

Like poison.

Like filth.

My breath hitched, and my fingers clenched so tightly around the porcelain that I feared it would crack.

The room suddenly felt too small, the walls creeping closer.

"Once we are wed, you will learn to obey and serve my purposes," Winston continued, his breath foul as it slithered across my skin.

He leaned in.

His lips were puckered and grotesque.

A thing pretending to be a man.

My stomach twisted—a violent churn of revulsion and panic.

I recoiled, my hand flying to his chest, a feeble barrier against the inevitable horror of him.

He laughed.

Low. Dark. Possessive.

"You'll learn your place," he murmured, his fingers tightening around my wrist, his grip a promise of torment to come.

"You'll serve your purpose, and in time…"

A pause. A leer. A cruel smirk slithered across his lips.

"You'll come to enjoy it."

The words coiled around my spine like a vice, bile rising in my throat.

I wanted to scream. To run.

To erase the feel of his touch.

But I sat. Trapped. Frozen.

And Lord Winston smiled.

"Don't bother resisting," he sneered, leaning in closer. "You're mine now. There's no escape from that."

A knock at the door fractured the moment, penetrating the silence.

The butler entered—his expression carefully schooled into indifference, but not before I caught the brief flicker of something else. Alarm.

"You are needed at once in the east wing, my lord," he announced.

Lord Winston's grip lingered for a heartbeat too long before he released me, his bony fingers trailing across my wrist like the legs of a spider retreating to its web.

"I don't want you to leave," he said, his displeasure barely concealed beneath the strained civility in his voice. His milky eyes locked onto mine, the unspoken command clear. "Look around. Make yourself at home."

Then, turning to the butler with a conspiratorial tilt, he added, "Mr. Pemberton, please show Lady Alexander around. Make her feel… comfortable. In the areas of the house deemed suitable."

Their gazes met.

A silent conversation. A shadowed understanding that curdled the air between them.

"Very well, my lord," Mr. Pemberton said, bowing slightly. His voice was measured, his posture obedient.

But his eyes—

His eyes never met mine.

I tightened my grip on the handle of my teacup, feeling its delicate edge dig into my palm—a small reminder that beneath the opulence, this place was nothing more than a gilded prison. And I, its unwilling captive.

An oppressive sense of impending doom clung to the air, draping over me like a funeral shroud within the decaying grandeur of Lord Winston's estate. My gaze flicked to Mary. In her eyes, I found my horror reflected.

"We'll look around, then leave," she murmured behind Mr. Pemberton's broad back, her voice barely more than a breath. "We don't want to anger Lord Winston."

"His home is a nightmare," I whispered, each word tight in my throat. "Gloomy. Musty. Death lingers in the walls." I glanced at the faded tapestries, the crumbling edges of what had once been luxury.

"It feels like ghosts are everywhere," Mary agreed, unease threading through her words.

"Let's take a walk in the gardens. Surely, it is better than the house," I suggested, pulling Mary with me to the terrace. I needed to escape.

And then—his voice, still ringing in my ears. Lord Winston's coarse, dreadful words. Words I couldn't bring myself to repeat.

I shut my eyes, drawing in a breath, feeling the sun on my skin, and for a fleeting moment, I thought of Lord Hassan. His warmth. His vibrance. When I married, I longed for love, passion, and desire—a younger man who would set my soul alight—someone like Lord Hassan. A wistful sigh slipped from my lips before I could stop it.

"Lady Alexander. Miss Mary."

Mr. Pemberton's voice cut through my thoughts, his tone brooking no argument.

"I must ask you, Miss Mary, to accompany me inside. His lordship insists."

Mary stiffened beside me. "Surely, I cannot leave Lady Alexander alone," she protested, her voice firm despite the worry creasing her brow.

"Lord Winston's orders are quite clear," Mr. Pemberton said, his expression as impassive as the stone statues standing sentinel over the withering gardens.

Mary cast me a troubled look, hesitation flickering in her eyes before resignation settled over her features. She leaned in, her breath warm against my ear as she whispered, "I'll be back in five minutes. I promise."

And with that reluctant assurance, she turned and followed Mr. Pemberton, vanishing into the dim maw of the house.

Left alone in the thorny embrace of the neglected gardens, I inhaled the scent of rot and wilted blooms. Once vibrant, the roses drooped with neglect, their petals falling like silent eulogies to a long-forgotten past.

With each step through the overgrown garden, prickly brambles snagged at my skirts as if trying to ensnare me, to tether me to this place of slow, creeping ruin. The gnarled branches stretched toward me, skeletal fingers grasping at the empty air, their brittle thorns whispering of misery.

And then—

A sound.

A scream.

Not the distant echo of wind through broken windows, nor the rustle of leaves, but something raw. Agonized. Human.

The cries sliced through the quiet, sudden and precise, shattering the hush settling over the garden. My pulse lurched, a cold sweat gathering at the nape of my neck. The wretched wails did not fade. They did not cease.

Drawn by a force I could not name, I stepped forward, my feet moving before my mind could protest.

Tucked away beyond the overgrown hedges was a small, dilapidated outbuilding, its crumbling walls barely holding themselves upright. The door hung ajar, revealing only darkness beyond its splintered frame—but I knew he was in there, waiting.

A foul stench seeped from within—iron, sweat, fear. It coiled through the damp night air, clinging to my lungs with every shallow breath.

I should have turned away.

I should have fled.

Instead, I edged closer, the screams pulling me in, my fear eclipsed by something far more dangerous.

Morbid curiosity.

Peering through the grimy window, my gaze fell upon a macabre scene that would haunt even the most ghastly of nightmares. There was Lord Winston, towering over a naked man whose body bore the evidence of merciless brutality. His skin was mottled with bruises and lacerations, each one a testament to the cruelty he had endured.

Lord Winston's smile was like a grotesque gargoyle, full of malice and sadistic pleasure. In his hand, he held a knife, its blade catching the dim light as he carved cruel lines into the man's face. A wicked grin spread across his mouth as he spat out the words. "You're nothing but a filthy Timeborne," he hissed with venomous delight, his eyes blazing.

"Every second I wait hones the edge of what's coming. I will break you—slowly, methodically. And when you finally beg for mercy… it still won't come. Because there's a special kind of pleasure in watching someone realize how much agony they can survive—only to learn it's still not enough."

The helpless man's eyes fluttered closed, his body limp from the agony he had endured. Something shifted in Lord Winston then—something feral and monstrous. I could feel it rather than see it, a pulse of depravity in the air that made my stomach turn.

I looked away.

I couldn't watch.

But the sounds—the sounds would haunt me forever. A low, guttural growl. The rustle of fabric. The sickening rhythm of violence. My breath caught in my throat, and the world tilted around me—the trees blurring, branches swaying like they too wanted to look away. The air felt too thin, the earth unsteady beneath my feet. I wanted to scream, to run, to rip the moment from time itself and bury it where it could never reach me again.

A soft rustle stirred from the shadows.

A young maid stepped out from behind a crumbling partition, where the broken remains of old shelves slouched against the wall, emerging slowly, her eyes wild and glassy, her grin split too wide, too wrong. It was the smile of someone who had long since abandoned their soul.

"Oh, my lord," she whispered, her voice packed with something sick, something corrupted. Her gaze dropped to his blood-smeared hands, and a tremble rippled through her body. "Seeing you like this… it drives me mad."

She moved toward him like someone hypnotized.

"Fuck me," she begged.

A sound clawed its way from my throat, strangled and hoarse. I couldn't stop shaking.

Lord Winston's face twisted into a mask of wickedness—hunger without conscience, lust without humanity. He seized her, pulling her against him with violent fervor.

And then, before the broken body on the floor, they consumed each other—two beasts lost in their shared madness.

I staggered back, bile rising in my throat, the world tilting violently around me.

How could such evil exist?

How could I be bound to it?

The trees seemed to shudder, their gnarled limbs arching

inward as if the very earth recoiled from the sickness festering inside.

And in that moment, a single, brutal truth seared through me—I could not, would not, shackle myself to this monster.

But panic held me in its iron grip, rooting me to the spot. A petrified statue. A prisoner of my horror. My gaze remained locked on the macabre tableau beyond the grimy glass as if my body refused to believe what my mind already knew.

Lord Winston's twisted, satisfied grin burned itself into my memory, branding him as something beyond villainy—something unholy.

I didn't wait. I turned and ran.

Branches clawed at my sleeves as I fled through the overgrown path, heart pounding like a war drum in my chest. Only when the shadows of the outbuilding were safely behind me did I stop, gasping for breath.

"Lady Elizabeth, what's wrong?"

Mary's voice broke through the haze—crisp, urgent. She hurried toward me, jarring against the horror I just witnessed.

"You're as pale as a ghost!"

She skidded to a stop as she appeared before me, her eyes wide with concern. My lips parted, but my voice barely made it past my throat.

"We have to leave. Now."

It was little more than a whisper, no louder than the squeak of a mouse.

But my hands—shaking, desperate—found hers, gripping with a force that betrayed the storm raging inside me.

I pulled her with me, stumbling, nearly tripping over the uneven ground as we fled toward the carriage. My pulse roared in my ears, my breath ragged, my body fighting to expel the images seared into my mind.

Bless her. Mary asked what had happened. She pleaded for answers, but the words wouldn't come.

Some horrors could not be spoken of.

Some nightmares refused to be named.

The ride back was a fever dream.

The countryside blurred into meaningless streaks of green and gold beyond the carriage window, the world spinning past as if it wanted to rid itself of what I had seen. But the horror clung to me. Burrowed into me.

No matter how tightly I shut my eyes, the images returned—Lord Winston's grotesque smile imprinted deep into my mind like a wound that would never heal. The glint of his blade. The sick, eager moans. The dying man's ragged breaths were swallowed by the depravity taking place beside him. Gods above. The woman. That woman.

What were they?

What kind of wretched souls found pleasure in such perversion?

The carriage lurched to a stop, but I did not wait for the footman.

I flung the door open, stumbling onto the gravel. My legs carried me before I could think, my breath coming quick and ragged as I ran. Away. Away. Away. But there was no outrunning the filth in my mind, no tearing free from the memory dragging me back into that dim, suffocating room.

When I reached my chambers, my hands shook violently, so I could barely latch the door behind me.

The walls closed in, smothering—but at least they were mine. At least here, in this gilded cage, I could pretend I was safe.

But my body betrayed me. Tremors racked my limbs, my pulse an erratic drumbeat against my ribs. I placed my hands to my cheeks, ice-cold with terror, desperate to ground myself, to find something real beyond the nightmare clawing at my thoughts.

"I can't marry him. I can't. I can't."

The words spilled from my lips, a fragile, useless mantra—a whispered plea.

I had no choice.

Not unless—

A name flickered in my mind, a lifeline in the darkness.

Lord Hassan.

Where Winston was filth and decay, Hassan was something else entirely—something I needed to believe in.

He had offered me refuge—a sanctuary in his townhouse.

But could I trust him?

Or was I only grasping at cobwebs, weaving a foolish dream of escape in a world where men—no matter their charm or promises—only ever took what they wanted?

CHAPTER 8

AMIR

The late afternoon sun slanted through the windows of my London townhouse, gilding the mahogany bookshelves and velvet drapes in molten gold. Yet, the light never reached the corners. Shadows pooled there, untouched, as if the walls refused to relinquish their secrets.

I stood in the study, scented with aged parchment and ink, though beneath it lurked something fouler—something steeped in blood and suffering. The broad oak desk before me bore more than ledgers and maps; it was our war table, our battlefield before the real one began.

"Speak," I commanded, my voice cleaving through the tense silence.

One by one, my men delivered their reports. The words dripped like poison, painting a twisted portrait of the city I had sworn to purge.

"Abandoned factories, Pasha Hassan—littered with the bodies of Timebornes and Timebounds," rumbled a hulking figure, his voice tight, his eyes still haunted by what he had seen. "Derelict houses, underground chambers... all soaked in blood. Bones scattered like trophies. A graveyard without names."

A map was unfurled, its crude lines marked with red circles, each one a site of horror. My fingers traced the inked paths, feeling the malevolence pulsing beneath the paper, a vile heartbeat that throbbed through the very streets of London.

Disgust coiled in my gut like a serpent.

"Destroy them." The order left no room for hesitation. My voice was steel. "Every last den of those depraved Timehunters. If you find any of the Timebornes or Timebounds alive, save them. But make no mistake—the nests of evil must be scorched."

A murmur of assent rippled through the room, but one voice rose above it.

"Pasha Hassan, are you certain there will be survivors?"

Doubt. Skepticism.

I fixed him with a stare that brooked no argument. "I doubt it. But if souls are clinging to life amidst the carnage, we will not abandon them. Rescue those who breathe. But let the fires cleanse this blight from our streets."

A moment of silence. Then, they saluted—a quiet acknowledgment of the burden I had placed upon them.

The study held its breath as if the walls bore witness to our mission's gravity. The air crackled with unspoken resolve.

Then Ilyas stepped forward.

His rugged features were lined with exhaustion, his broad frame wound tight with something unreadable. His dark eyes, honed by years of surveying enemy territory, fixed on me with cautious intensity. One hand hovered near the hilt of his dagger, fingers twitching—a rare tell of unease.

"Pasha Hassan..." His gruff voice fractured the stillness. "We found something... strange."

I lifted an eyebrow. "Strange?"

"A small cottage, five kilometers from the Alexander manor. It looks abandoned, but there are signs of life inside."

Intrigue cut through my focus. "Signs of life? Explain."

"Plants, sir. Too many of them. Growing wild, creeping up the walls, choking every inch of the place." He hesitated, choosing his words with reluctance. "And inside... rows of vials and flasks. Glass everywhere. The kind you'd see in an alchemist's den."

A sharp intake of breath. Alchemy.

"Did you enter?"

"No, sir." His grip tightened on the dagger. "We suspected poison."

Smart.

I nodded. "Very well. Spread out. Burn every last Time-hunter den to the ground." My voice was quiet but absolute. Then, after a beat— "But leave the cottage to me."

Murmurs of assent rippled through my men as they absorbed the directive. But Ilyas lingered, his gaze locked with mine.

"The cottage is well-hidden, buried deep in the western woods," he said. "It's strange—close to the Alexander estate, yet nothing like its outbuildings."

My fingers drummed against my chin. "Indeed?"

Alexander had always denied any involvement with alchemy. He hadn't just been evasive—he had lied. And now this? A secret lair tucked away on the fringes of his land.

"Intriguing."

"Pasha Hassan, despite its abandoned facade, the place is active," Ilyas continued on. "Jars. Tools for mixtures. Fresh-cut plants and flowers. Whoever tends it isn't just passing through— it's a healer's or an alchemist's sanctuary."

I straightened, and the decision was made. "Then it warrants investigation. Leave it to me."

The room barely had time to settle before rapid, delicate footfalls echoed up the staircase, each step creaking in frantic succession.

Every man in the room went rigid.

Then—the door burst open.

It slammed against the wall with such force that the wood groaned, the crack of impact reverberating.

My hand went to my dagger, instinct kicking in before my mind registered the blur of silk, the tumble of wheat-blond hair—

Elizabeth.

Disheveled. Breathless. Eyes wild with something unspoken.

"Leave us."

The words were barely out before my men obeyed, slipping from the room without hesitation, vanishing like shadows at dusk.

"Elizabeth! What has happened?"

My voice was a low growl, rough with concern, not anger.

She was frozen in the doorway, her breath shallow, her blue dress reduced to tattered remnants. The delicate embroidery, once pristine, was now smeared with dirt and something darker. What had formerly been a symbol of refined elegance—her Caraco jacket—slipped from one shoulder, the lace edging torn and undone.

"Lord Hassan..." Her voice trembled, struggling to hold onto the last remnants of formality. But her fear crushed the words before they could fully take shape.

I stepped forward, my touch light as I held her shoulders. Beneath my fingers, I felt the tremor of her body—small, violent quakes betraying the horrors she carried within her.

"Please, call me Amir," I murmured, my tone gentler now. "There's no need for formality here."

She swallowed hard, her breath hitching as if fighting to hold herself together.

"I need to talk to you," she whispered.

I let my hands slip from her shoulders, trailing down until they closed around hers. I held her cold, trembling hands gently, as if that could still the fear I felt pulsing through her skin... or mine.

"What happened?" My voice was quiet now, careful, afraid that too much force would startle her fragile composure.

She hesitated, then exhaled shakily.

"Something happened at... at... at Lord Winston's."

Her eyelids fluttered shut as if trying to lock the memory away. But her body betrayed her—the way she stiffened, and her breath hitched unevenly.

The stillness that overtook her was more than fear.

It was petrification.

"What did you see?" I asked, my voice gentle, my thumbs stroking the tops of her hands. A feeble attempt to ground her, to siphon away a sliver of the terror attached to her like a second skin.

Her eyelids flew open, panic stark in the depths of her gaze.

"It's something I can never unsee!"

Her voice cracked, raw, and uneven.

"Come. Sit down with me."

I guided her carefully, leading her to the corner chaise nestled beside the bookshelves. My grip was firm but gentle, as though she might collapse from the horror of what she'd seen.

The office, though designed for strategy and statecraft, suddenly felt too opulent for grief. The warm firelight cast light over war maps and antique daggers mounted along the walls— remnants of a past I once took pride in. Now, they bore silent witness to a different kind of battle before me.

But Elizabeth…

She did not belong in such a setting.

She sank into one of the plush velvet settees, yet the opulence did nothing to comfort her. Her hands gripped the armrests as if the solid wood might stabilize her, her breath shallow, her eyes darting—searching, pleading for an escape from a prison that wasn't made of stone but of memory.

"Tell me," I urged again.

The room's grandeur made the space between us feel vast, an abyss neither of us dared to cross.

"Talk to me, Elizabeth, darling." The endearment slipped from my lips unbidden. "You're safe here."

A lie, a promise spoken in a house built on shadow.

But when she looked at me—wide, trusting, searching for anything to hold onto—I felt something stir in my chest.

A flicker of warmth.

Unexpected. Unwanted.

Because in this world, warmth was a weakness.

And I could not afford to be weak.

Elizabeth swallowed hard, her hands still gripping the armrests as if she feared the room might collapse. When it came, her voice was fragile, her words stumbling like a child lost in the dark.

"I went to tea at L-L-Lord Winston's house with my maid Mary," she began, her syllables fractured, her breath coming in shallow gasps. "He was called away. I was told to wander... to familiarize myself with his—his despicable, dark home. His butler accompanied me."

Her fingers clenched into fists, her knuckles whitening, the pearls strung around her neck trembling with her.

"But he... the butler..." Her breath hitched, her chest rising and falling too quickly. "He snatched Mary away. His eyes..."

She shuddered, her hand flying to her mouth, pressing so hard against her lips that I thought she might tear them open.

"His eyes glinted with malice. With... vile pleasure. He said it was Lord Winston's command."

A muffled whimper slipped through her fingers, raw and involuntary—a sound torn from the depths of her breaking.

I leaned in.

"You're safe here."

Another lie.

It was a hollow reassurance—one monster offering comfort to the only soul he could never see as one.

But she needed something to cling to, even if it was only an illusion.

And so, I gave it to her.

Slowly, she uncurled from herself, but her voice remained a ghost, a whisper drifting on the edge of breaking.

"I stumbled upon this wretched chamber..."

Her breath hitched, her fingers twisting into the fabric of her ruined dress. "Lord Winston... that malevolent monster... stood over a man. His twisted form contorted in sadistic pleasure, his blade gleaming—slicing—mercilessly. The sight—" her voice cracked "—it was a nightmare made flesh. A symphony of agony and despair, one that seared itself into my soul, never to be undone."

The tremor in her voice vibrated through the space between us, and I could feel it—like the bite of something cold just before it pierced the skin.

The grandfather clock in the corner beat a slow, ponderous

rhythm, a reminder of time slipping between our fingers. A cruel echo of truth—that while she sat here, the world outside remained unchanged. Wicked men still roamed. Horrors still unfolded in dim-lit rooms.

"Keep talking, Elizabeth," I urged, my voice barely more than breath. Encouraging her. Coaxing her to unburden herself. To give voice to the nightmare that had stolen the light from her gaze.

Her lips parted, but no sound came.

She tried—gods, she tried. But the words refused to form, choking her from the inside.

"They had…"

Her hands clenched against her lap, fingers digging into the fabric, nails pressing into her skin as though the pain might tether her to the present.

"He, um… the man was—"

Her head shook, frantic, desperate. As if she could shake it loose, dislodge the horror from her mind. But it clung to her.

Her eyes squeezed shut, lips pressed into a thin, bloodless line. A dam, barely holding back the flood.

I exhaled slowly, carefully, measuring my next words.

"Did Lord Winston have…?" I hesitated. Even with all the wickedness I had seen in this world, knowing the depths of depravity men were capable of, I struggled to form the question. "Did Lord Winston have carnal relations with the man?"

The words hung between us, a grotesque wound cleaved into the silence. But I needed to know.

Her breath hitched, a choked noise catching in her throat before she buried her mouth against her palm.

And then— "Yes!"

It was more than an answer. It was a sob, a confession ripped from something too dark to name.

"He did it when the man was dying."

The tremor in her voice dissolved whatever restraint I had left.

"He stripped himself naked and—"

She couldn't finish—the words trailed off, lost in the space between us. But I didn't need to hear the rest. The picture was already painted in blood and suffering.

My pulse pounded, a murderous drumbeat.

She shuddered, her fingers trembling against her lips. "Then this woman came in—she was dressed like a maid. They… they had intercourse with each other while the man was still bleeding, still gasping."

The words tumbled from her in broken fragments as though speaking them out loud might lessen their weight. But nothing could lighten something so vile.

Something so unforgivable.

The cold fury that settled over me was absolute. A quiet rage that coiled around my ribs and sank its claws into my bones.

My hands itched—ached—to wrap around Lord Winston's throat, to crush the life from him slowly, to make him feel the horror he had inflicted upon another soul.

But first…

First, I had to shield the fragile creature beside me.

Because even monsters—even me—could dream of being a hero, if only for a moment.

Elizabeth's voice cracked the silence like thin ice underfoot.

"I can't marry him, Amir. I can't live with someone capable of such evil. I need your help… please, help me escape this."

Her words hung between us, as heavy as a noose waiting to claim its victim.

I wanted to destroy the society that had birthed such iniquity. To scorch their wicked halls to the ground and scatter their ashes to the wind. To wrap my arms around her and swear that no harm would ever touch her again.

But she was the daughter of my enemy.

And my embrace—my protection—could be just as perilous as the evils she fled from.

The tension coiled around us. The only sound was the slow, methodical ticking of the grandfather clock, measuring the seconds of our shared torment.

Then, as though gasping for air after being submerged for too long, Elizabeth lifted her gaze to mine.

Her eyes—pleading—were liquid solace, beckoning me into their depths.

"I can tell you're not like the men in my father's society," she whispered.

The words struck me like a blade, unexpected and unearned.

"Like" them?

I had been forged in the same darkness. Born of the same bloodstained cloth, stitched into a tapestry of monsters.

"What makes you think I'm different?" My voice was rough, edged with something bitter. "What makes you think I'm not a brute like the others?"

Her answer was a breath. Soft. A flicker of faith amidst the gloom.

"I can feel in my heart you're not a beast."

She spoke it as if it were truth. As if belief alone could make it so.

But she didn't know.

She didn't know what I had done.

She didn't know what I was capable of doing.

How wrong she was. And how cruel it would be to let her believe otherwise.

"Oh, my dear Elizabeth," I murmured. "I'm a creature of darkness, too. I do despicable and horrific things."

The words sat heavily on my tongue, leaden with the truth I carried—the truth she must understand. I had no salvation—no hero lurking beneath the shadowed exterior.

I expected her to recoil, avert her gaze, see me for what I was—and shrink away.

But she didn't.

Instead, she stood. A flurry of restless energy, her breath quickened, her fingers curling into her skirts as though bracing herself against an unseen wind.

"Forgive me, Lord Hassan," she said, reverting to my formal title—a calculated shift, like a wall sliding into place. "But I refuse to believe you share the same cruel intentions as my father's society."

Her voice wavered, but her conviction did not.

She stepped back, ready to flee, to take the warmth of her body, the trust in her eyes, and the intoxicating scent of her skin away from me.

I couldn't let her go.

Not when I had tasted the possibility of her.

Standing swiftly, I caught her wrist, pulling her back against me, her breath escaping in a soft, startled gasp. The second our bodies collided, heat erupted between us—scalding, undeniable. Her chest against mine, her pulse frantic beneath my fingertips, her lips parting on a shuddered exhale.

I didn't think.

Didn't hesitate.

I took her.

My mouth crushed hers, desperate, claiming. Her moan was swallowed by the kiss, a sound that sent fire racing through my veins. She melted against me, her fingers tangling in my hair, nails scraping along my scalp, sending sparks skittering down my spine.

I pushed her against the wall, hard—closing every inch of distance between us, making sure she felt me, every solid, aching part. My hands roamed her body, memorizing the curves, the softness, the way she shuddered when my fingers skimmed over her ribs, her waist, lower.

She gasped, her back arching as her thighs parted just enough to let me slide in close—pressing against her with slow, tantalizing rhythm, every movement a promise whispered through touch.

Her breath hitched, a whimper catching in her throat, her hands gripping my shoulders as if she didn't know whether to pull me closer or push me away.

I traced my lips down her neck, teeth grazing her skin, feeling her shiver beneath me. She was intoxicating, a heady mix of silk and sin, and gods help me. I wanted to unravel her and see what she became when she stopped thinking and let go.

Her corset was in my way. The laces, the fabric, all of it— too much. My hands slid beneath her skirts, fingers tracing up her thighs, her skin fever-hot against my palms.

She gasped, her head falling back, her lips parting in wordless surrender.

I didn't need her to tell me what she wanted.

I could feel it.

In the way her body moved against mine, in the way her breath came quicker, in the way her nails raked across my back, demanding, desperate.

I lifted her, her legs wrapping around my waist instinctively, pressing her deeper into the wall, pinning her against me.

Her moan was sinful, wrecked, a sound that sent fire racing through my veins.

And I devoured it.

Tasting the hunger, the raw, desperate need building between us since our worlds collided.

She was fire, and I wanted to burn.

I would burn.

"Elizabeth," I murmured, my voice strained, betraying the war inside me. "I shouldn't... we shouldn't—"

"Please, Amir," she whispered, her lips brushing mine with every word. "Allow me this moment. I have never felt want or desire until you."

At her words, the last remnants of restraint crumbled.

I didn't care about the consequences. Didn't care about the chaos we were inviting, the ruin that would inevitably follow.

All I cared about was her.

I pulled her back into my arms, crushing her against me, my lips slanting over hers in a kiss that was fierce, unrelenting, all-consuming. There was no hesitation, no second-guessing—only raw need.

"I desire you, Elizabeth. I can't deny it."

The confession was guttural, ripped from somewhere deep inside me, but she already knew. She could feel it in the way my hands roamed her body, memorizing every curve, every dip, every shudder that coursed through her as she arched into me.

Her moan vibrated against my lips, her body molding against mine, needing more.

And fuck, I gave it to her.

Our mouths moved together in a frantic dance—lips, teeth, tongues colliding in a frenzy of need, want, and hunger.

I took advantage of the exposed skin, my lips trailing down the delicate column of her throat, sucking, tasting, biting.

"Amir..." she gasped, the sound raw, breathless, utterly intoxicating.

Her fingers tangled in my hair, nails scraping against my scalp as she pulled me back to her, desperate for more.

And gods, I wanted to give her everything.

I rolled my hips into her again, and she whimpered, a sound so soft yet so utterly undone that it nearly drove me to madness. She arched her body into me, her breath coming in ragged little gasps that threatened what little control I had left.

She was ruining me.

I was losing myself.

The world beyond these walls no longer existed—only her lips, her body, the way she melted into me, offering herself completely.

With every desperate kiss and touch, I felt the last remnants of my restraint slipping away.

It became harder to remember why we shouldn't be doing this—why I should push her away and return to the shadows where I belonged.

My senses reeled as I tore myself from her, gasping, burning; the intoxicating swirl of her scent and the softness of her lips seared into my memory like a brand.

The room was suddenly too small, the air too thick with desire, with longing, with something I could not afford to name.

I couldn't yield to this.

Not when so much was at stake.

"Why did you stop?"

Her voice cracked, a fragile whisper that threatened to break me completely.

I squeezed my eyes shut, fists clenched, fighting the aching need to take her back into my arms.

"Because I am a monster," I said, the words like ash on my

tongue. "Just like Winston. Just like your father and the men who serve him. You should stay away from me."

It was a plea. A command. A desperate, final attempt to save her from the darkness that clung to my very bones.

"No, no, no!" Her voice rose, frantic. "You can't be like them. Please, you're just saying that!"

Tears streaked down her cheeks, hot and unchecked, and her pain slashed through me—a knife twisting deep into a wound I had long since stopped feeling.

"You don't know me, Elizabeth." My voice was frayed—callous and cracked. "You don't know what I'm capable of."

I turned away, fists flexing, muscles coiled so tight they might snap.

"Leave now. Before it's too late."

The beast within me howled, clawing, fighting, screaming to take her back, claim her, lose myself in her warmth, touch, and undeniable need for me.

But I knew the truth.

I knew the darkness that lurked beneath my skin.

I had seen what men like me could do—what I had done. What I could become.

A maggot-infested man.

A devourer of souls.

"I don't care what you've done, Amir."

Her voice trembled as she came in front of me, but her gaze held mine.

"I don't believe you're a monster."

Her words stung, cutting deeper than any blade, cracking something inside me that I had long thought dead.

I clenched my fists, forcing my breath to steady, forcing my heart to turn to stone.

"Go... Elizabeth... leave this place now before I corrupt your soul."

The rejection tore me apart, a death sentence to my own heart—but it was for her good.

A muscle ticked in her jaw, her lips parting as if to fight

back, challenge me, and force me to see what she saw. But then, something shifted.

The fire ignited in her eyes, the kind that could forge a new path or burn everything to the ground.

"Fine! I'll figure this out on my own."

Without another word, she spun on her heel, the skirts of her dress whipping around her as she vanished through the door. Her footsteps echoed down the corridor, a slow, devastating dismantling of my world. And I let her go.

The moment the door slammed behind her, my choice crushed me.

I sank against the wall, my chest heaving, my hands shaking as if the ghost of her touch still lingered on my skin.

I had done the right thing.

I had to believe that.

But every instinct inside me howled to chase after her, to beg for her forgiveness, to fall to my knees and tell her that I needed her more than I needed my next breath.

A sudden knock at the door jarred me from my despair.

My pulse lurched.

Elizabeth?

Had she come back? Had she seen through my desperate attempt to push her away? Had she returned to fight for me and plead for my aid again?

I rushed forward, heart hammering, hands already reaching for the handle, ready to cast aside everything if it meant I could have her back, if I could claim the sliver of hope that she might still want me.

But as the door swung open—

It wasn't Elizabeth standing before me.

It was Balthazar.

I froze, shock locking me in place.

The last time I had seen him was amid flames and screams— when Mathias' school was reduced to ashes.

And now, standing in my doorway, he was a storm brewing on the horizon, dark and unrelenting.

"Amir," he said, his voice carrying an ominous weight that filled the threshold.

I was utterly unprepared for this ghost from my past to appear at such a moment.

Before I could react, Balthazar shoved past me, his hulking form moving into the dimly lit foyer with the confidence of a man who feared nothing—not consequences, not me.

His sneer was a familiar poison, twisting his lips into something cruel, something vile.

"Well, well, well," he taunted with mockery, his eyes gleaming with something far more dangerous than amusement. "Is it possible you've stumbled upon love at last?"

My jaw clenched.

"That woman who just fled your home… she's alluring in a way that stirs a craving for mischief." He smirked, his words slithering like a serpent coiling around my throat. "She resembles an apple, ripe for the picking. Tempting me to take a bite as well."

The disgust that filled me was instant, and all-consuming. My fists curled, rage thrumming through my veins like an untamed beast ready to strike.

"Stay away from Elizabeth. Leave her alone!"

The words roared from my throat, bouncing off the high ceilings and shaking the house's very walls.

Balthazar only laughed, a jagged, grating sound that scraped at the edges of my sanity.

But then, as quickly as it had come, his mirth vanished, his gaze locking onto mine with a cold, devastating intensity.

"I should kill the bitch the same way you took the school from me," he sneered, his voice laced with venom.

I felt something snap inside me.

"I had intricate intentions for that school—dreams etched into every stone, every corridor!" His voice rose, filled with a force just as dangerous as rage—obsession. "You were well aware of my vision! And yet, you burned it to the ground with flames of betrayal. I found not even a whisper in the ashes of what was once mine. My aspirations, my legacy, reduced to cinders!"

The fury in his voice was absolute, a force that vibrated through the air.

I stepped closer, the heat of my rage matching his, threatening to consume me whole.

"Balthazar shut the fuck up!" I snarled, my breath coming in ragged bursts. "How could you want that school?"

My control was fraying, the beast inside me rattling its cage.

"Mathias was despicable," I spat, my hands trembling as I fought to hold myself back. "Transforming his school to suit your purposes wouldn't have given you the satisfaction you wanted."

His smirk twisted into a snarl, lips curling back to reveal too-white teeth, sharp with malice. His eyes simmered with something feral, something sick.

"Oh, but it would have!" he hissed. "You took that from me. You think you won, don't you? But guess what?"

He leaned in, his breath hot with cruelty.

"I found Mathias' daughter, Alina."

A slow, deliberate pause.

"And I didn't just fuck her once."

My stomach turned, but he wasn't finished.

"I took her over and over again until she was nothing but a mindless shell."

The sickening glee in his voice sent ice through my veins. He relished it, drank in his own horror, and made like a man starving for wickedness.

A hollow, humorless laugh tore from my throat, dripping with bitter disbelief.

"You are beyond foolish, Balthazar." My voice was honed to a lethal edge, slicing through the rotting air between us. "How can you betray everything we stand for by crawling into bed with the enemy's daughter? You claim to be different from Mathias, but your actions scream otherwise. You were supposed to destroy his legacy, and instead, you fucked his daughter, and what—thought that would make her yours forever?"

His nostrils flared, a muscle jumping in his jaw, but I wasn't done.

"Are you so deluded to think that fucking her would make him suffer? Mathias wouldn't have cared. Not one fucking bit. You didn't ruin him, Balthazar—you became him."

The air between us crackled.

In a blink, his hand shot out, slamming into my chest, shoving me back hard against the cold marble of the fireplace.

The impact sent pain ricocheting down my spine, but I barely felt it—because his next words detonated like a bomb between us.

"I'm going to kill your beautiful Elizabeth."

And just like that—humanity left us.

We became monsters.

A snarl ripped from my throat, deep and guttural, as my body shifted, bones elongating, skin stretching as darkness consumed me.

Balthazar mirrored the change, his form warping, his frame growing broader, more monstrous, eyes flaming red like a beast starved for blood.

We circled each other, muscles coiled, jaws clenched, the room shrinking from our rage.

"You dare put a hand on her," I growled, voice now a low, guttural warning—a death sentence hanging between us.

I felt the poison surge beneath my skin, black and deadly, itching to be unleashed.

"And I will send you to a place worse than hell."

I stepped closer, slow, restrained, the air teeming with the scent of war.

"I will use poison so dark your skin will melt from your bones."

Balthazar lunged first, and I met him with equal fury.

We collided, claws and wrath entwined, our monstrous forms tearing into each other with a force that shook the foundation beneath us. Teeth bared, talons slicing through flesh, the room became a blur of snarls and shadows, of unrelenting violence born from centuries of hate.

His roar shook the air, a sound laced with unbridled rage—one that threatened to consume everything.

"You dare threaten me, Amir?" His voice was a growl, his breath hot with venom. His claws raked across my ribs, but I barely felt it. The raw power surging through me made me stronger, made me faster. I forced him back, slamming him into the wall with a thunderous crack, but he only laughed—that cruel, jagged sound of a man who relished the fight.

His eyes burned into mine, an inferno of unholy hatred.

"If you ever cross me again, I will make sure Elizabeth suffers a slow and agonizing death at my hands!"

The words hit me in the chest—swift, merciless, and unrelenting.

A snarl ripped from my throat, my claws tightening around his neck, ready to end him—

But in an instant, he was gone.

Vanishing in a sulfurous cloud of smoke.

I stood there for a single heartbeat, my breath ragged, my pulse hammering, the room still vibrating with the violence we had unleashed.

But then—Elizabeth.

A new kind of terror seized me that had nothing to do with Balthazar or the monster I had just battled.

I spun, bolting for the door, my body shifting back as I ran into the descending twilight.

She was out there, alone, unprotected.

And men like us—monsters like him—were always waiting in the dark.

I had to find her.

Before he did.

CHAPTER 9

AMIR

The cobblestones glistened under the fading light as dusk settled over London, a city veiled in shadows and secrets. I prowled the streets, a silent predator searching for Elizabeth, my every step guided by an instinct I could not ignore.

The night deepened, impenetrable, as if it conspired to swallow her whole, to cloak her from my vigilant gaze. The rain came in hesitant droplets at first, a tentative caress against the city's skin. Then it grew bolder, more insistent, falling in sheets that darkened my coat and traced rivulets down my temples. The cold seeped into me, but I welcomed it—let it carve clarity through the haze and fuel the hunger that burned beneath my ribs.

And then—her.

A willowy figure slipped through the labyrinthine alleys ahead, her stride hurried. The downpour did not slow her. She did not seek shelter or turn toward the safety of her heart and home. Instead, she continued forward, deeper into the city's bones.

Toward the dead.

The iron-wrought gate loomed before her, its rusted hinges groaning a protest as she pushed through. Beyond it stretched an expanse of silence and stone—a graveyard where time seemed to mourn.

I followed, a phantom draped in the vestiges of night, swallowed by the storm.

She moved through the rows of the departed, rain-soaked and fragile yet utterly indomitable. Then, she stopped.

Before a cluster of graves.

I stepped closer, unseen, my gaze drawn to the names etched upon the weathered stones.

A woman. Two young men.

A single name bound them all.

Alexander.

The night held its breath.

And so did I.

The dates on the gravestones were fresh, their deaths recent enough that grief still clung to the air like an unshaken specter. The woman—her mother. The young men—her brothers. Lives claimed by that masked imposter's indiscriminate hand, taken on foreign soil.

Elizabeth's voice broke the hush, a fragile whisper carried by the wind.

"I'm so sorry."

Again and again, the words spilled from her lips, a litany of apologies, as soft as prayers, spoken for the dead who could no longer hear her.

A storm raged inside me.

I yearned to step from the shadows, gather her in my arms, and shield her from this world's cruelty. To press my lips to her hair and promise that she was not alone.

But I was bound elsewhere.

Another cause. Another master.

Lazarus held my loyalty in his grasp, and through that bond, the fates of many teetered on a knife's edge.

Elizabeth deserved more than a man whose hands were stained with the ghosts of his past. More than a creature chased by shadows, relentless pursuits, and whispered betrayals.

And so, I remained silent.

A guardian was unseen. A specter who could only exist in the hush of falling rain and the watchful gaze that never left her.

She lingered a moment longer, head bowed, fingers tracing the cold edges of the stone before she turned.

Her silhouette receded, fading into the cemetery's somber embrace, growing smaller as she neared the looming facade of the Alexander estate.

I lingered.

Hidden in the darkness, unseen—until—

A voice shattered the night.

It was harsh and reprimanding, each word laced with judgment and disappointment.

"How dare you abandon the hallowed halls of Lord Winston's estate without a proper goodbye?"

The venom in his tone cut through the rain, his voice a force of pure indignation.

"You've disgraced our lineage with your betrayal. And look at yourself! Cloaked in grime and neglect—standing before me like some wayward beggar."

Lord Alexander was rigid, his fury lashing out like a whip meant to break or humiliate.

Elizabeth halted.

Her back to me, her shoulders tightening as though bracing for a blow that had not yet come.

Something inside me snapped.

Before I could stop myself and consider the wisdom of my next action, I stepped forth from my concealment, boots striking the cobblestones with purpose.

"Lord Alexander."

My voice cut through the space between us, carrying across the courtyard with clear intent.

Elizabeth whirled around.

Her eyes—wide, startled—locked onto mine, an unspoken question flickering in their depths.

I held her gaze for half a second before focusing on her father.

"Forgive my unannounced arrival at your home," I continued smoothly, my voice unwavering.

A calculated pause.

"Her carriage broke down, and then the rain started," I said, the words falling effortlessly, a half-truth meant to shield her. "I happened to be running errands nearby. I had her and her maid stay at my estate until the weather cleared. Elizabeth informed me that Lord Winston had other matters to attend to, so I offered my home as shelter."

Lord Alexander's posture shifted—rigid, unreadable.

Surprise flickered across his face for a moment before cooling into something far more dangerous—reluctant gratitude shadowed by distrust.

"Lord Hassan."

The formality in his tone was clipped and assessing.

"I had no idea."

He turned to Elizabeth, his gaze piercing.

"Elizabeth, is this true?"

The air between us thickened, every second stretching unbearably taut.

Her answer would mean everything.

A faint nod was her only concession, subtle yet weighted with all the unspoken words between us.

"Yes, Father. Thank you so much, Lord Hassan. I appreciate your hospitality and kindness."

Her voice was steady, but I heard the tremor beneath it, the strain of maintaining the ruse.

I inclined my head, a brief, silent acknowledgment—our unspoken pact.

As I turned to depart, her voice—subdued, yet resolute—halted me.

"I'll be retiring to my room, Father."

"Nonsense." Lord Alexander's command cracked through the night, his tone brooking no argument. "Tell me how your day was with Lord Winston. And why did you choose to leave in such haste? You'd better have a convincing argument to justify your disgraceful actions."

A soft sigh escaped her lips.

Resignation.

Defeat.

She followed him inside, each step a solemn echo, a prisoner walking to the gallows.

And I—I was left alone with the night once more.

But not for long.

As silent as the mist curling through the garden, I circled the house, a ghost among the ivy-clad walls. Then, there—

Her window.

Soft light spilled from within, a golden glow against the veil of darkness, promising solitude and sanctuary.

I let the shadows consume me.

And then I was inside.

Her room was warm and scented with lavender and old parchment. A few pieces of paper lay upon her desk, their ribbed texture a testament to craftsmanship long lost to time.

I grabbed the quill, the feathered end brushing against my fingers before the ink-kissed paper.

A single note.

A whisper of all I could not say aloud.

Forgive me, love. I wish things were different.
—Yours, A.

The note lay bare upon the desk, a token from me, a confession rendered in ink.

With one last look at the room that held traces of her essence —the scent of lavender, the warmth of candlelight, the ghost of her lingering touch—I vanished as silently as I had come, leaving nothing but a whisper of what could never be.

Dawn had barely touched the sky with its pale fingers when I set out, cloaked in the guise of the Black Wraith.

The clouds hung low and oppressive, a heavy curtain of gloom stretching over the city as if the heavens themselves mourned something unseen. The air was damp, waiting.

But the unease in my gut had nothing to do with the storm brewing overhead.

It was the cottage.

"Remember," I instructed the few men who knew of my dual existence, my voice low. "If I am not back by late afternoon, come find me."

Their nods were tight, their lips grim lines. No questions. No doubts.

They understood the dangers that lurked in the shadows of our world.

The forest was a labyrinth, its paths winding and deceitful, the air overflowing with the deceptive murmurs of unseen things. The undergrowth clawed at my boots; the silence was fractured only by the occasional rustle of creatures.

Minutes turned to hours.

Frustration gnawed at me.

Had I been led astray? Was this another ghost, another elusive strand in the tangled web of deceit surrounding Elizabeth?

But then—

I saw it.

Nestled deep within the trees, half-swallowed by nature itself.

A solitary shamble, its form hunched beneath time.

The windows were coated with dust, clouded with the haze of neglect.

Yet—

Something about it felt wrong.

Not merely forgotten.

Not merely abandoned.

Something lived beneath its quietude.

Something waited.

With one firm push, I forced the locked door open. The hinges groaned in protest, a jagged screech that echoed through the stillness.

My senses flared—scanning for the scent of poison, the tell-tale residue of traps, the invisible dangers that lurked in places meant to deceive.

The interior was deviously quaint.

Bunches of dried herbs dangled from the rafters, their fragrance mingling with the acrid bite of sulfur. A wooden table dominated the center of the room, its surface arranged with meticulous care—vials, flasks, and instruments of alchemy laid out in a method that spoke of obsession rather than neglect.

Whoever called this place home wanted the world to believe it was untouched, forgotten.

But I was not so easily misled.

My gaze drifted to a tall shelf.

Rows of glass vials and flasks stood like silent sentinels, sealed with wax or cork. Some were clouded, stained with the remnants of past experiments, while others held liquids that gleamed with an unnatural luster—like they contained something more than mere compounds.

Beside them, a tarnished copper alembic rested, its curved neck poised to distill not just elements but essence itself.

On a nearby table, I traced my fingers along a mortar and pestle, its bowl dusted with the fine residue of crushed minerals. Sulfur. Possibly cinnabar. A heavier pestle sat beside it, meant for breaking down metals—its surface still gleaming from recent use.

A set of brass scales rested, perfectly balanced, near the table's edge. Tiny fragments of mercury and salt clung to its surface—symbols of alchemy's eternal pursuit—transformation, the line between ruin and rebirth.

I moved toward the furnace. Its dormant heat brushed against my skin as I leaned down to peer inside. The air still carried the faint scent of scorched metal.

A pair of soot-stained tongs lay discarded nearby, their edges blackened with residue from something recently extracted. Just behind them, a set of bellows rested, its handle worn smooth from years of use, waiting to stoke the fire into a roaring blaze.

But the scrolls unsettled me the most.

Hung on the walls, rolled and pinned with care, filled with symbols, diagrams, formulas—many of which I couldn't decipher. Their meanings eluded me, but their significance pressed against my chest.

This wasn't the simple workshop of a healer.

This was a place of secrets.

Of experiments.

Of someone teetering on the edge between science and something far darker.

I let my fingers brush the worn leather cover of a manuscript, the grain of it rough beneath my touch, as if time had etched warnings into its surface. My gaze wandered to the large retort on the adjacent table, its snake-like neck poised to condense vapors into liquid gold—or so the legends promised.

A soft hiss reached my ears—something bubbling in one of the alembics, its sound hypnotic, alive, full of potential.

The air here was thick, with something more than heat and alchemical residue.

It breathed.

This wasn't merely a study in transmutation; this was a place where ancient philosophies met modern ambition, where the impossible—the Philosopher's Stone, the elixir of life—felt, for a moment, tantalizingly close.

I prowled deeper into the room, muscles taut, every sense attuned for the unexpected.

And then—I saw it.

A flower.

Suspended within glass, untouched by time.

Its petals were silver and black, spinning slowly as though dancing to an unheard melody.

A prickle of unease crept up my spine.

This was no ordinary bloom.

It was the Noctyss flower.

Rare. Forbidden. A harbinger of death.

My pulse quickened.

This—this was the handiwork of the one who had unleashed death upon the Timehunters' orgy in France.

A confirmation. A warning. A threat woven in delicate petals and dark magic.

My gaze flicked across the room, catching on to something that made the breath stall in my lungs.

A book.

Old—ancient—its spine cracked, its pages containing the scent of centuries. The ink had faded in places, but the title remained legible.

The Sacred Alchemy of Solaris: Secrets of the Celestial Forge.

A bolt of ice shot through my veins.

Solaris.

My homeland.

The world I had been torn from, the legacy I had been forced to leave behind.

Slowly, reverently, I reached out, tracing the embossed letters with a touch that felt almost… devotional.

What secrets did this tome hold?

What knowledge had been plundered from the sacred halls of Solaris?

With the book clutched tightly, I knew—this was more than an abandoned cottage.

I had stumbled upon a nexus of past and present, a bridge between who I had been and what I must become to protect those ensnared in the web of this unfolding tragedy.

My fingers flipped through the brittle pages, parchment whispering under my touch.

And then—I found it.

A recipe.

A poison so malevolent, so unforgiving, that it did not simply kill—it decapitated, melted flesh, deformed bones.

My breath stilled.

I traced the list of ingredients, my eyes narrowing—until they landed on one.

Noctyss flower.

The Bloom of Death.

A single petal capable of slaying the darkest of lords and ending Timehunters with a mere drop in the bloodstream.

A slow, crawling shiver etched down my spine.

This—this was an assassin's dream. A toxin so absolute that no mortal body could withstand its wrath.

But the revelation darkened.

The only known antidote—

Snake venom.

Lazarus' cure.

The very substance he had once used to heal me.

The irony clawed at my ribs, a bitter, twisted truth that left a knot in my chest.

A human who dared hope against such a toxin—who thought they could fight against its creeping death—would find none.

They would succumb.

They would die.

My grip tightened on the book as my gaze fell upon another list—a litany of impossibilities, of forbidden flora not meant for this world.

Frost Bloom.

Sunspire Root.

Time Weaver's Root.

Each name burned into my mind.

These were plants from Solaris.

A realm thought lost, unreachable to those who dwelt in shadowed secrecy.

Yet—here the Noctyss flower was.

How had it been procured?

Who had crossed the boundary between worlds?

Who wielded the power to bridge realms, to steal from Solaris itself?

The answer hung in the air, unseen.

Waiting.
And I had every intention of finding it.
I turned the page.

The Noctyss flower
Mind corruption. Soul devourer. Magic suppression. Deformity.

A death sentence—not just for the body, but for the very essence of a being.

My fingers trembled as I read the warning, scrawled in jagged red ink across the margins—

To tamper with the Noctyss is to gamble with fate itself. Only the foolish or the damned would seek its full potential.

The ingredients were listed with the cold exactitude of an execution order:

—One petal of the Noctyss flower
—Five drops of Darkness blood
—10 mL of charcoal-distilled plant extract
—A dried sprig of mugwort

Beneath them, the instructions were laid out in careful, meticulous detail—each step a pathway to something far beyond a mere poison.

The warnings were more harrowing:

—The blood of a Darkness increases the poison's potency and danger to the alchemist. Use extreme caution.

—Avoid direct skin contact and ensure all tools are properly disposed of or purified.

—This poison is a weapon of unmatched lethality—its misuse could unleash chaos.

I held the alchemy book open, my gaze locked onto the ink-stained page, my pulse pounding.

I had always known the raw power of the Noctyss flower—how its mere essence could unravel the strongest minds, devour the souls of those who dared wield it and suppress magic at its very core.

But now—

Now, I realized what it became when combined with the blood of a Darkness.

Not just a tool of death.

A force of absolute annihilation.

A poison so potent, so damning, that it could shatter the invincible, unmake the unbreakable.

This was not simply an assassin's blade.

It was the undoing of the gods.

Then—an intrusion disturbed the stillness.

The truth of my discovery had barely settled when the door groaned open, its creaking hinges slicing through the quiet.

My head snapped toward the entrance.

In one fluid motion, I vanished into the shadows, the journal clutched tightly to my chest, my breath slowing to a controlled hush. Years of survival, of lurking in unseen places, guided my movements, rendering me nothing more than a ghost in the dark.

The intruder entered, draped in black.

A mirror image of myself.

My pulse pounded as I took in the familiar cut of the dark fabric, the precise way the hood draped over the face.

I had seen this before.

In France.

Among the chaos of the Timehunters' demise, amid the spilled blood and whispers of Noctyss-born death.

Whoever this was—

They belonged here..

They moved through the space with ease, each step calculated, unhesitating, as if they had done this a hundred times before.

The true keeper of this hidden lair.

My breath hitched as they pulled back their gloves, the dark fabric sliding from their fingers in smooth, practiced movements. Then—the cloak fell away.

And the world stopped.

A shockwave of disbelief tore through me, my grip tightening around the alchemy book as though it could tether me to reality.

Elizabeth.

Her name rang through my skull, an unrelenting echo of denial and realization colliding.

Elizabeth Alexander.

The woman I had sought to protect.

The woman whose quiet strength had drawn me to her, whose every movement I had memorized in the briefest encounters.

She stood before me—no longer the shy, reserved lady confined by the world's expectations.

Here, bathed in the glow of flickering candlelight, she was something else entirely.

A woman etched in secrets, molded by the darkness I thought I alone carried.

Not delicate. Not fragile.

An enigma cloaked in night.

My world tilted, torn between the gravity of what I had uncovered and her undeniable pull on me.

Elizabeth Alexander, the keeper of alchemy's greatest weapon.

And she had no idea I was watching.

The scent of crushed herbs drifted through the air, mingling with the lingering traces of sulfur and age-old parchment.

Elizabeth worked with practiced ease, her slender fingers stained green and brown as she crushed the herbs into a fine paste. Every motion was purposeful, her actions instinctive—this was no idle hobby.

This was mastery.

This was her sanctum—a place where nature's gifts were transformed, where potions of healing and destruction were woven from the same hands.

A sudden knock broke the stillness.

Elizabeth froze, her grip tightening around the mortar.

"Who's there?" Her voice, usually composed, carried a thread of alarm.

"It's me, sweetheart. Agnes Holloway."

The tension in her shoulders eased.

"Oh! One moment, Mrs. Holloway."

She wiped her hands hastily on a rag, smearing plant residue across the fabric before hurrying to the door.

The old wood groaned as she pulled it open, revealing an elderly woman cloaked in years of wisdom and time.

Silver hair framed a face lined with deep creases, each etched with the tells of experience. A cane supported her frail frame, yet there was a keenness in her gaze, a clarity that spoke of a mind untouched by age's cruel hand.

"My dear," the woman greeted, her voice warm yet expectant. "I've been waiting patiently for my next herbal concoction —my hands feel much better. Where have you been?"

Exhaustion crossed Elizabeth's face, too fleeting for most to notice.

"Oh, my father had me otherwise occupied," she replied, her tone gentle though it carried an undercurrent of fatigue.

From my shadowed vantage point, I remained still, my mind a war zone of conflicting revelations.

This was the same woman who had easily handled the Noctyss flower and uncovered the darkest formulas of alchemy.

And yet—here she was, a healer, offering comfort to weathered hands that reached for hers in gratitude.

Two sides of a coin.

One who could mend—and one who could destroy.

Which was her true nature?

Or, more dangerously—

Was she both?

"I have prepared you another concoction for your hands, and I hope it will last longer," Elizabeth assured the older woman, her voice carrying a promise as delicate as the lace at her collar. "I promise I will stay in touch better next time."

"Thank you, sweetheart. You're such a powerful healer," the woman praised, her voice warm with gratitude. She shuffled toward the door, stepping out into the creeping dusk.

Elizabeth sighed, leaning against the closed door

She never saw me coming.

I stepped forward, emerging from the darkness like a specter of truth, a shadow cast in flesh and intent.

Our eyes met.

Horror.

It flashed across her face, her blue eyes wide with the terror of being discovered.

She didn't breathe.

She was a doe caught in a hunter's sights for a single heartbeat—frozen, waiting, calculating her escape.

Then—

The sound of boots on the forest floor.

Elizabeth's gaze snapped to the windows, her body rigid as the realization sank in.

My men had arrived.

They were an unrelenting force, surrounding the cottage like wolves closing in on their prey.

The net was tightening, and at its center was Elizabeth Alexander—vulnerable, exposed, no longer the enigma hidden beneath layers of secrecy.

"So, you took over my role in France."

My voice was devoid of hesitation, betraying none of the inner turmoil being near her evoked.

Her lips parted, but she didn't speak.

She knew what I meant.

"You're the one who threw the poison. The one who wiped out the entire French Timehunter society."

The accusation hung between us, as damning as the Noctyss flower she had wielded.

Elizabeth shook her head, her breath sharp and shaky.

"No!" she cried, her voice slicing through the tension. "I'm not part of my father's vile game."

Tears glistened in her eyes, but her chin lifted in defiance.

A challenge.

A plea.

I couldn't suppress a scoff, though something inside me quailed at the idea of her innocence.

"But here you are," I continued, my voice cold and biting, as I gestured to the alchemy tools strewn across the room. "Creating powerful concoctions, working with forbidden knowledge, leaving traces of your work in France."

My eyes narrowed, watching her, waiting for the cracks to form.

"I read your notes, Elizabeth."

The name seared on my tongue.

"You're involved."

She shook her head desperately, eyes wide, hands trembling.

"I promise you, I have nothing to do with this!"

I didn't blink.

"We shall see."

The words sliced through the air—calm, merciless, stripped of warmth.

"One way or another, I will loosen your lips."

Her breath hitched.

"And if you refuse to cooperate—"

I stepped closer, towering over her, watching how her body tensed.

"You'll regret it."

A flicker of fear passed through her gaze—but she didn't back down.

Not yet.

Then—the sound of boots.

My men stepped forward, their appearance swallowing the small cottage like an inevitable fate.

Elizabeth's breathing turned shallow and erratic, her body coiling as if preparing to flee—

Then, she screamed.

A sound raw and unfiltered, like a wounded animal's final cry, tearing through the trees, desperate and wild.

But there was no time for hesitation.

There was no room for doubt.

"Take her to my dungeon," I ordered, my heart steeling against the surge of pity that tried to creep into my chest.

Elizabeth struggled, eyes fiery, fury mixing with terror—but it was too late.

With a whispered incantation, darkness coalesced around us, swirling, pulling tight, wrapping Elizabeth in its unforgiving embrace.

And in the blink of an eye, we were gone—

Vanished into the abyss.

To a place where secrets would unravel—

And truths would be laid bare.

CHAPTER 10

ELIZABETH

I awoke to the stench of mold and the skittering of rats, their tiny claws scraping against damp stone.

Decay's aroma sullied the air, and each breath filled my lungs with the cold, rotting moisture of a dungeon that seemed to swallow all light and hope.

I shifted, instinctively testing my limbs— only to feel the bite of iron securing my wrists and ankles to a heavy wooden chair.

Panic bloomed in my chest.

My heart hammered in an erratic rhythm of pure dread.

Then—the memories seeped in, slow and insidious, like poison working its way through my veins.

The Black Wraith.

A masked nightmare in my alchemy cottage.

He had been an omen— and now, I was here.

But where was I?

How had I gotten here?

No one knew where I was.

No one was coming for me.

A movement from the shadows sent a jolt through my system.

I snapped my head up, my breath catching—

From the darkest corner of the room, he emerged.

The Black Wraith.

A figure forged in darkness, a silhouette of power and menace.

My breath hitched, terror's icy fingers clawing at my throat as he closed the distance with slow, deliberate steps—like a predator that had already decided the outcome of this hunt.

He stood there—taller than I remembered, cloaked in shadow, the faint scent of smoke clinging to him like a warning. But it was the mask that stole my breath.

Bone-white, cracked like old porcelain, it molded to his face with unnatural perfection. The sockets were nothing but black voids, swallowing any existing light, swallowing *me*. I couldn't see his eyes, but I felt them—felt his stare like cold hands around my throat.

The mouth was fixed in that twisted grin. Those jagged teeth looked like they were meant to bite, to punish, to mock.

This was it. I was going to die here, and no one would ever come for me. These were my last moments on this earth.

The man loomed over me, swallowing the room, his power caressing me like a second skin.

A gloved hand reached out—

Fingers brushed my jaw, a touch as cold as winter's first frost.

I shuddered, the contact scalding with icy cruelty, its agonizing slowness a brutal reminder of how powerless I was beneath him.

His voice followed, a low, menacing growl that coiled around me like a noose.

"I'm going to make this simple."

I swallowed hard, pulse pounding against my ribs.

"You answer all my questions, and I'll let you go—without hurting you, without killing you."

The words should have been a reprieve, but they were anything but.

Because then came the promise, the real threat, that sent my insides twisting into knots.

"But if you don't comply..."

His grip tightened, just for a moment.

"I will make your life a living hell."

The scent of leather and sandalwood surrounded him, intoxicating, inescapable.

His eyes—cold, unreadable, merciless—bored into mine, his stare a command, a silent demand for obedience.

And in that moment, as the walls pressed in, as the darkness breathed around us—

I knew.

There would be no mercy.

"Where did you get the Noctyss flower, the Bloom of Death?"

Each word dripped with threat, with malice, making it clear that if I didn't comply—if I hesitated—I would suffer for it.

A flutter of panic erupted in my chest, wild and erratic, searching for escape.

"I don't know what you're talking about."

The lie tumbled too quickly from my lips, a weak, feeble thing that I barely believed. I willed myself into the innocent, demure, compliant facade I had perfected over the years—

But the quiver in my voice betrayed me.

I choked down my despair, but it clung to me, settling like a cloak of inevitability.

I had never been a convincing liar.

And now, as I tried to deceive this dominant beast, as I stared into the cold abyss of his eyes, I felt guilt, terror, and something else—something primal and dangerous—crushing me.

How long could I keep this up before it all crumbled?

Before he undid me completely?

His voice came low, cruel, as intent as a blade sliding beneath the skin.

"Stop lying to me, Elizabeth."

My name on his tongue felt like a violation, an invasion, stripping me bare.

"I know it was you who released the poison in France. A nightmarish hell unleashed on monstrous men—yes. But did you think I wouldn't find out?"

The accusation cracked through the air like a whip, leaving no room for evasion or pretense.

"I know it was you. And now, you will pay for your crimes."

A shudder racked through me, my body instinctively recoiling, the iron chains biting against my skin.

"How do you know my name?" I gasped in a desperate, frail attempt to regain control, to turn the interrogation around.

But he didn't flinch.

He didn't hesitate.

"I make it my business to know my enemies."

His tone was ice, devoid of heat and pity, as if my life, existence, and secrets were trivial matters to be collected, used, and discarded at his will.

He stepped closer, his shadow swallowing me whole.

"You're just like that flower, Elizabeth."

I stiffened.

"Trapped in eternal suspension. Beautiful. Alluring."

A pause—calculated, suffocating.

"But hiding a venomous sting."

His words coiled around me, an unspoken threat more damning than any blade he could wield.

"No!"

The word erupted from me, a feeble protest, weak and hollow, swallowed by the darkness around us.

I twisted my wrists, the chains clinking in a cruel mockery of my desperation.

His hand found the back of my neck.

Not a strike.

Not a choke.

A cradle—a touch paradoxically tender and terrifying.

My eyes snapped shut, and every muscle tensed.

Was he going to kiss me?

The unbidden, horrifying, visceral thought sent a shudder through me.

But no lips came.

Instead—his breath.

A whisper of heat against my skin, setting me ablaze with a

fear-fueled desire so foreign it unnerved me more than his threats.

"I came to France to destroy the Timehunter society."

His voice was low, venomous, controlled rage barely leashed.

"Instead, I find them already dead. Maimed. Deformed. Their bones misshapen, their skin melting from their bodies like hot wax."

The horror of his words seared through me, a new kind of terror, one that dug deep—because I knew it to be true.

Yet I could not escape his grasp.

Or the corrosive touch of the truth.

His fingers seized my chin, wrenching my face toward his darkened stare, forcing me to look at him.

"I don't like being lied to."

His words snapped like a whip, raw with danger and warning.

"Tell me the truth, Elizabeth—now."

I swallowed hard, my pulse thudding in my throat.

"I know nothing," I persisted, voice shaking, fragile beneath his scrutiny.

But I had to keep my secrets.

His laugh was low—vicious and devoid of warmth.

"I was there, Elizabeth."

His voice turned into something deadly, cruel, yet intimate, like an inevitable storm.

"That quaint little cottage of yours? I walked through it all—saw your potions, your bottles, flipped through every page of your precious alchemy book. I read every single word."

His rage burned, controlled but lethal, an ember smoldering beneath the surface.

"Tell me, how did you come into possession of the alchemy book of Solaris?"

The words struck like a physical blow.

"Where did you get such a powerful book?"

His gaze bore into me, dark and merciless, his posture coiled like a serpent poised to strike.

I stayed silent, my breath uneven, my mind racing for an escape, a distraction, anything.

But he was undeterred.

"Alright."

His voice dropped lower now, silk wrapped around iron resolve.

"You want to play games with me?"

A shift.

A glint of metal in the dim light.

A knife.

The sound of the blade sliding free was deceptively soft, a whisper of menace that sent my stomach plummeting.

He held it easily as if it were simply an extension of himself, the razor edge catching the faint flicker of light as he methodically turned it between his fingers.

"Do you know what this is for?"

His voice was a silken promise of pain, laced with cold, calculated intent.

I said nothing.

I could say nothing.

His fingers traced the blade's edge, his grip relaxed, yet nothing was casual about the threat curling between us.

"I won't hesitate to use it."

A simple statement.

A fact.

"If I have to."

He stepped closer, the blade glinting between us, a quiet, insidious reminder of the violence he was capable of.

"There are far more..."

He tilted his head, watching me, studying me as if trying to decipher a puzzle that refused to yield its secrets.

"Effective methods than death to get answers."

The dungeon's chill coiled around me—into my skin and bones—making me shudder.

"Please don't hurt me," I whispered, my voice a fragile thread in the oppressive silence.

"I didn't want to hurt anyone in France. It was an experiment... gone wrong."

His expression did not change.

His eyes—cold, unflinching—remained fixed on mine as though peering straight through my soul.

"Then tell me what you know."

His voice was forged of steel, every word a blade, every breath a sentence—as unforgiving as the stones that trapped me in this hell.

I faltered, the reality of my predicament crushing me.

He did not like hesitation.

With one swift motion, he slashed the air, the blade flashing dangerously close to my face—a warning, a threat wrapped in the silent, deadly display.

"Do you want me to hurt you?"

The snarl in his voice sent a violent tremor through my body.

The blade hovered—just inches from my throat, its deadly promise taunting my skin.

"Because I will. Tell me what you did, Elizabeth—or I will carve the truth out of you."

A sob tore from my throat, my entire body racked with terror.

"No! Please!"

I broke, the fight crumbling inside me as tears streamed hot down my cheeks, flaming against the dungeon's cold.

"I'll tell you! I'll tell you everything!"

My plea hung in the air, trembling, fragile, the last remnant of my fading resistance.

He did not move.

But the energy between us changed—a crackling wire of impatience, his frustration, and urgency tangible in the dimly lit cell.

"I am not known for my patience."

His words slithered over my skin like a live current, waiting, demanding, giving me nothing but the certainty that one wrong move could end me.

His posture was tense, coiled, lethal—a beast poised to strike, and devour every last truth I possessed.

Each second that passed stretched unbearably, the tension between like a knife against my neck before he touched me.

I forced down the sob clogging my throat, grasping for control, for anything to cling to in the face of my undoing.

"I found the flower... with my mother."

The words spilled out, raw, fragile, my voice hoarse from my betrayal.

"It was a long time ago... in the mountains."

A shuddering breath.

A moment of hesitation.

And then—

His grip tightened.

"Keep talking!"

The Black Wraith's patience frayed, his voice cleaving through the air.

"She learned about the Noctyss flower. The Bloom of Death."

The words felt foreign on my tongue, memories rising from the depths of my past like corpses from a forgotten grave.

"My mother was fascinated. She spent years studying it."

My gaze remained fixed on the floor, unable to meet his, my fear writhing with the echoes of a story I had never spoken aloud.

"And how did you create the poison?"

The question landed like a clean, unrelenting blow.

I felt my throat tighten, the burden of a truth I had buried strangling me like a noose.

I had never told anyone.

"My mother created it."

The confession came out in a trembling breath, my hands shaking, my body bracing for judgment.

"She... she found an old alchemy book. Buried in the dirt."

The memory was a phantom, whispering its cruel reminders into my ear.

"There were strange messages... written in blood. About Solaris. About how to use the flower."

The Black Wraith didn't move, but I felt his focus intensify, his being like a dark tide swallowing me whole.

"She crafted it to kill my father. To destroy his society."

A bitter laugh escaped my lips, hollow, devoid of mirth.

"She thought she could control it."

A pause.

A silence so dense it felt like the walls themselves held their breath.

"But it killed her."

My voice broke, splintering under the words.

"That's how she died. She didn't know how to use it safely."

The dungeon was deathly silent, and the air was taut and heavy, charged with something that felt too vast and too dangerous.

The Black Wraith leaned in, his shadow stretching over me like a phantom, swallowing the dim flickers of light that dared remain.

"So." His voice was a low, menacing rumble, resonating through the stone walls.

"Your mother couldn't control it—but you took over."

It wasn't a question.

It was an accusation.

I nodded, my lips parting as I dragged in a shallow, uneven breath.

"I had no choice!"

The words tumbled out, broken, raw with desperation and grief.

Tears slid down my cheeks, unbidden, unstoppable, staining my already fragile resolve.

"I was trying to master it! To use it for good!"

I gasped, my heartbeat pounding like thunder in my ears.

"I didn't want anyone to die! I only wanted to stop those monsters from their cruelty!"

My chest heaved, my world spinning, my confession like iron shackles.

"You crafted something you didn't understand," he accused, his gaze slashing straight through me. "And in doing so, you killed your brothers."

Panic fluttered in my chest like a trapped bird. "No! That wasn't my intention! You set the fire," I shot back, my voice trembling despite my attempt at bravery.

"Yes," he admitted, his voice a menacing whisper. "I am a killer. A ruthless, efficient killer. I destroy societies for a reason —because of what they do. But you?" His eyes gleamed with something cold, something final. "You had no right to interfere. You don't understand the power you've unleashed or the game you're playing."

His words coiled around me like a noose, tightening with each syllable. There was no remorse in his tone, no hesitation— just the conviction of a man who had seen, had done too much, and would not be stopped.

Memories of fire and screams tore through my mind like jagged glass. My heart thundered as the words clawed their way out. "How did you survive France? I threw the last of my poison at you. No one walks away from that—the rest ended up broken, twisted... or dead."

His laughter echoed off the stone walls, jagged and cruel. "Do you want to know how I survived, my sweet venom?" His voice was almost mocking, his eyes dark with something unnatural. "Snakes. Deadly Inland Taipans, to be exact. They slithered over me, injecting their venom again and again until it ran through my veins like liquid fire."

I froze. "Snakes?" I breathed, barely able to comprehend. "That should have killed you."

"Indeed. They would have killed an ordinary man. But I am not ordinary." He stepped closer, his voice smooth, assured. "I am a Darkness."

A shiver traced down my spine, as cold as the stone walls around us, yet heat pooled deep within me. "Darkness?" My voice barely rose above a whisper. "What do you mean?"

He was close now—too close. His breath warmed my skin,

sending every nerve into chaos. "A Darkness is a creature that kills every day to survive," he murmured. "I inhale a person's soul to keep my strength."

My stomach tightened, dread curling like a serpent within me. "You kill to survive? You... inhale souls?" The words trembled from my lips, laced with terror—and something else—a dark curiosity.

"Every day." He said it so simply, as if he were stating the time, and at that moment, I understood the true meaning of fear. And it wore the face of the Black Wraith.

Yet, despite the terror, something deeper—something far more dangerous—pulled me toward him. He was a contradiction, a monstrous and magnetic force, and I was caught in his gravity.

His fingers tangled in my hair without warning, yanking my head back with ruthless force. A gasp escaped me, sudden and unbidden. My neck lay bare before him, vulnerable, exposed.

Though the mask concealed most of his face, something in the way he looked at me—his stillness, the tilt of his head, the subtle tension—made it clear. His hunger was palpable. Behind the wicked teeth of the mask he licked his lips, slowly, as if savoring the anticipation of a feast.

I should have been repulsed, should have recoiled. But instead, something ignited within me—a wildfire of fear and fascination. The terror twisting inside me blurred into something far more dangerous—desire.

"I'm not a killer," I whispered. "I never meant for it to go that far. They were corrupt—vile—but they deserved justice, not death." A tear slid down my cheek, but I didn't look away. "The poison was meant to stop them, not... that fire. That was you. You turned retribution into a massacre. You burned them alive."

The Black Wraith's breath ghosted over my skin, sending a shiver through me. "I put them out of their suffering," he murmured, his voice rich with something intoxicating. "Elizabeth, we are reflections of each other in this dark mirror of life. We both wield the power of death." His tone was laced with dangerous certainty as though he were speaking an undeniable truth. "You may cloak yourself in righteousness, but our hands are equally stained."

I shuddered in his grasp, but his fingers were iron, unrelenting. "No," I hissed. "You know nothing of my heart."

His laugh was low, cruel, knowing. "Ah, but I do."

Pain lanced through my scalp as he tightened his hold, the ruthless tug forcing my head back further. My chest rose and fell rapidly, betraying the storm inside me.

"Your father's ignorance of your true nature is a fragile shield, Elizabeth," he murmured, his lips barely grazing mine as the jaw of the mask seemed to separate, the heat of his breath igniting something deep within me. "And should it shatter, his wrath will be merciless."

Then, without hesitation, he seized me.

His mask hard against my face, the protrusions biting into my skin—then his mouth found mine, desperate, unrelenting. It wasn't just a kiss. It was fire crashing into fire, a raw, devouring claim that pulled me into the storm with him. I felt his hunger, his fury, the way he stripped me bare with every breathless second.

I gasped against him, and he swallowed the sound, leaning over me as I sat shackled to the unyielding chair. His hand traced down my body with a boldness that sent shivers tearing through me.

There was no patience, no tenderness—only possession, only need. My body arched, instinctively seeking more, a treacherous fire began low in my stomach, coiling tighter with every brush of his tongue against mine.

This was no act of love.

It was dark, desperate, a sin-soaked surrender.

His fingers tightened in my hair, yanking my head back with a ruthless dominance that sent a molten shiver down my spine. "You crave it, don't you?" he whispered against my lips, his voice a velvet trap of seduction and danger. "The darkness in you begging to be claimed by mine."

I should have denied it. I should have pushed him away. But my traitorous body moved closer, my lips parting in silent invitation.

He growled, a sound deep and guttural, his teeth grazing the sensitive skin of my jaw before trailing lower, his mouth marking a path of fire along my throat. I moaned, a sound that betrayed me entirely.

Gods, what was this? This ache, this feverish desperation for more, for him?

He stepped between my legs, rubbing his thigh against me, and I nearly shattered—my breath catching as delicious friction sent white-hot need flashing through me. Shackled to the chair, I couldn't move, couldn't run. His hand roamed with expert ease, mapping every shiver, every unsteady breath.

Then—just as my control began to slip entirely—he pulled away.

I gasped, breathless, and aching.

Though I couldn't see his mouth, I felt the smirk in his voice as he took in my disheveled state. "You're more dangerous than you realize," he murmured, his tone sinful.

I exhaled shakily, forcing a smirk, though my legs still trembled. "And you're not?"

He leaned in again, the lower edge of his skeletal mask shifting just enough to expose his mouth. His lips ghosted over mine—a cruel, calculated tease that sent another wave of need crashing through me.

"Oh, I know exactly what I am." His voice was a promise— dark, wicked, dripping with temptation. His teeth grazed my bottom lip, a sinful tease before he pulled back just enough to make me ache. "The question is… can you handle it?"

I forced my voice to steady, though it quivered like a leaf in the wind. "We can work together. Stop my father and Lord Winston before their plans unfold. Their society is hunting you, but I can help you. Let's bring them down—together."

He scoffed, shaking his head, the movement curt and dismissive. "I work alone. You might as well confess your every betrayal to your father because he remains blissfully blind to the true nature of his daughter. He sees only obedience."

A slow, cold smile ghosted behind the skeletal mask, the kind that sent a thrill of dread down my spine. "I could strip away that illusion with a mere whisper in the right ear. Shatter his trust in you without ever stepping into the light."

My hands clenched involuntarily, nails biting into my palms. "You wouldn't dare!" I snapped, but the fear curling in my stomach betrayed my confidence.

"You think this is a game, love?" His voice dipped into something dangerously soft, a velvet snare. "You're playing with forces that could devour you whole. You don't understand the depth of this world—the power, the peril. And you are not ready for it."

The words lashed against me like a storm, a stark reminder that I had stepped onto a battlefield where the pieces were moved by shadows and whispers, not brute force.

I swallowed hard, my pulse a frantic rhythm in my throat. "Who are you?" The question tumbled from my lips. "Why do you hide behind that mask?"

Before I could move, his hand was on me—cold, immovable, seizing my chin in a grip that sent a jolt of dark electricity coursing through me. His touch was possessive and commanding, forcing my gaze up into the abyss of his eyes.

"Because monsters don't need faces, my sweet venom. Only power," he whispered, his voice an unnerving caress that slithered down my spine, a phantom touch I could feel even where his fingers didn't linger.

Then—the world twisted.

Darkness unfurled from the depths of his cloak, a living shadow that swallowed the space between us. It coiled around me like writhing, cold, insidious tendrils, a whispering abyss that pulled me under. My breath hitched as the sensation wrapped around my body—velvet and void, sin and sorcery. I clenched my eyes shut as if I could will away the impossible.

When I dared to open them again, the dungeon was gone.

I was no longer trapped in stone and shadow but seated

before my vanity. The air damp and frigid replaced with the familiar scent of my chamber. The candlelight flickered, uncertain as if sensing something still lingered in the air.

But when I lifted my gaze to the mirror, my breath caught.

Not my own startled reflection but his. The Black Wraith's haunting image burned through the glass, so tangible it sent a shudder rippling through me.

"You should have stayed away, Elizabeth." His voice was a whisper in my mind, in the air, in the very marrow of my bones. "I'll be watching you, my sweet venom."

A gasp tore from my lips, my pulse a frantic, erratic thing as I twisted around—but he was gone.

Vanished like a specter, like smoke slipping through my fingers, like the whisper of a dream that lingers just long enough to haunt you.

The silence was deafening. My chest heaved, my body still humming with the aftershock of his touch.

How did he do that? How could he disappear so effortlessly, like a ghost untethered by the rules of this world?

But worse—far worse—was the way my body still ached from his touch.

The kiss. The threat. The revelation that this masked man knew everything—about me, about my father, about the deadly poison I had created.

I shuddered, my fingers grazing my lips as if to erase the memory. But it was there, seared into me—a dangerous dance of desire and dread.

"How could I be so reckless?" I whispered to the empty room.

But the truth was far more damning.

I wasn't just reckless. I was captivated.

And the worst part? I wanted more.

The thought stole my breath, tightening its grip on my sanity. I craved what I should have feared.

The realization sent a violent shudder through me. No. No more.

I stood abruptly, knocking over the chair in my haste. It clattered to the floor, the harsh crash a stark reminder of my situation's fragility and the perilous tightrope I walked. I was tired—so exhausted—of being a pawn in their games.

Of men who sought to dominate. To dictate. To control me.

"No more."

The words were steel against my tongue. My reflection in the mirror was no longer that of a frightened girl but of something colder, harder. Deadlier. My blue eyes darkened into shards of ice, steeled, unbreakable.

"I won't let him, or any man control me again."

My hands trembled—not from fear, but from rage. It coursed through me like molten fire, igniting something deep within, powerful and waiting to be unleashed.

I inhaled, steadying my breath, my resolve solidifying like tempered glass.

"I will rise from the shadows."

The words spilled from my lips, quiet but lethal, the first droplet of a venomous concoction forming in my mind.

"I will create the most dangerous poison."

The vow settled in my chest, a dark promise, a fate already written in blood.

"I will join my father's society—but on my terms. I will infiltrate his world, his Timehunter empire, and tear it apart."

A slow, dangerous smile curved my lips, my reflection smirking back at me as the pieces fell into place. If the Black Wraith thought he could break me with a single kiss or a few words, he was mistaken.

He had no idea what he had awakened.

I was far more dangerous than he could ever imagine.

My alchemist's mind, once shackled in obedience, was now free. It pulsed with lethal possibilities, each more ruthless and deadlier than the last. The dormant hunger for vengeance unfurled in me like a creeping vine, twisting its way into every fiber of my being.

This was no longer about rebellion.

This was about war.

I would no longer be their pawn. I would be their reckoning.

And when the time came, I would make sure the Black Wraith watched as I crushed every chain and expectation and remade myself into something far more dangerous than any man had ever dared to imagine.

A Queen of Poison.

And I would not bow.

CHAPTER 11

ELIZABETH

The soft caress of the morning sun danced across my eyelids, coaxing them to flutter open like butterfly wings stirred by the first breath of dawn. Its warmth traced lazy patterns over my skin, whispering promises of a new day, painting my chamber in hues of honey and amber.

For a fleeting moment, I let myself sink into the golden embrace of morning, but then—reality.

My mind, still caught in the tangled web of the past few days, spun too fast to grasp anything solid. Yet one memory refused to fade, clinging to me like the scent of rain on parched earth—the kiss with Amir.

His lips had been a revelation, igniting something deep, something untamed within me. It was a kiss that wasn't just a kiss but a whispered promise, a fleeting taste of something forbidden—something I hadn't known I was starving for. It had branded me, a spark setting every nerve alight, making the clumsy, forgettable peck from Peter—the baker's son—seem laughably insignificant in comparison.

How could a kiss like that exist?

It had unraveled me, shattered me, and made me ache in ways I had never experienced before. But as I savored its lingering heat, a bitter truth crept in like an unwelcome ghost.

He had pulled away first.

Leaving me breathless. Alone.

Amidst the ruins of that brief, intoxicating encounter, I was left with nothing but questions. Why? When every fiber of his being had seemed so fiercely entwined with mine at that moment, why had he withdrawn? What held him back?

What shadows lurked behind those dark, intense eyes?

I lay there, tangled in my sheets, my heartbeat still betraying me with its unsteady rhythm. I couldn't ignore the way Amir had stepped between me and my father's wrath, how he had followed me home, a silent shield against the storm. And then—he lied for me.

Why?

He was an enigma—all razor-cut angles and guarded walls, his clipped words and stoic veneer daring me to look deeper, to see what he wouldn't show.

Could a man indeed be as dangerous as he claimed yet still choose to protect me?

Or was the real danger not in him—but in what I was beginning to feel for him?

The questions spun through my mind, a tangled web of uncertainty, each thread leading back to him. Lord Amir Hassan, with his swarthy Mediterranean complexion—a face carved from the shadows he battled—remained a mystery. And yet, despite the secrets that surrounded him, something unseen tethered him to me. An invisible thread binding us together in ways I was only beginning to understand.

I propped myself up on the downy pillows, reaching for my diary—hidden beneath their soft embrace. My fingers brushed against the folded note within its pages, the inked words "I wish things were different, my love," bleeding into the parchment like a wound too deep to heal.

The word "love" lingered, curling around my heart like an incantation, filling me with an ache that refused to subside. What would it feel like if Amir truly wanted me? If he let go of whatever restraint kept him at arm's length and surrendered to the undeniable pull between us?

But deep down, I knew.

These were nothing but daydreams, fragile illusions that could never bridge the chasm between fantasy and reality.

And yet, I clung to them.

Every stroke of ink, every curve of his handwriting, tethered me to a different possibility—one where I could flee from Lord Winston's looming shadow and into Amir's enigmatic embrace.

Why couldn't it be different?

The question seared through me as I closed the diary with a soft thud, unspoken dreams pressing down on my chest. I longed to shed the shackles of betrothal and duty, run wild and free, and choose my own fate.

To choose him.

A shudder rippled through me—not from the morning air's chill, but from the memory that slithered through my consciousness unbidden.

The Black Wraith.

His kiss had been a storm—violent and consuming, leaving destruction in its wake. It burned as fiercely as Amir's own, yet where Amir's touch was restraint warring with desire, the Wraith's was pure, unbridled possession.

It was danger wrapped in seduction, an intoxicating connection that had left my lips bruised and my soul aflame.

I sucked in a breath, my pulse quickening. Two men. Two dangers.

And I was caught between them, drawn like a moth to a fire that could devour me whole.

In the sanctuary of my chamber, I allowed myself a moment of indulgence—a fleeting marvel at the boldness I had unearthed within myself. An innocent virgin, once destined for an arranged, loveless marriage, now teetered on the precipice of reckless desire.

Passion called to me. Temptation whispered promises in the dark.

A life untouched by disgust. A life where I would not wilt in the shadow of duty but blaze in the light of my choosing.

"Elizabeth," I chided myself, the sound of my name a reprimand, a tether meant to pull me back to reason. I had been careless. Foolish. My heart had become a battlefield, torn between the storm that was Amir and the abyss that was the Black Wraith.

But as I rebuked myself, the truth slithered through my mind, undeniable and relentless.

I craved the fire.

I wanted to be consumed by it, to feel something real before I was snuffed out by fate's cold, merciless hands.

The thought of submitting—of bowing my head, folding my hands, and accepting a future of cold duty beneath Lord Winston's loathsome touch—made my stomach churn.

I would not bear it.

No.

I would chase the inferno. If only to blaze for a moment before the darkness claimed me.

A quick breath, a shake of my head—a futile attempt to silence the thoughts spun by men who had no right to linger in my mind.

"Men! Bah!" The whispered exclamation slipped from my lips, fierce and defiant.

Let them haunt me, let their touch linger on my skin like a ghost—I had more important matters than the war waged in my veins.

A new vow coiled within me, dark and unforgiving.

The elimination of my father's society.

The destruction of Lord Winston.

They perched atop my intentions like carrion birds waiting to feast, but I would not be their victim. I would be their undoing.

I needed to craft the perfect poison—a concoction as potent and final as the resolve that now steeled my heart.

No more hiding.

No more fear.

Today, I became something else.

Something formidable.

∽∾

As Mary entered to dress me, I stood tall, my movements no longer that of a girl shackled by duty but of a woman who had set herself free.

And when I descended the grand staircase, my simple gown whispering against the polished wood, it was with purpose in every step.

My father awaited me in his private sitting room.

He had no idea what was coming.

"Good morning, Father!" My voice was almost too bright—like the sun spilling through the gauzy curtains, warm and deceptive. The scent of his black coffee curled in the crisp morning air, mingling with the faint hint of ink from his newspaper.

Surprise flashing across his features, he looked up before it melted into something softer. Something pleased. The paper crinkled in his hands as he set it aside, his full attention settling on me like an embrace I had once sought but now endured.

"Elizabeth," he greeted, his tone infused with warmth. "What brings you down so early?"

I stepped forward, leaning in to press my lips to his cheek—a daughter's affection or perhaps the prelude to a betrayal yet unseen.

I met his gaze as I sat across from him at the small table where he took his solitary meals. "I have been thinking, Father," I said, smoothing my hands over the fabric of my gown as if to still the storm beneath my skin. "I realized you were right. I want to take on my responsibilities. I want to join your society."

The words hung between us, weighty with unspoken truths, heavy with deception.

I saw it for the first time in my life—true pride flickering in his eyes, a rare and dangerous thing. He did not question me, did not hesitate. Because, in his mind, this was inevitable.

"You've made the right decision, Elizabeth," he declared, his voice swelling with paternal satisfaction. "I knew you would come around. You were always meant for this."

A chill slithered down my spine, but I forced a smile, tilting my head in a way that made me look demure and obedient. He saw what he wanted to see.

Good.

A soft knock at the door broke the moment, followed by the delicate hush of footsteps across the plush carpet. A maid approached, her gaze politely lowered. "Lady Elizabeth, what will you have for breakfast?"

"Just tea, please. And bread with butter."

My stomach was already a battlefield, twisting itself into intricate knots that could rival the finest lace. I doubted I could stomach anything more substantial—not when my mind was already steeped in something more consuming.

Across from me, my father had already returned to his paper, The Daily Courant claiming his attention again. I had just given him the greatest news—the supposed fulfillment of his ambitions for me—and yet, already, I was invisible again. The world's affairs ensnared him, his mind wandering through ink and print while I sat in silence, nibbling at the crust of my bread.

A daughter. A future heir. And yet, still, a shadow.

I was considering whether to break that silence when the butler's voice infiltrated the quiet, ending the fragile peace of the morning.

"My lord, Lord Hassan has arrived. Shall I see him in?"

I barely had time to react before my father nodded, glancing up from the page.

But I felt it.

A pulse—an unbidden rush of warmth spreading through me like fire in my veins, an embarrassing tide rising fast.

The door opened, and then… him.

Lord Amir Hassan.

The man who seemed to bend the air around us, shifting it into something heavier, something charged. The room had felt cool moments ago, but now, with each step he took, the temperature seemed to climb.

Damn him.

I clenched my fists in my lap, forcing my breath to steady, my pulse to slow. Stop. Don't have feelings.

I had to remind myself—he declined to help me. He was a murderer, just like Lord Winston.

He was a member of my father's organization. A killer. A man steeped in blood and shadow.

I repeated it like a prayer, a lifeline, something to anchor me against the tide of emotions threatening to pull me under.

And yet…

As I whispered those words in my mind, my heart betrayed me.

It fluttered—treacherous, reckless—like a bird desperate for escape.

I watched him, studied him, traced the contrasts that made up Lord Amir Hassan—his dark hair, swarthy skin, and chiseled features. A man built from shadows, mystery, and secrets too heavy to be spoken aloud. His eyes—gods, those eyes—had seen too much, held too much, yet they barely lingered on me before shifting to my father, nodding in polite acknowledgment.

"Lord Hassan," my father greeted, oblivious to the storm raging within me. "Please, join us for breakfast."

"Thank you."

His voice, that low, velvety timbre, slid through the air, smooth and disarming. He moved with a grace that belied his strength, a predator who did not need to flaunt his power because it was simply there—woven into every measured step, every precise movement.

I hated that I noticed.

I hated it more that I felt it.

Despite the logic screaming at me to turn away, I couldn't deny the pull—his undeniable gravity. The man who had stirred my soul, awakened something deep and forbidden and cast it aside as if it were nothing.

And yet, here I sat, caught between dutiful daughter and impassioned woman.

And I wasn't sure which terrified me more.

Amir took the seat next to me.

The table suddenly felt too small, too intimate—a prison of fine china and clinking silverware. The space between us was negligible, and the brush of his knee beneath the cloth sent a jolt through my body that I pretended not to feel.

I focused on the delicate porcelain of my teacup, watching the steam curl into the air as if I could lose myself in its fleeting tendrils. But his aura was tangible, a force, shifting the air between us like a silent storm rolling in.

The maid scurried around, placing food in front of Amir, and the silence stretched between us, crowded with unspoken truths, with ghosts of a past neither of us dared to name.

Then—

"I have excellent news to share, Amir."

My father set down his cup quietly, his expression aglow with unmistakable pride.

"My daughter has decided to join our society."

And just like that, the delicate balance I had tried to maintain teetered.

The room seemed to shrink, the air pressing in as if waiting for a reaction.

Amir's gaze finally found mine, dark, unrelenting—ablaze with something searing through my core. I felt it like a touch, a slow caress over bare skin, igniting something dangerous within me despite my desperate attempt to remain detached.

"Really? What excellent news!" His voice was smooth, but beneath the polished words, something lurked. Surprise? Or something else?

His head tilted slightly as if considering the truth behind my father's declaration. "And what will you be doing, Lady Alexander? What role will you play?"

I parted my lips, a flicker of nerves coiling in my stomach—

But my father's voice cut through the air with the finality of a guillotine.

"She will take over her mother's role—alchemy. Crafting poisons."

The words landed like a verdict, a future set before me in cold, absolute certainty.

Amir reacted instantly.

His posture shifted, muscles tightening beneath the fabric of his coat, tension rolling off him like a storm gathering on the horizon. It was subtle, but I saw the smallest crack in his impassive facade.

Was that concern flickering in his eyes? Or was it merely a reflection of my unspoken trepidation?

His cool gaze settled on me again, more piercing now, scrutinizing, assessing—as if searching for something he wasn't sure he wanted to find. The air between us seemed to quiver, stretched thin under unspoken words.

"How are you feeling about this, Lady Alexander?"

The formality of my title on his tongue was intentional, laced with something almost venomous—a reminder of the walls between us.

I refused to falter.

I lifted my chin, meeting his gaze with quiet insolence.

"Quite confident," I replied, my voice as smooth as silk, despite the storm.

Amir's eyes narrowed, assessing, challenging. "All the other societies have developed sophisticated poisons. They have superior alchemists at their disposal. How can you keep up?"

His words were a stone cast into still waters, sending ripples of doubt through the room.

But I refused to let him see a flicker of hesitation.

"I have secret ingredients," I said, letting the mantle of my legacy settle around me like a cloak. "The English society was once known for its poisons."

A shadow of a smirk toyed at the corners of Amir's lips, an unreadable glint flashing in his eyes.

Then—abruptly, purposefully—he changed course.

"Have you recovered since the last time I saw you?" His tone was casual, too casual. "You were so stressed when your carriage broke down."

His dismissive voice fanned the embers of irritation within me, the warmth of embarrassment flaring hot against my skin.

"Thank you for your concern, Lord Hassan," I bit back, the title laced with pointed venom, a subtle barb meant to wound. "I am feeling better, but I haven't been sleeping well. I'm far too restless."

His expression flickered with something unreadable, intrigue maybe. Then, with an almost imperceptible tilt of his head, he murmured, "Ah. Restlessness is said to be the sign of a coming revelation."

The words hung between us, delicate yet ensnaring, a spider's web spun from silk and shadow.

Was he mocking me? Or was there something more?

I yearned to press him, tear through the layers of mystery and indifference, and see what lay beneath. But the moment slipped away, leaving nothing but the ghost of unanswered questions.

Then—my father's voice broke the tension, breaching the silence with ease.

"Elizabeth, since you have decided to take your role in our society—and with Lord Hassan here—I think it's time I show you both my dungeon," he declared, his eyes glinting with an unsettling excitement.

A cold dread seized me, its grip tightening around my ribs like an iron vice. My breath hitched, and I forced myself to remain still though every instinct screamed for me to run.

The dungeon.

Gods.

I stiffened, the walls seeming to press inward, the moment suffocating. From the corner of my eye, I caught Amir's head tilting ever so slightly, his dark gaze flickering toward me— registering my alarm.

Yet his voice remained infuriatingly smooth, betraying nothing.

"I would be honored, Lord Alexander," he said.

Too eager.

The words rang hollow, too perfectly conveyed—as if he welcomed the opportunity to peel back yet another layer of the sinister web my father had woven.

Slowly, we rose from the table, and I followed their lead,

each step heavier than the last as inevitability bore down upon me.

Amir remained close—too close. His silent company contrasted with the churning storm within me. Whether he was a guardian or a witness to my undoing, I could not say.

We entered my father's study—a room as familiar to me as my thoughts. Or so I had believed.

He moved toward the towering bookcase, his fingers gliding over the polished wood as though performing a sacred rite. I watched, my breath shallow, as he knocked—once. Twice. Three times.

The hollow sound reverberated through the silence, a slow, ominous pulse.

Then, with deliberate ease, my father reached for the skull perched among the leather-bound tomes—a macabre relic of power and secrecy.

My stomach clenched as he twisted it.

A deep, resonant groan filled the study—the protest of something ancient, something weary, something meant to remain hidden.

The bookcase shifted, its movement slow and laborious, revealing nothing but darkness beyond.

A hidden chamber.

A secret buried within the very walls I had once thought safe.

My father's dungeon.

The breath I hadn't realized I was holding shuddered past my lips.

For a heartbeat, I was frozen. The revelation struck me dumb, a silent blow to my carefully constructed reality. While I had gone about my mundane routines all these years, something monstrous had lurked beneath my feet.

Fear slithered through me, coiling with the unmistakable sting of betrayal.

My father was silhouetted against the yawning void beyond the bookcase; his expression twisted in grotesque pride.

"Welcome to my torture chamber," he announced, his voice full of malicious pleasure.

I felt his gaze settle on me, searching—evaluating. Under his scrutiny, I felt exposed, as though he could see past my carefully controlled exterior, peeling back every layer until he found whatever darkness he hoped to lay within me.

"This, my dear, is not for the fainthearted." His voice was smooth and purposeful, brimming with a test I couldn't ignore. "But now that you have accepted your role and joined our society, it's time for you to witness what we are truly about."

A challenge. A threat. An invitation.

An initiation into a world of shadows and screams.

My resolve wavered.

But there was no turning back. Not now. Not with Amir watching.

He loomed beside me, a silent specter whose very existence reminded me of my choices. He said nothing, but I felt him—his quiet observation, his relentless scrutiny.

I inhaled quickly and stepped forward.

A chill coiled around us, wrapping like a shroud. The underground air was damp, bursting with the scent of cold stone and something more insidious—a lingering trace of agony past.

We descended.

Each flickering torch we passed hesitated, its light stark against the stone, a feeble protest against the devouring darkness. Shadows danced along the slick walls, stretching, contorting—watching.

The uneven stone steps bit into my feet, and my hand trailed along the wall for balance. The texture was rough and unforgiving as if mocking my hesitation.

My mind whirled with the unspoken horrors that awaited below, but my feet—traitorous, determined—continued forward.

Deeper.

Darker.

Down into the abyss.

Amir was a silent pillar beside me, his occasional touch at the small of my back both a steadying force and a confusing comfort. The subtle pressure sent ripples of warmth through the ice of my fear—a contradiction that unsettled me more than the descent itself.

He was both an anchor and a temptation—a reminder of safety yet a sign of just how deep I was falling.

With each fleeting brush of his fingertips, my heart betrayed me, aching to lean back into him, to seek refuge in his arms rather than in my defiance.

But I couldn't.

This path was mine to walk, and I would not cower.

The sum of my father's expectations loomed before me, the horrors I had yet to witness scraping against my skin like a phantom touch. Still, I couldn't stop myself from stealing glances at Amir, trying to read his expression in the dim torchlight.

What did he truly think of me—of us?

But his face remained an enigma, his features set in professional detachment. Yet the heat radiating from him, the charged intensity that simmered beneath his mask, felt anything but indifferent.

The stairwell finally ended, depositing us before a heavy iron door.

Centuries-old, marred by time and use, it was like a sentinel, guarding the secrets hidden within. Seeing it sent a fresh wave of dread curling through my stomach.

Amir's hand settled on my shoulder.

I froze.

The warmth of his palm burned through the fabric of my gown, his grip firm but not forceful—a silent pause, a moment just for us.

My father pulled a large, ornate key from his coat and fitted it into the rusted lock with practiced ease. The metallic groan of tumblers shifting filled the silence, a prelude to whatever lay beyond.

And then—a whisper.

A breath against my skin.

"Are you sure you're ready for this?"

Amir's voice was low and intimate, stirring the tiny hairs on the nape of my neck.

His words caressed my ear, a blend of concern and provocation.

"Your father said this is not for the faint of heart. When you came to me the other day, you told me what Lord Winston had done. You were afraid, scared. This, I fear, will be worse."

His tone was intoxicating, a dark melody woven with warning and temptation—a spell of danger and allure.

I should have recoiled from the seductive timbre of his voice. It should have chilled me and sent me running back up the stairs.

Instead, it drew me in.

Some part of me—the Elizabeth who still trembled and longed for innocence—wanted to flee, to pretend none of this was real.

But the woman I was becoming—forged in fire, shaped by betrayal and necessity—refused to break.

I lifted my chin, summoning a strength I wasn't sure I truly possessed, and met Amir's gaze.

"I'm not afraid," I whispered back.

The words tasted bittersweet, a lie dressed as defiance. It was more than just an answer—it was a declaration of war—a challenge hurled at my own fear, a banner raised against the abyss waiting beyond that iron door.

Amir said nothing, but his eyes lingered on mine for a fraction too long—a silent acknowledgment of my rebelliousness. Or my foolishness.

Then, with a resounding clunk, my father pushed the door open.

The door groaned, revealing the next chapter of my life—one written in shadows and etched with pain.

There was no turning back.

I stepped forward, my pulse pounding in my throat, and stumbled into a tableau of torment that seared itself into my mind.

The chamber was a cavern of horrors, where suffering was both an art and a science.

Racks stretched limbs to the breaking point.

Iron maidens stood with their spiked interiors bared, their jagged maws hungry for flesh.

In the dim glow of torches, branding irons pulsed with hellish heat, their edges shining like embers awaiting their next victim.

The air was overflowing with the stench of sweat, blood, and despair.

A sound rose through the chamber—a macabre symphony of agony.

Chained like twisted effigies, two women and three men hung from the walls, their bodies marred with bruises and welts, their raw wounds glistening under the quivering torchlight.

And in a shadowed alcove, another figure writhed upon a chair, the clank of his restraints punctuating his moans of pain.

I swallowed hard, my breath shallow, my fingers curling into fists at my sides.

This was it.

The heart of my father's empire.

And I was expected to embrace it.

My father moved through the chamber with the delight of a child unwrapping a coveted gift. He reached for an instrument hanging on the wall—cat-o'-nine-tails, its leather thongs ending in twisted knots—and without hesitation, he set to work.

The first lash tore through the air, followed by the sound of flesh breaking.

A scream tore from the man bound before him, the raw, agonized sound lodging itself into my bones.

My father's face was a mask of detached cruelty, his expression eerily serene as he worked as if this were a routine chore.

The image seared itself into my memory, a waking nightmare that would haunt me until my dying days.

My knees buckled. The room tilted, the stench of blood and burnt flesh coiling into my throat, threatening to drag me under.

Then—Amir's hand.

Warm. Steadying.

His fingers anchored my back, holding me upright, as if he

had expected this reaction—as if he knew what was coming before I did.

His voice cut through the cacophony, a low murmur weighted with something unreadable.

"This is what we do, Elizabeth. We are monsters."

His words should have been cold, but instead, they were final. Absolute.

"Lord Winston. Your father. Your brothers, when they were alive. Me."

I turned to him with a jolt, seeking—something. Anything.

A flicker of regret? A plea for understanding?

But his face was a wall, his expression unreadable.

Still, his grip on me lingered—a contradiction in itself.

My stomach churned, revulsion rising like bile. I forced my gaze back to my father, and then—the horror twisted deeper.

His arousal strained against the front of his trousers, a grotesque testament to the pleasure he took in this brutality.

Sickness crawled up my throat.

"This is disgusting," I spat, my voice barely above a whisper. "To see my father beating someone without mercy is—"

I couldn't finish.

Because before I could speak another word, another victim was dragged into view.

A woman—perhaps in her forties—was yanked forward by her hair, her feet barely catching the stone floor as she stumbled into the dim light.

She was battered but unbowed, her spirit not yet broken despite the constant tide of anguish that surrounded her.

"Here's another plaything, Thomas," the man sneered, shoving her at my father's feet.

Her body crumpled to the stone floor with a sickening thud, her breath ragged as she fought against her fate.

I couldn't breathe.

Twin pools of sadistic pleasure gleamed in their eyes—hungry, soulless voids that drank in her suffering with relish. My father paused briefly, his gaze sweeping over her trembling form, before indulging himself in the moment, savoring the power he wielded over her existence.

Then, with infuriating ease, he selected his next tool—a whip, its leather coils winding around his palm like a living thing. The weapon sang through the air, striking her bare skin with a crack that echoed through the chamber.

Her scream ripped through the oppressive gloom, a visceral sound that should have left no heart untouched.

And yet, it only fueled them.

My father's voice was calm, disturbingly casual, as if discussing the weather rather than orchestrating a scene of unspeakable horror.

"You're a filthy fucking Timeborne. You're going to have sex with this man while I destroy you."

His words, spoken with chilling nonchalance, struck harder than the whip itself.

The urge to flee clawed at my insides, a desperate cry of self-preservation tearing through my mind. Every instinct urged me to run, to erase this moment from my memory before it could consume me whole.

Yet—somewhere deep within me, something colder, deadlier, began to take shape.

A vow.

A seed of rebellion planted in the soil of my father's atrocities.

This empire of suffering that my family had built…

It would fall.

But not yet.

Not today.

The stench of blood and fear coated my tongue with a metallic tang that made me want to retch. I was rooted in place, trapped between disgust, terror, and the cruel reality of my helplessness.

I wanted to move.

To scream.

To fight.

But their cruelty shackled me.

"I can't do this."

The thought repeated in my mind, over and over—a frantic, silent mantra.

And yet, in the depths of that helplessness, I made a silent promise.

I would end this.

Even if it killed me.

Amir beside me was both a comfort and a torment—a silent guardian, a shadow of warmth amid the ice of horror.

Then—his voice.

Low. Intimate. A whisper that wrapped around my trembling core like silk and steel.

"You're not like this. You're too pure. Are you sure you want to be a part of this?"

His words were a lifeline—a rope dangled over the abyss, offering escape. But they were also an accusation. A reminder of the innocence I felt slipping away with every second I remained in this room.

I couldn't breathe.

I reached for him, my fingers clenching the fabric of his shirt, desperate for something—anything—to anchor me in this maelstrom of evil.

"I can't breathe," I gasped, the room spinning dangerously, the stench of blood and burning flesh coiling in my lungs.

Amir shifted closer, his breath warm against my ear, the hushed urgency in his voice slicing through the chaos.

"Elizabeth." A command. A plea. "You don't have to be a part of this world. Do you know what the English Timehunter Society is called?"

My heart slammed against my ribs, my breath hitching.

A test. A revelation. A warning.

I turned to him, my eyes wide, searching—begging for something, anything that could make sense of this nightmare.

Amir's gaze seared into mine, his next words sliding over my skin like ice and fire.

"The Executors of Agony. The Harbingers of Temporal Terror."

Each syllable dripped with dread, painting the society in strokes of horror darker than I had ever imagined.

A shiver slithered down my spine.

Not just from the words.

But from the way Amir spoke them.

As though he had known them intimately. As though the darkness had already claimed him.

I could feel the pull of a world that devoured everything good and left only shadows behind.

No.

No.

I would not allow this darkness to engulf me. I would not become another piece in this game.

With a strength born of fury, I straightened, my fingers releasing Amir's shirt as I lifted my chin and met his gaze head-on.

"Yes," I said, my voice a blade of ice. "I will be a part of this society."

Amir's expression shifted—not shock, not anger, but something more dangerous. Something unreadable.

I inhaled sharply, letting the rage crystallize into something lethal, something deadly.

"I will make a poison powerful enough to destroy men like you, my father, and Lord Winston."

The words fell between us like a guillotine's blade.

A declaration of war.

A vow of vengeance.

And yet—Amir didn't flinch.

Instead, he shifted, moving closer, his heat brushing against my side like a whisper of danger. His voice was low, husky, intimate when he spoke—the kind of sound that sent tremors through my body for all the wrong reasons.

"You should indeed kill me, my love," he murmured.

My love.

The words coiled around my heart like a snake.

"Because I am darkness. A ruthless killer."

The sentence struck like a thunderclap, shattering through my mind.

A memory. A voice. The Black Wraith.

He had said those exact words to me.

I spun around, the realization scorching through my veins like wildfire.

"You—your voice…" The accusation clawed at my throat. "You're the masked man. The Black Wraith."

Amir stilled. Then—he laughed.

His laughter was a sinister caress, curling through the air, settling over me like a shadow.

"Oh, darling," he hissed, his voice dripping with venom. "You think I'm the Black Wraith?"

The air between us was charged with something dangerous.

His dark gaze swept over me, lingering, calculating, devouring.

"I detest that creature with every fiber of my existence."

He stepped closer. Too close.

"I would never choose to be him," he continued his voice a blade disguised as velvet. "Especially considering your father and I are hunting him. Unless of course… you happen to know where he is?"

His fingers traced the blood vessel at my throat.

I shivered.

The pressure was light, teasing—a silent warning.

His gaze was heavy-lidded, dark, his lips curving into something that wasn't quite a smile.

"Or maybe…" He leaned in, his breath warm against my skin. "Maybe you've been in contact with him?"

His fingertip skimmed along my cheek, an agonizingly slow touch.

"Tell me, Elizabeth," he murmured, his voice a phantom against my ear. "Are you the one responsible for creating the poison that claimed countless lives in France?"

My breath hitched.

My eyelids fluttered shut.

The touch, the voice, the danger—it overwhelmed me.

"No."

The word barely escaped, lost in the shadow of his question.

But he wasn't done.

His lips hovered near mine, the space between us shrinking to a fraction—a breath, a heartbeat, a whisper of inevitability.

"You came to me begging for help, Elizabeth, and now, you stand before me, declaring your allegiance to your father's society and planning to annihilate us all."

His fingers curled at my jaw, tilting my face just enough to force me to meet his gaze.

"Are you truly working with the Black Wraith? Are you plotting our downfall?"

His voice was a velvet snare, each syllable laced with something dark, seductive, and lethal.

A dare.

A moment that could change everything.

But I did not waver.

I lifted my chin, locking my gaze onto Amir's, meeting the storm within his eyes with steely determination.

"I have never met the Black Wraith, Lord Hassan." My voice was steady, my words intent. "Nor do I have any intention of joining forces with him."

Amir studied me, his gaze narrowing, searching for weakness, lies, something I refused to give him.

The silence between us stretched, taut as a bowstring, humming with unspoken words.

Then—a flicker of something unreadable passed over his features. Dismissal. Amusement. Disdain.

With a casual glance at the brutal spectacle unfolding before us, he exhaled, his next words delivered with chilling indifference.

"Leave such matters to the men."

And then—he turned.

Without hesitation, without a second glance, he strode from the chamber, his silhouette swallowed by the shadows.

Leaving me behind.

Leaving me with the echo of his words, his arrogance branding my skin.

My breath trembled, but I did not break.

I would not break.

I stood there, surrounded by the stench of blood, by the sounds of suffering, and felt something hardening inside me.

Steel in my chest. Fire in my veins.

My lips parted, my voice a whisper of vengeance in the darkness.

"I will try with all my power to kill Lord Winston. This society. My father. And…"

The final name burned on my tongue, too bitter to swallow.

My voice broke.

I could not say it.

Amir.

Because even now—as I swore to end them all—his touch still lingered on my skin.

And I hated that I wasn't sure whether I wanted to kill him…

Or save him.

CHAPTER 12
AMIR

The harpsichord dominated my music room, its grand, wing-shaped body polished to a deep golden hue under the glow of candlelight. The legs, carved with exquisite detail, bore gilded accents that swirled along them like creeping vines, as if alive with some unseen magic.

My fingers trailed over the delicate floral patterns adorning its case, marveling at the artistry. When I lifted the lid, my breath caught.

Beneath it lay a pastoral scene, painted with such detail that I could almost hear the wind rustling through the rolling hills and whispering trees. Though faded with time, the colors still carried the vibrancy of an imagined world—a place untouched by this one's cruelty.

I sat upon the gilded bench, my hands hovering over the keys. Ivory was cold, smooth, and flawless beneath my fingertips. Gold leaf inlays shimmered faintly in the dim light, each an intricate masterpiece in its own right.

I played.

The first note unfurled into the air, silken, slow, a serpent uncoiling, poised to strike.

The only melody I knew seemed simple—a lullaby of deception, a masquerade of elegance. But beneath its charm lay something far more dangerous. Its magic thrummed through the air, sinking into the bones of those who heard it, ensnaring their senses, lulling them into surrender.

And when they succumbed—when the spell took hold, weaving euphoria through their veins—that was the moment I would take their life.

That was the moment I would feast upon their soul.

My fingers danced over the keys, each note wrapping the space around me in an intoxicating, suffocating pull. But my thoughts drifted, tangled in something else. Someone else.

Elizabeth.

Her voice echoed in my mind, the blade of her defiance slicing clean through the hypnotic spell of my music. It was her declaration—her vow to become the master chemist of her father's wretched society.

Such ambition.

Such ignorance.

She had no idea what path she had chosen, the depth of the abyss she was stepping into.

And worse—she did not understand the flower she now possessed.

The Noctyss.

The very bloom whose poison she had crafted with her own delicate hands.

She had no idea what it could truly do.

The harpsichord's melody faltered, the once-enchanting notes now discordant as my mind spiraled deeper into the dangers she did not yet comprehend.

"I need to know more," I muttered, the sound of my voice fracturing the spell that had lingered in the air.

The music was no longer a refuge but a distraction.

I stilled my fingers against the keys, the last note hanging like a specter in the silence, an unfinished whisper lost in the dimly lit room.

Where had she found the flower?

The question gnawed at me. There were layers to this game —pieces shifting in the shadows, invisible hands orchestrating a far more dangerous symphony.

If I intended to protect her—from her father, from Salvatore, from the very horrors she toyed with so naively—I needed to find that bloom before they did.

I leaned back, exhaling through clenched teeth as memories resurfaced.

Lord Alexander's torture chambers.

The screams echoing off cold stone. The stench of iron and despair, of bodies broken beyond repair.

Timebornes and Timebounds shackled, their gifts wasted on agony.

My skin crawled with revulsion. I had seen horrors before, had committed them in the name of power, in the name of war— but this was different.

It wasn't the violence that unsettled me. It was Elizabeth.

Her place amidst that darkness, her peril, her recklessness as she wove herself into a world that would swallow her whole.

"Be cautious, Amir," I whispered to myself, a warning for no one but the man I had long ceased to recognize. "You cannot betray who you are. Not now. Not when so many lives hang in the balance."

The stakes had risen.

Elizabeth's choices could be her downfall. Or worse—mine.

If she discovered my true nature and learned the full extent of my past and the complexity of my sins, there would be no going back.

And yet, she had done something far more dangerous than uncovering my secrets.

She had unknowingly mastered the Noctyss poison.

That flower was a curse, a weapon unlike any other.

And if Salvatore or Mathias learned of it, their wrath would be swift, merciless.

They would stop at nothing to kill Elizabeth.

And possess that flower.

My duty settled upon me, a burden I bore as shield and sword.

"Lazarus must know of this," I vowed.

The poison needed to be secured—soon. But how? When

every shadow could harbor an enemy, and every whisper could be a death sentence?

A knock jarred me from the storm of my thoughts.

I rose, spine rigid, every nerve sweltering with the promise of violence.

"Yes? What is it?" My voice carried the authority I wielded, yet a thread of urgency was coiled tight beneath it.

"Sir, Lord Alexander has requested a meeting."

The servant's voice was polite but insistent, filtering through the heavy wooden door like an omen.

A pause. Then—

"When?"

I rose from the bench, the image of that vile chamber, of shackles and screams, still clawing at my thoughts.

"At once, sir."

There is no room for argument. No room for hesitation.

I exhaled slowly, already running through the implications of this summons.

What game was Alexander playing now?

I swept my cloak over my shoulders, the dark fabric settling around me like armor against whatever twisted machinations awaited me.

I did not wait for further instructions. I stepped toward the door—ready.

The hooves of my steed echoed like distant thunder, striking the earth with rhythmic finality as I approached Lord Alexander's estate.

A house of power.

A house of monsters.

I dismounted with a fluid grace that belied the storm churning within my chest, handing the reins to a groomsman who barely met my eyes before scurrying away with my horse.

Cowards. They all were.

Each step I took onto the fine gravel path felt like an echo in the cavern of my thoughts—footfalls against the promise of treachery.

The door loomed before me, aged wood worn by time yet immovable, like the man who ruled behind it.

I raised my hand. Knocked once. Twice.

The sound rang solid through the silence.

The door swung open immediately.

They had been expecting me.

Without hesitation, I was ushered inside, into the dim corridors where the air felt crowded with the ghosts of hidden horrors.

The servant led me through halls I knew well—opulent, draped in finery meant to dazzle, to deceive.

But I knew better.

Every lavish tapestry concealed something.

A scream once stifled.

A body once broken.

A secret waiting to be unburied.

As I walked deeper into the lair of Lord Alexander, I prepared myself for the monster I was about to face.

The door to his study swung open, revealing the inner sanctum where power and depravity coiled together in a macabre embrace.

The hidden passageway to his dungeon loomed in the corner —a silent specter watching over the room, a reminder of its concealed horrors.

Elizabeth had walked down those steps.

Alone.

Armed only with her defiance and a name that no longer protected her.

My jaw tightened at the memory. She should not have seen what lay below.

She should not have been forced to carry that burden.

I wanted her safe—free from her father's dark ambitions. And yet, she moved closer to the flame, willingly stepping into the abyss.

And the abyss would swallow her whole.

Unless I stopped it.

The cloying scent of cigar smoke curled through the air, its stench wrapping around me like rot.

I didn't need to turn to know the source.

Lord Winston.

He fouled the very air, his bloated form spilling over the chair, lips slack around his cigar as if his body had long since given up the effort of holding itself together.

My stomach churned, repulsed by his stench, excess, and decay.

And yet—this was Elizabeth's world.

This was the lineage she was bound to.

And I would destroy it all before I let it consume her.

I forced my expression into careful neutrality as I turned to Lord Alexander.

"Lord Alexander."

My voice was cold steel wrapped in civility despite the bile rising in my throat.

His eyes met mine—a predator assessing another.

"Lord Hassan," he replied, his tone laced with unease.

Good.

Let him fear me.

He leaned back in his chair, fingers steepled, his gaze calculating. "Rumors reach my ears," he murmured, voice deceptively smooth. "Whispers of the Black Wraith's intentions to raze my dominion."

Of course, he was afraid.

The Black Wraith was not a ghost to him. He was a nightmare.

And nightmares were relentless.

I allowed a slow breath, ensuring my next words landed precisely where I intended.

"Which is exactly why the grand masquerade is crucial."

Lord Alexander's fingers twitched, but I did not give him time to interrupt.

"It will serve as the perfect lure."

I let the idea settle, let him feel the edges of its possibility, its inevitability.

"A gathering of such magnitude will draw him out. He cannot resist."

A pause.

And then, with methodical finality, I added—

"After all, he has his spies."

I met Lord Alexander's gaze, unflinching.

"Just as we have ours."

The words hung in the air, heavy and waiting.

I stood firm, my resolve steeling me against the filth of both this room and these men. Every instinct screamed to torch it all, to unsheathe a dagger and carve their monstrous arrogance from their bloated bodies.

But I did not.

Not yet.

This was a dance, a careful, intricate performance where missteps meant ruin—not just for me, but for Elizabeth.

I had to play my part.

The wet, muffled thud of Lord Winston's cigar hitting the ashtray made my stomach coil. His trembling hands relinquished the sullied roll of tobacco, his saliva gleaming on its end like a mother's nipple, wet from the suckling of a greedy babe.

Revulsion licked at my throat.

"Are you sure this will work?" Winston's ponderous voice dragged through the room like something dead being pulled through the streets. "He's stopped every trap we've set for him."

Doubt.

His skepticism was a burden I had neither time nor patience for.

I did not hesitate. "Certainty is a luxury we cannot afford," I said.

I had to project confidence and sell the lie as truth.

"But mark my words, he won't pass this by. He will be there."

I let the certainty settle, let it dig into their doubt like a parasite.

"He wants to stay abreast of the Harbingers of Temporal Terror."

At the mention of their society's name, I saw the faintest twitch in Lord Winston's expression—pride, greed, anticipation.

I held his gaze—unyielding.

Lord Alexander, ever the grand puppeteer of his sick theater, grinned.

A grin that could curdle blood.

"And they shall all be witnesses," he declared, his voice ripe with amusement as he turned toward Winston.

My stomach twisted.

Something was coming.

Something worse.

"When I announce your betrothal and elevate you as my successor, Phineas."

Silence.

A slow, suffocating silence.

Then—Lord Winston's lips stretched into a parody of joy.

"I can hardly wait," he wheezed, the air souring around him, packed with his perverse satisfaction.

The edges of my vision blurred. Elizabeth.

This was their game.

Their rotting plan.

"To display my beautiful bride and finally capture the Black Wraith."

His clouded, milky eyes gleamed with disgusting glee.

"We'll torture him before the society—no, before all the societies!"

Lord Winston's breath rattled, his ravenous anticipation bleeding out. "It shall be a spectacle to remember!"

I did not flinch.

I remained still.

A statue shaped from flesh and bone.

They spoke of me. Planned my demise. They wove their intricate web of death without realizing their target sat right before them.

"Elizabeth will prepare a powerful poison…"

Her father's voice slithered through the room, each syllable drenched in smug certainty.

"Something from her mother's teachings. We'll use it on him once he's captured. Let it rot him slowly—from the inside out."

Rebellion surged through me, icy and honed, like steel drawn in silence.

"A poison fit to kill a god."

Alexander's lips curled in malice.

"The Black Wraith will beg for death long before it comes—and we'll be there to witness every second."

A pause.

Then, the final nail in their wretched plan.

"I have also invited Mathias Alistair to witness this event."

Mathias.

The name hung in the air like a curse.

A slow, bone-deep shiver crept down my spine.

The room felt suddenly smaller.

Mathias' arrival would complicate matters significantly—a new variable in a game where I was already balancing on a knife's edge.

I could not afford his attendance.

I could not afford this trap tightening around me.

But before I could fully absorb the gravity of this revelation—

The door creaked open.

A servant entered, head bowed, shoulders tight with unease.

"Lord Alexander, I have news."

The quiet tremor in his voice slithered through the chamber, setting every nerve on edge.

Lord Alexander's gaze snapped toward the messenger, his lips peeling back in a snarl.

"What is it?"

A beat.

Then—

"We have received word that all your hideouts have been destroyed."

The words dropped like stones into a still lake.

Then—

Lord Alexander's face contorted, the slow shift from scorn to unbridled fury morphing him into something truly monstrous.

His fist slammed onto the desk, quills and parchments scattering like fallen soldiers.

The room rattled with the force of his fury.

A guttural roar tore from his throat, shaking the walls of his decaying empire.

Beside him, Lord Winston lurched to his feet, his bloated body swaying precariously, his jowls quivering as if the foundations of his world had been uprooted.

His voice rose in blind panic, full of rage and disbelief.

"How!" he bellowed, his spittle flying into the stagnant air. "How did this happen?"

The servant, already trembling beneath their scrutiny, stammered through his panic, his forehead slick with sweat.

"They were caught off guard, my lord," he stuttered. "The attackers knew precisely where to strike... The men who stood watch—perished. Every last one of them. There was no one left alive."

The room thickened with silence.

Death had come for them, swift and absolute.

A cruel satisfaction twisted deep in my gut.

My men had done their work.

Ruthless. Precise. Efficient.

Lord Alexander's breathing came heavy, his nostrils flaring like a beast poised to charge.

Then, he faced me, his eyes frigid and unflinching, slicing through the tension like steel.

"Lord Hassan, I must leave," he muttered, his tone all edges and finality.

He turned, boots striking the stone.

"Phineas. With me."

His cloak billowed behind him, his movements driven by fury and desperation, the wretched bulk of Lord Winston tottering in his wake.

And just like that—

They were gone.

Alone at last, I allowed myself a moment of grim pleasure.

Their empire was crumbling—brick by venom-soaked brick.

And I had laid the foundation for its ruin.

But I had no time to relish their downfall.

Now, I needed to slip away.

I must secure the Noctyss flower from Elizabeth's alchemy cottage—before she unknowingly placed a dagger at her throat.

Before her poison could find its way into mine.

A brush with death by her hand was a fate I intended to avoid at all costs.

Without a backward glance, I strode from the room, my boots soundless against the plush carpet. The hunt had begun.

Each step carried me closer to the cottage.

Closer to the flower.

Closer to her.

The night air was crisp, coiling around me like an omen. Above, the stars watched, indifferent to the sins unfolding beneath them.

The cottage stood ahead, bathed in pale moonlight, its edges softened by shadows. The damp earth swallowed the sound of my approach, my movements as silent as the secrets that lingered in the air.

Through the window, I saw her.

Elizabeth.

She moved with a fluid grace, her hands gliding over vials and beakers with effortless meticulousness.

A siren among potions.

And for a fleeting moment, I was merely a man ensnared by her beauty.

But time was an unyielding master.

And I was no fool.

Without hesitation, I burst through the door.

The impact sent a jolt of surprise through her slender frame. A gasp escaped her lips, and a vial slipped from her fingers, shattering against the wood floor in a cascade of glittering fragments.

She whipped around, wide-eyed, her chest rising and falling in quick succession.

"Oh, Lord Hassan, you frightened me."

Her voice trembled, betraying the force of her surprise.

"How did you find this place?"

I stepped forward, with quiet dominance.

"Your father told me," I said smoothly, my gaze flicking over the room, searching—hunting.

Where was it?

The Noctyss.

I let my eyes linger on her, feigning curiosity as my hands grazed over the cluttered wooden worktables.

"So, I see you're still going to join the society," I mused, tilting my head slightly as if amused by her reckless ambition. "Still determined to become an alchemist."

Her chin lifted in a silent challenge—defiance woven into elegance.

But I was already moving, prowling through the space like a hunter in a gilded cage. The room was a maze of glass and shadow, the air filled with the scent of herbs and something darker—something more potent.

And then—

There it was.

The Noctyss.

Sealed in a glass container, resting among an array of innocuous flora. Untouched from the last time I'd seen it. Unassuming. Deadly.

I lifted the Noctyss flower into the candlelight, slowly turning the sealed glass container in my hand.

The inky petals gleamed, their edges tinged with an unnatural iridescence, shimmering like something pulled from the depths of an abyss.

"My, my," I murmured, feigning ignorance.

Elizabeth moved with the same fluid elegance as the melodies I played upon my harpsichord.

Deadly. Controlled. It was a calculated step in our unspoken game.

She closed the distance swiftly, her gaze locked onto the prize in my hand.

"Lord Hassan, may I please have the flower?" Her voice was smooth, but there was an undercurrent of urgency she could not quite conceal. "It is rare and delicate, and I want to ensure its safety."

I tilted my head, watching her, studying her.

"It seems we have returned to formalities, Lady Alexander," I mused. "If I remember correctly, we once shared a passionate kiss, and you called me by my first name."

Her composure faltered, if only for a moment.

Then—she stiffened.

"That was a mistake, Lord Hassan."

A tremor laced her voice, though she fought to mask it.

"I don't know what came over me that day, but I assure you it won't happen again. Now, please, may I have the flower back?"

Lies.

Her words were deliberate, yet her demeanor betrayed her.

Her swift, instinctive movements.

The way her fingers flexed—not just with desperation, but something deeper.

Something she refused to acknowledge.

Our stolen kiss meant more to her than she dared admit.

I let the moment drag on, my gaze lingering on her, my silence speaking louder than words.

Then—a slow, knowing smirk.

"Apologies, my lady," I murmured, my tone polite yet laced with mock amusement.

But my true interest had shifted.

As my eyes roamed the cluttered wooden table, they landed on something more intriguing.

A book.

The Sacred Alchemy of Solaris: Secrets of the Celestial Forge.

The title alone sent a ripple of intrigue through me. It was time for another peek.

Without hesitation, I hurriedly plucked it from the table, flipping through its pages.

Elizabeth reacted instantly.

She stepped around, reaching for it, but I shifted my grip, holding it just out of her reach, amusement curling at the corners of my lips.

"Lord Hassan, return the book to me," she demanded, her voice firmer now—a thread of real frustration bleeding through her carefully composed mask.

I ran my fingers along the worn edges of the cover, my curiosity piqued.

"Hmm, it seems quite intriguing to me," I mused. "I've never seen one like it before," I lied.

Elizabeth's breath hitched—not from frustration, but something more.

A flicker of fear.

She knew this book was no ordinary text.

It was dangerous. Secretive. Forbidden.

Her fingers clenched.

Then—she abandoned formality entirely.

"Please, Amir," she whispered, urgency crackling between us. "Give me back my book. It belongs to our society. It's not meant for you."

A slow smirk curled at my lips.

"Hmm. You called me Amir. How forward of you."

I let my name settle between us, watching as realization flickered in her eyes.

She was slipping.

She was unraveling.

And she knew it.

I flashed her a mischievous grin. "I must insist on being addressed by my first name from now on."

Her lips pressed into a firm line, determination burning behind her gaze.

"Give it to me, Amir. Its secrets are dangerous."

Dangerous?

She didn't know the half of it.

But I couldn't resist the game.

"Oh, love. Now you care about me and how deadly this book is?" My voice dipped, laced with amusement. "Yesterday, you wanted to murder me. What are you going to do if I don't return it? Kill me?"

The space between us shrank, charged with unspoken desire.

With every lunge she made to retrieve the book, our dance grew more perilous.

My power surged.

Shadows coiled. Darkness obeyed.

I vanished in the blink of an eye—only to reappear across the room.

Elizabeth stumbled, reaching out—but I was already gone.

A cloud of dark mist curled around my form, shifting through the dimly lit space as I moved effortlessly between the shadows.

Each time she reached for me, I was elsewhere.

Each time she grew close, I disappeared.

Elizabeth's brow furrowed, her breath shallow as she spun to find me again.

"How are you doing that?" she asked, her voice tinged with awe and disbelief.

I gave her a slow smile.

Then—I vanished again.

She spun around, breath catching, frustration simmering beneath her skin. Her pulse thundered.

When I reappeared, her voice trembled—cracked with weariness.

"Amir… please. Give me back my book."

Her hands reached for me.

"I beg of you."

The desperation in her eyes and the unguarded urgency in her voice sent a flicker of satisfaction through me.

Our little game reached its crescendo.

She lunged again—this time, with more force.

Her body against mine, heat searing through the fabric between us, her breath tangled with mine.

The contact was a spark to dry kindling.

A fire ignited in my veins, dark and unrelenting.

Yet—just as quickly as she touched me, I was gone.

The shadows obeyed, slipping me away from her grasp as I reappeared across the room, the book still in hand.

"Amir, please stop!"

Her voice broke, frustration spilling into exhaustion.

"It's been a long and tiring day."

The pleading echoed in my ears, laced with something deeper than weariness—a frayed edge to her resolve.

But still, I could not escape the magnetic pull between us.

We collided in a tangle of limbs and unspoken desires, the fight dissolving into something far more dangerous.

Then—we fell.

The world tilted beneath us, and suddenly, she was atop me, her breath shallow, her luscious form against mine.

A jolt shot through me—raw, electric, darkly intoxicating.

Too close. Too warm. Too much.

The fire between us crackled in the air, unresolved, scorching, waiting to be consumed.

"Alright," I relented, my breath uneven, the proximity searing through my senses like an open flame.

Slowly, I surrendered the book, my fingers lingering a fraction too long against hers.

A hesitation.

A silent confession in touch alone.

I helped her up, though my hands were reluctant to let go.

She straightened, adjusting herself, but my gaze had already fallen elsewhere.

The Noctyss flower.

An opportunity. A risk. A prize.

With a sleight of hand honed by years of deception, I plucked the delicate, deadly bloom and slipped it into the folds of my cloak.

She wouldn't notice.

Not yet.

"I won't bother you anymore, love," I murmured, stepping

back toward the door, my voice smooth, easy—a lie dressed as reassurance.

Each step was heavy with untruths.

This was not our last encounter.

It could never be.

Our fates were bound too tightly, our desires too dangerously entwined.

With the poison secured, I stepped into the night, leaving behind a storm of emotions that raged as fiercely as any tempest.

But the truth was torturous.

I couldn't get Elizabeth Alexander out of my mind.

CHAPTER 13

ELIZABETH

The flickering candlelight stretched my shadow across the wooden floorboards, a distorted mockery of the solitude.

I sat hunched over the weathered alchemy book, my mind in turmoil, my thoughts entangled in Amir.

His piercing gaze haunted me.

A riddle wrapped in an enigma, unreadable and infuriating.

And yet—something about him stirred the embers within my chest.

A dangerous, smoldering curiosity.

The more I tried to untangle my feelings, the tighter their grip became.

At night, a different story emerged.

The dreams came.

Vivid. Unsettling.

The Black Wraith's mask danced through the darkness, its hollow eyes staring into my soul—an ominous portent.

During the day, my obsession with Amir only grew.

I would glance up from my work, half-expecting to find his dark, unreadable gaze watching me from the shadows.

But the cottage remained empty. Oppressively so.

Lord Hassan's absence from my father's house stretched into a full week, leaving a palpable void.

His attendance had once filled the manor with silent strength, an aura of control even in stillness.

Now, his absence felt like a missing heartbeat in a body that refused to die.

And I was left alone in my secluded cottage, pouring my restless thoughts into my craft.

The Noctyss poison.

If perfected, the mixture would glow with swirling hues of silver and gold, a beautiful, mesmerizing lethality.

But I had failed.

No luminous shimmer graced the bubbling liquid in the flask.

Only dullness. Disobedience. Frustration.

I sighed, my gaze falling to my hands, clad in leather gloves soaked in essential oils.

It was a necessary precaution when dealing with something that could instantly turn against its maker.

In my palm, I held the Noctyss flower—its petals delicate, unassuming, deceptively harmless.

A bloom so rare and demanding that taking more than one would leave the plant drooping listlessly.

Not dead.

But robbed of vitality.

Weak. Exhausted. Empty.

It would take months before it could bloom again.

I traced the fragile petal with a gloved fingertip, a flicker of understanding whispering.

The Noctyss was like me.

Depleted. Hollowed out.

Waiting.

But unlike the flower, I refused to wither.

Alchemy was a dance—a delicate, dangerous balance of taking and giving, extracting and nurturing. One misstep, one miscalculation, and creation became destruction.

As I sat there, my isolation pushing in, I couldn't escape the growing question—

Was it truly the poison I was trying to perfect—

Or was I seeking an antidote to the emptiness Amir had left behind?

The mortar lay abandoned on the worn table as I reached for another blossom.

The cottage held its breath with me.

Weeks had passed since I last harvested from the Noctyss plant.

Enough time, I had calculated, for it to regain its strength.

And yet—

Where a vibrant bloom should have stood, there was nothing.

A hollow space.

My breath hitched.

A ragged gasp escaped me, my heart slamming against my ribs as an awful, bone-chilling realization set in.

The flower had vanished.

I staggered back, my mind racing.

No one came here.

The ghost of my mother's touch lingered too heavily for my father to dare step inside.

And Mary—sweet Mary—would never cross the threshold without cause.

That left only two possibilities.

Each one was more terrifying than the other.

Amir.

Or the Black Wraith.

Had it been stolen by the liar who kissed me?

Or the phantom who haunted my dreams?

The answer might be the same.

A sudden knock at the glass jarred me from my spiraling thoughts.

"My lady, your father is asking for you to join him for lunch," Mary's muffled but clear voice said.

I whipped around, pulse still erratic, and flung the window open, desperate for a breath of air untouched by alchemical fumes—by the stifling scent of fear.

Mary stood below, her wide eyes drinking in my disheveled state.

I gripped the windowsill, forcing my voice into steadiness.

"Mary," I began, choosing my words with care, "have you ever been in this cottage by yourself?"

Her reaction was instant.

She recoiled as if struck, her hand flying to her chest.

"No, my lady. I would never."

The horror in her tone was unmistakable.

And I believed her.

Mary's loyalty was as unwavering as the northern star.

Which meant Amir had taken it during one of his little shadow-vanishing tricks.

"Of course," I murmured, more to myself than to her, the mystery of the missing flower deepening like a shadow at dusk. With a nod of acknowledgment, I signaled the end of our brief encounter and watched as she disappeared down the cobblestone path, leaving me alone with my thoughts and the whispering specters of suspicion.

Stripping off my gloves, I scrubbed my hands clean, ensuring every trace of Noctyss poison was gone. The water ran red before turning clear. Only then did I allow my breath to steady. I brushed through my golden hair, the waves cascading down my back, then straightened the simple gown clinging to my frame. It was time to face him—my father—and the sea of unspoken words that churned between us.

"Elizabeth," he greeted me as I entered the dining hall, his baritone rumble echoing off the stone walls. "How is the poison coming along?"

"Excellent, Father," I replied, the lie slipping easily from my lips. "You'll be most pleased."

The morning's frustration melted beneath the calm of deception. Lowering my gaze, I let my lashes cast shadows upon my cheeks—a subtle veil between us. "Father, it's been a while since Lord Hassan joined us. I hope he is well?"

Something—hesitation, perhaps—cracked his usual composed facade. "He's been unwell," he admitted. "Recovering. Perhaps it's the London air."

The realization hit—cold and cutting.

"Perhaps," I allowed, my voice laced with feigned concern. "Or maybe he inhaled something from my cottage. You shouldn't have sent him there." I exhaled, letting worry crease my brow. "He could have had an allergic reaction to one of the plants."

My father frowned, his brows knitting together like gathering storm clouds. "I never sent Lord Hassan to your cottage."

The truth struck with brutal force—Amir had been inside my haven, weaving lies. He had claimed my father had sent him. But how else could he have found my alchemist's cottage? It was impossible to locate unless one had already been there.

Further proof Amir was the Black Wraith. The way he moved through shadows—like they obeyed him—wasn't just skill. It was mastery.

The revelation coiled around me like a tightening noose. I barely touched my meal, my appetite as absent as the truth in our conversation. When the meal ended, my father excused himself, leaving me with untouched food and unanswered questions.

I found Mary in the observatory; her hands stained green from tending to the thriving plants within its glass walls.

"Mary, we need to go to Lord Hassan's house," I urgently said. "He took something from me, and I have to get it back before it's too late."

Her brow furrowed, concern darkening her features. "How do you plan to do that?"

"We go in secret," I whispered, the words cold with certainty.

Mary hesitated, her voice barely above a breath. "But how will we get in?"

"You'll invite yourself in as a guest. I'll slip inside while no one's watching," I replied with authority, my pulse thrumming against my ribs.

Her lips parted in protest. "That's dangerous." Fear warred with loyalty in her expression.

"I can't just knock on his door and ask for entry," I snapped, frustration edging my voice. "This has to be done quietly. If he finds out, everything will be ruined."

Mary let out a shaky breath, doubt flickering in her eyes. "And if we're caught?"

I swallowed hard, my certainty hardening like tempered steel. "We won't be." The words left my lips with more conviction than I felt. My tone softened, but the urgency remained. "Please, Mary. Just trust me. Get me in, handle your business, and then leave. I'll take care of the rest."

Mary's gaze searched mine, looking for the girl she once knew. She wouldn't find her. That girl was replaced by someone desperate, willing to play with fire.

With a slow nod, she sealed our course, and together, we stepped into the unknown—allies in a game where the pieces never stayed still.

As we neared Amir's estate, the sun dipped below the horizon, draping the world in the cool embrace of twilight. It was five o'clock. The city pulsed with its affairs, oblivious to mine.

I pulled my hood lower, letting the heavy fabric cast deep shadows over my face as Mary and I approached the grand wrought-iron gates. My heartbeat thundered in my ears, but my steps remained steady. Mary clutched the woven basket in her arms, playing the part of a dutiful servant delivering a token from Lord Alexander with grace.

The gatekeeper barely spared us a glance. The guise was too ordinary, too unremarkable, to warrant suspicion.

The first hurdle was behind us.

I met Mary's gaze, a silent exchange of understanding.

Leaning in close, my voice barely more than a breath, I murmured, "Straight to the kitchen. Keep them busy. I need at least twenty minutes."

Mary gave me a small nod, her lips a tight line. As we slipped through the servants' entrance, a wave of warmth enveloped us, bursting with the scent of baking bread and simmering spices. The kitchen bustled with movement, but Mary stepped forward with ease, her voice carrying just enough authority to command attention.

I lingered in the shadows of the still room adjacent to the kitchen, where the air carried the faint, familiar smell of herbs and sweet preserves. The space was cluttered, but not in a way that spoke of neglect—it was the organized chaos of purpose. Shelves lined the walls, filled with jars of jams, jellies, and dried herbs, their colors dimmed by the oil lamps that spilled soft light from the kitchen.

A large wooden table dominated the center, its surface strewn with mortar and pestles, glass bottles, and muslin cloths for straining. It reminded me of my alchemy cottage—where science and secrets intertwined. In one corner, copper pots bubbled gently over a low flame, steeping some remedy or tonic, their fragrances twining together—lavender, rosemary, and the faintest trace of currant preserves left to cool.

This wasn't a room of grandeur but of quiet craftsmanship— a retreat from the kitchen clatter, where skill and patience reigned over haste.

I inched closer to the doorway, straining to hear.

"This is a gift from Lord Alexander," Mary said sweetly, lifting the basket with a graceful tilt. "For the master of the house."

The cook, her hands dusted with flour, turned to her with interest. Her face brightened at the mention of Lord Alexander. "Oh, what a fine gift! Thank you, dear. I'll see that Lord Hassan receives it."

Mary hesitated for half a breath before soldiering on. "Is he here? Lord Alexander asked that I present the gift to him personally."

From my position in the shadows, I caught the briefest flicker of her glance—quick, subtle, intentional.

The cook waved Mary deeper into the kitchen, and I watched as she seamlessly fell into conversation. Within moments, the staff was fully engaged—discussing pastries, Lord Alexander's good fortune, anything but me. Their focus was elsewhere.

That was my cue.

Keeping my head low, I slipped past the kitchen unnoticed, my steps light against the stone floor. My pulse thrummed in my ears, a rhythm of urgency. Amir had taken something from me that could unleash immeasurable damage in his hands. I couldn't let that happen.

When I stepped beyond the kitchen's warmth, the silence became stifling. The vastness of the house swallowed me whole; it was quite unnatural, as though the walls themselves were holding their breath. The distant clatter of pots only underscored how hollow the space was.

Where were the footmen, the butlers, and the endless parade of attendants expected in a house of this stature? The kitchen had been running with a skeleton crew, and the rest of the estate felt… abandoned.

Did Amir truly live in this barren expanse?

My fingers grazed the polished wooden banister as I ascended the stairs, each step slow and stealthy. The air thickened as I climbed, heavy with dust and absence.

The upper halls mirrored the desolation below—not a single candle flickered, nor a voice carried through the air. Shadows clung to the walls, stretching long and eerie in the dim evening light.

I moved swiftly, methodically. The flower had to be here.

But dread twisted in my gut as I searched, opening drawers and scanning shelves. It was nowhere.

Desperation gnawed at me like a starved creature.

The emptiness chased me from room to room, each search yielding nothing but my mounting dread.

Until I reached the dungeon.

My breath hitched.

Unpleasant memories crashed into me.

Chains. Stone. The phantom bite of cold iron against my wrists.

I had been here before.

I knew this place.

A slow, dreadful realization settled in my chest like a poisonous bloom.

I had been here with him.

The Black Wraith had brought me here.

Amir.

The world tilted, my pulse hammering with a terrible certainty.

Amir was him and I could no longer deny it.

The man who claimed to hunt the Black Wraith was the Black Wraith.

Relief and terror warred inside me.

He was not my father's pawn.

But he was still a liar.

And then—my breath stilled.

Something glinted in the shadows.

Half-hidden beneath a wooden chest, nearly swallowed by darkness, something awaited me.

I dropped to my knees, my fingers trembling as I shoved the chest aside.

And there—

The unmistakable, haunting mask of the Black Wraith.

I snatched it up, gripping the leather edges, turning it in my hands, my heartbeat roaring in my ears.

The mask was shaped like a skull, but it didn't feel like something dead. It felt… possessed. Its surface was bone-white, not smooth but cracked—veins of shadow splitting across the forehead and cheeks like old wounds that never healed. I couldn't tell if it had been damaged or if it had always been this broken.

The eye sockets were the worst. Deep, black voids that swallowed the light, wide enough to lose someone in. Staring into them felt like falling. As if something inside was still breathing.

Its grin stretched across the jaw, frozen in place. Not a smile. A snarl. The teeth were jagged, uneven—too detailed, too human. Like whoever made it had studied pain and carved it into every curve.

There was nothing ornate about it. No markings. No jewels.

No color. Just white, black, and silence. And yet it radiated power. Sorrow. Rage.

A slow chill seeped into my bones.

This was it.

The proof.

No more denials. No more guessing.

Amir Hassan was the Black Wraith.

And he had been playing me all along.

In the cold air of the dungeon, where shadows twisted like specters of the past, I found a grim solace. The truth would come to light. And I would be the one to set it free.

Still frustration boiled beneath my skin—I hadn't found the flower.

I made my way out, avoiding the only rooms still bustling with life—the kitchen and servants' quarters. But something pulled at me, a force whispering for me to turn back.

A decision slithered its way into my mind.

I retraced my steps, moving with care.

Up the staircase I went, each step a silent plea for answers.

Back in the study, I stood before the large mirror.

Once, it had seemed ordinary. Innocuous.

But now—now it whispered of secrets.

Its smooth surface gleamed under the fading daylight, waiting.

Daring me to look deeper.

My gaze snagged on an inscription along the frame—"1 - 7" —a sequence begging for attention. Heart pounding, I pushed each engraved number in turn. A chime rang out with every press, the sound soft yet resonant.

One. Two. Three. Four. Five. Six—

There was a faint click.

Disbelief held me in place as the mirror swung open, revealing a hidden compartment.

And there it was.

The Noctyss flower.

Nestled within, its petals shimmered in eerie silver and black, pulsing with an almost unnatural vibrancy. My hand trembled as I reached for it, its significance sinking deep into my bones.

I closed the mirror with a muted thud, sealing away the secret it had guarded for who knows how long.

Then—

"Elizabeth..."

The voice, dark and razor-edged with fury, sent a shiver down my spine.

Through the reflection, I saw him.

Amir.

His skin was shadowed with anger, his eyes wild—a tempest barely contained.

"What are you doing here?" he demanded, his voice a snarl.

I spun to face him, my grip tightening around the mask I had found earlier. The Black Wraith's mask.

I held it up like a damning accusation. "How did you get this?" My voice was steady despite the fire raging in his gaze. "This mask belongs to the Black Wraith."

A slow, wicked smile curved his lips—dangerous, knowing.

"Did it, now? And what were you doing in France?" he asked, each word dripping with venom.

"And how, pray tell, do you know what the Black Wraith's mask looks like? Have you met him… personally?"

His eyes narrowed to slits, dark pools that saw too much.

I swallowed hard, realizing my mistake. I had given him something—a thread to pull. But I wouldn't let him unravel me.

Ignoring his question, I lifted my other hand, revealing the container that held the Noctyss flower.

"This is mine. You stole this flower from me."

Amir's jaw clenched, his muscles taut with barely restrained emotion.

"The flower, darling, is dangerous. And if you don't leave this place right now, you'll regret it," he growled, the warning hanging between us like a guillotine's blade.

With quiet defiance, I stepped forward, my pulse hammering, and placed the flower on the desk.

"I'm not leaving until I have answers." My voice was hard

now. "You stole my flower. You have the Black Wraith's mask. You knew where my alchemy cottage was, which could only mean one thing—"

I exhaled. "You're the masked man."

Something flickered across Amir's face for a moment—denial or something deeper. But it was gone as swiftly as lightning.

"I tracked down the mask maker responsible for crafting the Black Wraith's mask," he said smoothly. "I forced him to reveal its origins before ending his life."

His voice was even. Unapologetic.

"And yes, I took your flower."

My stomach twisted, but I held his gaze.

"Because in the wrong hands—or the right ones with enough knowledge—it's more than dangerous." His voice dipped lower, a quiet finality in the words. "It's catastrophic."

"Tell me the truth, Amir." My voice didn't waver this time. "How did you find my alchemy cottage?"

His gaze didn't flicker. "Your father told me where it was."

The lie curled between us, too smooth, too convenient.

"And as for the masked man," he continued, stepping closer.

His lips curved into something cold.

"Let me make one thing clear—I am not the Black Wraith."

I searched his face, my breath shallow, waiting for the hint of a lie.

Amir Hassan was an enigma. A fortress with walls too high to scale. He stirred fear and fascination within me, but I held the card now—I knew.

And I knew he was lying.

My voice cut through the silence, edged with accusation, echoing off the cold stone walls of his study. "Stop lying to me, Amir. I know you are the masked man."

His eyes darkened, but I didn't stop. I couldn't.

"My father never told you about my cottage… because you already knew. You were the one who captured me there. You and your men."

My hands trembled, but I held my ground, bracing for the truth that could shatter everything I thought I knew about him.

I sucked in a sharp breath, forcing the words past the knot in my throat.

"I was in your dungeon, Amir. It's the exact same place you took me."

His expression remained unreadable, but something shifted behind his eyes—a storm.

"And the mask I found in your dungeon… it's yours, not the mask maker's. Stop hiding. Tell me the truth."

I took another step toward him, my heartbeat thundering against my ribs. His eyes blazed, dark irises smoldering like embers fanned by an obstinate wind.

Then—

"The truth?"

His voice was low and dangerous, resonating with a slow-burning intensity that sent a chill down my spine.

"You want the truth?"

A step closer.

"The truth is dangerous."

The air between us crackled, heavy with unspoken things.

"Tell me," I pled. "Tell me who you really are."

I stood before him, my emotions a volatile storm, simmering beneath the surface, threatening to spill over. Confusion. Frustration. A tangled mess of feelings I could no longer ignore.

"Why do I feel this way when I'm around you?" The words tumbled out before I could stop them. "Despite your rejection and distance, I cannot stay away from you. This pull between us, dragging me toward you even as you push me away."

My breath hitched, my chest tightening. Tears threatened, but I refused to let them fall.

I just needed him to say something.

Amir's shoulders tensed, his entire body rigid, as if bracing for impact.

"You won't understand what I am." His voice was rough and restrained.

"Make me understand," I pushed, my voice softer now but no less determined. "I care for you, Amir."

Something in him snapped.

A growl rumbled deep within his chest—low, visceral, tormented.

"You don't know what I am." His voice was harsh, breaking at the edges. "You don't know the things I've done, Elizabeth. I am no hero. I am a monster."

"No." My voice didn't waver. "You are not the monster. The real monsters are Lord Winston and my father."

His jaw tightened, his fists clenched at his sides.

"I am darkness, Elizabeth," Amir said, his voice coated with barely restrained emotion. "Stay away, or it will consume you too. I kill to survive. I destroy everything I touch. You… you're light. And you don't belong in my world."

He meant to scare me. To drive me away.

But instead of fear—fire ignited within me.

I stepped closer, bridging the space between us until only inches remained. My heart pounded against my ribs, but I didn't retreat.

"You're wrong," I whispered, my breath mingling with his.

His gaze burned into me, filled with something I couldn't yet name.

"You're not a monster," I declared.

His throat bobbed, his breath shallow.

"You have no idea what I've done," he murmured, voice stripped bare.

His next words were quieter, almost as if he feared saying them aloud.

"Or who I am."

I didn't move, didn't flinch. My pulse roared in my ears. "I don't care. I'm not leaving until I know the truth."

The words spilled from me recklessly, binding me to him in ways I couldn't yet comprehend. "I understand enough. You push me away because you think you're protecting me. But you're not. I'm already in this, Amir. We both are."

His gaze locked onto mine, unwavering, endless.

"You want to see who I really am, Elizabeth?" he murmured as he stepped back, once again creating distance between us.

Then, before my eyes, he changed.

The air thickened, dark wisps curling around him, shadows swallowing the room's warmth. The edges of his form blurred, warping the space around him.

And then—

His flesh began to crack.

Thin fractures spiderwebbed across his face, splitting open like dry, decaying wood. Chunks of skin sloughed off, curling at the edges as they peeled away, revealing raw muscle beneath— wet, glistening, rotting.

I froze, horror rooting me in place.

Gods, his eyes sank into hollow sockets, leaving behind swirling pools of sickly green light, a ghostly, unearthly glow where life should have been.

I wanted to scream, but the sound caught in my throat as his lips peeled back—blackening, rotting—before his teeth crumbled away in jagged, decayed shards.

His body convulsed as if something was draining the life from him in real-time. His frame collapsed inward, his shoulders caving, his form shrinking, shriveling, until he was barely more than a wraith of himself.

His hands—

No longer human.

Elongated. Skeletal. Twisted. The flesh clung tightly over bone, splitting at the knuckles, leaking foul, black ooze that splattered onto the floor in gelatinous, nauseating drops.

Then the stench hit me.

Rot. Mold. Decay.

A putrid wave so strong I gagged, my hand flying to my mouth, my stomach lurching violently.

His hair thinned in patches, falling away in brittle clumps, revealing a blistered, oozing scalp.

He stood before me, no longer a man but something caught between life and death, a walking corpse suspended in an eternal state of rot.

I had never seen anything so horrifying.

Yet—I couldn't move.

I was trapped in that moment, watching as the last shreds of humanity peeled away from him, layer by layer, until only the nightmare remained.

My hands flew to my mouth, stifling the gasp that threatened to escape. But not out of fear.

No—fear had no place here.

Not when my father was the real monster. Not when Lord Winston embodied cruelty in its purest form.

Amir, this man before me… he was not a monster.

His dark form loomed, a specter of every nightmare, yet all I saw was the pain carved into the lines of his being—a soul suffering beneath his darkness, mistaken for the thing it feared becoming.

His shadowed figure trembled, the air overflowing with the manifestation of the curse that clung to him.

"Look at me!" His command shattered the silence, raw and jagged, his voice laced with bitter self-loathing. "This is what I am."

His voice was a rasp, a confession, an executioner's final verdict.

"I destroy everything I touch. I am no better than the monsters you despise."

My heart ached at the torment in his voice. This was not the voice of a monster—this was the voice of a man drowning in suffering.

Slowly, I stepped forward. Closing the distance between us.

Between light and dark.

"No." My voice was soft but resolute. "You're wrong."

His eyes simmered like dying embers. "You should hate me." His tone hardened, daring me—begging me—to turn away.

And yet—I didn't.

Leeches clung to his decaying skin, feasting on the rot. Carrion beetles skittered along his exposed bones, antennae twitching as they burrowed deeper, seeking nourishment from the remains of a man who breathed.

I should have been repulsed. Horrified. Sick with fear.

But revulsion was the furthest thing from what I felt.

"I don't," I whispered.

Slowly, intently, I reached out, my fingertips grazing the contours of his face—the hollow ridges where the flesh had withered, the cool, spectral skin beneath.

"I love you, Amir Hassan."

His breath hitched.

"You are my beautiful monster."

He flinched at my touch as if my acceptance wounded more than rejection ever could.

"You can't mean that, Elizabeth," he grated. "You barely know me."

I stepped closer, our bodies separated only by the veil of shadows clinging to him.

"I know enough to trust my own heart."

Our breaths mingled—my warmth seeking his chill, refusing to be repelled.

"We are the same, you and I," I whispered against the hollow of his cheek.

Then, as if sealing a vow I could not take back, I kissed the darkened flesh there.

His silence was a plea, an unspoken cry for something he did not dare name.

So, I kissed him.

What was left of his mouth.

A seal over the bond that had formed between us despite—or because of—the shadows.

I pulled back just enough to look into his eyes, dark whirlpools of agony and disbelief.

"I understand why you hide your true identity," I said, lifting a hand to cup his cheek and turning his face back toward mine. "But I also know that you're not a monster, Amir. You have a good heart."

His gaze searched mine, desperate, uncertain—scouring me for the smallest sign of deception, of disgust.

But he found none.

He shuddered, a breath escaping him like a man who had spent a lifetime drowning and had finally broken the surface.

Then, slowly, he leaned forward.

His forehead rested against mine—moist with exposed muscle and blood, raw and real.

"Even in this nightmare form… Do you still love me? You still desire me?" His voice trembled like the edge of a blade, poised between longing and disbelief.

I didn't answer. I didn't need to.

His body trembled, and then—it changed.

Bones knit together, muscles and sinew stretching, reforming.

A layer of smooth, unbroken skin replaced the tattered remains.

His teeth reformed—perfect, whole, gleaming white.

His thinning hair darkened and thickened, cascading to his shoulders in rich, silken waves.

And in the flickering lamplight, he stood before me whole.

Still him.

Still mine.

"I love you, Amir," I whispered, my lips grazing his, teasing, taunting. "I desire you. Every part of you."

His breath hitched, his body tensing as though my words had shattered something inside him.

"You and I," I murmured, my body flush against his, feeling the hard planes of his chest, the heat radiating from his skin. "We're fighting the same battle. I know you're the Black Wraith. And I want to help you destroy my father's society."

The admission hung between us, electric, charged. But before he could respond, I claimed his lips, devouring him.

He growled into the kiss, raw, untamed, dangerous. His hands gripped my waist, fingers digging in, pulling me harder, closer, deeper.

I gasped as he pushed me against the nearest wall, pinning me there with his body, his lips traveling down the column of my throat, kissing, biting, claiming.

The world beyond this room ceased to exist.

Only his touch, his taste, the fire between us.

I moaned as his teeth grazed my skin, his tongue flicking over the sensitive spot just beneath my ear. "Amir..." I sighed, my hands sliding up his broad shoulders, feeling the taut muscles beneath my fingertips.

His breath was ragged and heavy with restraint—restraint I wanted him to lose.

"Tell me to stop," he rasped against my neck, his voice loaded with hunger, his control fraying with every second.

"Don't stop."

I felt his entire body tense—then snap.

With a deep, feral growl, his hands roamed me without hesitation, without mercy. Exploring, kneading, claiming. His fingers slid down my spine, dragging slow, teasing paths that made me shiver beneath his touch.

His lips were everywhere—my throat, my collarbone, the curve of my shoulder—each kiss searing, marking, and branding me as his.

I gasped as his teeth grazed my skin, pleasure tangled with the aching pull of desire. His hands slid beneath the fabric of my dress, palms hot and demanding against my bare thighs.

I arched into him, my body surrendering to the aching, pulsing heat between us.

"Amir," I moaned, my fingers tangling in his dark hair, pulling him closer, my nails scraping down his back.

His chest rose and fell in uneven, desperate breaths. "You drive me mad." His voice was hoarse, wrecked.

"Then lose control," I whispered against his lips. "With me."

Something broke in him.

With a guttural sound, he lifted me effortlessly, my legs locking around his waist, my body molding to his like I was made for him. He pinned me against the wall, his body a solid, smoldering force against mine, and his lips crashed into me with hunger so deep, so consuming, I forgot how to breathe.

I gasped into his mouth, my fingers digging into his hair, pulling, needing, demanding.

"Amir," I whispered, breathless, reckless. "Every part of me desires you."

His growl rumbled through me, vibrating against my skin. His hands slid up my thighs, fingers branding my flesh, holding me in place like I was something precious and fragile—yet meant to be completely devoured.

I met his eyes, dark and fiery with something primal.

"I've always dreamed of marrying for love," I admitted. "Of feeling this… this fire between a man and a woman. And when you kissed me—"

He nipped at my bottom lip, his teeth teasing, his tongue following, soothing, seducing.

"You set that fire ablaze within me."

I shuddered as his fingers traced a slow, dangerous path up my inner thigh, stopping just shy of where I needed him most.

"But… are you certain this is what you want, my love?" I asked.

His gaze darkened, his control hanging by a thread.

Slowly, deliberately, he took my hand and placed it firmly against the throbbing heat straining through his breeches.

I gasped.

Thick. Hard. Hot.

A deep, low groan left his lips as I touched him, feeling his sheer power.

"Does this feel uncertain to you?" he asked, his voice dripping with hunger.

My fingers curled around him through the fabric, and his entire body tensed—like a beast barely restrained.

"If you say yes, I won't be able to hold back. I'll take you— again and again—until I am lost in you, until you are crying my name in pleasure, until I have marked you so deeply that no man, no force in this world, will ever claim you but me."

Gods.

The world tilted, spun, and burned as heat spread low in my belly, a molten ache throbbing between my thighs.

I had never touched a man like this before, never been this

close, but I couldn't stop. My palm explored, curious, emboldened, drawn to him like gravity.

His breath hitched, a ragged, intoxicating sound that lit a firestorm beneath my skin.

"Tell me no, Elizabeth," he groaned, his forehead on mine. "Because if you don't, I swear to the gods, I will ruin you."

"Ruin me, then."

My words were his undoing.

A low, guttural growl tore from his throat as he seized me and swept me into his arms like a conqueror taking his spoils.

The world blurred as he carried me through the dimly lit corridor, each step a promise, a descent into something visceral.

My pulse thundered, anticipation and hesitation tangling inside me—a battle between craving what lay ahead and fearing the depth of what I was about to surrender to.

But as Amir reached his private chambers, his fingers tightened on my body, his lips brushing against my ear in a whisper that sent shivers cascading down my spine.

"There's no turning back now, my love."

And I didn't want to.

CHAPTER 14

AMIR

I laid Elizabeth on the bed, her delicate form sinking into the whisper-soft linen, her breath a gentle sigh that mingled with the stillness of my chamber. My heart hammered fiercely against my ribs; each beat echoing the raw urgency thrumming through me. As I hovered above her, my body pulled tight with desire, I felt my arousal ignite—hotter, fiercer, more consuming than anything I had ever known.

Centuries had passed me by, marked by fleeting indulgences and hollow encounters. Yet here, with Elizabeth beneath me, her eyes locking onto mine, something deep and powerful unlocked within me. I cared for her—truly, achingly—in a way that terrified me. Vulnerability was a blade I had never let near my heart —until now.

My throat tightened, dry with words I dared not speak. She lay bathed in silvery moonlight, shadows caressing her face, but it wasn't enough. I needed to see all of her, to memorize every curve and line, to etch her into my soul.

Silently, I moved to the wall sconces, summoning a flicker of flame at my fingertips. A soft glow bloomed, filling the room with amber light that danced over her golden skin. Her eyes, the color of a summer sky, shimmered, reflecting the flame, revealing flecks of resolve beneath the tenderness.

This moment was a precipice. I stood at the edge, ready to

plunge into an abyss of emotion and desire—a place foreign to a man who had always commanded but never surrendered. Yet, as I looked at her, the general who once led armies found himself helplessly falling, willingly captured by the quiet strength of the woman before him.

Doubt prickled at the edges of my consciousness, a whisper of resistance that faltered against the storm of need roaring through me. I was a master of seduction, a puppeteer who played on the desires of women, bending them to my will with charm and deception. But with Elizabeth, I wanted none of that—no games, no illusions. All I craved was her, to feel her bare soul against mine.

Could I truly allow myself this indulgence? My heart slammed against my ribcage, each pulse echoing the throbbing need tightening in my core, demanding release.

Her vulnerable gaze sliced through my armor, exposing the man beneath the monster. Her hands fisted in the sheets, knuckles pale with anticipation, while her legs dangled over the edge, feet tapping a frantic, uncertain rhythm. She bit her lip, that small act of innocence igniting a potent fire.

"Is this truly what you want, Elizabeth?" My voice was a growl, torn from my chest—a final tether before I lost myself completely. "Once I begin, there will be no mercy, no stopping. I will take you, claim you, make you mine in every way."

Her breath hitched, her chest rising and falling with the acceptance of her decision. But her voice was unwavering, sweet yet resolute. "Yes, Amir. I want you. I need you."

The beast within me roared, its chains broken by her words. All pretense of control evaporated. A primal hunger surged to the surface, consuming every shred of restraint. I was on her in a heartbeat; the distance between us obliterated as my body pressed against hers, heat radiating from every point of contact.

My hands trembled as they found her waist, fingers digging into the delicate curves that fit so perfectly against me. Her skin was soft, warm, and intoxicating, and I was lost—drowning in her scent, the taste of her anticipation lingering in the air.

"Stand," I commanded, my voice rough and predatory. She obeyed, rising before me, vulnerable and breathtaking.

I traced my thumb over her lips, swollen from where she had worried them moments before. My mouth followed, claiming hers with a savage hunger, my tongue demanding entry as she surrendered to me. Her taste was intoxicating, her every sound and shiver pulling me deeper, until the fire in my chest roared to life and I couldn't get enough of her.

My hands roamed lower, unapologetically exploring, memorizing every curve and hollow, every delicate contour that made her mine. Her body quivered under my touch, arching toward me, craving the pleasure only I could give. She was mine—to touch, to worship, to ruin. And I intended to do all three, relentlessly, until she knew she belonged to me.

Control slipped through my fingers, crumbling to dust as need took over. I was no longer the calculated general, the master of strategy and discipline. I was a man, undone and ravenous, burning with a desire that threatened to engulf us both.

I would claim her, body and soul, until her screams echoed my name, until she was marked as mine, bound to me in ways she would never escape.

Her gown hugged her curves, teasing me with the promise of what lay beneath. It was plain and practical, a testament to her devotion to alchemy over vanity. But to me, it was an obstacle that needed to be removed. My fingers traced the neckline slowly, teasingly, before I slid the fabric from her shoulders, watching as it cascaded to the floor in a whisper of linen around her feet.

Her bare skin glowed in the candlelight, flawless and inviting, a vision of temptation that made my mouth water. My lips found her neck, trailing hot, open-mouthed kisses along the delicate line of her throat. Her pulse fluttered beneath my tongue, quickening with anticipation, and a shiver ran through her as I grazed her skin with my teeth.

A breathless apology fell from her lips, a confession that she owned nothing finer, nothing more seductive. I silenced her with a growl, my hands tightening possessively on her hips, pulling her against me, making sure she felt every hard, throbbing inch of my need for her.

"You don't need silks or lace to seduce me," I murmured, my voice low, rough with desire. "You don't need anything at all."

Her blush deepened, her innocence igniting a fire within me, and I claimed her mouth in a hungry, dominating kiss, my tongue exploring, tasting, owning. She melted against me, her body pliant and eager, her hands clutching at my shoulders as if to anchor herself against the storm I was about to unleash.

My fingers found the ribbons at her waist, pulling them loose impatiently. The petticoats fell in soft folds, slipping down her legs, brushing against her bare thighs as they descended to the floor. I kicked them aside, clearing the way and making room for what would happen.

I touched her everywhere, my hands greedy, intent, sliding over her curves, learning every inch of her. Her body was soft, warm, inviting, and I explored it without restraint, my palms caressing the curve of her waist, the swell of her hips, the smooth expanse of her thighs.

A needy moan escaped her, her back arching as her body sought mine, and my name fell from her lips, breathy and pleading, driving me to the brink of madness. I watched her as she surrendered herself to me and offered everything she was, everything she would ever be.

I would take her—slowly, thoroughly. I would claim her, over and over, until her body bore the mark of my touch, until my hands molded her very essence. She would scream my name, a symphony of surrender, echoing off the walls until her voice was raw, until she was utterly, irrevocably mine.

Body and soul. Forever.

With a swift, fluid motion, I tore off my leather jerkin, the heavy garment dropping to the floor with a dull thud, a forgotten relic of who I was before this moment. My cravat was next, yanked free and discarded carelessly, the knot unraveling as I stripped away every barrier between us. The linen shirt followed, pulled over my head, leaving me bare, exposed to her hungry gaze.

She was already naked—gloriously so. Her body was a masterpiece, with soft curves and smooth skin, delicate and powerful, illuminated by the dim, flickering candlelight. Her hair tumbled over her shoulders, cascading around her like a halo of temptation.

Her eyes were wide with desire, pupils dilated as they roamed over me, taking in every scar, every line etched into my flesh. Her lips parted, a soft gasp escaping as she drank me in, her cheeks flushing with need, her chest rising and falling with rapid, shallow breaths.

"Your scars..." Her voice was a whisper, trembling with fascination. Her fingers reached out tentatively, brushing over the raised lines that mapped my battles, the wounds I had endured and survived. Her touch was delicate and reverent, sending electricity crackling through my nerves, igniting a fire that burned hot and fierce.

"Every mark is a story," I murmured, stepping closer, the air charged with unspoken intimacy between us. "A reminder that I survived... to find you."

Her eyes flicked up to mine, shimmering with emotion, her lips parting with a soft gasp. "Amir... you're beautiful."

Her words shattered something inside me, leaving me vulnerable, and hungrier than I had ever been. I needed her— needed to feel her, taste her, consume her.

I captured her mouth with mine, a searing kiss that left no room for doubt, my tongue sliding between her parted lips, tasting her, claiming her. She responded with fervor, her hands clutching at my shoulders, her bare body against me, soft curves molding to my hardness.

With one hand tangled in her hair, holding her in place, my other roamed downward, tracing the delicate line of her throat and the elegant curve of her collarbone. Her pulse raced beneath my fingers, quick and frantic, and I followed its rhythm, my lips moving to her neck, my tongue tasting the salt of her skin.

She whimpered, her body arching into mine, her skin electric beneath my touch, desperate for more.

I answered her plea, my hands gliding lower, exploring the

curves that had haunted my nights, the softness that drove me to madness.

"Amir…"

My name fell from her lips like a prayer, breathless, yearning, drenched in desire.

It shredded the last remnants of my control.

I growled against her throat, my teeth grazing her delicate skin, nipping, tasting, marking her, claiming her.

Mine.

Only mine.

Her fingers tangled in my hair, pulling me closer. Her soft and yielding body molded to mine, igniting a fire that destroyed every rational thought.

I wanted to devour her.

To feel her break beneath my hands, shatter beneath my mouth, to hear her cry my name again and again until there was nothing left but us.

I sank to my knees before her, my hands sliding along the smoothness of her legs, exploring, savoring.

I touched my lips to the tender skin of her thigh, savoring the way she shivered beneath the heat of my mouth, my voice low, rough with need.

"Sit down, my love. Relax. I want to worship you."

Her breath caught, her chest rising and falling with ragged anticipation. Slowly, she stepped back, her eyes locked on mine, heat and trust fiery in their depths. With a soft exhale, she lowered herself onto the edge of the bed, her movements graceful—each shift of her body a silent invitation.

Her legs parted slightly, the moonlight catching the sheen on her skin. Her hands gripped the sheets beneath her. She looked utterly undone yet poised—a trembling masterpiece before me, waiting, wanting, ready to be claimed.

And I was going to take my time with every inch of her.

My fingers traced delicate patterns along her skin, teasing, igniting, claiming. Her eyes fluttered shut, her lips parted, and a soft sigh escaped her—a sound that nearly drove me to ruin.

Gods.

I was lost, completely addicted to the electric sensation of her touch, the way her fingers explored my shoulders, my chest, her nails grazing my skin, leaving feverish trails in their wake.

I couldn't breathe, couldn't think—only feel.

My mouth followed the path of my hands, kissing, tasting, and worshiping the body that was driving me to madness.

She was my addiction, my undoing, my everything.

She consumed me—my body thrumming with need, my heart thundering as I waged war between restraint and the overwhelming urge to take her, claim her, make her mine.

Her voice cut through the haze—soft, hesitant, vulnerable.

"Amir… have you ever felt something so overwhelming it devours every part of you? Like a fire blazing inside, but instead of pain, it's… something else entirely?"

Her words lingered in the air, fragile yet charged—an invitation, a confession, a plea.

My gaze locked onto hers, my chest tightening at the sight of her—cheeks flushed, lips slightly parted, eyes searching. Beautiful. Devastatingly beautiful.

I leaned in, brushing my lips over hers, my voice low, bursting with unspoken emotion.

"I have. It's a feeling so intense it steals your breath," I murmured, my lips grazing her skin, "Like the world ceases to exist… and all that is left is this—the sensation, the connection."

Her breath hitched, lashes fluttering as my hand slid up her thigh, my fingers tracing lazy, teasing patterns that made her shiver beneath my touch.

"I've never… felt anything like that," she whispered, her voice trembling with longing and fear. "I've always wondered if it's real—or just something people imagine."

I cupped her face, thumb grazing her cheek, my touch gentle, reverent.

"It's real, Elizabeth."

My voice dropped to a whisper, heavy with meaning.

"But it's not just about the feeling—it's about trust, about surrender. Losing yourself in a moment… and finding something even more powerful in return."

Her eyes met mine, wide and vulnerable; her soul laid bare.

"How do you let go like that?" she asked, her voice barely a breath. "How do you give yourself over to something so completely?"

My fingers lingered at her jaw, tilting her face to mine, eyes locked.

"You let go," I murmured, my lips brushing hers, "when you feel safe—when you know the person holding you will catch you, no matter how far you fall."

Her breath shuddered, and I felt it—the way her body softened, yielding to me, surrendering completely. Trust wrapped around us like a silken thread, unbreakable.

Her lips met mine, soft and warm, igniting the fire between us again—but I didn't hold back this time.

I kissed her deeply, hungrily, claiming her mouth, tasting her breath, drinking in the moans she gave me. My hands roamed, exploring every inch of her skin, while my mouth worshipped her with the kind of reverence reserved for gods. My body against hers, hard and needing, our rhythm syncing, instinctual and ancient—older than time, older than reason.

She was everything.

And tonight, I would show her exactly what that meant.

Her scent overwhelmed me—sweet, intoxicating—a drug I craved with every breath. I lowered myself between her legs, my hands spreading her thighs wide, and hovered there, letting my breath ghost over her slick heat. She gasped, her hips lifting in a silent plea.

I answered.

My tongue flicked out, teasing her folds before sliding over her clit, tasting her, devouring her. Her moan was raw, desperate, her fingers tangling in my hair, tugging me closer, deeper.

She arched beneath me, writhing, her thighs trembling as I worked her clit in slow, torturous circles—alternating between soft licks and firm pressure. Her body responded like dry tinder to flame, hips grinding against my mouth, her slick heat coating my tongue as I feasted on her, insistent, hungry, lost in her.

My cock throbbed painfully hard, still trapped in my

breeches. Every gasp, every helpless cry she made sent a jolt straight through me, igniting something wild and uncontrollable in my blood.

Her legs locked around my head, pulling me tighter, her moans rising—breathless, wanton, raw. I slid a finger inside her slow and teasing, savoring the way her tight, wet walls clenched around me, her body jerking in response.

She was unraveling.

Her skin aflame under my hands, her taste slick and sweet on my tongue, her body trembling on the edge of oblivion.

I didn't stop. I didn't let her breathe.

I devoured her until she shattered—legs quaking, cries spilling from her lips like a prayer, like a surrender. And then, I licked her through it—slow, deep, consuming—tasting every pulse of her release, feeling every tremor of her thighs as she fell apart in my arms.

She was undone.

Writhing. Wrecked. Mine.

Her body trembled beneath me, breath ragged, chest rising and falling as she lay utterly spent—flushed, sweat-slick, her thighs still quivering from the force of her release. I rose slowly, savoring the sight of her—disheveled, glowing, ruined most exquisitely.

I licked my lips, tasting her still on my tongue, her sweetness lingering—addictive, intoxicating, a flavor I never wanted to forget.

Her eyes locked onto mine—dark with lust, wide, dazed, lips parted as she reached for me. She tugged at my breeches, frantic with need, her touch igniting me like kindling to flame. I groaned, barely holding on, and tore the fabric away, freeing my cock—hard, throbbing, the head slick, aching for her.

She gasped, her breath catching, eyes fixated on me, and then her hand wrapped around my length—slow at first, then faster, her grip confident, claiming, owning me. I hissed, hips jerking into her touch, every nerve alight, my control lost by her hand alone.

And then—her voice.

Soft. Trembling. Honest.

"Amir…" she whispered, eyes vulnerable, and fierce. "I've never been with a man before."

My breath caught, her words slicing through me—raw, sacred, a gift I hadn't expected.

But she didn't stop—her touch, her voice.

"I want to feel everything. I want all of it—all of you." Her voice grew bolder. "Don't restrain yourself. Don't hold back. I desire you, Amir. Take me. Completely."

My mind snapped. My body flamed.

I seized her mouth, crashing into her with a kiss that devoured, no longer soft, no longer patient—it was feral, carnal. Our tongues tangled, breaths stolen, lips bruised as I drank her in, consuming every moan from her throat.

My hands moved over her body, possessive, worshipful, sliding over sweat-slick skin to cup her breasts—full, flushed, heavy with arousal. I groaned against her lips, rolling her nipples between my fingers, feeling her arch, offering herself to me.

I broke the kiss only to trail my mouth down her throat, biting, sucking, marking her—mine, only mine—her gasps like music, her fingers fisting in my hair, urging me lower.

I slid down, lips finding her breast, wrapping around her nipple, sucking her into the heat of my mouth. I groaned as her body bowed beneath me, her moan desperate, her back arching, offering me everything. I worshipped her with my mouth, tongue flicking, teeth grazing, my hand kneading the other breast, fingers pinching, teasing until she writhed beneath me.

I was going to take her apart again.

And this time—I wouldn't stop until I had every part of her.

She cried out, her back arching herself against my mouth, offering everything I craved. My tongue flicked over her nipple, slow and sinful, circling her peak before I sucked hard, drawing a ragged, breathless moan from her throat. Her legs writhed beneath me, thighs parting wider, body pleading without words, begging for more.

I shifted to her other breast, biting lightly, then soothing the sting with slow strokes of my tongue. Her nipple pebbled beneath my mouth, her body trembling as I worshipped her—thorough, persistent, tender. Every inch of her was alive beneath my hands, my lips, mine to savor.

"You're mine," I growled against her skin, my voice rough and thick with hunger. "Every inch of you... belongs to me."

She moaned, her hands in my hair, guiding me, holding me to her chest as though separation would tear her apart. Her breath came in hot, broken pants, hips grinding against me, slick with need, soaked with want.

I trailed kisses down her body, slow, torturous, savoring every tremor, every hitch of breath as she writhed beneath my touch. Her skin seared under my lips. Her scent, taste, and surrender were all I could breathe. All I wanted.

She'd asked for everything. And I was going to give her more than she ever imagined.

Her body quivered, slick with sweat, skin flushed, breasts rising and falling from the worship I'd lavished upon her. Her nipples—swollen and sensitive—peaked from my attention, her thighs parted in open invitation, her core glistening, dripping with desire.

I hovered above her, breath ragged, my cock hard and pulsing, veins tight with need, aching to be inside her for the first time—no restraint, no gentleness... just the unrelenting need to claim her completely.

She looked up at me, dazed, undone, lips parted. "Amir... please..." Her voice trembled, her eyes wide with trust, with need.

I gripped her thighs, spreading her wider, drinking in the sight of her—wet, perfect. I dragged the head of my cock along her slick folds, teasing, circling, letting her feel every inch she was about to take. She squirmed, hips rising, trying to pull me in.

I leaned down, crushing my mouth to hers, devouring her moans as my cock poised at her entrance.

"You want everything?" I growled into her lips. "Then feel everything."

I thrust into her—slow, devastating—my cock stretching her

tight, velvety heat, inch by inch, her slickness welcoming me, coating me, pulling me deeper. Her head fell back, lips parting on a moan, her back arching as I sank in, her body clenching, gripping me like she'd never let me go.

"Gods… Amir," she gasped, nails dragging down my back, leaving hot, stinging trails. "You're so deep… I can feel you everywhere."

I buried myself to the hilt, fully inside her, our bodies fused, breaths tangled, hearts pounding like war drums. Her walls pulsed around me, slick and hot, every muscle quivering, begging for more.

I held her, buried deep, savoring the way she wrapped around me like silk and flame—so tight, so perfect, her body clutching me as if she'd been made for this moment, made for me.

I crushed my mouth to hers, kissing her slow and deep, tongues tangling, teeth grazing, stealing every moan from her lips as I began to move.

Long, punishing strokes—slow at first, dragging almost out, the head of my cock just barely teasing her entrance before I drove back in with a groan that tore from my throat. Her body responded like a flame to oxygen—hips rising to meet me, thighs tightening around my waist, skin slick with sweat. Her core fluttered around me, squeezing, pulsing, coaxing me deeper with every thrust.

I watched her unravel beneath me—face flushed, lips kiss-swollen, her eyes fluttering shut with every slow, deep stroke. She gasped my name, voice cracking, desperate, pleading, her hands clawing at my back as if her sanity depended on holding onto me.

I picked up the pace, hips snapping forward with a brutal rhythm, the sound of our bodies colliding filthy and perfect, echoing through the room like a song of sin. I gripped her ass, lifting her hips off the bed, slamming deeper, harder—finding that spot that made her scream, her cries raw, unrestrained, intoxicating.

"You're mine," I snarled against her ear, voice rough, undeniable as I thrust deep. "Say it. Tell me."

Her voice pitched, high and breathless. "Yours!" she cried, her body shaking violently. "I'm yours, Amir—only yours!"

Her words lit me on fire, burning through the last thread of my control. I drove into her mercilessly now, our rhythm wild and desperate, my cock pistoning into her soaked heat, her moans turning to helpless screams, her nails digging into my shoulders, claiming me right back.

I reached between us, fingers finding her clit, circling fast, knowing. She fell apart beneath me—coming hard, her body convulsing, muscles clamping down, her core milking me, slick and tight, soaking me as her cries pierced the silence, pure ecstasy in every sound.

I roared her name, hips jerking, spilling deep inside her, pulse after pulse, my release ripping through me like fire, like salvation. I collapsed over her, our bodies slick, ruined most perfectly, hearts hammering together, breath tangled, souls utterly consumed.

Lying entwined in the hazy afterglow, I cradled Elizabeth against my chest, her soft and warm body fitting perfectly against mine. A heavy silence draped over us, broken only by our synchronized breaths and the faint hiss of dying candles. Shadows clung to the room like secrets but no longer felt menacing—not with her in my arms. The amber glow flickered across our skin, stubbornly defying the dark.

I brushed a damp lock of hair from her face, marveling at how the moonlight kissed her skin, turning her into something ethereal, almost unreal. My heart thudded beneath her fingers, beating with a strange mix of triumph and vulnerability. She had undone me quietly, completely. Something ancient inside me—hardened, hidden—had cracked open under her touch.

As if she sensed the storm of thought within me, Elizabeth shifted closer, her fingers tracing slow, idle patterns across my chest, leaving trails of heat in their wake. Her voice, when it came, was soft but certain.

"I want to know everything about you, Amir. Who are you?"

Her words settled between us, heavy and intimate. It wasn't just curiosity—it was an invitation into the sanctum of my soul. To answer would be to strip away the centuries of armor I had built, to expose the wounds, the battles, and the bloodstained purpose that defined me.

"Everything is… vast," I said quietly, my voice hoarse, laced with a rare hesitance. "But I'll give you pieces of me—as long as you give me your truth, too."

She looked up at me, her eyes shining in the low light, filled with wonder—and something deeper. A challenge. A promise.

"Everything," she whispered, her smile soft, vulnerable, and bold all at once. "I'll tell you everything."

She curled tighter against me, drawing the covers around us to seal us in that moment. I felt it—the shift—the pull of something far greater than lust or desire.

I was crumbling.

And as the memories surged—painful, beautiful, unstoppable—I knew I had to start. Somewhere. Anywhere. Before I drowned in everything, I had never told a soul.

CHAPTER 15

AMIR

Lying amidst the tangled sheets, I wrestled with the chaos inside me. Emotions I had long buried crawled their way to the surface—jagged and achingly human. It was terrifying and unfamiliar. These sensations made me feel exposed and vulnerable.

Elizabeth's fingers ghosted over my chest, a touch so light yet heavy with a tenderness I didn't deserve. She unsettled me, stripping away my defenses layer by layer. I didn't know how to handle it—her, this, us.

Her voice broke the silence, soft but piercing. "Who are you, Amir? Is Amir your real name?" Those storm-washed eyes searched mine, unwavering, reaching for truths I didn't know how to give.

I closed my eyes, shame curling through me. Damn, Lazarus, I shouldn't have let her get this close. I shouldn't have let her look past the surface. But she did. She saw the darkness that festered beneath my skin, the shadows that twisted my soul. And still, she stayed. Unafraid. Curious. Hopeful.

A bitter laugh scraped my throat, burdened with self-loathing. What a fool. Opening my eyes, I met her gaze, my chest tightening as I prepared to test whatever fragile bond was forming between us.

"I am a Darkness," I confessed, my voice hoarse, raw. "I don't belong in this world... or any other."

Her breath hitched, shock rippling across her delicate features, but she didn't pull away. Her hand remained over my heart, warm against my cool skin.

"If not here... then where?" Her words trembled, the slightest fracture in her voice betraying her fear, her intrigue. She was braver than I ever gave her credit for.

The truth weighed heavy, suffocating. I wanted to lie, to protect her from the storm I carried, but there was no point. She deserved the truth, even if it destroyed whatever illusion she held of me.

A deep, shuddering sigh escaped me as my vivid, merciless past flooded back. Solaris. My home. Once beautiful—now corrupted. The unforgiving memories in my mind, dragged me into the shadows I had fought so hard to escape. I could almost see it again—not lit by the familiar sun, but by an immense, otherworldly clock whose face mirrored the moon. I could hear the laughter that once echoed through the citadels, feel the way life used to pulse with purpose.

But that was before. Before darkness seeped in, twisting everything it touched... twisting me. My voice came out jagged, fractured. "I come from a place called Solaris... a once-magnificent realm. A place of light, purpose, and hope. But that is long gone—shadows have since tainted everything, and corruption has sunk its claws into the very heart of my world."

The memories unfurled like a cruel tapestry, threads of joy ripped apart by loss and betrayal. My chest tightened as faces I once loved flashed before my eyes—faces now long gone, reduced to ashes and echoes. "Solaris was the realm of time travelers, ruled by the House of Timebornes and Timebounds... protected by the House of Shadowbornes." My voice wavered, the pain too real, too raw. "We were guardians. Heroes. Until we became monsters."

I swallowed hard, the taste of regret bitter on my tongue. "An evil queen ruled Solaris once, her cruelty poisoning the land, driving it into chaos. Under her tyranny, everything fell apart. I fought... I fought so damn hard to protect it. But I failed." My gaze fell, shame searing through me. "I lost my army. I lost my home. I lost... myself."

I looked past Elizabeth, my vision blurring as I stared into the abyss of my past. Solaris had been my paradise, my purpose. And now... it was nothing but dust and ruins.

I looked at her, searching her eyes for understanding, for any sign of fear. But all I found was a blazing curiosity and trust I didn't deserve.

"How much do you know about your father's society?" I asked, my voice low and edged with steel. I needed the truth. No more lies. No more secrets. "I need to know. How much do you know?"

Her eyes locked onto mine, unflinching and fearless. Her voice was laden with pain. "I know more than I should. My father is a destroyer... a ruthless hunter of Timebornes and Timebounds. He's merciless. Cold. Obsessed with eradicating them, like they're a plague that needs to be wiped out." Her gaze faltered, a flicker of confusion breaking through her bravery. "But I don't understand why. I don't understand his obsession. And as for time travel... it's just a myth to me. A fairy tale."

Her words hung between us, a cruel twist of irony. Time travel was a fairy tale. To her, maybe. But to me, it was everything—the reason for every scar on my body and soul.

I looked at her, really looked at her. Her innocence was a purity I could never touch without staining. Yet, she was tangled up in this darkness—in my darkness. Her father was a monster, and I was no better.

A cringe tightened my muscles, a bitter laugh threatening to break free. It was incomprehensible to me—this disbelief of something so intrinsic and vital to my existence. "How can you not believe it?" my voice was a whisper, low and splintered.

"It's as natural as breathing. It's in my blood, my bones. It's who I am."

She leaned closer, her curiosity tinged with awe and just a hint of fear. "Can you... can you time travel?" Her voice was fragile, a whisper that tore down the walls around me.

"Of course," I breathed, the truth tasting bittersweet on my tongue. My curse. My gift. My prison.

Her gaze softened, fascination swirling in her eyes. "How? How is that possible?"

A shadow passed over me, ancient and insistent. "When a Timeborne is born... so is the Darkness," I confessed, my voice raw, haunted. "We are two halves of the same coin. A black dagger appears by our side, born of shadows and blood. The blade is etched with sacred inscriptions intertwined with a curse and a blessing. And when the full moon rises, we speak the words... time bends to our will. We slip through the cracks of reality, defying fate itself."

Elizabeth's eyes widened, her lips parting as she absorbed my words. Her pulse raced, her heartbeat echoing in the heavy silence between us. I could almost taste her fear... her awe.

For a moment, she was silent, her mind weaving through impossible possibilities. Then, with a voice that trembled with wonder and hesitation, she asked, "Where have you traveled in time?"

My chest tightened, memories crashing into me—images of worlds lost, and futures shattered, faces long gone, and battles fought in the shadows of time. A bitter smile twisted my lips. "The real question is... where haven't I traveled?" I met her gaze, letting my past sink into the space between us. "I've seen empires rise and fall. I've watched the birth of legends and the death of hope. I've stood in the ashes of worlds that no longer exist. And through it all... I remained a shadow. A ghost passing through time, never truly belonging."

Her breath hitched, her eyes wide and shimmering with an emotion I couldn't quite name. She wasn't just looking at me— she was seeing through me, and it was terrifying. I had built walls so high that I sometimes forgot what was on the other side. Yet, at this moment, her gaze reached places I thought were long buried.

My hand moved almost instinctively, fingers tracing the soft skin of her arm. It was a grounding touch, delicate and unconscious as if I needed something real to anchor me to this world—to this moment. Memories began to surface, uninvited and unending. I felt the shadows stir within me, restless and uneasy.

"Alina," I began quietly, my voice softer than intended. Her name felt heavy on my tongue, like an old wound reopening. "The dark queen of Solaris... she was powerful. More powerful than any ruler before her. And she craved more. Always more."

Elizabeth's eyes remained locked on mine, wide and curious. Her gaze had no fear, only a genuine need to understand. It made my chest tighten. She deserved better than my darkness, better than my past. But she was here, warm and steady, and for once, I didn't have the strength to push her away.

"She wanted the Blade of Shadows," I continued, my fingers still absentmindedly brushing her arm. "A weapon of unimaginable power. With it, she could have ruled all of Solaris... and beyond. Nothing could've stopped her." A chill ran through me, the old fear resurfacing. "She would have destroyed everything to get what she wanted."

Elizabeth's lips parted, her breath catching. But her gaze softened, compassion flickering in her eyes. She reached up, her fingers tracing my jawline, and the gentle touch made my chest tighten painfully. It was too tender, too kind. I didn't deserve this.

"Her daughter, Isabelle..." I swallowed, the memory bittersweet. "She saw the darkness in her mother and feared what would happen if Alina got her hands on the blade. So, she did the only thing she could—she separated the blades, breaking their power... and she ran."

I let out a breath I didn't realize I was holding. Isabelle's choice had changed everything. She had been brave and selfless. And I had failed her.

I glanced at Elizabeth, expecting pity, maybe fear. But her eyes were filled with understanding, a quiet strength that made something inside me ache. Her fingers traced light patterns across my chest, her touch grounding and calming. She shifted, facing me fully, her expression open and curious.

"What was your role in all of this?" she asked, her voice

gentle but firm. She wasn't demanding answers; she was inviting me to share them.

I hesitated, the words heavy on my tongue. I had spent so long hiding the truth, even from myself. But she felt safe and honest. She was willing to listen, even if she couldn't understand, and I found myself wanting to tell her.

I took a steadying breath, my fingers tightening slightly against her skin. "I was the leader of the House of Shadowborne," I admitted, my voice quiet, almost fragile. "I commanded the Shadowborne army. I followed orders from Lazarus, who protected the last king and queen—Isabelle and Armand."

The names felt distant, like echoes from another lifetime. Saying them aloud felt strange, almost surreal, like speaking of ghosts.

Her expression softened, sympathy flickering across her delicate features. But she didn't interrupt. She listened, her hand resting over my heart, a silent reassurance.

"I thought I was doing the right thing," I continued, my voice wavering. "I thought I was protecting Solaris... protecting them. But I was wrong. I was so... blind. I didn't see the darkness growing. I didn't see it until it was too late."

Her fingers tightened over my chest, warm and comforting. Her eyes held no judgment, only quiet understanding, which made the pain a little more bearable.

"And how did you end up here, in this world?" Elizabeth's blue eyes searched mine as if trying to unravel the mysteries of Solaris hidden within their dark depths.

My hand found hers against my chest, stilling the hypnotic motion of her fingers. "When Isabelle shattered the Blade of Shadows, chaos followed. We were cast from Solaris—flung into this world with no way back. All of us, scattered like ashes on the wind." I hesitated, my next words pressing against my ribs. "The book in your alchemist's cottage—*Sacred Alchemy of Solaris: Secrets of the Celestial Forge*—comes from my realm."

Her lips parted slightly, absorbing the revelation. "The Timehealers... they became the Timehunters in this world. They hunted us. Hunted me." My mission loomed between us, an unspoken specter in the dim light. "Lazarus, my master, tasked me with eradicating these ruthless societies. Since the day I was thrown here, I have waged war against them—leaving a trail of ruin and destruction across countless timelines. But when I arrived in France, ready to continue my mission..." I exhaled, my voice dropping to a whisper. "You, my love, had already beaten me to it."

I paused, running my tongue over my lower lip, my thoughts dissolving into questions I dared not ask. "Did I know I would meet you? That I would fall for the daughter of my enemy? No. Was I surprised to find you possessed the Noctyss flower? Absolutely."

The words poured forth, a confession filled with wonder. Drawn by something unseen—something inevitable—I leaned in, placing a trail of kisses along her neck, each one a silent vow, a tether binding me to the fate neither of us had foreseen.

"How did you come to possess such a powerful flower?" I asked between kisses, my voice rough with desire. "The Noctyss only blooms in Solaris. Where did you find it? You have to be honest with me."

I needed to know. The Noctyss was no ordinary flower—it was a relic of my lost world, a passageway back to Solaris, back to a home shattered in time.

Elizabeth hesitated as if gathering the fragments of a distant past. "A long time ago, my parents took my brothers and me to the Carpathian Mountains."

Recognition flared within me. Ah. So that is where the realm opens. Excitement surged through my veins, so potent it felt like I could tear through the veil of time and return to Solaris instantly.

Her voice softened, tinged with something I couldn't quite place. "My father took my brothers hunting. My mother and I wandered the mountains, searching for rare blooms." A flicker of something—pain, perhaps—darkened her expression. "She was an alchemist of great renown in my father's society. She believed we might find something... useful."

She hesitated, then exhaled, the memory unfurling like a long-buried secret. "I wandered away from her and stumbled upon an unusual flower. It stood apart from the others as if waiting for me." Her fingers curled slightly against my chest. "I picked it. And then... I saw them. A row of identical flowers led away into the forest like a trail of fallen stars. But the moment I plucked that single bloom..." She swallowed. "All the others died."

A hush settled between us. I listened, enthralled, imagining her as a child—innocent, unaware that her small hands had disturbed something far greater than she could comprehend. The Noctyss did not simply die. It responded. It reacted.

It chose.

Elizabeth's voice softened, touched by memory. "My mother found me, and we followed the path of flowers. It led us to an engraved stone. It was so strange." Her gaze met mine, shimmering with the same awe she must have felt that day.

We lay there, two souls intertwined by destiny, bound by secrets that traversed realms. The span of history imposed on us was as tangible as the touch of skin on skin.

I furrowed my brow, my mind piecing together fragments of an ancient puzzle. "Did you ever tell your father about the flower or the stone?" The question hung between us, delicate yet charged, a thread that might unravel more than we were prepared for.

"Never." Elizabeth's response was immediate. Her fingers traced the outline of an invisible book in the air, as if conjuring the memory itself. "We found the ancient tome beneath a peculiar rock—a rock that seemed to levitate ever so slightly above the ground, as if imbued with power itself."

She mimicked the motion of brushing dust from its cover, lost in recollection. "It was so close to that strange monument. To us, it looked like a door—one leading to a healer's cottage hidden within a stone wall. Yet, no matter how we searched, we could find no way in. It was as if we had stumbled upon the remnants of someone's abandoned sanctuary."

A chill swept through me, despite the warmth of her body

against mine. The pieces aligned, revealing a truth neither of us had spoken aloud.

That wasn't an ordinary stone, nor was it a door—it was a gateway.

Elizabeth's eyes met mine, clouded with secrets long kept from her patriarch. "We immersed ourselves in the flower's mystery when we returned home. We devoured every script, every scroll, every alchemical record within *The Sacred Alchemy of Solaris*—searching for answers. And there, hidden among its ancient pages, we found it. The Noctyss. Its name, its image. And so, we began our experiments, testing the formulae it revealed."

My thoughts clashed like steel on steel, the implications striking harder than I could comprehend. Finally, I asked, "How was it possible for your mother to master such an art? Did she inherit the necessary bloodline? And how did she acquire the key ingredient—the blood of a Darkness? Where did she get it?"

Elizabeth's hand trembled as she looked up at me, fear flickering. She opened her mouth to speak, but her voice faltered.

I reached for her, my touch gentle, steadying her trembling fingers. "You never have to be afraid when you're with me. I will protect you from any monster that dares to come your way."

Her expression softened, but the shadow of uncertainty still lingered.

I exhaled, my breath uneven, my mind still reeling from the revelation.

"Your poison may not have been flawless, but it had an effect. A powerful one. If you had perfected it, the people of France would have been forced to flee—it's that dangerous." I hesitated, the question clawing its way to the surface. "Who was your mother? What was her name?" My voice was barely a whisper, bracing for the truth I hadn't known I was seeking.

Elizabeth's answer came, unaware of the storm it would unleash.

"Isolde Ravencroft."

Lightning shot through my veins. My breath caught. I jolted, muscles tensing with the thought of the name that echoed through history.

"The Ravencroft family," I murmured, the words tasting of revelation. My pulse pounded in my ears. "Your kin hail from Solaris. They were Timehealers—their essence allowed them to create perfection where others found only failure."

The past had never truly been buried. It had only waited—through bloodlines and legacies—until now.

Elizabeth's gaze held mine, searching. "Were you acquainted with the Ravencrofts?"

I propped myself up on one arm, turning fully to face her. "I only knew of them. The Timehealers possessed an innate connection to the natural world—a bond so profound that their touch could heal and soothe life. They carried an energy that calmed, nurtured, and balanced. That is how your mother was able to do what she did. Her bloodline carried the essence of a Timehealer, giving her the power to craft both deadly poisons and miraculous remedies."

I hesitated, my voice dipping lower. "But I never had the honor of personally knowing any of your family. My path was forged in darkness, far from the light of your mother's healing world."

Reaching out, I traced my fingers along the curve of her cheek, a silent question lingering between us. "Can you tell me more about her alchemy practice?"

Elizabeth watched me, absorbing my words as they reshaped the narrative of her past. A silent understanding passed between us—a bridge built from opposing legacies, light and dark, bound together by the unrelenting pull of Solaris.

Lying there, tangled in the crumpled sheets that bore witness to our shared revelations, I studied her face as she spoke.

Her eyes, heavy with the sorrow of loss, held a glint of something else.

Pride.

"My mother taught me her craft," she said softly, almost wistfully.

She drew a breath, the memory haunting her. "Mother

always employed a helper—an assistant. She was meticulous in every precaution, ensuring every step was taken with the utmost care. But no matter how careful they were… they always died. The poisons claimed them, without fail."

Her words lingered in the space between us, heavy with implication.

My brow furrowed. "And yet, these assistants perished—but not your mother. Not you. You've handled the deadliest substances, yet here you are, untouched. Do you know why?"

Elizabeth hesitated before responding. "I wear these leather gloves," she murmured, lifting her bare hands as if to show me. "I douse them in essential oils. It's a protective measure."

I shook my head, exhaling sharply. "No, love. I'm certain your mother's assistants did the same. But that's just a myth. The scent-covered gloves do not prevent the death lurking in those poisons."

My heart pounded as the realization struck me like a bolt of lightning. My gaze locked onto hers, and the answer unraveled before me.

"It's because you and your mother are Timehealers. Your bloodline doesn't just grant you the ability to create these poisons—it grants you mastery over them. To wield them. To survive them."

Her breath hitched, but I wasn't finished.

"And for the poison you crafted—the one meant to drive the people of France to their knees—you needed the blood of a Darkness."

I leaned in, my voice low, edged with a demand for the truth.

"Tell me, Elizabeth… whose blood did you use to craft the poison?"

Elizabeth took a deep breath before revealing the source of the blood of darkness.

"The blood my mother used… belonged to a man named Mathias."

A shiver ran down my spine at the mention of his name. The air between us charged with something unspoken, something that set my nerves on edge.

I swallowed hard, trying to process her revelation. A chill swept through the room as if nature recoiled at the power of Mathias' blood and the horrors it could create.

"Mathias?" I repeated, his name tasting like bile on my tongue. The urgency in my voice made Elizabeth flinch. "How did your mother know him?"

Her breath caught as she hesitated. "He is—was—a family friend," she stammered, startled by the sudden storm in my eyes. "He hasn't returned since my mother died. But… that's how she made the poison."

Tears welled in her eyes, spilling over and tracing silent paths down her cheeks.

"My mother thought once she acquired the final ingredient, the poison would be complete." Her voice trembled, heavy with sorrow. "But she made a mistake. A fatal one. She inhaled the lethal fumes… and within a week, she was dead."

"But are you sure it was a mistake?" he said, his tone low, skeptical. "Your mother was a Timehealer. A single breath of poison wouldn't kill her that easily—not unless something else was at play."

The confession settled between us.

Her eyes flickered at my words—clouded with grief, but not doubt. It was like the thought of something darker, something intentional, hadn't touched her mind.

I watched her closely. That same hollow look clung to her face, like sorrow had wrapped its fingers around her throat and wouldn't let go. She was too far gone in mourning to consider the possibility that her mother's death was more than a mistake.

But I couldn't let it go.

A Timehealer? Dead by poison? No. That didn't sit right. It clawed at the back of my mind like a whisper I couldn't ignore.

She blinked, slowly—like she was dragging herself out of a place I couldn't follow. Then she went on, voice flat, mechanical, untouched by what I had just said.

Like the truth hadn't reached her yet. Or maybe... she just didn't want it to.

"With her death, our family fractured. My father and brothers… became more ruthless in pursuing power. Their thirst for control knew no bounds."

Her hands clenched into fists as her voice hardened with conviction. "But I refused to follow in their footsteps. I vowed to put an end to their corruption."

She drew in a deep breath, steadying herself before continuing. "The poison needed years to ferment, to reach its full potency. And when it was finally ready… I traveled to France to begin my mission."

Her words lingered in the silence that followed—a declaration of defiance, sacrifice, and war she had waged alone.

And now, I understood.

She wasn't just fighting against corruption; she was fighting against the legacy that ran through her veins.

I reached for her, brushing a strand of hair from her face. "And how is it that you did not die, my love?" My concern for her safety momentarily overshadowed the storm of questions swirling in my mind about Mathias.

Elizabeth shifted, lifting herself onto her elbow to meet my gaze. "I waited until the poison had fully matured," she said, her voice quiet yet resolute.

A flicker of something darker crossed her expression. "There were moments when guilt consumed me, whispering doubts, making me question whether I was inflicting suffering on innocent lives. But then I would remind myself of the atrocities committed by Lord Winston, by my father—true monsters and sadists who thrived on pain and power."

Tears welled in her eyes, spilling over as memories resurfaced, raw and unrelenting. Without hesitation, I reached for her, pulling her into my arms. She melted into my embrace, her body trembling as she released the emotions she had buried for so long.

"You did the right thing," I whispered against her hair, my grip tightening around her. "You had to protect yourself. You had to stop them."

Her grief was a tangible force, tugging at the threads of my soul.

Slowly, she pulled back, her tear-streaked face lifting to meet mine. Her eyes, filled with an aching vulnerability, searched my own.

"Amir, you have been my protector, my solace. You have shown me kindness and comfort, shielding me from my father's fury." Her voice wavered, but the truth in her words was undeniable. "Despite your claims of being darkness... of being a monster... there is so much more to you. I've always seen the man beneath it all. But here, lying beside you, it's undeniable. You're strong, brave... and far kinder than you let the world believe."

She exhaled shakily, her fingers tracing the line of my jaw.

"You would have been a wonderful father," she whispered.

The words hit me like a blade to the chest, carving through the walls I had spent years fortifying—a father. The thought had never crossed my mind. Duty was always my priority—loyalty to Lazarus, the mission, the war. There had never been room for such dreams. And yet, something stirred within me, something unfamiliar and dangerous.

I swallowed. "If I ever had sons, I would raise them to be fearless warriors. They would embody honor, bravery, resilience, and heroism," I declared, my voice steadier than the storm raging inside me.

Elizabeth tilted her head, curiosity flickering in her gaze. "What would you name them?"

For the first time, I imagined a life beyond bloodshed, beyond vengeance—a future where I was more than a weapon.

"My sons would have powerful names," I mused. "One would be Roman. And if I had another, I would name him Marcellious."

She smiled softly, then asked, "And what if you had a daughter?"

A daughter.

The thought nearly unraveled me. I had always envisioned raising warriors and preparing them for battle. But at that moment, I saw her—a girl with Elizabeth's strength, fire, and gentleness—a daughter who would be fearless, resilient… and unstoppable.

"She would be just as strong as her brothers," I replied, my voice quieter now.

Elizabeth's fingers traced slow, thoughtful patterns on my chest. "What would you name her?"

I exhaled, the name forming on my lips like a prayer. "Reyna," I whispered.

A single tear slipped down my cheek.

Because I knew I would never have her.

I would never have any of them.

The fantasy burned through me, leaving only ashes. Duty would always come first. Lazarus had forged me into something that did not belong to this world—into a future of love and family.

But then Elizabeth's fingers intertwined with mine, her touch impossibly soft, like the petals of a rose. She leaned closer, her breath mingling with mine—a sweet blend of lavender and vanilla. The world around us faded to insignificance as her lips met mine, a gentle caress that spoke of longing and tenderness— a whispered promise, a silent vow.

At that moment, time stood still. None of the weight of war, bloodshed, or duty mattered. All I felt was her. The warmth of her love wrapped around me like a comforting embrace from the heavens.

When we finally pulled apart, her gaze scorched into mine with conviction.

"Amir, I want to help you take down my father's society—and others like it." Her voice was firm, unwavering. "We can work together. I'll perfect the Noctyss poison and use it at the masquerade. Together, we can be free from my father and Lord Winston. We'll be partners in destroying these oppressive societies."

I stared at her, my heart swelling with something dangerous —something I dared not name. This woman was delicate in appearance yet carried a strength rivaling any warrior I had ever known.

"No," I whispered, the word scraping against my throat, aching in my chest. "It's too dangerous, Elizabeth. Do you know the forces you're dealing with?"

Her chin lifted defiantly. "I know some."

I let out a breath, cold and tight in my chest.

"Salvatore," I said, the name alone sending ice through my veins. "He will stop at nothing to destroy you. He's powerful beyond comprehension. You need to forget about the flower. Forget about the poison. If he or Mathias discovers you have it..."

I swallowed hard, gripping her hands as if I could physically hold her back from the edge she was so willing to walk.

"They will destroy you."

"But Mathias is our friend," she said, tears spilling down her cheeks, raw with lamentation.

I exhaled harshly. "He's not a friend, Elizabeth. He is crueler than your father. And Salvatore… Salvatore is powerful beyond compare."

Reaching out, I brushed away a tear with the pad of my thumb. "He's formidable. I don't want you to destroy lives only to be destroyed in the process." My voice was firm—but inside, I was anything but. The thought of losing her after finding something so unexpectedly tender in this bleak existence was unbearable.

Elizabeth's eyes blazed, her fire undimmed by my words. "I want to be by your side and fight your battles with you." Her fists clenched the crumpled sheets beneath us, her voice a raw mix of anger and desperation.

I gritted my teeth, suppressing a growl of frustration. Every word from her lips was like a dagger, stabbing into my already burdened mind. How could I let her step into my hell, into the world of shadows where innocence was a weakness and mercy was a liability?

But she refused to back down.

"You keep shutting me out," she accused, her voice trembling with emotion. "But I won't give up on you. You're not a murderer. You have a kind heart."

I turned my face away, jaw tight.

She reached for me again, her touch searing through my defenses. "If I can't concoct the poison, let me help you find the missing Blade of Shadows. Let me help you stop this madness."

Desperation seeped into every syllable, her words laced with something dangerous—hope.

And as much as I wanted to push her away, to keep her from the abyss that consumed me, her unyielding determination shook me to my core.

But I couldn't let her into my darkness.

I shook my head, slow and heavy. "I have been tasked with eliminating the Timehunter societies. It is someone else's fate to find and reunite the Blades."

Her frustration coiled between us like a living thing, restless and desperate. "I want to be with you, Amir. I want to be part of your life."

"No." The word tasted like ash in my mouth. "I can only give you darkness."

It was the truth—stark, unwavering, inescapable. To pretend otherwise would be to invite ruin upon us both.

But her response was immediate, a whisper of defiance laced with something softer. "Then I will embrace the darkness. I want to help you."

Her fingers trailed up my arm in a feather-light caress, igniting something deep within me, something I had long believed to be dead.

She was an angel, too pure and bright for the shadows that clung to my existence. And yet here she was, pleading to step into my world instead of running from it.

"Don't push me away," she murmured, her voice threading through my defenses like a siren's call. "Allow me to be part of your darkness—your world."

The twist in my heart ached, deeper than I was prepared for.

She spoke of darkness as something to be embraced, not feared. As if she truly believed she could walk through the fire and emerge unscathed.

Her naivety was both endearing and terrifying.

My body betrayed me, drawn to her warmth, touch, and unwavering resolve. Every fiber of my being screamed to shield her, to keep her safe from the abyss I had long since surrendered to.

And yet, a more dangerous part of me—one I had no control over—craved her. Needed her.

Because in her arms, for the first time in my existence, the darkness felt less like a curse…

And more like home.

"My sweet venom," I rasped, my voice full of desire, raw with possession. My hands found her waist, dragging her closer until nothing was left between us—not space, hesitation, or reason.

I silenced any further discussion with a fierce, unrelenting kiss—a brand upon her lips. There was no gentleness, no restraint, only hunger clawing its way to the surface, demanding release. As our bodies entwined, I surrendered to the wildfire she ignited within me, allowing myself to be consumed by the need that raged between us.

Words became meaningless.

Only sensation mattered—the clash of light and dark, the push and pull of something ancient, something inevitable.

I should have stopped.

But I didn't.

The thought of indulging in my reckless desires loomed in the back of my mind like a gathering storm, a dark cloud ready to burst. I knew there would be consequences. There was no escaping the fallout of what I was about to do.

And yet, the temptation was unbearable.

It was like standing on the edge of oblivion, knowing one step forward could send me plummeting into ruin—and still leaning into the abyss, daring to fall.

The uncertainty, the thrill of it, consumed me. Right and wrong blurred into nothingness, swallowed by the fire she fed with every breath, every touch, every desperate pull of her body against mine.

Would this cost me everything?

Would I wake tomorrow with nothing but the ashes of this moment, of her?

I didn't know.

And I didn't care.

Because for the first time in my life, I wasn't thinking of tomorrow. I wasn't thinking of duty, of war, of consequences.

I was thinking only of her.

And I was ready to burn for it.

CHAPTER 16
AMIR

The morning light filtered through the shutters' slats, casting angular patterns across the study floor. I sat there, elbows braced against the desk, head cradled in my hands, trying to piece together the chaos of the past few days.

Elizabeth's pale-blue gaze haunted me—a maddening contradiction of fragility and determination—a woman too delicate for my world yet too relentless to be ignored. I had spent years moving through the shadows, unburdened by attachments, but now she lingered in my thoughts refusing to be silenced.

How could I reconcile her with the mission at hand? How could I protect her and still do what needed to be done?

It seemed impossible.

I exhaled, shaking my head to dispel her image. There was no time for distractions. Five Timeborne and Timebound prisoners languished in the depths of Alexander's estate—a miracle they had survived this long—a complication I could not afford to ignore.

The path before me was clear. I had to save them.

"Shadow Falcons," I called, my voice slicing through the hushed stillness of the townhouse.

They entered without hesitation—grim-faced, battle-hardened, ready for orders.

"Alexander holds five prisoners," I began, wasting no time. "Timebornes and Timebounds."

A ripple of unease passed through them. It wasn't just their status that set them on edge—it was who held them captive.

Thomas Alexander's name inspired fear among the most ruthless. The man did not grant mercy.

"I will get them out," I said firmly.

One of my men stepped forward, his voice tight with concern. "Pasha Hassan, this is a trap waiting to happen."

He wasn't wrong.

I met their gazes, reading the same hesitation in each set of eyes. They knew what I was walking into.

"I am the only trusted man within that household," I reminded them. "I will exploit that trust, set them up, and walk through their doors, not as myself—" I let the words settle before finishing,

"—but as the Black Wraith."

A beat of silence.

"Too risky," one of them countered. "You're walking straight into the lion's den."

They were right, of course. But hesitation was a luxury we couldn't afford—not with lives hanging in the balance.

"Risky, yes," I conceded, my tone brooking no argument. "But necessary. I can move through the shadows, slip in and out unnoticed. Get the prisoners to safety before Alexander suspects treachery."

Their expressions remained grim, concern carving lines into their hardened faces. But beneath what I was asking, I saw something else—trust.

Trust in me.

Trust in the Black Wraith.

Trust in the cause.

Finally, the first man exhaled and nodded, "Alright." The others followed suit, one by one.

"Good," I said, hardening my voice. "Prepare yourselves. Once I have the prisoners, I will signal. Be ready to move quickly."

As they dispersed themselves, I turned toward the window. The light had shifted, spilling fully into the room, illuminating everything in stark contrast—the dawn of a new day.

But this was no ordinary morning. It was a day edged with danger, its promise tainted by the ever-present threads of fate. Even the best-laid plans could shatter in an instant.

My fingers tightened around the quill as I brought it to parchment. Every stroke of ink was a calculated deception, a carefully placed lie.

"Meet me at the Sable Mare Tavern," I wrote, the words precise, despite the duplicity bleeding into them.

"I am the Black Wraith. I've heard you're looking for me."

Instead of wax, I sealed the missive with a smudge of soot and shadow—a mark that would be understood by those who needed to see it.

I turned to the boy waiting in the corner, his wide eyes betraying fear and understanding. He was young but had long since learned the way of the world he moved in.

"Deliver this," I instructed, placing the note into his palm. "Do not linger. Do not speak. You were never here."

He swallowed hard and nodded, vanishing into the corridor as swiftly as he had come.

As nightfall draped its ebony cloak over the city, I slipped through the secret passageways of Alexander's estate with practiced ease. The corridors were familiar, their shadows wrapping around me like old companions. Outside, my men—phantoms in their own right—waited along the perimeter, poised for the strike.

The plan was simple—free the prisoners, signal my men, and extract swiftly.

But my mind—my mind wasn't on the mission.

It was with her.

Elizabeth.

The enemy's daughter. The woman I should've never touched, never trusted. And yet, last night, I had done both. I let my guard down. I let her in not just to my bed, but into the locked vault of my past.

I told her things no one else knew—about the scars no one saw, the army I lost in Solaris, the man I used to be before this war hollowed me out.

And then she said something no one ever dared.

"You would have been a wonderful father," she'd whispered.

The words continued to hit me like a blade to the chest, carving through the walls I had spent years fortifying—a father. The thought had never crossed my mind. Duty was always my priority—loyalty to Lazarus, the mission, the war. There had never been room for such dreams.

And now, here I was, crawling through corridors with her still in my head. I had made a mistake.

I allowed myself to want.

Approaching the dungeon, every nerve in my body sharpened, attuned to the slightest sound. Something was off.

The door was ajar.

An ill omen.

A shiver crawled up my spine. My pulse quickened—not with fear, but with the thrumming pull of anticipation. Something had gone wrong.

I stepped inside. The torches blazed, casting flickering light against the damp stone walls. Chains dangled from their iron clasps, swaying slightly, empty.

Not a soul stirred.

I exhaled slowly, the sound barely more than a whisper.

"Too late."

The words charred as they left my lips. A bitter taste coated my tongue. I had come for five lives; instead, I found only silence.

Anger simmered within me, a slow-building fire. The room was too clean, too empty. They hadn't merely taken the prisoners. They had erased them. A cold, methodical execution.

I moved deeper into the labyrinthine corridors, my every step echoing against the stone. And then—

I found them.

A chamber deeper within, their bodies strewn across the cold floor like discarded remnants of a life that no longer mattered.

The Timeborne prisoners—silent, unmoving, their last breaths stolen before I could reach them.

A slow exhale escaped me, controlled—because if I let the rage take over, it would consume everything.

I knelt beside the nearest fallen man, his face frozen in the stillness of death. Reaching out, I closed his sightless eyes with a gentle touch.

"Forgive me," I murmured, the words falling like ash.

"I was too late."

A door loomed at the far end of the chamber, slightly ajar—a silent, ominous invitation—a maw of darkness beckoning.

My pulse hammered as I strode toward it, rage bursting from my veins. With one swift motion, I thrust it open.

Smoke.

A choking cloud billowed out, swallowing me whole. My vision blurred, my throat ached, and my eyes stung with the acrid sting of something unnatural. Poison.

Coughing, I staggered forward—just as the door slammed shut behind me.

Click.

A lock. A trap.

"Fuck—" The curse barely left my lips before realization struck.

Belladonna.

A slow-burning assassin's toxin, crafted for cruelty. It was designed to paralyze, incapacitate, and leave its victim aware just long enough to savor their impending doom.

And now it was in my blood.

I reached inward, grasping for the shadows that had always been mine to command—but they were distant, slipping through my fingers like mist.

Laughter—low, mocking—echoed from the smoke-filled abyss. A voice packed with malice, one I knew far too well.

"The famous Black Wraith."

Mathias.

I forced my body to move, but every limb felt heavier than the last. The air thickened, and the walls closed in.

"Did you truly believe you could outsmart us?" His voice slithered through the darkness, close now, a whisper against my fading senses.

I tried to respond, summon some rebelliousness, but the words collapsed on my tongue—

—as did my body.

I hit the cold stone floor, breath ragged, limbs failing.

The shadows that had always been my refuge—gone.

And I knew then, with sickening clarity, that I was no longer the hunter.

I was the prey.

Mathias' silhouette emerged through the acrid smoke; a phantom conjured from my worst nightmares. The cloth covering his nose and mouth shielded him from the poison, a cruel reminder of how thoroughly I had been outplayed.

"You thought you could destroy us?" His voice slithered through the air, low and mocking. "You're a fucking fool."

The Belladonna surged through my veins, a relentless riptide dragging me away from consciousness. I fought against it, clinging to lucidity, but it was like thrashing in quicksand—every struggle only hastened my descent.

"Did you think you could waltz in here and save those filthy fucking Timebornes and Timebounds?" Mathias continued, his form shifting at the edges of my blurring vision.

I gritted my teeth and tried to move, to force my body to obey me. Rise. Fight. Anything.

But my limbs had turned to lead.

Mathias advanced, his movements slow, deliberate, savoring his victory. With infuriating ease, he gripped my collar and hauled me upright, my body no more than a marionette with cut strings.

The cold bite of steel snapped around my wrists.

Chains rattled, locking me in place against the harsh stone wall.

Footsteps.

More intruders.

My vision swam, narrowing to slits as two figures stepped into view.

Lord Alexander. Lord Winston.

Alexander's piercing blue eyes, devoid of empathy, regarded me with the cold detachment of a man who believed himself untouchable. He looked at me the way one looked at the filth on one's boots—something to be scraped off and forgotten.

Winston's expression, however, seared with something else entirely—a sickening satisfaction.

"Did you think you could outmaneuver us?" Winston's voice was shrill, each syllable a scalpel meant to carve through my pride. "Imagine my amusement when I received a cryptic little note about the infamous Black Wraith appearing at a tavern. Did you truly believe we would take such bait?"

He scoffed, shaking his head.

"Gentlemen," Mathias cut in smoothly, his voice laced with cruel amusement, "let's finally see the face of the man who has haunted our shadows for far too long."

His fingers curled around the edge of my mask.

One swift motion—ruthless, unforgiving.

The mask was gone.

A charged silence followed, thick with realization.

Their synchronized gasps punctuated the moment like the final note of an execution drum.

Mathias recovered first, his tone a mixture of disbelief and morbid curiosity. "Well, well... what a surprise. Amir Hassan himself." He tilted his head, studying me as if I were some rare beast caged for his amusement. "How is this possible?"

Alexander's lips twisted into a smirk, his amusement growing as the pieces clicked into place. "Good gods, it all makes sense now." A slow chuckle rumbled from his chest. "You came here to trap us. Oh, this is rich. We knew your letter was a ruse, a desperate attempt to draw us out. But why? Why would the Black Wraith reveal himself in public?"

He began circling me, a slow, creeping poison.

"And then it became clear," he continued, his voice laced with satisfaction. "You weren't luring us out."

He leaned in, his breath hot against my ear.

"You were trying to get us away from here… so you could save them."

Their laughter filled the dungeon, hollow and mocking, reverberating off the cold stone walls—a cruel symphony of my failure.

A groan escaped my lips, heavy with my recklessness. Lazarus. Elizabeth. My men. All of them were betrayed by my arrogance, ensnared in a trap I had set upon myself.

The iron against my wrists burned, not from heat but from the bitter realization that I had given my enemies exactly what they wanted.

"Tell me," Mathias' voice slithered through the air, a viper's hiss laced with venomous amusement, "do you know who you've lured here?"

His gaze flicked to Winston and Alexander—silent sentinels of doom, standing in cruel judgment.

"He is darkness incarnate," Mathias continued, lips curling with disdain. "A vestige of my past teachings."

Then, his expression darkened further, suspicion slicing through his features. "Are you and Balthazar working together? Is he near?"

Balthazar.

The name rang in my head, absurd in its intrusion. How had Mathias' mind wandered there, now, of all times?

Even in victory, he remained shackled to his delusions. A fool chasing ghosts.

But his mood snapped in an instant.

"Enough of this," he barked, impatience seething beneath his words. "Sedate him. More Belladonna. Let him drown in his misery."

The order was given, and its execution was swift.

A sting pierced my neck—a needle, a dagger's kiss of poison. The dim room blurred at the edges as the venom sank into my veins, curling through my body like a viper. My thoughts fractured, slipping through my grasp like water, and the figures before me melted into grotesque silhouettes, their movements twisting in the flickering torchlight.

I hung there, suspended in agony, my mind reeling from pain, from betrayal, from the cruel hand of fate. And then, mercifully—

Darkness.

∞

Consciousness returned, but it was no mercy.

The air was a putrid mix of decay, sweat, and the lingering stench of old blood. My head lolled forward, my vision swimming as I entered my new prison.

A torture chamber.

A gallery of horrors where each instrument bore silent testimony to the agony it had inflicted.

I shifted, rusted chains rattling against stone, their echo joining the rhythmic, merciless drip of water in the shadows. It was a macabre symphony, each note promising suffering.

My gaze landed first on the tools of this wretched theater—pincers and tongs, their metal jaws stained with the ghosts of past victims; a rack looming in the corner, its wooden rollers warped and splintered, glistening with the sweat and screams of those who had known its cruel embrace.

Against one wall stood an iron maiden, its spiked interior waiting, patient and hungry. The door was left ajar like an invitation to hell.

Nearby, knives of every shape and size gleamed dully in the dim light—some curved like the crescent moon, others jagged, designed not to kill but to carve, to linger.

And then the ones whose purpose was more insidious—screws meant to crush, clamps meant to tear.

Every instrument in this chamber whispered a promise—an assurance of pain.

A symphony composed of sadistic minds, each tool a musician waiting to play its part on my flesh.

This was where hope came to die.

Where the darkness was not just a shroud but a living thing —crawling through the stone, slithering into the bones of every soul who had dared to resist.

And there I was, the unwilling centerpiece of this macabre tableau strung up and awaiting the conductor of my torment to begin his work.

The door to the interrogation chamber creaked open with a low, agonized moan.

Three silhouettes loomed against the dim glow of the corridor before morphing into Lord Winston, Lord Alexander, and Mathias as they stepped into the grim chamber.

Alexander's words came as a hiss. His eyes gleamed with a twisted cocktail of triumph and sadistic pleasure as he towered over me, drinking in the sight of his prisoner.

"So," he sneered, "you're the infamous Black Wraith. The destroyer of our world."

The smirk curling his lips was cruel and gleaming with savage satisfaction.

"You thought you were clever—slipping into our midst, pretending to be one of us. But we saw through your facade all along."

A slow, mirthless laugh bubbled from my throat despite the ache lacing every inch of my body.

"So, you saw through my carefully crafted facade all along, Thomas?" I sneered, tasting blood on my tongue, irritation flaring at his insufferable smugness. "Funny, considering you were the one who summoned me from Anatolia, desperately seeking my help. If you truly saw through me, why did it take you this long to catch me?"

Fury ignited in Thomas' eyes.

His smug veneer splintered.

And then—a sudden, vicious strike.

The slap landed with a resounding crack against my cheek, snapping my head to the side. Pain blossomed across my jaw, hot and immediate, but I didn't give him the satisfaction of a reaction.

Instead, I exhaled slowly, the faintest smirk curling my split lip.

Finally.

The ever-composed Thomas Alexander had fractured.

He leaned in closer, his breath hot and acrid against my skin.

"Your grand plan failed, and now you will pay for your arrogance."

His voice slithered over me, each word dripping with cruel delight. "You are the embodiment of the darkness we despise, and I will relish every moment of your suffering."

His words lashed at me, but they couldn't pierce through the armor of resignation I had already wrapped around myself.

"You're all brainwashed by Mathias," I rasped, forcing the words past the power of the Belladonna dragging me under. The poison still coiled through my veins, making each syllable a battle.

Alexander's face contorted into a wicked grin, his eyes gleaming with malice.

"We will annihilate you," he vowed, his tone final, merciless. "You will beg for mercy, but we will give you none."

I held his gaze, unflinching. I had long since stopped expecting mercy from men like him.

"And your downfall," he continued, savoring every syllable, "will be a public spectacle."

A sadistic gleam entered his gaze.

"We will strip away your facade, Amir. We will reveal the true monster within."

Then, he twisted the blade deeper.

"And my daughter—" his grin widened, "she will bear witness to your destruction. She must see the evil that lurks in your soul."

His breath fanned over my face, the sickly warmth of it sending a shiver down my spine.

A slow, creeping horror unfurled in my chest.

Elizabeth.

The thought of her witnessing this farce—seeing me brought

to ruin by men like them—sent a jagged spike of agony through me.

I should have acted sooner, not confided in her, and not let myself get entangled in the web of the enemy's daughter.

In trying to protect her from the world she was trapped in, I had failed her most cruelly.

The insidious darkness compressed in, curling around me like a vice, choking.

Regret tore through my chest, a cruel reminder of my choices.

The lingering taste of self-loathing was concentrated on my tongue—a bitter cocktail mixed with the venom that coursed through my veins.

Love—that cursed weakness—had led me to my inevitable destruction.

And now, I was drowning in it.

Not in battle. Not in war. Not by a worthy hand.

But in a cage built from my own mistakes.

And this, I realized with bone-deep certainty, was just the beginning.

CHAPTER 17

AMIR

I hung there, the cold iron chains biting deep into my wrists, each link a cruel tether to my suffering. The pain was no longer a fleeting sensation—it had settled into my bones, an endless specter whispering of my fragility.

The stench of my blood permeated the air, mingling with the damp rot of the torture chamber—a sickly reminder of the torment Mathias had unleashed upon me.

His knives, thin as whispers, had carved wounds into my flesh, each stroke a signature of his cruelty. His brands, heated in the inferno of his hatred, had seared my skin, marking me with the fire of vengeance. The whips had sung against my back, embedding their venom deep into my flesh, while hammers crashed against stone—a symphony of agony played for his twisted pleasure.

Yet, through it all, one name throbbed like a heartbeat through my soul.

Elizabeth.

Her voice—a soft melody. Her eyes—alight with defiance, with warmth. She was the balm to the brutality, the tether that kept me from succumbing to the abyss.

My heart clenched—not from pain, but from a love so deep, so fierce, it became the only force capable of defying the gravity of this hell.

With every strike, every act of cruelty Mathias devised, I withdrew into myself, retreating into the sanctuary of my memories. I clung to them as a soldier clung to his last weapon, even when my body begged for surrender.

I was chained, but I was not broken.

I would not grant Mathias the satisfaction.

Centuries of discipline, of training my mind to bend but never break, stood as my last defense. Pain became a distant echo, a dull roar at the edges of my consciousness, something to be acknowledged and dismissed.

But my body told another story.

Bruised. Beaten. Lacerated.

Every breath was a battle; each inhale laced with the taste of iron and misery. My torso—a grotesque canvas of purples and raw reds—bore the brutal artistry of Mathias' torture.

But I would not be destroyed.

For Elizabeth. For Solaris. For all that I had lost and all that remained to be saved.

The pain might erode my body, but my spirit was an impervious citadel, an unshaken fortress built upon rebellion. And from that indomitable will, I found the strength to whisper her name through bloodied lips.

"Elizabeth."

My vision swam. But then—her face. Emerging through the haze of agony, soft eyes, quiet strength, the only oasis in this desert of torment.

I clung to that image, forged myself into something unbreakable.

The heavy door groaned open.

A shadow loomed.

Mathias.

He stepped forward, surveying his work with twisted satisfaction. "Look at you, Amir. All broken. All powerless."

His voice dripped with disdain, the words slithering into the cold air like a death sentence.

I lifted my head, tasting blood and insolence.

"You're wrong."

With grim determination, I gathered the crimson pooling in my mouth and spat it at his feet—blood, teeth, and the last remnants of anything he thought he had taken from me.

"I may be chained, Mathias, but that won't stop me. I will destroy your society. I will tear down everything you've built."

Thunderous laughter.

Mocking. Deafening.

"Bold words for a man in chains," he taunted. "You don't understand, do you? You're already finished."

I let out a slow, ragged exhale, a bloody grin carving across my battered face.

"Is that what you think?"

Pain laced every word, but I savored it—a reminder that I was still here, still breathing, still fighting.

I studied him through swollen eyes, drinking in his arrogance, his belief that he had already won.

Then, I shattered it.

"I see the bigger picture, Mathias." I let the words settle and sink into his carefully curated certainty. "I know you're working with Salvatore. I know everything. You want to reclaim Solaris and rule it with darkness."

And for the first time—his mask cracked.

It was there, a flicker of uncertainty.

His breath hitched—a subtle shift.

His voice was no longer dripping with absolute confidence. "You have your memories from Solaris?"

"I do."

Each word was a battle, yet I forced them past the rawness in my throat. "You thought it was Balthazar who destroyed your School of Darkness. But it was me. I've been one step ahead of you this whole time, and I will continue to tear down every single one of your Timehunter societies."

Mathias stepped closer, his instruments of agony glinting menacingly in the dim light. "You'll regret those words."

But I held his gaze, unflinching. "You're terrified, Mathias. You and Salvatore both. Because you know when the end comes, Lazarus and I will claim Solaris. And when we do, you'll be nothing more than a forgotten name in a history of failures."

His expression darkened, but his voice remained cool, dismissive. "Salvatore is more powerful than Lazarus. You will never defeat him."

I exhaled, every breath infused with pain, but I refused to let him see weakness.

"We shall see whose power prevails."

Mathias chuckled, a low, mirthless sound. "Says the man chained to the wall, at my mercy."

"Mathias," I spat. "You act as if I know nothing. But do you understand why you've always despised me?"

The chains rattled as I shifted against the stone, the metal biting into raw flesh. "It's jealousy in its most elemental form. In Solaris, I was chosen to lead the House of Shadowbornes, to command the Army of Shadowbornes. Me. Not you."

I let the words hang between us.

"Zara chose Balthazar over you. And you've never recovered from that. You were always the pawn, Mathias—never the mastermind, or leader."

A muscle ticked in his jaw. Rage flickered deep in his eyes, barely restrained.

I smirked through my pain. "I will find a way to obliterate everything you've corrupted."

Mathias' face twisted in fury. His hands curled into fists, nails digging into his palms.

"I will kill you myself, Amir," he seethed. "But not before I let everyone witness your demise."

His voice rang out like the toll of a funeral bell. Cold. Final.

I exhaled, slowly, a bloody grin lingering on my lips.

"Your arrogance blinds you," I rasped, my breaths shallow but determined.

"In the end, it is you who will fall."

Mathias chuckled, the sound hollow and drenched in mockery. "Really? You believe you and Lazarus are a step ahead?" His dark and cruel laughter echoed in the chamber. "The evil queen has been reborn. My daughter, Alina, controls Balthazar.

And Queen Isabelle? King Armand?" He leaned in, his breath teeming with triumph. "They're gone. Killed by my hand. And they won't be returning. Ever again."

His words should have been a dagger, slicing through my resolve. But instead, I laughed—a brittle and bitter sound that rattled through my broken ribs. As my body screamed in protest, I let the laughter spill forth, mocking.

"You think you have everything figured out," I grated, spitting blood at his feet. "But in the end, we will prevail. And you…" My gaze locked onto his, unflinching. "You will die."

Mathias' expression darkened, twisted by fury.

A storm unleashed.

Pain struck like a whipcrack—his hand moving in a blurred arc, sending fresh agony rippling through my battered frame. I choked on the sensation, my body convulsing against the chains, but I did not break.

And then—the poison.

He administered another dose. A searing fire in my veins promised a torturous descent into oblivion.

I bit down hard, refusing to cry out.

Then—another voice, cutting through the haze.

"Mathias."

Ice-cold. Commanding.

Lord Alexander stepped forward, his aura heavy and oppressive, magnifying the dread that clotted the air. His fingers caressed the cat-o'-nine tails, the leather tassels whispering against one another like serpents, hissing in anticipation.

His lips curled into a cruel smirk. "Shall we indulge in some entertainment with our prisoner?"

"I would not dream of denying you pleasure," Mathias murmured, a wicked gleam in his eyes. "I want to savor this."

And then it began anew.

A symphony of suffering orchestrated with a conductor's precision.

They struck with methodical cruelty, each lash, each blow, calculated—not just to hurt, but to unravel me.

The room became a blur of agony, the walls pulsing, shifting, darkening, until I could no longer tell where I ended and the pain began.

And then, finally, they left.

I hung there, a marionette with its strings cut, my body broken, my breath ragged.

But I was still breathing.

Still alive.

Because surrender was a luxury I could not afford.

Even in the dark, as despair threatened to devour me whole—

A last vestige of resistance still smoldered deep inside me.

Time had become an enemy, stretching each second into an eternity of anguish. The cold stone of the torture chamber leeched the last remnants of warmth from my body, leaving me shivering, brittle, and alone with my torment.

Pain was my constant companion, whispering lies of defeat, coiling around me like a serpent, constricting.

And then—

A sound.

Soft, almost imperceptible.

A rustling, like the wind stirring the dust of forgotten ruins.

My battered heart, beaten into silence by agony, stuttered to life.

Elizabeth.

She seeped into the room like a salve against the raw edges of my spirit.

"Amir?"

Her voice was fragile, a delicate thread weaving through the stifling air of the chamber.

"Oh, Amir… what have they done?"

Her sobs broke against the walls, the sound carrying her anguish, her despair. She looked at me—eyes wide with horror, with disbelief, with a grief so deep it hollowed the space between us.

"What have they done to you?" she cried again.

I tried to move, every muscle in my body protesting, screaming.

Through the blur of my pain-clouded vision, I saw her—a wraith of hope and desperation, shimmering in the dark.

I forced my lips to move, my voice barely more than a whisper cracked and broken.

"You shouldn't be here."

Elizabeth ignored me.

With trembling hands, she retrieved a damp cloth from the folds of her skirt, gently dabbing at the blood and bruises marring my skin. Each touch was a whisper of tenderness against the brutality that had carved itself into me.

"Oh, Amir," she gasped, her voice laced with heartache, tears slipping down her pale cheeks. "I swear on everything I hold dear, I will make my father pay for this. For every wound. For every moment of suffering."

"Shhh, my love," I said through my battered lips. "You shouldn't have come."

"I had to."

Her hands cupped my face, light as a feather yet heavy with unspoken promises. "I couldn't leave you like this."

I clenched my jaw, mustering what little strength I had left. "Go! Do not stay." My voice, though weak, held the urgency of a dying man.

This place was no sanctuary for angels; it was a pit for monsters and martyrs.

But Elizabeth—fierce, unrelenting, my light in the dark— refused to yield.

"No!" she snapped, her voice clinging to fury and desperation. "I am here to save you! To heal you!"

My name trembled on her lips, and when she pulled me into her arms, I nearly collapsed against her warmth.

I should have resisted. I should have fought against the comfort she offered.

But I didn't.

I couldn't.

"Elizabeth..." My voice wavered a broken plea. "You can't be here. They will return. Any moment now, they will come back to continue their work."

Images of them—their twisted faces, their insatiable cruelty —flashed through my mind, burning behind my eyes with merciless force.

I swallowed hard, my breath shuddering.

"I… I am a monster."

The words spilled from me, raw, tainted with shame.

"I'm sorry, Elizabeth. I'm sorry I couldn't protect you from them."

The words sat heavy on my tongue, laced with guilt, poisonous in their truth.

My failure crushed down on me.

But she didn't recoil.

She didn't flinch.

She only held me tighter.

Her fierce blue eyes burned with an intensity that made the pain momentarily fade—a fire, raging against the darkness that sought to consume us both.

"No."

The word cut through the air.

"Stop saying that."

Her grip tightened as if she could hold me together through sheer force of will.

"I will fight alongside you. If you are trapped here, I will take the battle to them. We will tear those men down together and reclaim our freedom."

A bitter chuckle rattled through me, tinged with something dangerously close to despair.

"You have no idea what you're saying."

The words felt cruel, but they had to be.

I lifted my head, forcing her to see the truth in my battered face, in the blood that stained the floor beneath me.

"They don't just want to kill me, Elizabeth. They want to make an example out of me."

My voice was raw, hoarse, laced with something darker than pain—acceptance.

"They want to break me, display my ruin for the world. They

want to prove that the Black Wraith is nothing more than a shattered man, a whisper of rebellion crushed beneath their boots."

But the thought of losing her—of her standing in their line of fire—was a wound I knew I wouldn't survive.

I needed to make her leave.

For good.

Before it was too late.

CHAPTER 18

ELIZABETH

I huddled in the corner of my alchemist cottage, the scent of crushed herbs and minerals in the air, clinging to my skin like the ghosts of failed remedies.

Tears streaked down my cheeks, etching clean paths through the grime smudged across my face. I had tried not to cry. I tried to block out the echoes that slithered through the night, but Amir's cries reached this far—my supposed sanctuary, deep within the woods.

Every sound from the dungeon was a brutal reminder of his suffering, his torment, and his slow undoing at the hands of my father.

I placed a shaking palm against the wooden worktable, peeling myself from the wall. Alchemy. I had to focus. I had to do something.

But as I reached for my tools, my body shuddered, a silent rebellion against the horrors unfolding beyond my reach.

My father had become more demanding.

Tasking me with poisons day and night, new brews, stronger venoms, deadlier weapons.

And now—his latest command chilled me to my very core.

I was to craft a poison stronger than Belladonna—one meant for Amir.

I stared at my hands, at the trembling fingertips hovering over the mortar and pestle. I had the means to obey.

But I also had the means to raze everything to the ground.

The Noctyss flower.

Nestled within my grasp like a death sentence ready to be rewritten.

With it, I could obliterate them all. My father. His men. The entire wretched Timehunter society.

I reached for the pestle, but my hands trembled too violently. It slipped from my grip, clattering to the stone floor with a deafening crash.

I couldn't do it.

Each motion felt like a betrayal.

The thought of harming Amir shredded what remained of my already tattered heart.

Memories flooded my mind, unwelcome but desperately clung to.

Amir shielded me from my father's wrath that stormy night, his arms a fortress around me.

His body and soul had met mine in his sleeping chamber, searing away the cold fear with something raw, unbreakable.

The whispered vows of vengeance we had spoken in the dark.

The plans we had woven together, our rebellion a tapestry of justice and destruction.

But now…

Now, those plans felt like distant dreams.

Dreams torn from my grasp by the cruel hands of my father.

And by the man I was meant to marry—

Lord Winston.

I was trapped. Caged.

The word circled like a vulture over carrion, persistent and suffocating. Trapped by duty. By blood. By love.

I was Elizabeth Alexander, daughter of Thomas Alexander— forced to choose between the man who gave me life and the one who made that life worth living.

No more.

With determination hardening in my bones, I brushed away the remnants of herbs from my hands and set to work. Grief could not save Amir. Despair could not change my fate. Action would.

Once unsteady with sorrow, my fingers now moved with tenacity honed by love.

"I love you, Amir," I whispered into the silence of the alchemist's cottage. "I don't care about my father. I'm going to heal you. He won't torture you anymore."

The words, spoken aloud, solidified something within me.

I turned to my shelves, hands carefully selecting only the most potent healing agents—roots of renewal, elixirs of restoration, powders that could mend flesh and stave off infection.

I filled the vials one by one, sealing them with wax and setting them aside with the tenderness of a promise.

But healing him was not enough.

I needed a way to reach him.

The glass vials and dried herbs before me were no longer mere ingredients—they were allies of subterfuge, instruments of rebellion.

The soft grind of mortar and pestle became the drumbeat of my defiance.

A sleeping draught.

I worked quickly, combining elements with careful attention, adjusting the mixture until its consistency was perfect—potent enough to numb the most hardened man.

I was ready when the evening unfurled its dark cloak over the estate.

I moved like a wraith through the halls, invisible, unheard, the vials tucked carefully within the folds of my dress.

The smoking parlor awaited.

And so did the brandy bottle.

An unwitting accomplice to my silent rebellion.

With sure hands, I uncorked the decanter, pouring the clear liquid into the amber spirits, watching as my betrayal dissolved seamlessly into the depths.

A part of me marveled at the ease of it.

Another part quaked at the implications.

Retreating to the front parlor, I picked up my embroidery hoop, the delicate fabric stretched taut beneath my trembling fingers. The needle moved in and out—a mindless, rhythmic dance that belied the chaos within me.

Yet, my focus lay elsewhere.

Every sense was attuned to the sounds beyond the room, my pulse counting the moments until Lord Winston's arrival.

And then—the doorbell tolled.

Deep. Ominous.

A knell rang out through the hollow silence of the house.

I forced myself to remain seated, my hands never ceasing their work, though the stitches grew erratic with anticipation.

Through the veil of my lashes, I watched the maid scurry past, her footsteps swift as she hurried toward the grand entrance.

Now.

I slid from the parlor, melting into the dimly lit hallway. The silk of my skirts barely whispered against the polished floors as I pressed myself into the shadows.

Then—his footsteps.

Heavy. Ponderous.

Each step echoed through the hushed halls, a dreadful cadence of power and arrogance.

Lord Winston had arrived.

"Ah, Thomas," his low, crawling voice slithered through the air. "Let us retire to your esteemed smoking room."

My father's response was a murmur, indistinct, but their footsteps soon merged as they moved down the corridor. I did not need to see them to know what would follow.

I could envision the two of them settling into the leather chairs, brandy in hand, to discuss the ruin of lives.

Unaware that swift and unforgiving sleep was already curling its fingers around their throats.

I did not breathe.

I did not move.

I slipped away only after their footsteps faded, quick and quiet, no more than a shadow swallowed by the night.

Back in my bedchamber, I waited.

The heavy fabric of my gown lay around me, its folds closing in like the petals of a flower shrouded against the dark.

"Patience," I whispered to the restless spirit within me.

"For Amir, you must be patient."

Time trickled by, each second stretching into a cruel eternity. I paced back and forth, my breath shallow, my pulse hammering against my ribs. The wooden floor beneath me groaned as though it strained under my thoughts.

Then—silence.

A profound, eerie stillness settled over the house, a hush so absolute it felt as if the world held its breath.

This was it.

With cautious steps, I slipped from my chamber, my fingers brushing along the cool banister as I descended. The touch anchored me in a sea of uncertainty.

The smoking parlor loomed before me, its door a silent sentinel guarding the truth of my actions.

I placed my ear against the polished wood, my breath shallow, my heart a tireless drumbeat.

Nothing.

No murmurs. No shifting movements.

Just silence.

A tentative tap of my fingertips against the door yielded no response. Emboldened, I curled my fingers around the handle and opened it.

And there they were.

My father. Lord Winston.

Slumped across the chairs, tangled in their limbs, oblivious.

The brandy had done its work.

Their chests rose and fell in a slow cadence—the breathing of men too deep in the clutches of an enchanted slumber to dream, conspire, or stop me.

Relief surged through me, but I couldn't bask in triumph. Not yet.

There was still so much to do.

Clutching a torch, its flame flickering in time with the urgency pounding in my veins, I moved.

Toward the dungeon.

Toward Amir.

The corridors twisted and darkened as I descended, the air growing colder and heavier. The shadows stretched toward me like hungry hands, reaching and grasping.

But my determination flamed brighter.

Brighter than the fear. Brighter than the dark.

And no shadow could quench the fire that raged within me now.

"Amir."

His name left my lips in a whisper, barely more than a breath.

My knees hit the cold stone floor, the impact jarring but insignificant compared to the pain tearing through my chest. He was a ruin before me—bruised, broken, reduced to a mere shadow of the man I knew.

I gathered his battered hands in mine, holding onto him as if I could tether him back to life.

"Amir, I shouldn't have left you yesterday. I should have come sooner."

His eyelids fluttered, his breath shuddering from his lips. "Elizabeth… why did you return?"

"Shhh," I hushed him, brushing damp hair from his fevered forehead. My fingers trembled against his clammy skin. "My father is under a sleeping draught. He won't know."

I reached for the vials I had spent the night crafting—my weapons of salvation, my last defiance against the cruelty that had left him in this state.

I administered them individually; each sip met with a wince, and each swallow a battle. His resilience, even now, left me breathless.

"Rest now," I murmured, rubbing a cool cloth against his burning skin. "Let these mend what cruelty has tried to break."

His eyes drifted closed. For a moment, peace.

And then—

His eyes snapped open.

Torches flickered, their unsteady glow casting jagged shadows across the torment carved into his face.

His breathing came fast, ragged, his fingers curling into fists. A war waged within him—against the pain, against me.

And then, in a voice hoarse with suffering and something far worse—regret—he rasped, "I was foolish to fall in love with you."

The words sliced through me.

"You weakened me," he gasped, every syllable wrought from agony as if each one tore from his soul. "You brought me to my knees. I should never have let you in."

A choked sob clawed its way up my throat.

"No, no," I whispered, my hands trembling as they cradled his face as if I could hold him together through sheer will alone.

"You can't mean that. I am your strength, Amir. Not your weakness."

His head jerked, shaking violently as though trying to expel some terrible, unbearable thought. "No," he croaked, his voice a raw wound. "You must leave this place. You must go to the Americas, my love. It's safer there than here. The only way to escape the grasp of the Timehunters."

His eyes held me captive, desperate.

"Pack your bags and go with Mary," he demanded, his eyes smoldering with something deeper than pain—dread and resignation. "Leave me to face this nightmare alone."

His plea cut through me sharper than any blade.

"I won't leave you," I hissed, my voice like a drawn wire, trembling.

"I will recreate the Noctyss poison. I will bring it to the masquerade. I will annihilate them all. They will not win. They will not break you."

A shudder racked his body, but it wasn't pain that caused it. It was something darker. Something festering deep inside him.

"You were my downfall," he growled through clenched teeth. "My one weakness."

The words struck like a whip, carving into me, but I did not waver.

"I promised we would destroy them together," I countered, my fingers finding his, gripping them tight despite the tremors agonizing me.

His skin was cold, clammy, weakening.

"No. We can't," he whispered. "I should never have agreed to that. Salvatore and Mathias are too powerful. Your father will kill you."

His breath hitched, his fingers tightening around mine like this was the last time he'd ever hold them.

"Escape, Elizabeth. Go. Start anew somewhere far away, where no shadows lurk in doorways. You are young. Beautiful. You deserve a kind husband and a happy home. Leave these monsters behind."

I stiffened.

The words—get away, escape, leave it all behind—felt vile on my tongue, foreign and wrong.

"Get away?"

I spat the words, my revulsion abundant in the air between us. "You think I could ever run? That I could ever abandon you?"

I shook my head, fire searing through my veins, my fury a beacon against the oppressive gloom of the dungeon.

"No, Amir. I will not run. I will make sure this masquerade happens. I will find a way to release you. You can't stop me."

My grip on his hands tightened.

"I will kill them."

Every. Last. One.

Amir tried to shake his head, but the effort was futile—his movements hindered by the shackles of both his wounds and the unforgiving chains that bound him.

"Elizabeth..."

His voice was weak, stripped of its usual steel, his once-commanding being diminished by captivity and his concern for me.

I leaned closer, so close that my lips nearly brushed his ear.

"I am not the girl you think you need to protect," I whispered, my breath a vow against his skin. "I am the woman who will stand with you against the darkness."

And at that moment, I swore to myself—I would walk through the fire, become an instrument of vengeance before I would ever let them harm him again.

No more waiting.

No more fear.

I retrieved the vial, its contents shimmering faintly in the dim light. The liquid caught the torch's glow, swirling like molten gold in my palm.

I held it to Amir's parched lips, my hands firm despite the storm.

The potion slid down his throat—a silent prayer, a final rebuttal against the ruin they had tried to carve into him.

For a moment, nothing.

A breathless pause in the cold hush of the dungeon.

Then—color.

Gradually, the ghostly pallor of his skin gave way to a fragile warmth, the deathly sallow replaced by the faintest flush of life.

His chest rose and fell with more purpose.

Hope flickered.

I clutched his hand, my grip fierce. "You can't stop me. Regain your strength."

His eyelids fluttered, those dark, haunted eyes regaining their fight.

"I can't regain my strength."

His words were sluggish, edged with something raw. "I haven't killed..."

The sentence trailed into a grimace, the truth too bitter to fully voice.

A chill slithered down my spine.

"What do you need?" My voice was urgent, willing him to ask for anything but that.

His jaw clenched, his fingers tightening around mine.

"I need to kill."

A grate, hollow and irrevocable.

"I must inhale the souls of the dead."

His admission was a death knell, spoken with the resignation of a man who knew his nature too well.

A cold shiver coiled through me—but I didn't flinch.

Didn't hesitate.

Didn't question.

I locked away the moral quandary for another time, burying it beneath the urgency of what needed to be done.

I met his gaze without flinching. "I'll bring them," I said, my voice unshakable, born from something deeper than mere conviction.

Worthless men would be a small price for his recovery.

As I exited the dungeon, the flicker of my torch sent twisting shadows slithering along the stone walls, mirroring the darkness unfurling inside me.

This was the path I had chosen.

No turning back now.

The next day, as I lingered outside Father's study, the muffled voices within sent a different kind of chill.

Lord Winston. His voice, as grating as ever, dripped with arrogance.

But the other—a voice steeped in cruelty—made my breath still in my chest.

Mathias.

"We can just gut Hassan," my father's voice came, casual, careless, as if he were discussing the pruning of an overgrown hedge rather than the brutal execution of the man I loved.

A cold hand gripped my heart.

"Out of the question," Mathias countered, his tone one of absolute control. "We want a public execution."

My stomach twisted.

"We will show the people what happens to those who stand

against us," he continued, his voice dripping with malice. "They must fear me. They must fear us."

Each word was a dagger.

A blueprint of Amir's suffering, of his staged, bloodied downfall.

No.

They would not have their spectacle.

Not while I still drew breath.

A fire erupted in my chest, and before I could temper the fury clawing its way through me, I shoved the study door open with enough force to send it slamming against the wall.

All eyes snapped to me.

A moment of silence, as thick as a storm cloud.

"Elizabeth!"

My father's voice cut through the air, edged with disapproval. "Where are your manners?"

Manners?

They plotted a public execution, and he dared to chastise me for decorum?

I swallowed my revulsion, inhaled slowly, and then let my voice spill into the room—mocking, hollow, poisoned with ice.

"Forgive me," I murmured, feigning breathlessness, my heart hammering beneath my corset.

Then, I tilted my head, eyes locked onto Mathias' soulless gaze, mimicking his chilling words back to him.

"Yes, let's make a spectacle out of Lord Hassan's suffering."

Let's see if they could stomach the taste of their cruelty.

Lord Winston's face twisted into something wickedly delighted, his milky eyes gleaming with sick satisfaction as if he had just witnessed a prized possession come to life.

"You're finally coming around, my darling! This is wonderful!"

The words coiled around me like a noose.

I smiled, letting false enthusiasm coat my voice like honey over poison.

"Yes, my lord! I have seen the light."

The endearment tasted like bile. A reminder of the role I must play.

"We will make this masquerade truly unforgettable," I purred in a light voice, eyes gleaming with a fire they mistook for ambition. "We will strike fear into everyone."

Father's gaze settled on me, pleased, his eyes glinting with approval. Mathias, standing beside him, let a smirk curl on his lips.

"This is wonderful." He exhaled, pleased. "How you've grown, Elizabeth! You and your husband will rule the English society. You will make a fine wife to Lord Winston."

My stomach turned.

The very thought made my skin crawl and my hands tremble with the urge to tear him apart.

But I masked it. Smoothed it over with a serene, practiced smile.

"Yes, Mathias." I nodded as though I were truly honored. "I will ensure the masquerade is a masterpiece of fear."

Father leaned forward, interest piqued.

"Tell me, Elizabeth, how is the poison coming along?"

I did not hesitate.

"Very well! It will destroy our prisoner," I said, my voice clear, betraying not a single crack. "His suffering will be talked about for years."

Their satisfaction was palpable.

As I turned to leave, I could feel their expectant gazes on my back, my departure a final act of obedience to their vile plans.

But once I stepped into the night, back into the cool silence of the forest, the mask cracked.

I ran.

Not in fear—but in desperation.

When I reached my alchemist's cottage, deception no longer throttled me—it fueled me.

In the dim candlelight, my fingers found the velvety petals of the Noctyss bloom.

Lethal. Unforgiving.

"I'm going to make the most powerful poison."

The words slipped from my lips, not a whisper, but a promise.

I would orchestrate this masquerade.

I would be the unseen hand, guiding them toward their demise.

I closed my eyes and pictured Amir—walking free from his chains, his strength restored, his enemies crumbling around him.

And then I pictured my father.

Lord Winston.

Their lips parted, gasps of agony spilling forth as their bodies succumbed to the venom I would slip into their veins.

A masterpiece of ruin.

I exhaled, slowly, my resolve hardening into something unbreakable.

"I will be the one pulling the strings."

CHAPTER 19

ELIZABETH

A week had trickled away like sand through my fingers, each grain a moment stolen from me—a moment I hadn't spent with Amir.

The herbs I had left him—a desperate concoction of comfrey and willow bark—were nothing more than a feeble balm, a temporary salve for wounds that demanded something far darker to heal.

I knew the truth.

I had always known it.

He needed to kill. He needed to consume souls.

And I had promised him I would bring him the worthless—the men who deserved no mercy.

But time, that unyielding thief, had slipped through my grasp.

The masquerade loomed just days ahead, approaching like a rising tide, swallowing me whole.

My father had chosen me as the organizer of the affair, not out of trust or admiration but because he knew my dutiful nature would ensure his grand vision came to life.

So, my days were spent wading through the suffocating tedium of preparations.

And my nights—my nights belonged to the poison.

A lethal elixir, crafted under the hush of candlelight, a silent assassin waiting to be unleashed upon those who had orchestrated Amir's suffering.

I was the conductor of this firestorm.

The household erupted into a frenzy from the moment my father announced the date—a Thursday, to avoid clashing with the Countess' ball.

Servants scurried through the halls, each seeming to grow an extra pair of hands.

Invitations were sent within the week.

Handwritten by Mr. Gainsborough, his script was flawless, and every swirling letter sealed fate upon fate.

Each envelope bore the family crest in red wax—an emblem of power, dominance, and the illusion of control.

But they had no control.

Not over me.

Not over what was coming.

The estate, though grand, could scarcely contain the flood of Timehunter guests and their insufferable "plus ones" who had eagerly accepted our invitation.

Thus, Kew Palace was chosen—an opulent jewel on the outskirts of London, a venue renowned for its grandeur, gilded excess, and deceptive beauty.

A place fit for kings and queens.

A place that would soon become a graveyard of the unsuspecting.

As I entered, the chandeliers dripped with light, diamonds splintering across the polished floors. Servants bustled like ants through golden corridors, ensuring that every detail—from the placement of roses to the arrangement of seating—was executed with meticulous care.

A spectacle of perfection.

It was a performance for those who had no idea they were walking straight into the final act of their existence.

The palace itself became a stage.

Garlands of fresh greenery—rosemary for remembrance, lavender for fleeting peace—were woven through the balustrades, filling the air with a false sense of serenity.

The silver was polished to a mirror shine, reflecting the faces of men who believed themselves untouchable.

The chandeliers in the grand ballroom were cleaned, new candles refitted, ready to cast a golden glow upon the unwitting damned.

Outside, I commanded the footmen to sweep the front drive until every speck of gravel was aligned.

Carriages would arrive one after another, delivering lambs to the slaughter.

And I would be there, smiling, welcoming them to their fate.

My attire took no small effort.

Madame Beaulieu, London's most sought-after modiste, had sent her assistant for the final fitting of my gown.

A vision in pale-blue silk.

Pearls embroidered along the bodice—tiny, delicate things, like tears frozen in time.

Exquisite.

Restrictive.

A masterpiece of beauty meant to stifle.

Mrs. LeClair, my hairdresser, promised to arrive early on the day of the event to sculpt my hair into an elegant tower of ribbons and feathers.

I would be painted, adorned, and transformed into the perfect image of grace and poise.

It was a beautiful lie.

For beneath the lace, beneath the silk, beneath the carefully applied powder and rouge—

I was a storm waiting to break.

Yet, before the storm could come, I had to perfect the illusion.

The menu planning became my battlefield, a silent war over silver platters and gilded table settings.

The cook and I debated for hours.

Should the pheasant be roasted or braised? Would a venison pie be too rustic?

Would they suspect poison in the turtle soup?

Ultimately, we settled on roasted peacock, turtle soup, and decadent pastries that rivaled the king's table.

But the true indulgence?

Fresh strawberries.

It was outrageously expensive this early in the season, but I dismissed the cook's protests with a flick of my wrist.

"It will set the right tone."

Death deserves a touch of luxury.

The music had to be perfect.

Musicians were hired—not just any musicians, but the best.

A quartet for dinner, a harpsichordist for the dancing that would follow.

I designed the dance cards, embossed with gold filigree, a small extravagance justified by the deception at play.

Still, I would not allow innocence to suffer alongside guilt.

The musicians would be gone before the poison touched a single goblet.

There was no sense in spilling blood that did not deserve it.

In the solitary confines of my cottage, I toiled.

The flickering candlelight bore witness as I worked, its feeble glow illuminating the cold alchemy of vengeance.

The grind of the pestle against the mortar was a slow, rhythmic dirge—a death knell in motion.

Every grain crushed, every liquid distilled, was another step toward the inevitable.

And yet, as my hands moved with practiced ease, my thoughts drifted.

To him.

To the dungeon's cold embrace, where Amir languished.

I could almost feel the chill of the damp stone against his skin, the bruises forming beneath his chains.

I ached to go to him.

To press the vials into his trembling hands, to whisper promises of escape against his fevered skin.

But the dungeon was forbidden to me.

Sealed off by my father's iron decree.

"Elizabeth," he had said, his voice a steel trap snapping shut around me, "your place is here, overseeing the final touches. We cannot afford distractions."

Distractions.

That was what he called Amir.

As if he were a mere inconvenience. As if he were not my very heartbeat.

Though spoken under the guise of concern, his words were nothing more than chains—meant to keep me locked away in duty.

But shackles could break.

And soon, very soon—they would.

I retired to my room each night, but the rest never came.

The pain of longing pushed against my chest like an iron shackle, unrelenting.

I yearned to slip through the shadows, vanish into the night, and find my way to him.

To Amir.

He was trapped in that dungeon, and yet, it was I who felt imprisoned.

I was a prisoner in my own home, bound by duty and expectation—by the hidden eyes watching my every move, whispering my father's will.

I fought in the quiet hours before dawn when the world held its breath.

Fought the war between responsibility and love.

The masquerade demanded my focus.

But it was Amir's suffering that claimed my soul.

And with every beat of my heart, it murmured a promise.

Find a way.

Find him.

The masquerade loomed over me like a tempest cloud, its preparations an intricate dance of deception and death.

But death required meticulousness.

I unlatched the weathered door to my alchemist's cottage, slipping inside the only place where I could shed the facade of the dutiful daughter and embrace the monster I was becoming.

Upon the workbench, the Noctyss poison lay in wait in the dim candlelight.

Nearly complete.

All but for one final, crucial ingredient.

The blood of darkness.

A chill ran down my spine.

There was only one way to obtain it.

Mathias was beyond my grasp—a phantom lurking in the periphery of shadows.

But Amir…

Amir was close.

Amir's blood would serve as the key.

I inhaled, my decision forged in the fire of necessity.

Under the cover of night, I would seek him out.

I would draw forth the darkness from his very veins.

For the poison to be complete—he must bleed.

Days blurred together, an endless tide of orders and arrangements.

And then, my father presented a solution.

A solution as twisted as it was fortuitous.

"We have new hands to assist us, Elizabeth," Father announced, his voice curling with amusement, his eyes gleaming with something cold, something cruel.

"Lord Winston's staff will join our ranks."

A slow, dark smile curled at the edges of my lips.

Perfect.

"Surely, Father, their number is insufficient for grandeur as you envision," I countered smoothly, feigning concern as my mind sharpened with purpose.

I knew full well what Lord Winston's servants truly were.

Creatures whittled from the same rotten wood as their master.

Men soaked in sin, stained beyond redemption.

"Ah, but they are well-versed in our... unique requirements," Father assured me, his words slithering through the air like serpents.

A plan unfurled within me, slow and deliberate, like the petals of a night-blooming flower.

A plan steeped in dark promise.

"Perfect," I murmured, my heart quickening with wicked anticipation. "I shall see to their integration myself."

A simple sentence, innocuous in sound—but beneath it lay an unspoken vow.

I would bring them to Amir.

The very filth that served Winston, that obeyed without question would serve another purpose now.

Their tainted, corrupt souls would be his sustenance.

And then—he would rise.

The masquerade would not be a triumph of social graces.

It would be a reckoning.

With the stage set and the players unknowingly cast, I retreated to my chambers, my carefully woven deception pressing against my skin.

Each tick of the ornate clock upon my mantel was a heartbeat—Counting down.

To the moment I would unleash Amir's might upon them all.

That night, I stood at my chamber window, watching.

My father. Mathias. Lord Winston.

Three monsters cloaked in wealth and power slipped into their carriage like vipers retreating into the dark.

The heavy curtains fell shut, sealing them inside—conspirators bound by whispers too grave for my ears.

Their secrets evaporated before they could reach me, carried away in the cold night air.

The horses snorted impatiently, their breath curling into the darkness, and with the snap of the reins, the carriage rolled away to some clandestine rendezvous.

Let them scheme.

Let them believe they were untouchable.

They had no idea what I was preparing in their absence.

I turned from the window, my pulse even, my resolve honed to a deadly edge.

There was work to be done.

My gaze swept the corridors until it landed upon her.

The maid.

The one who eagerly warmed Lord Winston's bed, her laughter too free, too bright for this house of horrors.

She was the perfect offering.

And I felt no guilt.

None.

I approached her, my voice smooth, coaxing. "Come."

She hesitated, brow furrowed.

"There are items we require from below."

The others followed.

Lord Winston's newly-arrived staff—filth from a decaying estate.

They exchanged uneasy glances, their expressions flickering between ignorance and suspicion.

One of them, braver than the rest, cleared his throat. "We know not the way to this vault you speak of."

A pathetic attempt at resistance.

I tilted my head and let my lips curve into a slow, knowing smile. "Follow me."

My voice was not a request.

It was a summons.

And so, they obeyed.

We descended.

Down the spiraling staircase, deeper and deeper into the bowels of our home.

With every step, the air grew thicker.

Darker.

The flickering torches cast shifting shadows along the damp stone walls, an eerie waltz of light and dread.

They did not yet know—did not understand where I was leading them.

Not to some harmless vault of treasures.

But to something far worse.

At last, we reached the heavy door—a barrier between the living and the damned.

living and the damned.

I rested my palm against the cold iron, my pulse thrumming in anticipation.

On the other side, Amir waited.

And tonight, he would feed.

"In here."

My unwavering voice carried through the dungeon as I gestured toward the cell where Amir was held.

They hesitated.

Lord Winston's men—wolves in their own right, now fumbling, uncertain.

Their gazes passed between one another, searching for some unspoken assurance, some silent order that would not come.

They did not yet understand.

But they would.

"Inside," I commanded again, the finality in my tone leaving no room for argument.

Reluctantly, they obeyed.

I stepped in behind them, and before the last of them could turn, I slid the heavy bolt into place.

Locked. Sealed.

Their fate was set in iron and stone.

A shudder raked through my hands—not fear.

Something far more potent.

Something wild.

As the last echo on the stone faded, I turned.

To Amir.

His chains dangled loosely from the wall like serpents waiting to strike, and in the dim glow of flickering torchlight, I saw the slow rise and fall of his chest.

A predator lying in wait.

"What are you doing?" one of the men stammered, his voice brittle with unease.

"Silence," I snapped.

They huddled together now—frightened sheep, sensing the wolves closing in.

"Amir."

His name was a whisper, a call.

I stepped forward, closer to the shadows within shadows.

And then—his eyes found mine.

Dark. Hollow. Waiting.

A flicker of life burned there, an ember within the abyss.

His voice was rough, edged with exhaustion, but beneath it, there was something else—admiration.

"Elizabeth."

The way he spoke my name sent a pulse through my veins.

"What have you done?"

I pushed them forward.

Trembling. Weak. Prey.

"I've delivered Lord Winston's forces," I declared, my voice strong with purpose.

"I want you to kill them."

They stiffened, the truth dawning upon them.

"You're getting weak, Amir. You need to regain your strength," I said, forcing steadiness into my voice as worry coiled in my chest. "The success of the masquerade depends on you."

But more than that—I could not bear to watch him suffer another day.

The pain in my chest was an ache too deep to name.

"And, truly, I cannot live knowing how you are suffering, my love."

A slow, satisfied exhale left him.

"Ah, my sweet darling venom."

His voice slithered through the dungeon, a sound both affectionate and lethal.

He struggled to rise, his movements slow, strained.

But in his eyes—anticipation.

Hunger.

A promise of strength renewed.

And then—he smiled.

Not a cruel smile. Not entirely.

But something dark still lurked behind it.

"I have never met such a determined woman," Amir murmured, his voice bouncing off the stone walls.

"I do not deserve your kindness."

"Don't say that," I countered, my tone hardening like tempered steel.

"I would do more," I whispered, the words catching on the edge of a breath. "Whatever it takes."

I stepped forward, brushing my fingers along the rough stubble of his cheek before pulling a small, hidden key from my pocket.

The key to his freedom.

I put it into the iron lock, meeting his gaze.

"Be free," I whispered.

The metal clinked.

He rose.

Unsteady at first, his body was a battlefield between hunger and weakness.

But his eyes—

His eyes were alive.

Smoldering.

And then—he moved.

The first to fall was the woman.

Her lips parted in a breathless gasp—but it never became a scream.

His hands closed around her throat.

No hesitation. No mercy.

Her body convulsed, the death rattle barely leaving her lungs before the silvery coil of her essence began to rise.

Drifting from her skull, curling, shimmering.

Amir breathed it in.

His muscles tightened. Swelled. Strength surged through his veins.

His hunger was no longer a whisper.

It was a storm.

And he was just getting started.

The remaining staff stumbled backward, their faces carved in sheer terror.

But I did not move.

I stood still—watching.

Captivated. Entranced.

This was no mere slaughter.

This was art.

Every motion of Amir's body was precise, the embodiment of lethal grace.

And when he fed—

It was reverent.

A ritual long-practiced—devotion to the darkness within him.

And something within me…

Stirred.

In the farthest corner of the dungeon, two figures huddled.

The last of them.

One was slight and ugly, his body curling inward like a worm trying to burrow itself into stone.

The other, a heavier man, his breath wheezing from lungs filled with too much fear.

The slight one begged.

His voice was frantic, fractured, pathetic.

"Someone help me. This demon is going to kill me."

His plea hung in the air.

Unanswered.

Because no one would save him.

Not the gods.

Not fate.

And certainly not me.

I could not move.

But it was not fear that rooted me in place.

It was something else.

Something unnamed.

Something that pulsed beneath my skin, warming me from the inside out as I watched Amir advance.

There was no hesitation in his steps.

Only certainty.

The certainty of death's embrace.

Like a harvester reaping his yield, Amir took their lives.

Their silvery, fragile essences unfurled from their flesh, drawn forth by his touch—

And he drank them in.

Their souls coiled into him, binding with his own.

And as the last wisp of life faded from the air, Amir stood transformed.

No longer weakened.

No longer starved.

But reborn.

Silence filled the dungeon.

The only sound was our breath—his, steady and whole. Mine were uneven, shaken by what we had done.

And as it all pressed against my chest, I realized—

We had crossed the threshold.

There was no turning back.

Our freedom would be bought in blood and darkness.

The last echoes of deathly silence shattered under something primal, something insatiable. Amir turned to me, his dark eyes alight with a hunger that hadn't been there before. Power rippled off him in waves, a force both intoxicating and dangerous. I was still drowning in the aftershock of his resurgence when he stepped closer, erasing the space between us with a predatory grace.

"Elizabeth," he murmured, his voice a low, velvety rasp that slid over my skin. "Your aid is… invaluable."

Before I could respond, his lips crashed against mine, searing, consuming, a kiss that decimated the hesitation and left only raw, aching need. It was not tender. It was possession—fierce, unrelenting. His fingers tangled in my hair, tightening just enough to steal my breath, to make my pulse hammer with something wicked. He tasted of dark promises and whispered sins, of power barely leashed beneath the surface.

I melted into him, my hands clutching the fabric of his shirt as if it could anchor me against the storm of his desire. He pushed me back until I was trapped between him and the cold stone wall, his body a furnace of heat against mine. Every shift and movement sent sparks racing across my skin, stoking the smoldering fire between us.

I wanted more. More of his darkness, control, and touch's dangerous allure. But with a gasp, I forced myself to break away, my lips ghosting over his in a lingering tease before I spoke.

"I'm going to release you and—"

Amir pulled back quickly, his grip on my arms firm and unrelenting yet not cruel. The air between us cracked with something heavy, something unspoken.

"No," he commanded, his voice low and final, laced with a force that struck like a blow. That single word sent a tremor through me, igniting something deep and primal. His voice had once rallied armies—a sound that allowed no rebuttal.

His gaze locked onto mine, dark and demanding.

"You can't release me," he continued, his tone measured but edged with a quiet ferocity. "I will stay here. I will pretend I am still broken." His fingers ghosted over my pulse, his touch both a caress and a warning. "You will go to my men. Tell them what happened. They will believe you. Tell them to surround the building. They must be anywhere and everywhere. They will blend in."

A dark smirk curved his lips, the barest flicker of amusement breaking through the calculated coldness. "I will come to the masquerade. You can be certain of this."

His hands slid down my arms, teasing, possessive, before settling at my waist. His grip was light—deceptively so—but there was no mistaking the control in his touch.

"Put poison in their food and drink," he murmured, his voice a dark caress against my ear. "But be careful, my love. I couldn't bear it if harm came to you."

The warning shivered through me, a stark reminder of our fine line. The stakes were high; every detail of our plan was crucial to its success. One wrong move, one misstep, and we would be the ones to fall.

Amir's hands lingered at my sides, grounding me. "Stay away from Mathias," he added, his tone dropping lower. "Women are his weakness. We must ensure this ball is filled with other beautiful women to distract him. He likes to play with them."

His words were strategic, but beneath them lay something unspoken. Perhaps concern, or simply the calculated care of a man who knew that misdirection was key to survival.

Then, almost imperceptibly, his expression softened. "Although none will be as captivating as you, my love."

The warmth in his voice was fleeting, quickly replaced by the cold focus of a man prepared for war.

"Stay as Lord Winston's obedient betrothed."

It settled over me. We were stepping into something irreversible, weaving a web of deception that, if tangled, could be the death of us both. The walls of this society were closing in, and we had only one chance to bring them down from within.

I swallowed, steadying myself before I met his gaze. "Amir," I whispered, my voice hushed. "There's one thing I still need from you."

His eyes darkened slightly, assessing me, reading the unwavering determination behind my words.

"I need your blood to complete the poison."

The request lingered between us like a whispered oath, a dark covenant binding us in ways neither dared to name. He didn't flinch, didn't hesitate. Instead, he extended his arm with practiced grace, the flickering torchlight casting jagged shadows across the lines of his face.

My pulse quickened.

I glanced around the dim dungeon, my breath shallow, until my gaze landed on a jagged shard of stone jutting from the crumbling wall—crude but lethal enough.

I wrenched it free, the rough edges scraping against my palm. The sting barely registered. My focus was locked on him, on the unwavering trust in his gaze and the quiet dominance in the way he watched me—waiting.

The cold stone tore against his skin as I dragged it down in a shallow cut. His breath hitched. A single, ragged intake—so brief it was almost imperceptible—but I felt the tension that coiled in the air between us.

Crimson welled against his swarthy complexion, blooming in a slow, hypnotic trickle.

My fingers slid between the curves of my breasts, grazing flushed skin as I retrieved the glass vial nestled there. I pulled it free, its warmth proof it had been resting against me for far too long. Holding it beneath his wound, I watched, transfixed, as each drop of his essence fell into the vial, swirling like liquid rubies.

Something visceral stirred in me. I should have looked away and been clinical and methodical, but I wasn't. I was entranced. I was mesmerized by the way his life bled for me willingly, as if he'd surrendered something deeper than flesh—something twisted, sacred, and utterly his.

Once I had his blood, I corked the vial and tucked it back between my breasts. My gaze drifted to Amir's hand—his blood still trickling, dark and warm. Desire curled in my belly. Slowly, I lifted his hand to my lips, breath trembling, heart pounding, as I pressed a kiss to the wound before letting my tongue taste him.

The metallic tang of iron flooded my mouth, rich and intoxicating. His blood—hot, vital—seeped into me, igniting something deep, something raw. It spread through my veins like fire, like power, a wicked hunger unfurling in its wake. I shuddered, my entire body alight with something dark and insatiable, something heedless of consequence.

A deep, guttural sound escaped him—a growl, a warning, a surrender. His eyes burned, wild and untamed, locking onto mine with an intensity that frightened and thrilled me. It was as if an otherworldly force had taken hold of us, binding us in a feverish madness where desire and destruction were indistinguishable.

His scent—sweat, leather, raw need—wrapped around me, pulling me into his gravity like a moth to a flame. And when his lips crashed onto mine, it was violent, desperate, unrelenting. There was no gentleness, no hesitation—only hunger, only need. His mouth claimed me, his tongue tangling with mine in a battle as fierce as the fire raging between us.

I gasped into him, my hands clawing at his chest, at his

shoulders, pulling him closer, needing more. He pushed me back against the cold stone, his hands rough and insistent, pushing my skirt higher, fingers burning against my bare skin. My hands fumbled at the laces of his breeches, trembling with urgency. The ache between my thighs was unbearable, maddening—I didn't just want him; I needed him, like air in my lungs, like the blood that had just passed between my lips.

His body crushed against mine, hard, and hot. Through the thin barrier of clothes, I could feel him—every rigid, aching inch. My breath hitched as his hands gripped my hips, bruising, possessive, demanding. My fingers found him, wrapped around him, feeling the pulse of his need, the way it mirrored my own.

His forehead against mine, his breath ragged, his control slipping like sand through his fingers. "Do you feel this?" he grated, his voice rough, guttural, laced with torment and pure, unfiltered lust. "This is what you do to me."

Then, with a swift, commanding motion, he lifted me, his hands gripping me with bruising possession. My back hit the cold stone wall, but I barely registered it—because in the next breath, he drove into me.

A raw, animalistic groan tore from my throat. "Amir—"

Never before had I felt so unchained, so free. Something vital and untamed had awakened inside me, something I couldn't explain—something I didn't want to explain. I could only surrender, wrapping my legs around him, pulling him deeper, gasping as he filled me.

"More," I whispered, my nails raking down his back, desperate, greedy. "Don't stop."

A dark, approving sound rumbled from his chest, low and feral, vibrating through me like a violent storm. His fingers dug into my hips, holding me as he thrust again and again, each movement brutal and demanding. I gasped at the intensity, the way he stretched me, the way he claimed me. I felt split apart, overwhelmed—yet I still wanted more.

"Look at me," he ordered, his voice a razor's edge of dominance.

I did.

His eyes were ablaze, wild with something that bordered on madness, his pupils blown wide with unrelenting hunger. The flickering torchlight cast shadows over his sweat-slicked skin, over the tension rippling through every muscle in his body. He looked like a god of war, a conqueror—and I was his spoils.

And I wanted to be conquered.

His pace turned relentless, each movement a savage demand that sent pleasure crashing through me like a raging tide. Every nerve in my body seared, the fire growing hotter, devouring me whole.

The world outside this moment ceased to exist.

There was no time. No morality. No reason.

Only this. Only him. Only us.

"Elizabeth," Amir hissed before capturing my lips in a bruising, possessive kiss. His teeth scraped against my bottom lip, dragging a whimper from my throat as he owned my mouth the same way he owned my body.

"Amir," I groaned when I came up for air, my head tilting back against the cold stone. I needed him. I needed the way he filled me, stretched me, and drove me to madness with every brutal thrust.

The intoxicating symphony of heat and desire between us was unstoppable, unbreakable.

I raked my nails down his shoulders, my fingers digging into his skin, leaving fire trails in their wake. His head snapped back, a low, guttural growl rumbling from deep in his chest. The unrestrained sound sent another bolt of heat coursing through me, the kind that devoured, wrecked, ruined.

We were tangled in a maelstrom of passion—dark, desperate, delicious. Each movement pulled me deeper into the storm, into the abyss of him, where only pleasure existed. His thrusts turned merciless—faster, harder, deeper. Every stroke was a claim, a demand, a silent vow that said I was his.

And gods help me—I never wanted to belong to anyone else.

The pleasure built, winding tight, a blistering, unbearable crescendo. His name tore from my lips in a breathless, broken plea. He was ruthless, and I was helpless against the force of him, against the overwhelming pleasure that shattered me.

We unraveled together.

My body clenched around him, my climax ripping through me like wildfire, stealing the breath from my lungs. Amir followed, his body stiffening before he let out a deep, throaty groan—a sound of pure, unbridled satisfaction—as he buried himself inside me, spilling his pleasure into me like he never wanted to let me go.

For a long moment, neither of us moved. We were wrecked. Breathless. Bound by something neither of us could name.

And then I felt it—the filth beneath me, the decay of the dungeon around us, the stench of death clinging to the air. How had we found love in a place so tainted by despair?

But love we had found. Dark. Twisted. Unstoppable.

"Elizabeth," he growled, his voice still rough with lingering desire, still edged with that untamed, animalistic hunger. It reverberated through the stone chamber, through me.

"Together, we will conquer the world, and you and I will be free."

I met his gaze, my lips curling into something sinful, something knowing. "I can't wait," I murmured.

The scent of blood clung to the air, mingling with the damp rot of the dungeon. The dead bodies strewn across the stone floor were a silent testament to our fight—a macabre declaration that we had stepped beyond the point of hesitation.

There was no turning back.

Mathias, Lord Winston, and my father were likely toasting their victories in some candlelit tavern, oblivious to the storm brewing beneath their feet. They had no idea what was coming.

Amir and I rose in unison, the eerie stillness settling like a final benediction.

"Well?" I asked, casting my gaze over the carnage as I straightened my skirts, my fingers still slick with the night's work.

Amir merely shrugged. "Warriors do as they must."

With effortless strength, he reached down and seized the arm of a lifeless man, dragging him toward the dungeon's darkest recesses. His movements were practiced. This was not the first time Amir had hidden bodies in the shadows, and it would not be the last.

I stepped over the corpse of the woman who had been with Lord Winston, a flicker of something jagged twisting in my chest. Pity? Regret? No. Those emotions were as dead as the bodies at our feet.

Side by side, Amir and I worked in silence, concealing the evidence, stuffing them beneath the rotting husks of the countless Timebornes who had been tortured here before them. Our victory crushed me, suffocating, exhilarating.

I had no idea if our plan would succeed.

I had never done anything like this before.

But I would not falter. I would not fail.

Not Amir. Not my mother's dying breath.

Not the promise I made to scorch my father's wicked society to the ground.

I had already stepped into the abyss.

Now, I would set it on fire.

CHAPTER 20

AMIR

The cold stone of the dungeon walls was nothing compared to the heat that surged within me. It was the night of the masquerade—the night everything would change. As I paced like a caged beast in the dimly lit cell, I could feel the power thrumming through my veins—a gift from Elizabeth—her alchemy, her sacrifice.

She had given me what I needed—the bodies, the strength, the will to rise again.

I halted mid-stride, every sense going taut as Elizabeth's silhouette appeared in the archway. The light from the corridor beyond framed her, casting a golden glow over her pale skin and wheat-blond hair. In the dimness, her blue eyes gleamed—not with hesitation but with shared understanding.

I crossed the space between us in an instant.

My hands found her face, firm and grounding. Our eyes locked briefly before our lips met in a kiss with urgency and unspoken promises. It was not a kiss of hesitation or doubt—a seal upon the night ahead, a confirmation of the storm we would unleash.

When we pulled apart, my fingers lingered against her cheek, tracing the delicate contours of her face—the face of a woman who had not only stood by my side in whispers and shadows but in blood and fire.

I let my forehead rest against hers. "Elizabeth," I murmured, my voice low and full of promise. "Once this night ends, once we have torn down the tyranny that shackles us, I long to see a world where we are finally free."

It was not just a wish. It was a vow.

She exhaled softly, a whisper of fabric against stone, as she stepped back into the shadows, her presence receding but never gone. She was in me now—in my pulse, in my breath, in every fiber of my being.

Tonight, we would bring ruin upon those who had kept us in chains.

And nothing—not power, fate, or death—would stand in our way.

The stillness of the dungeon ended with a whisper.

"Amir, the men are ready."

Elizabeth's voice sliced through the darkness, quiet but firm. The promise of what lay ahead clung to every syllable, yet fear did not linger in her tone. As the faintest quiver ran through her hands, her gaze scorched with insolence, unwavering in purpose.

"The poison is made," she continued, locking eyes with me. "And it is perfect."

Something clenched deep in my chest at the sight of her standing before me, caught between fear and unshakable determination. She had never done this before. But she would not break. She was too strong to shatter.

"I know you're nervous," I murmured, stepping closer, our breath mingling in the cold, damp air. "But you have the strength of the fiercest warrior and the heart of the purest soul. You will not fail."

She drew in a breath, a quiet nod her only response, but I saw it then—the shift, the straightening of her spine, the tightening of her grip.

"We will succeed," she whispered, as if speaking it aloud solidified it into existence. "The poison is ready. It will be in their food and drink. Everything is falling into place."

"As it should," I said, voice low, firm.

I reached out, fingers brushing against her cheek in a fleeting moment of solace. A touch meant to ground her, to remind her she was not alone in this.

Her eyes met mine one final time, and then our lips collided in a fierce, fleeting kiss that carried no softness, only purpose.

A vow. A promise sealed in the dark.

Then, without another word, she was gone.

But her warmth lingered, a ghost of a promise hanging in the cold air.

I slipped my hands into the waiting shackles, the cold bite of metal closing around my wrists. My body sagged, my head bowed, every inch of me transforming into the image of a man beaten, broken.

But beneath it all, my blood thrummed with fire and vengeance.

"Play your part," I whispered to myself, letting the illusion take hold, sinking into the guise of frailty.

The shadows would be my ally.

They would not see the warrior within.

Not until it was far too late.

The dank air of the dungeon clung to every surface, a miasma of decay and rot so thick it felt alive. I had grown accustomed to it—the way it curled into the lungs, settled into the skin —until it became as much a part of me as the iron bite of my shackles.

But their faces twisted in disgust when Lords Winston and Alexander descended into my fetid prison.

"Good lord, what a smell!" Lord Winston's voice cut through the gloom, his delicate sensibilities affronted by the filth they had left me in. He was a specter of rot himself, yet the irony of his repulsion was utterly lost on him.

"It is fitting for the likes of him," Lord Alexander sneered, his cold disdain ricocheting off the stone walls. Both men held perfumed handkerchiefs to their noses as if such a feeble barrier could protect them from the reality of their sins.

Their laughter—a hollow, chilling sound—filled the chamber. It was the kind of laughter that mocked the dead who could no longer take offense.

I remained motionless—a broken thing in their eyes.

But inside, the fires of retribution seared hotter than any torch they could bring against me.

Lord Alexander remained out of reach.

"Did you know you were planning your death?" His voice slithered like a serpent, full of venom and dark amusement. "When you came to us all those weeks ago, speaking of this grand masquerade... who knew? You were designing your execution."

He stepped closer, relishing the moment, eyes gleaming like a wolf scenting blood.

"We're going to break you, Amir. Slowly. Every last one of us will take a piece of you. We will carve your disobedience from your bones, burn you, make you beg for death."

His lips curled into a wicked grin, feeding off his cruelty. "And then, my dear Elizabeth will add the finishing touches— with her poison."

My stomach coiled at the mention of her name, but I did not move. Did not speak.

He thought he had won. He thought I had lost.

A rumbling laugh escaped him, deep and cruel, before he turned and bellowed into the shadows—

"Guards! Bring me the gilded cage!"

The command reverberated off the stone walls, a cruel decree meant to herald the spectacle they intended to make of me. Yet beneath their arrogance, a secret thrill coiled in my veins.

For this masquerade was mine.

And the final act had yet to play.

The dungeon's air echoed with the sound of approaching boots, the cadence menacing—a funeral march for men who did not yet know they were dead. Shadows stretched long and distorted against the damp walls, crawling forward like specters ushering in their doom.

Then, with a grating echo of metal against stone, the gilded cage was dragged into my cell.

It was a grotesque display of opulence, its golden bars

gleaming in the dim light. It was a mockery of imprisonment meant to parade me through the streets like a captured beast. But the fools had yet to realize that this prison was not my tomb.

It was their pyre.

Six men struggled beneath its weight, their breaths ragged, their muscles straining. The putrid stench of death curled through the air, clinging to them, thick enough to choke. One of them—a broad-shouldered brute—stumbled mid-step. His face twisted in revulsion, his body convulsing.

Then, with a violent gag, he doubled over and retched.

Satisfaction curled at the edges of my lips. Good. Let them taste the rot they had cultivated.

"Good gods," Lord Winston wheezed, his voice taut with disgust. He clutched a silk handkerchief to his lips, his aristocratic repulsion writ across his pale features. His gaze turned to mine, meeting my eyes for a fleeting second—before he looked away.

Coward.

"Alexander, let us leave at once," he muttered, swallowing against the bile rising in his throat. "These men will do their job and transport him to Kew Palace."

Lord Alexander did not move immediately. His icy gaze lingered on me, as cold as a dagger's edge, a silent promise of suffering yet to come.

I did not look away. Let him watch. Let him believe.

But whatever taunt he had prepared died before it could leave his lips. The stench overpowered his sadistic amusement, and with a final glance, he turned on his heel.

They retreated as hastily as dignity would allow, their silks and arrogance wilting under the decay that clung to this place.

They thought I was caged.

They thought I was defeated.

But soon, very soon, they would learn—

A gilded cage did not make a man tame.

It made him patient.

And patience was the deadliest weapon of all.

The front of the cage swung open with a creak, a sound that

might have signaled captivity—but to me, it was the sound of inevitability.

I let my body slump forward, every movement slow, designed to deceive. To sell the illusion. A man beaten, broken, stripped of the fight that once made him dangerous.

They wanted to believe it.

And so, I let them.

The guards sneered as they shoved me forward, their laughter grating against the dungeon walls, full of cruelty and arrogance.

"Get in there, you sorry excuse for a rebel," one barked, shoving me into the metallic enclosure with a force that might have meant something had I truly been as weak as they thought.

I offered no struggle.

No protest.

My limbs buckled on command, my body crumbling onto the cage's cold floor like a hollow shell of the man I once was.

They jeered at my pathetic collapse, watching with smug satisfaction as I curled into myself, nothing more than a relic of defiance.

Fools.

They saw a prisoner.

They did not see the embers smoldering beneath the ash.

With a grunt, the guards hoisted the prison onto their shoulders, removing me from the dungeon's depths into the crisp night air. The cold bit into my skin, starkly contrasting to the heat thrumming beneath my ribs—the fire of what was coming.

The cage rattled, the metal groaning beneath the shifting weight. Every footstep sent vibrations through the bars, the clanking of iron against cobblestone ringing through the streets like a death knell.

They grunted, their breaths puffing in the chill as they labored to carry their demise.

They did not know it yet.

But I did.

With each jolt of the wagon as they loaded me into its darkened belly, my body swayed with the motion, but within—my heartbeat was constant.

A drum of impending retribution.

They thought I was being delivered to my execution.

But I was being delivered to theirs.

I let out a low, guttural moan, feigning pain, my voice weaving through the wooden slats of the wagon, threading weakness into the night. Each sound was a deliberate note in the symphony of deception, a carefully crafted illusion meant for any watchful ear lurking in the shadows.

The ride was brutal, each jolt and lurch rattling my cage, throwing my body against the iron bars. I let it. Every shudder, every groan was a calculated performance.

But beneath the veil of frailty, strength pulsed through my veins.

I was no longer the hunted.

I had become the hunter, lying in wait.

As the wagon rumbled to a halt, the deafening roar of a bloodthirsty crowd greeted me. Their cheers surged through the night, an orchestra of cruelty, a prelude to the final act of this masquerade.

Kew Palace loomed before me, bathed in golden light—ornate, gleaming, decadent. It was a palace built on power and corruption, its grand halls now serving as the stage for my supposed downfall.

Rough hands clawed at me, dragging me from my confines, their fingers digging into my arms as they paraded me before the sea of masked faces. Laughter swelled, a hideous revelry, each jeer a celebration of my suffering.

And then I saw her.

Elizabeth.

Radiant, poised—a blade wrapped in silk.

But my breath caught, my heart constricting at the sight of Winston's gnarled fingers curled around her wrist.

The sight of his hand upon her was a slow, agonizing poison.

Her gown cascaded around her, a waterfall of silk and lace—

a portrait of innocence, yet her eyes told another tale. Steel cloaked in velvet, fire smothered beneath constraint.

And in that instant, my determination hardened into something unbreakable.

Lord Winston did not yet know it.

But after tonight, his hands would never touch her again.

A slow, burning fury coiled in my gut, its heat spreading through my limbs, but I did not move. Not yet.

Instead, I exhaled, soft, patient.

"Stay strong," I whispered, the words barely leaving my lips, a silent vow carried on the wind.

For now, I would play the part of the puppet in chains.

But soon—very soon—

The strings would be cut.

And vengeance would be mine.

Lord Alexander's voice thundered over the revelry, each syllable honed like a blade.

"Ladies and gentlemen," he proclaimed, his tone slicing through the noise, demanding absolute attention. "Thank you for gathering here tonight for this momentous engagement—a union of two powerful families that will solidify our strength and secure our future.

"The wedding will occur next week, and you are all invited to witness this historic alliance. But tonight—"

He paused, his gaze sweeping over the room—cold, calculating. He let the tension coil tighter, feeding off the anticipation.

"Tonight, we celebrate!"

The crowd erupted into applause, their cheers emboldened with the excitement that only power and cruelty could inspire.

Then, Lord Alexander raised a single hand, silencing the room. His voice dropped, weighty and intentional.

"As you all know, our society has been ruthlessly hunted, our ranks ravaged by a shadow in the night—by the infamous Black Wraith."

A murmur rippled through the gathering, uncertainty slithering beneath their gilded masks.

"But tonight—" he continued, his voice rising with

triumphant certainty, "the reign of terror ends. Thanks to the unwavering efforts of Mathias Allistar, Lord Winston, and myself, we have captured the Black Wraith!"

He extended a hand toward me, a grand gesture to mark my fall.

"Tonight, you no longer need to fear this ghost."

The crowd erupted into a tempest of sound—gasps, cheers, wild applause. Their hunger for spectacle contorted their faces into grotesque masks of glee and contempt as they came closer, the pulse of their collective malice swelling.

A few brazened souls spat in my direction, their disdain flung through the air.

Most missed.

One did not.

A wad of spit slapped against my cheek, sliding down my skin like an insult made flesh.

The roar of approval was deafening, their perverse pleasure swelling at the sight of my supposed humiliation.

But I did not move.

I remained as still as stone, my expression unreadable.

I let their hatred wash over me like rain against a mountain—irrelevant, passing, incapable of erosion.

This was not the time for anger.

This was the time to endure. To outlast.

A single word from Lord Alexander split through the cacophony.

"Silence!"

And just like that, they obeyed.

Every eye snapped back to him, every breath hitched in waiting. He held them in the palm of his hand.

"Now that he is caught," he continued, "you will all partake in his torture and death."

A new kind of stillness filled the crowd—one bursting with anticipation.

Lord Alexander turned, his gaze flickering briefly to his daughter. Elizabeth.

His voice darkened, dripping with sick pleasure.

"My daughter, our next alchemist, has created something powerful."

A murmur of intrigue swept through the gathering.

"We will watch as his skin melts away. And then—"

He smiled.

"We will cut him apart. Piece by piece."

The horror of his words settled deep into my bones, an echo of the depravity that had ruled this place for far too long. Yet outwardly, I gave them nothing.

These people—these monsters in silks and masks—knew nothing of justice.

They mistook cruelty for strength and savagery for power.

They relished in mutilation, not understanding that their thirst for blood would soon remain unquenched.

Lord Alexander's voice boomed with unrestrained glee.

"We will begin this grand event with a toast!"

A raucous cheer erupted from the crowd, their lust for my suffering thickening the air like smoke. Faces blurred together, distorted by their revelry, the heat of their excitement swirling.

My gaze cut through them, seeking her.

Elizabeth.

The one thread of light in this tapestry of shadows.

"Let's drink!"

The roar swelled, clinking crystal, and bubbling anticipation as servers scurried like ants at a feast, pouring champagne into eager glasses.

"To the death of the Black Wraith!" Lord Winston bellowed, his voice slicing through the merriment like the fall of a guillotine.

As one, they lifted their glasses.

A crystal sea caught the flickering candlelight, glimmering like a thousand knives poised above my throat.

And amongst them—Elizabeth stood still.

Her chalice untouched.

Her complexion pale beneath the golden glow, her lips frozen just above the rim of her glass.

Then, her eyes met mine.

I held her gaze, unwavering—a fortress of silent strength.

Her own wavered for just a breath, a flicker of vulnerability masked beneath steely resolve.

She had done her part.

Now, it was time for me to do mine.

The moment stretched, taut and trembling, teetering on the precipice of fate.

And then—Lord Alexander turned.

Laced with authority, his voice snapped the tension like a blade slicing through the cloth.

"Mathias, I give you the honors to start first."

A hush fell over the crowd.

Mathias moved forward—a shadow harboring death.

He approached with the confidence of a man who believed he held fate's strings.

His dagger glinted—a sliver of moonlight against the abyss of his dark attire.

He raised the dagger, its steel catching the glow of the chandeliers, the cruel smirk of a man certain of his power.

And yet—he had no idea his demise was already at hand.

"Balthazar and I have a history," he snarled, my mentor's name dripping from his tongue like venom. "But you… you took my School of Darkness. You carry memories from Solaris. That's a problem. You need to be eliminated."

His words were meant to unnerve.

Instead, they only fed the fire smoldering within me.

He turned, snapping his fingers toward the guards lurking in the shadows.

"Get him out of this cage so I can begin the torture!"

Six men advanced, their movements mechanical, without hesitation as they wrenched me from my gilded prison. I did not resist.

I let my body slacken, a portrait of a man truly broken, my limbs yielding to their grasp as though spiritless—a ruse woven of necessity.

But beneath the surface—every muscle coiled.

Every fiber of my being braced for the storm.

Mathias' grip tightened, the dagger trembling ever so slightly in his grasp, its poised edge a viper ready to strike.

But the fangs would never reach me.

Because before steel could taste my flesh—pandemonium erupted.

A collective shudder rippled through the crowd, the gaiety of moments before twisting into something else—something horrific and unnatural.

Confusion. Horror. Convulsion.

A murmur of unease became a cry of agony.

Bodies jerked, hands clutching at throats, backs arching grotesquely as realization struck too late.

The venom of betrayal flowed—not from Mathias' blade—

But within the very veins of the assembly.

Elizabeth's masterstroke.

The champagne.

Her silent ally in this masquerade of death.

Mathias' eyes widened as the first lord collapsed, his noble facade writhing in agony, his lips frothing.

Then another.

And another.

Lords and ladies crumpled where they stood, their limbs contorting in unnatural shapes.

Their wretched symphony rose, screams, gurgles, and bodies collapsing like marionettes with their strings severed.

Mathias turned, his voice tight with panic, fury, and disbelief.

"What the fuck is going on?!"

He stood frozen, dagger still raised, but his power—his moment—had already been stolen.

The great lords of this society—the ones who had called for my torture, who had toasted to my execution—

Were now dying before me.

The illusion of their power collapsed in real time, and their wealth and titles became meaningless as they choked on their arrogance.

I did not waste the moment.

With predatory swiftness, I lunged to my feet, my hand snapping around Mathias' wrist like a vice.

He gasped, startled, his once-unshakable confidence now a thing of the past.

The room spun as my body fought against its own exhaustion. Darkness crept at the edges of my vision, whispering for me to succumb, but I would not.

I anchored myself to this world, to this moment.

Towering over the chaos, I stood defiant as the nobility writhed at my feet.

"You forgot about the powerful alchemist in France," I bellowed, my voice a blade, slicing through the terror.

"You thought it was me. You should have listened to my warning."

Mathias' wild eyes darted across the room, desperately trying to piece together the nightmare before him.

He lashed out—a frantic, uncoordinated attempt at control.

But the poison was merciless.

It stripped him of his precision, his balance—his very dignity.

His blows were weak and ineffectual, a pathetic display of a man who had once believed himself untouchable.

His strength bled out of him with every passing second.

And then, I moved.

Surging through the convulsing masses, an apparition of vengeance.

The air reeked of death and dying grandeur, their once-opulent laughter now guttural gasps, choked screams.

Still, my thoughts flitted to Elizabeth.

The architect of our salvation.

She had vanished.

A clawing sense of unease stirred in me, but there was no time to falter. I needed to gather my men.

I needed to seize control of the chaos.

And then, I saw them.

Alexander and Winston.

The titans of this society were now nothing more than writhing corpses-in-waiting.

They twitched and convulsed on the opulent floor, their power stripped, their wealth offering no salvation.

I loomed over them, my shadow stretching long and mercilessly over their tormented forms.

"You should see your faces," I snarled, my voice a dark hymn, each word dripping with finality.

"You seemed to have forgotten my warning when I first entered your home. You were so focused on destroying the Black Wraith that you failed to fear the one true force that could undo you. The powerful alchemist in France. Perhaps you should have spent less time hunting me—And more time fearing them."

Alexander's eyes, wide with horror, darted helplessly, his mind frantically searching for an escape that did not exist. His lips parted in a silent scream, but no words came. There was nothing left to say.

They had played their game.

And they had lost.

I leaned close to Mathias, my breath warm against his paling skin, my voice a low growl laced with triumph and warning.

"You are nothing but a pitiful fool," I whispered, each syllable a dagger sliding between his ribs. "Barely worth a second glance."

Mathias shuddered, his body betraying the terror he refused to voice.

I let the moment hang, savoring his helplessness.

Then, I smirked.

"If only Balthazar could see you now. The sheer delight it would bring him to witness your downfall would be… immeasurable."

A choked gasp rattled from his throat, but he had no strength left to fight.

"Another of your so-called societies lies in ruins," I continued, my tone almost mocking, a slow dismantling of everything he once stood for. "And no one is coming to save you."

I let the silence stretch, watching his composure crack.

"No one."

His breath hitched.

The fear in his eyes deepened, widening into something close to understanding.

Too late.

"This is how you meet your end," I said, my words dropping like a stone into the abyss of his fading consciousness. "Crumbling. Defeated. Forgotten by all."

I straightened, letting my gaze drift over the wreckage of the men who had once ruled with impunity.

"In the end, Lazarus and I will reclaim Solaris as our own."

I watched as the last flickers of resistance faded from his trembling form.

"And you—you and Salvatore will fade into eternal oblivion."

I took a step back, my eyes cold, unforgiving.

"Erased from existence."

Mathias' eyes flickered with the last, dimming light of comprehension as the poison turned his veins into rivers of fire.

His lips parted, a final, strangled breath escaping—a useless plea to a world already leaving him behind.

And then, something darker than the room emerged from the shadows.

Salvatore.

He did not step into the light. He annihilated it.

The glow of dying candles seemed to recoil from him, shrinking away as if his being devoured illumination.

His cloak draped over his hunched frame, its tattered ends dragging like funeral veils across the cold marble. The fabric hung from him like decay incarnate, as if he had been stitched together from the remnants of old kingdoms and forgotten nightmares.

And his face—carved from vengeance itself.

A mask stretched too tightly over angular bones; skin pulled thin where veins slithered like blackened tributaries beneath the surface. The creases etched deep into his flesh were not from age alone—they were the scars of a man who had ruled through terror, who had built an empire on the bones of the fallen.

His eyes—glacial, endless, distant—gleamed with something inhuman.

Not madness.

Not cruelty.

Something worse.

Something that knew far more than any mortal should.

And then—he smiled.

It was a ghastly thing, the corners of his lips tugging back ever so slightly, revealing teeth yellowed with time and stained with something older than wine or rot.

He did not speak.

He did not need to.

The room felt smaller beneath his existence.

A moment passed—one heartbeat stretched into eternity.

Then, he rolled his neck, the tendons pulling taut beneath his paper-thin skin—

And roared.

The sound was not human.

It ripped through the chamber, an earth-shattering, marrow-deep bellow that threatened to tear the very foundation apart.

The walls trembled.

The floorboards groaned.

The air seemed to crack and shudder beneath that sound.

Every muscle in my body seized.

And my heart—

My heart lurched.

Because Elizabeth was nowhere in sight.

"Elizabeth," I breathed—barely a whisper, yet it pierced the chaos.

Bodies collapsed around me—choking, convulsing, dying. The masquerade we had so carefully crafted was dissolving into ruin with Salvatore here. Poison laced the air, its scent acrid and metallic, a twisted symphony of death. Screams echoed, then faded into silence, one by one.

And she was gone.

Nowhere by my side.

Nowhere safe.

Then—through the swirling mist of death—I saw her.

Across the ballroom, her silhouette emerged. She was cloaked in black, her face masked, the same attire she wore in France.

In her hand, the final vial. The last of the poison.

And she was aiming it at him.

Salvatore.

"No," I whispered, horror freezing my blood. "Elizabeth... don't."

She moved.

Poised with deadly accuracy, she threw the vial at him.

"ELIZABETH!" I roared, surging forward, sprinting toward her—toward them. My heart was pounding, and desperation was clawing at my throat.

But the vial had already shattered.

A noxious cloud exploded through the air, rushing out in all directions. I was too close—too slow. The poison hit me like fire, slicing into my lungs. I gasped, choked, staggered.

No—no—NO!

Salvatore reeled back, shadows erupting around him. He moved fast, slipping just beyond the edge of the poison, escaping into the dark like a serpent.

He didn't inhale it.

I did.

I stumbled, but through the burning and haze, I saw him strike.

His hand shot out—grabbing her.

Elizabeth's body jerked in his grip, and before I could scream, before I could reach her, he hurled her across the ballroom.

Her body hit the wall with a sickening crack.

She crumpled to the ground—motionless.

"Elizabeth!" I tore across the room, falling to my knees beside her. My lungs singed, my vision swimming, but none of it mattered. Nothing mattered but her.

Her skin was pale, and her breath shallow. Blood stained her lips. Her eyes fluttered open—just barely.

"I'm here," I choked out, gathering her in my arms. "You're okay—you're okay—I've got you—just stay with me—please—"

Her lips moved, but her voice was gone. Her body trembled in my hold, fading, fading...

With an inhuman roar of unrestrained fury, Salvatore seized Mathias' lifeless body, lifting it high above his head with an iron grip.

His knuckles turned bone-white, his sinewy arms tensed like iron cables, and every muscle in his form coiled with unearthly power.

And then he screamed.

Not a sound.

Not a mere shout of anger.

A bellow of wrath so raw, so volcanic that it tore through the very bones of the palace.

The air itself trembled.

And then—the explosion.

A blinding detonation of rage, a shockwave of destruction that ripped through the grand hall with a force that defied nature itself.

The world shattered.

The remaining walls detonated outward, massive slabs of stone and brick hurtling through the air like cannon fire. The earth quaked beneath Salvatore's fury as though the palace screamed in its final moments.

The lime plaster blew off the walls, revealing the crumbling skeleton of the structure beneath.

The boiserie—the intricate, gilded wooden panels—shattered into a thousand deadly splinters, turning into a hurricane of wooden daggers, piercing flesh, marble, and glass alike.

What had once been a palace of decadence, power, and tyranny—

Was now a war zone.

I clutched Elizabeth to my chest, shielding her broken body

from the chaos around us. Blood coated my hands, but I didn't let go.

The world tilted. The palace trembled—stone groaning under destruction.

And then—

Lazarus.

He burst from the ruin like a phoenix from flame, dust, and debris parting around him. His eyes locked onto Salvatore's with the force of a lightning strike—pure, unrelenting fury.

The air between them crackled, charged with ancient energy, something older and darker than the crumbling stone, and spilled blood around us.

Salvatore sneered, lips peeling back to reveal jagged, decayed teeth—a predator savoring the kill. With a flick of his hand, shadows slithered forth, curling around Mathias' broken form. In a breath, the body vanished, swallowed whole by the darkness—erased from this place, claimed by Salvatore's void.

And then—he moved.

With a sweeping gesture, his hands sliced through the air, fingers carving an intricate and monstrous pattern like a curse written in motion.

The world answered.

A sickening hiss, low and venomous, slithered through the chamber. The walls shuddered, and cracks spiderwebbed across the ceiling.

And then came the flood.

From shattered stone and blood-soaked earth, they rose—

Serpents.

A writhing tide of scales and fangs spilled across the ruined floor like a living nightmare. They surged forward, over corpses, over the dying, over the barely breathing.

Screams pierced the air—the last survivors scrambling, desperate to escape.

But there was nowhere to run.

The vipers coiled around limbs, their fangs sinking into flesh. The scent of venom and blood overwhelming.

I tried to hold Elizabeth, tried to pull her closer—

But my grip slipped.

My body—betraying me. The Noctyss poison that had invaded my veins was tearing me apart, sweltering like wildfire, hollowing me out with every breath.

Then—

Lazarus appeared.

His form blurred, flickering through my failing vision, but his voice was solid.

"I've got you, Amir."

His grip was iron, unyielding, anchoring me when everything else fell away.

And then—the shadows came.

A void darker than night, blacker than ink. An abyss that swallowed light, sound, everything.

Salvatore's fury.

The dying screams.

The writhing serpents.

All gone.

The world was erased in an instant.

I felt myself slipping—falling into the dark.

And for the first time since this nightmare began—

I let it take me.

When I awoke, Anatolia greeted us with its timeless serenity—a world untouched by the devastation we had left behind.

The air was crisp with ancient power, and the very stones beneath me hummed with history. It was a place of refuge, of forgotten strength.

But none of it mattered.

Elizabeth lay beside me, deathly still.

Her skin, pale as moonlight, seemed almost translucent beneath the celestial glow of this sacred place.

And her breath—

So faint. So fragile.

Panic surged through me.

"Lazarus!"

My voice came out as a desperate croak, raw and broken.

A sickness still curdled in my veins, tendrils of poison twisting through my lungs like malignant fog.

I tried to inhale, but each breath was a battle—ragged, wheezing, drowning in my own body's failure.

Every gasp burned. Every movement sent agony lancing through me.

But none of it mattered.

Only her.

The shadows stirred.

Lazarus emerged, silent and composed, both a balm and a warning.

I couldn't read him.

Not now.

Not when I was unraveling at the seams.

"Please," I rasped, my voice scraping against the silence. "Heal her. Save her."

My words echoed off the walls, a command and a prayer entwined in desperation.

I didn't care what it cost.

"Whatever you do, save her."

The words hung between us, heavier than the very history of this place.

My vision blurred, darkness creeping in once more, tugging at the edges of my consciousness.

I reached for Elizabeth, my fingers trembling, my strength draining away.

My body betrayed me, the last of my willpower gave way to exhaustion, poison, grief.

And just before the void pulled me under—

I held onto one final, desperate hope.

That Lazarus could undo what Elizabeth had sacrificed herself to achieve.

And then—

Oblivion took me.

CHAPTER 21

ELIZABETH

I awoke to the caress of silk brocade beneath my fingertips, the fabric cool and unfamiliar against my skin.

A dim glow surrounded me—countless candles flickering in their sconces, their flames casting eerie shadows across the vaulted ceiling.

My head throbbed with crushing pressure as if it were caught in a vise, each pulse of pain sending waves of disorientation through me.

Where was I?

Fragments of memory swirled in my mind like scattered leaves in a storm.

The masquerade—bright masks, laughter like chimes of crystal—

And then, chaos.

I had been the alchemist of that ruin.

The thought struck hard, cutting through the haze and leaving only regret behind.

With a soft groan, I turned to my side, curling into myself, seeking comfort in a place that held none.

The room was vast and oppressive in its splendor—its walls were lined with intricate gold leaf carvings that shimmered in the candlelight. The air seemed to pulse, alive with something unseen.

There were no windows.

There was no way to measure day or night.

Only the endless stretch of stone, its grandeur stifling rather than beautiful.

Tapestries of legendary battles and mythical beasts hung like silent sentinels, their embroidered figures almost shifting in the low light, watching.

I tried to rise, but my limbs refused to obey.

Heavy as lead, my body was unresponsive, bound by a fatigue that felt deeper than flesh.

"Easy, Lady Elizabeth."

The voice rumbled above me.

I turned my gaze toward the source and found him—

A man who seemed to fill the room.

The deep creases etched into his face betrayed age and experience, but his eyes held a power that defied time.

Something was commanding about him. Something undeniable.

Yet beneath that, there was a peculiar sense of protection.

"Who are you?" My voice came soft, unfamiliar.

"Why am I here? And where's…?"

The question died on my lips.

His hands guided me gently back onto the plush divan.

"Shh… rest now."

The words weren't just spoken.

They settled over me, sinking into my bones like an enchantment.

"You are safe. I am trying to protect you."

His voice dipped lower, shifting into something ancient, resonant, otherworldly.

He uttered an incantation—a language not meant for mortal tongues.

"Lost to the void, hear my call. By shadow's grace, find new life in the vessel before me. Return and walk among the living."

His fingers moved quickly, each stroke dragging hidden forces into being.

Glyphs of power, ancient and unreadable, burned into my skin.

Something stirred beneath my consciousness.

Something was pulling me back.

Something that did not belong to me.

A creeping frost coiled around my bones, spreading through my veins and wrapping around my ribs like iron vines.

Shadows—thin, spectral, alive—slipped beneath my skin, twisting through me like living whispers of darkness.

My body recoiled in instinctual terror.

This was not healing.

This was not protection.

This was something else entirely.

Panic clawed at my chest. I thrashed weakly, my limbs useless against his unshakable grip.

"No—stop!" My voice was a raw whisper, barely escaping my throat.

My eyelids fluttered, yet my mind screamed against the horror before me.

Then I saw it.

The gash across his chest—seeping, bleeding.

And his forefinger, drenched in his blood, dragging those cursed symbols across my flesh.

He was using his blood.

To inscribe me.

A fresh wave of revulsion surged through me.

I tried to sit up, tried to shove him away, but my body betrayed me.

I could only watch as warm, wet crimson landed on my forearm, tracing lines I did not understand or want to understand.

The sight sent a raw terror flooding my system.

I wrenched my arm free, my breath coming in shallow, panicked gasps.

Rune-like symbols sprawled across my skin—etched in blood.

Then—

A pinch.

A sting bloomed against my wrist.

A needle.

He was taking my blood.

"Stop!" My voice broke into something close to a sob as I thrashed beneath his hold. "Why are you taking my blood? What evil symbols are you inscribing on me?"

He did not flinch.

His voice was a low hum, unwavering.

"Easy, child. The symbols are not evil. They hold the key to your future."

His gaze pinned me, deep-set, willing me to understand.

To accept.

But I could not.

Not when my life essence trickled into the glass vial clenched in his hand.

"Wh-what are you doing?" My voice shook.

His dark eyes met mine, unshaken by my panic, his expression unreadable.

And then, with an infuriating calm that only deepened the terror in my chest, he said—

"I'm taking your blood to protect you."

His words were soft, assured.

But they did nothing to quell the storm rising inside me.

"Protect me? From what?"

My breaths came fast, shallow, desperate.

A battle I was already losing.

"Shh," he murmured, his voice a whisper of smoke and shadow.

He swiped his palm before my face, slow, purposeful.

My eyes fought to stay open.

And then—his blood.

Still warm, still slick with something unholy, he dragged it across my forehead in a single, binding stroke.

"I bind the soul to this new life by my blood and shadow's might.

"Rise, be born anew, and walk the path once more."

The words slithered through me, coiling around my bones, sinking into the marrow.

I exhaled a long, shuddering sigh.

A lull pulled at me, a sweet oblivion, an enchanted embrace whispering surrender.

No.

Don't succumb.

I clawed my way back, forcing myself to hold on, to fight.

"Where's Amir?"

The question ripped from my lips before I could stop it, the urgency of a living, breathing thing inside me.

"What happened to him?"

There was a pause—too long, too heavy.

And in that breath of silence, I knew.

I knew before he spoke, before his lips formed the words.

And it gutted me.

"He didn't make it. He's dead."

"No…" My voice broke. "Amir!"

His name tore from my throat—an uncontrollable wail of pure agony.

The sound bounced off the walls of this gilded tomb, filling the space with my grief.

No.

No, no, no.

This couldn't be real.

A scream ripped through my throat, raw, broken, shattering me from the inside out.

I thrashed beneath the old man's grip, my body twisting in futile rebellion, as if fighting hard enough could undo his words.

Could bring Amir back.

But there was nothing.

Just this unbearable truth swallowing me whole.

"Amir!" I sobbed, my vision blurring with tears that would never be enough to mourn him.

The pain—gods, the agony.

It filled me and devoured every crevice of my being until I was nothing but loss and ruin.

"Please, child."
The old man's voice no longer commanded—it pleaded.
His touch, once cold and foreign, softened.
But no hands could hold me together.
Not when everything inside me was coming undone.
And then—
A bitter taste bloomed on my tongue.
Something touched my lips.
A foreign liquid coaxing me to swallow, to yield.
I tried to fight.
I tried to spit it out.
But the world was already tilting, my limbs growing heavier, my body sinking.
The old man, jailer, and savior watched as the darkness took me.
And I—I could do nothing but fall.
In the abyss of unconsciousness, nightmares found me.
They did not creep in gently.
They tore through me, ravenous.
I saw Amir—
Stoic.
Dissolving.
His dark eyes—once full of unspoken strength—stared, empty, unseeing.
His flesh peeled away in slow, agonizing strips, exposing raw sinew and gleaming bone.
His arms, his legs—once powerful, once familiar—contorted into grotesque angles, twisting, breaking, mocking the proud warrior he had been.
I screamed for him.
I begged.
But my voice came out raw, hoarse, useless.
He did not hear me.
He did not move.
He was vanishing.
Fading.
Until all that remained was emptiness.

And the aching echo of what we had lost.

I woke with a violent start.

My chest heaved. My pulse pounded in my ears, a frantic drumbeat against my skull.

But Amir was gone.

The dream—the nightmare—clung to me like sticky cobwebs, its poison still in my veins.

My bedroom wavered into existence, familiar yet distant, as though I had been gone for an eternity and returned to find everything slightly… off.

I wasn't alone.

Mary.

She sat beside me, a silent tether to reality.

Concern etched into her face, her hands folded in her lap, but her eyes mirrored my fear.

"Mary..."

Her name barely scraped past my lips, a whisper, a ghost of a voice that no longer felt like my own.

Reality's embrace was tenuous at best, the line between waking and nightmare dangerously thin.

I tried to sit up.

The world tilted violently, blurred at the edges.

My limbs were heavy, unresponsive—like lead weights dragging me down.

Mary's hands were there.

Gentle. Placing me back onto the cool linens.

Lavender.

Faint. Familiar.

A scent that should have grounded me but felt distant, disconnected.

"Easy now, Lady Elizabeth," she soothed, her voice a balm against my fractured mind.

"You've been quite ill."

Ill.

The word felt foreign. Inadequate.

This was not an illness.

This was something else.

Something stolen.

Something lost.

My thoughts spun, untethered, drifting through a haze of broken memories.

Searching for reality.

Finding only pieces.

Memories. Fragments.

A dream too vivid and cruel to be only a nightmare.

"Mary… was there… a man?"

The words felt foreign and hesitant, as if speaking aloud would pull the shadows from my mind and make them real.

"An old man. With power in his eyes.

"He was drawing these… blood symbols on me.

"He said he was protecting me…"

Mary's expression shifted, the lines of concern on her brow deepening.

She shook her head.

"No, my lady. You've been here in your bed.

"It's been a month since the masquerade.

"I've not left your side."

A month.

The revelation punched through me, swift and unforgiving.

A whole month.

Lost to this bed.

To shadows that danced behind closed eyelids.

My breath hitched. I tried to cling to Mary's words, to the comfort she provided.

But they slipped through me like sand.

And Amir—

Was he truly dead?

Or had it all been a fever dream?

"Mary, the masquerade."

The word seared my tongue like a brand, memories rising in jagged fragments.

Dread. Poison. Chaos.

But there was something else—

A shiver crawled down my spine.

The ghost of satisfaction.

A whisper of something dark, something buried beneath the horror.

"I saw things that night." My voice caught, the memories too vivid, too raw. "Terrible things."

My hands trembled, my breath shallow.

"But when the poison took hold of me, I fled."

I swallowed hard, fear and uncertainty twisting like a vice around my ribs.

"Do you know what happened after? What became of everyone?"

A pause.

A silence thick enough to smother.

And then—

"What became of..."

The name caught in my throat.

I couldn't say it.

Not without breaking.

Mary's hands stilled.

She tucked the blankets around me again, the soft rustling of fabric the only sound between us.

And when she finally spoke, her voice was softer than before.

"Much has happened, my lady."

Silence settled between us, intentional.

"But rest now."

Her eyes shimmered with sorrow.

Not just grief but understanding.

The kind born only from witnessing the unspeakable.

"We can speak of it later. Your strength must return before we face the past."

A chill settled in my bones.

The past.

Something had been left unsaid.

Something that could not be confronted until I was strong enough to endure it.

My mind reeled, drowning in a tempest of confusion, half-formed questions, and the creeping sense that the truth was far worse than I could comprehend.

But Mary's hands anchored me.

And for the moment, I let go.

I let her pull me back into the quiet embrace of convalescence, trusting her to guard the gateways to a reality I was not yet ready to acknowledge.

The coverlet felt heavy on my legs as I shifted, trying to ease the stiffness that clung to my muscles like iron restraints. I fought against the lingering pull of unconsciousness, struggling to surface fully—to return to the world I had left behind.

Mary sat nearby, an embroidery ring clutched lightly in her hands. She stabbed the needle into the cloth—once, twice—then set it aside as soon as she saw my eyes flutter open.

"You're back," she said softly, a small smile breaking across her weary features.

"I'm trying to be back," I murmured. My voice felt foreign —thin and frayed at the edges. I pushed myself upright with effort, plumping the pillows behind me, needing the stability they offered.

"You must tell me what happened."

Mary's expression shifted. The light in her eyes dimmed, a shadow passing over her as the past caught up to us both.

"Nearly all perished that night," she said quietly. Then her gaze dropped to the coverlet, fingers worrying a crease in the fabric.

"Lord Hassan…" Her voice faltered.

"He is gone…"

"Gone?" The word hit me like a blow, and tears came, fast and hot, blurring the room's edges.

She nodded, her eyes glossy with unshed sorrow.

"He hasn't been seen since that night. It's whispered his body was found with the others."

I couldn't breathe. I couldn't move. My world tilted beneath me.

Amir. Gone.

The room closed in, and the coverlet was suddenly unbearable.

Mary spoke again, her voice a fragile tether.

"Your father—he survived. But…"

I snapped my gaze up.

She hesitated only a moment, then finished.

"He's paralyzed."

A chill traced down my spine.

"Paralyzed? But… he's alive?"

The words stumbled out, twisting in my throat, refusing to make sense.

Mary nodded solemnly.

"Yes, Lady Elizabeth. He cannot walk anymore… but he's still with us."

I sat in silence, a storm churning beneath my skin. My father —the man who had ruled my life with an iron fist, cold commands, and colder punishments—now bound to a chair.

His own body severed his power.

I didn't know if I felt justice… or fear.

"Tell me more," I whispered, the words catching like thorns in my throat.

Emotions warred inside me—grief, disbelief, a bitter tangle of relief and guilt.

The past hadn't let me go.

And now, I would have to face it.

Mary exhaled slowly, her gaze drifting to some distant point of sorrow, her voice softened by memory and dread.

"There's not much to tell.

"Most didn't survive the night… the masquerade."

Her hands trembled slightly as she clutched her chest as if trying to hold herself together.

"The dead were… grotesquely deformed. Misshapen.

"There were great efforts to keep the news from the public.

"I only heard whispers.

"From the staff.

"It was… awful."

Her words trailed off, choked by what couldn't be said aloud.

My heart skipped, then pounded violently against my ribs, a drumbeat of dread.

"And Lord Winston?"

The name tasted bitter, foul on my tongue, a reminder of hands that had never touched me without leaving scars.

Mary's lips thinned, the briefest flicker of relief—or perhaps disdain—shadowing her features.

"He didn't make it."

She exhaled, slow, controlled.

"He's gone to his maker in hell."

I sagged back into the pillows, my body limp with confusion and release.

Relief washed over me—brief, treacherous.

And then—guilt. Crushing, choking guilt.

The burden of lives lost—claimed by my creation—settled on me like a mountain, stealing the air from my lungs.

A terrifying thought struck me like a hammer to the chest—

Had I killed Amir, too?

Was it my poison that ended him?

The notion coiled in my gut, a serpent of regret and terror, tightening around my heart until I feared it would break.

My hands—once balanced, sure instruments of healing and alchemy—

Now stained with destruction.

How many had fallen?

How many had been killed by my hand?

"The fact that you survived is a miracle."

Mary's voice pulled me back from the abyss.

I stared at her, empty. Numb.

"Is it?" I murmured, my gaze shifting to the wall, to nothing.

"I should be dead, too."

The words hung in the air.

In my mind, I was pulled back—to that chamber of shadow and gold, where opulence met nightmare.

Underground.

Somewhere else.

And the old man…

His voice, his touch, the symbols etched in blood.

"I keep remembering... I was somewhere else," I whispered.

"Underground. There was an old man. He… was taking care of me."

"Elizabeth."

Mary's hand found mine—warm, grounding, real.

"You've been here this whole time. You've been ill, but you never left this room. It's only your fevered dreams that took you elsewhere."

Her words struggled to settle, fighting the storm still raging in my mind.

"Then how—"

The question died on my lips.

Because the answer had already bloomed in my heart, cold and bitter.

"My father…"

Mary's expression didn't waver.

"I told you. Most died that night."

Her voice was even, but beneath it, I sensed a quiet fury, a grief too long carried.

"Your father survived, but he is a changed man. Bitter. We've lost nearly everything. The estate is in shambles. Most of the servants are gone—frightened away by him. It's a miracle this house, our home, hasn't been taken from us already."

I lay there, absorbing her words.

A miracle.

It felt like a curse.

Miracles were for saints and martyrs.

Not for women like me, who had toyed with death in glass

vials, whispered forbidden incantations over open flames, and lost everything.

Mary's eyes darted away, and a shadow flickered across her face.

"What is it?"

The edge in my voice was thin, frayed by fear.

Her hesitation hung between us, like the heavy drapes that locked out the sunlight I craved.

"Elizabeth."

My name broke on her lips, trembling like the last leaf clinging to an autumn branch.

Her hands tightened around mine.

As if to prepare me.

"I need to tell you something."

A pause.

A breath.

"You're with child."

The words hit me like a storm.

A gasp ripped through my throat, raw, ragged—leaving me breathless.

I yanked my hands from hers, covering my eyes as if to block out the world.

But it was too late.

Tears spilled over, tracing silver paths down my cheeks.

Amir's child.

But now he was gone.

Lost to the darkness that had claimed him—and now, part of him lived on within me.

My heart pounded a frantic rhythm of dread and help-lessness.

"My father will kill me," I whispered, the words barely audible above the thunder in my chest.

Mary's face paled.

"Does he know?"

"No, my lady."

Mary's hand rested gently on my arm, her touch grounding.

"I convinced the doctor that his suspicions were due to your stress. He's mistaken, I told him. No one knows but me."

Relief warred with dread in my chest, a storm of contradictions I could barely contain.

Mary's gaze searched mine, her voice barely a whisper.

"Could it be true?"

The question hovered, a ghost on her lips.

But she already knew.

We both did.

"Yes."

The word scraped from my throat like a shard of glass.

"Amir and I… we fell in love."

Mary's eyes lit with wonder, a smile blooming across her face like sunlight after a storm.

"That's wonderful!"

She squeezed my hand.

"He left you a gift. This baby."

But her joy couldn't pierce the cloak of sorrow wrapped tight around me.

Not when the world had already taken him.

Not when this child would be born into ruin.

Suddenly, a cacophony exploded from the hallway—shouts, crashing, the jarring clatter of something heavy.

Mary's head snapped toward the door, her hand tightening on mine.

Then—

The door burst open.

It slammed against the wall with a force that echoed in my bones.

My father appeared in the doorway, propelled forward by a servant, his face a twisted mask of fury.

He sat in a wheelchair, an iron-rimmed chariot of suffering, more prison than a tool.

Sunlight streamed through the tall windows, bathing the room in gold—but it felt wrong, offensive against the darkness he brought with him.

His once-proud visage was a ruin of angry scars, unrecognizable, a remnant of the man I once feared and loved.

His gnarled left hand clutched the armrest with a bone-white grip, the veins bulging as though the wood might splinter beneath his wrath.

His right arm lay limp and lifeless, twisted awkwardly in his lap, a cruel mirror of the power he'd lost.

The man who had once lifted me high on his shoulders, who had filled our halls with laughter—before it turned to commands, punishments, and fear—

Now filled the room with raw, unspoken fury.

I couldn't move.

I couldn't breathe.

His eyes burned into mine, and in the stillness between us, I felt it—

The tremble of the room, or perhaps just my bones, under his rage.

"Elizabeth."

The word scraped from his throat, each syllable a shard of broken glass dragging across my nerves.

A shiver cut down my spine—cold, sudden, involuntary.

I told myself—I should not be afraid.

It played in my mind like a fragile mantra.

But it couldn't silence the pounding of my heart, a frantic, erratic beat that echoed the throbbing guilt coursing through me.

He was my father.

And yet—

The scars etched across his face, warped and angry, had remade him into a stranger.

A man sculpted by bitterness, loss, and rage.

"Father," I managed, the word barely a whisper, foreign on my tongue.

Then he exploded.

The words erupted from him like a loud, violent, and lethal volcanic blast.

The sinewy cords of his neck strained, veins bulging with fury.

"I heard Mary say you're with child!"

Spittle flecked his twisted lips, the sound ripping through the room like a weapon.

"Lord Hassan's child."

His legs, as limp as broken branches, hung uselessly beneath him—a grotesque reminder of the power he'd lost.

"You whore!" he thundered, voice cracking with venom and fury.

"How dare you disgrace our house!

"How could you consort with the enemy—the very man who razed our society to the ground!"

He spat Amir's name as though it charred him, the syllables loaded with poison and hate.

I flinched, the barrage of accusations hitting with the force of daggers, each one aimed at my heart.

The man who once made me believe I could touch the stars—

Whose laughter used to chase away every shadow—

Now he looked at me with eyes void of warmth—

Eyes glazed with a cold, inhuman fury.

Eyes I barely recognized.

"Stop it!" I screamed, my hands flying to my ears as if I could block out his venom, his hate, his voice.

"Amir is not the monster you paint him to be!

"It is not him—it is you!

"You are the monster!"

I choked on the bile rising in my throat, every word tearing from me like shrapnel.

"I did what I had to do—to destroy your society.

"I am the alchemist who crafted the poison.

"I brought the French Timehunters to their doom."

Silence.

A terrible, gaping silence.

It swallowed the room, sucked the air from my lungs, and left only the deafening pound of my heartbeat in my ears.

Then—

His face twisted.

Contorted with a wave of fury so raw and feral, I thought the earth might crack beneath us.

"Destroyed France? Destroyed my society? Murdered your future husband? Did you kill your brothers? You?"

His voice was disbelief turning to a snarl of rage.

"How dare you stand there and claim such treachery!"

"Because it's the truth!" I screamed, my voice jagged with grief and fury and despair.

"I am the alchemist behind it all. Not Amir. It was my hand that wrought this devastation. Not his."

His face darkened, red as blood, the scars warping with every word, twisting him into something demonic—something no longer human.

"I want you out of this fucking house. Now!"

His roar shook the air, the words like an incantation to banish demons—only I was the demon now.

"I disown you. You are no longer my daughter. You are dead to me. Get out of my sight.

"You have one hour to leave this house."

With a violent jerk of his head and a tremble in his crippled hand, he signaled the servant.

The young man, eyes wide with shock, stepped behind the wheelchair, his fingers quivering on the worn handles.

I pushed myself up from the bed, the motion instinctive, desperate. I stood—frozen—tears blurring my vision, the world around me cracking, crumbling with every breath.

His words still rang in my ears—words of dismissal, exile, betrayal—as I reached out to the man who no longer felt like my father.

"Father, you can't mean that!"

My voice cracked, broken, raw.

"I have nothing—nothing with which to live!"

Desperation clawed through me, but he met it with a gaze of stone.

His voice dripped with venom, each word a blade to the heart.

"You should've thought about the consequences before unleashing something deadly."

He sneered, eyes narrowing.

"And now look at you—pregnant with an illegitimate child, your lover dead, and without a home to call your own.

"You're completely on your own now, Elizabeth."

His voice cut through my sobs like a knife, slicing deep, leaving nothing untouched.

There was no warmth in his eyes.

No glimmer of the father I once knew.

Just cold, merciless disdain.

His words cast me adrift, and I felt the terrifying pull of an uncertain future, of a life ripped apart.

"Father, please," I begged, reaching for him one last time, grasping for a scrap of the man who'd once loved me.

"I did this for us.

"What you were doing—it was despicable."

But my plea bounced off the walls, unheard, unwanted.

His fury boiled over, a storm unchecked.

"Shut up! Get out! Pack your bags! You're no longer welcome in this house."

His eyes blazed into mine.

"I will tell the authorities if you don't leave within the hour. One word from me, Elizabeth, and they'll come for you.

"With orders to eliminate you on sight.

"And I'll enjoy every second of it. Watching you meet your end."

He jabbed a finger toward the hallway, his lips curled in hatred.

The servant turned the chair abruptly, wheels shrieking against the floor.

And then they were gone—swallowed by the corridor, leaving only silence.

A silence filled with ruin.

And I—alone. Pregnant. Homeless. Hunted.

The chamber around me seemed to tighten, its walls heavy with betrayal and abandonment.

But there was no time for grief.

There was no room for shock.

My limbs ached with weakness, but urgency seared through me, pushing my body into motion.

"Mary," I gasped, my voice raw, but insistent.

"We must pack. Quickly."

Her eyes met mine—a flicker of fear, then resolve. She nodded.

We moved in tandem, our hands trembling, every movement swift, frantic, necessary.

A few changes of clothing—wrinkled, hastily folded.

Hidden beneath the loose floorboard, a small pouch of coins was now our only wealth.

The locket—my mother's portrait inside—pressed to my chest before being tucked away.

Each item hurled into worn leather satchels, their weight crushing as though we carried the remnants of a life severed by force.

"Be quick, Mary," I whispered, the panic climbing in my throat.

My heart pounded like a trapped bird, frantic and helpless, its wings slamming against my ribs.

The house—once my sanctuary—now felt like a tomb.

Every creak of the floorboards screamed danger.

Every breath, every whispered instruction, felt like a spark in a room full of powder.

Outside the door, the mansion stirred, muffled voices and footsteps unaware of the exile unfolding behind these walls.

We moved like shadows, our steps cautious but propelled by the ticking clock of my father's threat.

The corridors, once familiar, felt alien now—cold, vast, and merciless.

The mansion that had cradled my entire existence was now hostile ground, its grandeur a mockery of the life we'd been forced to abandon.

With our satchels slung over our shoulders, we carried not

just possessions, but the burden of survival, loss, and beginnings forged from ruin.

"Stay close," I whispered to Mary—my only constant in a world that had turned its back on me.

Together, we fled the place I once called home, our shadows fleeting and forlorn.

Behind us, the door clicked shut—a soft, merciless, full stop to everything that had been.

It was over.

Ahead lay only the unknown, wrapped in morning mist and fear, as we hastened away from the crumbling edifice of my past.

The stables loomed—a rough sanctuary in our escape, smelling of hay, sweat, and freedom.

We burst through the wide double doors, our breaths ragged, desperate.

"Harry!" I called, my voice urgent, echoing off beams and rafters.

From the shadows, the stable hand emerged. His face was smudged with dirt and sweat, and his eyes narrowed as he took us in.

"Lady Alexander?"

Suspicion coiled in his tone, his gaze darting between our disheveled appearances.

A flicker of insolence gleamed in his eyes, and a smirk tugged at the corner of his mouth.

"What's the meaning of this?"

"Prepare a carriage. Now."

The command cracked through the air like a whip, my voice leaving no room for defiance.

His expression didn't falter, but I saw the shift behind his eyes.

The calculation. The hesitation. The thrill of power, if only for a moment.

"Seems the high and mighty can fall after all," he quipped, leaning lazily against a wooden post, dirt-streaked fingers toying with a bit of straw.

I stepped closer, my gaze hard.

"Listen to me, Harry."

My words were razor-edged with urgency.

"This household is dissolving into dust. Let me go—and get out of here yourself."

His smirk faltered, fear flickering across his face like a crack in his armor.

My words settled into him, and whatever satisfaction he'd found in my downfall shriveled beneath the truth.

He moved quickly, hands trembling as he fumbled with bridles and harnesses, the echo of his mockery gone.

Mary and I exchanged a glance—silent understanding forged in fire, refined under years of shared fear and loyalty.

The morning light filtered through the stable's slats, casting long shadows that seemed to chase us here.

The carriage groaned as Harry hitched the horses, every creak a countdown to freedom or capture.

When it was ready, we threw our satchels onto the seat— each thud a punctuation mark to our frantic, pounding hearts.

I climbed to the driver's bench, hands trembling as I seized the reins, the leather biting into my palms like a vow.

Mary followed, sitting beside me like a lifeline, a thread anchoring me to sanity in a world undone.

"Where are we going?" she whispered, as if afraid that speaking might shatter our fragile escape.

I clucked to the horses.

They lunged forward, hooves striking the ground with a fierce, eager rhythm.

Just like us—ready to run.

"To the cottage first," I said, my eyes fixed on the winding road ahead.

"Then... we go to the Americas."

A beat of silence.

The words tasted foreign but strong.

An unfamiliar sense of peace settled into me—hard, cold, unshakable.

I had been forged in betrayal. In fire.

Now, I would rise from the ashes.

And across oceans, beyond the reach of my father's shadow, the next chapter waited.

One I would write in my hand.

The carriage wheels crunched over the gravel path, each rotation a thunderous reminder of all I'd lost.

We arrived at the cottage—

A place that once whispered secrets now stood eerily silent, its door ajar like an open wound.

I dismounted, heart thudding against my ribs, panic clawing at my throat.

Inside, chaos reigned.

Drawers ripped from their places, glass vials shattered, bundles of herbs strewn like corpses across the floor.

A violent search. A desecration.

A mirror of the turmoil inside me.

"Elizabeth?"

Mary's voice floated from the doorway, thin with worry.

I didn't answer.

I couldn't.

Desperation moved my limbs, each step frantic as I tore through the wreckage, searching for two sacred things—

The Noctyss flower, once preserved beneath the glass.

And my mother's alchemy book, the legacy of everything she was.

Gone.

Both gone.

My breath hitched—

A sound of grief, of failure.

They had taken everything.

I had destroyed my father's Timehunter society—yes.

But that wasn't the promise that mattered.

There had been one sacred vow I made to my mother as she lay dying—

And I had failed her.

No flower. No book. No legacy.

I stood there, ruins at my feet, my hands trembling at my sides.

But I couldn't stay here.

Not in this grave of memories.

I held a hand to my heart, choking back tears.

"I promise you, Mother," I whispered.

"I will fulfill your dying wish… when the time comes."

A vow—

Not broken. Delayed.

"Mary," I called, my voice hollow.

"Before we go, I must say goodbye to my father."

She stepped into the light, her face shadowed with sorrow.

There was no need to explain.

The need for closure.

The faint hope for something human in him—

It was all laid bare in my eyes.

"Are you certain, Lady Elizabeth?"

Her words were soft but heavy—weighted with the hopeless-ness we both felt.

I nodded, the tremble in my lips betraying the pain.

"I need to."

We climbed back into the carriage, the horses sensing our urgency. Their hooves struck the dirt road with a restless rhythm as they carried us toward a farewell steeped in dread and longing.

I clung to a sliver of hope—not for forgiveness but for clar-ity, to clear the air soured by secrets, lies, and bloodshed.

The carriage jolted violently over a rut, nearly pitching me forward.

I gripped the seat's edge, my knuckles white, breath shallow.

Outside, the landscape blurred, trees and hedgerows racing past.

I saw none of it.

My mind was fixed on the house.

And the man inside it.

Every mile closer felt like a stone against my lungs.

I should have been relieved to leave it behind—his rage, his contempt, his damnation of me.

I should have embraced freedom, the promise of a new life beyond his reach.

But instead—I turned back. Unable to let go without one last word.

What was I hoping for?

A kind word?

That man was gone.

Buried beneath bitterness.

Rage.

And scars that ran deeper than flesh.

But still—

I had to face him.

One last time.

And still, some part of me couldn't stop hoping.

Hoping that if I just explained—

Why I did what I did.

Why I couldn't be the perfect daughter he demanded.

Maybe he'd understand.

Or at least… stop hating me.

I wasn't sure I could bear leaving without trying.

Without saying goodbye to the man he had once been—

And the girl I had been when I still believed he loved me.

The road curved, and the house came into view—dark, unwelcoming, crouched beneath a dull gray sky like a grave marker.

My stomach twisted.

He'd just thrown me out like a stray dog, his voice still echoed in my ears—full of fury, full of finality.

I told myself this was a mistake.

That I should turn around and keep going.

Never look back.

But my mouth stayed shut.

And the carriage rolled on.

I didn't know what I'd say when I saw him.

I didn't know if I could weather his anger again.

But I had to try.

For myself, if nothing else.

To leave without trying felt like abandoning the last shred of love or loyalty I still had for him—no matter how much it hurt.

The mansion loomed larger, a monument to everything we had been—and everything we'd lost.

My resolve wavered.

But loyalty to the man my father once was nudged me forward.

It was a duty born of love—however fractured.

A final act.

A daughter to her father.

Before the last threads between us unraveled completely.

The mansion's shadows clung to me like a second skin as I slithered through its silent, treacherous halls.

Each step was heavy—each breath taut with the a choice.

To confront.

Or to flee.

My heart was a storm—thunderous, erratic, betraying my every doubt.

I reached the threshold of his study.

The familiar scent of aged leather, scorched tobacco, and old mahogany enveloped me, pulling me back into old rhythms—of obedience, of fear.

Then—

A voice. Not his. Piercing. Otherworldly.

"Do you know who I am?"

The words sliced through the stillness like a blade.

My pulse kicked. A jolt of alarm surged through me.

It wasn't my father.

Inside, his brittle reply echoed—defiant, shaking.

"No. Should I? Why the fuck should I know you?"

That rasp—arrogant on the surface, but I heard the fear buried beneath.

And then, the name dropped like a guillotine.

"My name is Salvatore. I am your master. Mathias reports to me. Where did you get the Noctyss poison?"

Every syllable was a poisoned barb.

Salvatore.

Amir's warning hit me hard—a memory laced with dread, cold and unforgiving. It struck like lightning, illuminating the shadows I thought I'd buried.

I tried to face him once before.

Tried to stand against him... and I failed.

The memory clawed its way back—Salvatore's eyes burning into mine, his power bearing down until I could barely breathe. The vial in my hand. The fear. The recklessness. The consequences.

And now—

Here he was again.

I froze, breath caught in my throat, my limbs heavy and unwilling to move—pinned by the gravity of his authority, the terror of his voice.

Inside, silence.

My heart a drumbeat of panic.

Then—

My father's voice cracked through the stillness like thin ice beneath a heavy step.

"I don't know what you're talking about," he said, strained. "I know nothing about a Noctyss poison."

A lie.

A weak one.

But it was all he had.

Salvatore's laugh followed—cold as a tomb, the sound of death scraping stone.

"You are living proof of the Noctyss poison," he hissed. "I can smell it. Feel it. It's lodged in your broken, misshapen bones."

A pause followed—slow and cruel, heavy with unspoken threat.

"Your society was powerful once—herbs, fear, reputation. Until your wife died."

His voice darkened, each word dipped in venom. "So, I'll ask again—who created the poison?"

Silence stretched, razor-thin, every breath a risk. The air around us was a noose.

"It was Lord Hassan," my father said.

A lie.

A shield.

Cast over me like armor I didn't deserve.

My eyes widened, breath faltering, heart lurching in my chest.

Why?

Why would he protect me—after everything between us?

Our relationship—a tangled tapestry of control, rebellion, and pain—suddenly bore a single thread of sacrifice.

I pushed closer to the door, peering through the narrow crack. My fingers were ice-cold, my breath held hostage, my soul trembling in its cage.

Salvatore stood still. Unmoving. Yet the air shivered around him, as if reality itself recoiled before him.

Then he spoke—

Low. Venomous.

"No... it was not Lord Hassan. The alchemist was a woman."

His head tilted slightly, eyes narrowing like a predator scenting blood.

"Where is your daughter... Elizabeth?"

My breath caught, the world spun sideways.

"She's dead," my father answered, his voice hoarse. "She didn't make it."

Silence.

A beat of stillness that stretched the air razor-thin.

Then Salvatore screamed—a sound of pure rage and inhuman fury, the kind that fractured stone.

"Lies!" he bellowed, and the walls themselves quaked beneath the force of his wrath.

I stumbled back from the door, spine hitting cold stone, heart slamming in my chest like a drum of doom.

Salvatore moved—like death given form.

Silent. Inevitable. Unstoppable.

A flash of steel.

A wet, broken gurgle.

And then—my father collapsed.

A man who once ruled over everything... reduced to a lifeless heap.

The world fell to stillness. Blood pooled across polished floors, soaking into the silence like a curse.

"I will find out where your daughter is hiding... and kill her!"

Salvatore's roar splintered the air—a nightmare loosed upon the world.

Horror gripped me, rooted me in place, paralyzed my limbs for a single, eternal heartbeat.

Then instinct took over.

I turned—ran.

My skirts whispered against the marble like ghosts, feet barely touching the ground as I fled. My heart pounded, my blood boomed in my ears.

Bursting into the daylight, I threw myself into the carriage beside Mary.

"We need to leave. Now!" I gasped, voice raw, a desperate scrape torn from a throat tight with fear.

The horses whinnied, sensing the storm in my chest, hooves hammering the ground like war drums as we surged forward— toward the docks, toward escape.

My mind raced ahead—over the ocean, across an expanse vast and unknown.

To the Americas.

A refuge...

Or another battlefield.

I didn't know.

I didn't care.

There was no time for doubt.

Only survival.

Only escape.

Only the road ahead.

CHAPTER 22

AMIR

I awoke to the sensation of fire coursing through my veins—raw, consuming, alive. Each jolt of pain was more agonizing than the last, stealing my breath, dragging me back into a world I no longer recognized.

The pit was alive.

A writhing mass of serpents coiled over me, their slick bodies sliding across torn skin, scales gleaming, fangs bared. They struck without mercy, again and again, piercing deep, their venom a torment I could not escape.

I screamed, hoarse and ragged, as their bites tore through me like searing needles. But beneath the agony, I could feel something else—something darker, something purposeful.

The venom.

And the antidote.

Twisting together inside me like enemies locked in war.

It surged through my blood, battling the poison that had infected me, fighting to cleanse it. Their healing was no act of mercy—it was as savage as the sickness it sought to destroy.

Between the convulsions, my mind shattered into fragments.

Elizabeth.

Her face haunted me—those pale, frightened eyes etched into memory—the last time I saw her. I could still feel her slipping from my arms, still hear her voice in my bones.

Was she safe?

Did she escape?

I didn't know.

And the not knowing was its own kind of torture.

All I could do was endure.

I writhed beneath the swarm, powerless, as the serpents moved with single-minded purpose—each one a tormentor, a savior, a curse and a cure in the same breath. Their mission was etched into the pain they inflicted, a language of suffering I could no longer fight.

Then—suddenly—they stopped.

One by one, the serpents slithered away, disappearing into the shadows of the pit, leaving me alone in the silence they abandoned. I lay there, drenched in sweat, my body trembling, skin torn and bruised, marked by a thousand wounds. Each breath felt foreign, each heartbeat uncertain—a question I had no answer for.

Broken—but purified.

Time unraveled around me.

Reality blurred, slipping at the edges of my awareness, until the tremors inside me dulled to a distant roar—quiet enough to breathe, to think, to move.

With a guttural groan, I rolled onto my side, pain screaming through every muscle, my body a ruin barely stitched together by will. I crawled toward the edge of the pit, dragging myself inch by agonizing inch.

Each movement was a battle.

Each breath, a victory.

At the edge, I braced my arms and forced myself upright, staggering to my feet as my legs shook beneath me. A caftan lay crumpled on the cold stone floor—a shred of dignity amidst the carnage. I seized it, slipped it over my battered frame, and without looking back, left the snake pit behind.

One thought dominated all others.

Elizabeth.

"Where is she?"

The words tore from my lips—hoarse, broken—a vow and a question fused in desperation.

The underground palace stretched out before me—shadowed, silent, forsaken. Every hallway felt endless, every shadow a threat, every breath too loud against the stillness.

My heart hammered, a frantic drumbeat in my chest as I tore through corridor after corridor—room after empty room—shouting her name into the void.

"Elizabeth!"

My voice echoed back at me—hollow, mocking, a cruel mimicry of hope against the silence.

Desperation clawed at my insides, gripping tighter with every step. She wasn't here. She was nowhere.

And in that deafening silence, a dreadful truth bled through me—

I might have lost her.

I roared again, "Elizabeth!"

The sound ripped from my raw throat—a savage, broken plea.

No reply.

Only the oppressive hush of ancient stone, its stillness a tomb for my hope.

My mind reeled.

Had she died?

Had I failed her again?

The venom in my veins still scalded, but it was nothing.

Nothing compared to this.

Her voice.

Her face.

Her glacier-colored eyes—filled with fire and fear—gone.

Elizabeth, forgive me.

I should've been there.

I should've protected you.

I stumbled forward, each step heavier, burdened by loss and a love that felt doomed from the start.

I stormed through the labyrinth, the echo of my footfalls

chasing me like a hound at my heels. Torchlight flickered across the stone walls, casting shadows that danced along the corridors—taunting, fleeting, just beyond reach.

Every corner turned.

Every hall searched.

No closer.

No answer.

The dread inside me coiled tighter, a knot of grief and fury pulling me under—threatening to consume what little strength I had left.

Then—at last—I found him.

Lazarus.

Seated in his study, quill scratching across parchment, his eyes fixed on the page as if the world outside his door wasn't disassembling. As if I wasn't standing there—ablaze.

He didn't look up.

Didn't flinch.

Just wrote.

Calm. Detached.

As though none of it mattered.

"Elizabeth," I breathed. Her name slipped from my lips, barely more than a whisper, a question, a plea.

"Is she—?"

"Alive." His voice was flat, unaffected. He didn't pause, didn't lift his gaze.

"She's back home. Recovering. Her father lives too—though paralyzed. She is not alone. Her maid tends her."

Relief hit me like a wave—hot, blinding.

It seared through my veins like the serpents' antidote, stinging, cleansing, overwhelming. A weight lifted—but only to be replaced by another.

Urgency.

Need.

Her.

"I have to go to her," I said, the words ripping from me, half-prayer, half-declaration. Her face filled my mind—sky-blue eyes, wheat-blond hair—etched into my soul.

I needed to protect her.

I needed to see her.

"No, Amir."

Lazarus' voice cut through my thoughts—leaving no room for argument.

He looked up. Finally.

Eyes like ice, gaze honed enough to flay me where I stood.

He rose slowly, every movement deliberate, authority cloaking him like armor. The quill slipped from his fingers, forgotten.

"You will stay away from Elizabeth," he said.

His voice was iron. Final.

"That's an order."

Silence thundered between us.

My heart pounded, fury igniting like dry tinder. Every fiber of me rebelled.

"What?" The word tore from me—a half-snarl, half-wound.

Lazarus didn't blink.

"I've been watching you, Amir. Since the moment your mission in England began."

His voice was unnaturally calm. Controlled to the point of menace.

A stark contrast to the storm raging inside me.

"Getting involved with the daughter of your enemy?"

Lazarus' voice was low, but the accusation hit hard, each word laced with quiet condemnation. He shook his head slowly, disappointment settling in his eyes—cutting deeper than any wound I'd ever taken in battle.

"And now," he sighed, "Lady Alexander is revealed to be a Timehealer. One who has crafted a potent poison meant to ensnare Salvatore."

My heart pounded, each beat like a war drum battering against his words.

"If Salvatore or Mathias see you together," Lazarus warned, his voice hard, "they'll connect the dots. Instantly. And she—she will meet her demise."

He paused, gaze sharpening.

"He will spirit her away, torture her for her secrets. She will die, Amir. Do you understand this?"

For a breath—just a heartbeat—his tone softened. A rare fracture in the armor of the man who had shaped every step of my life.

"I'm sorry. I know you love her," he said quietly. "But you must let her go."

The words hit like steel, twisting in my gut, tearing something raw and sacred inside me.

My fists clenched at my sides, the stoicism I wore like armor beginning to fracture beneath his demand.

"Love demands sacrifice, Pasha Hassan," he added—almost idly.

But that phrase…

It hung like a noose between us.

Letting her go…

My voice was a whisper carved from stone.

"It might be the hardest battle I've ever fought."

"Indeed," Lazarus said, turning back to his desk, dismissing me—as if my agony was nothing more than collateral.

"But it is one you must endure—for her sake."

The heat inside me ignited, fury surging beneath my skin.

A wildfire.

Uncontainable.

"None of this—none of it—would have happened if you had controlled Isabelle. If she hadn't separated the Blade of Shadows."

My voice thundered through the study.

Righteous fury propelled every word.

"This disaster rests on your shoulders, Lazarus. You have cursed me—condemned me to a life of darkness, of unfulfilled longing. I can never truly be happy, never find love in this wicked world."

I could feel the truth in my veins, in every syllable.

"With the Blade of Shadows severed, Isabelle and Armand are dead. And now—Alina of Solaris has returned from the grave. And you—what do you do, Shadow Lord?"

I stepped closer, voice rising like a battle cry.

"You sit idly, barking orders... while our world burns."

The words had barely left my lips when he struck.

The blow wasn't just flesh and bone—it was power, raw and ancient.

Dark energy surged through his fist, through me, and agony exploded across my face.

Pain blinded me, and then my lungs seized.

I staggered back, hands clawing at my throat.

Invisible manacles—tight, unrelenting—strangling the life from me.

Panic tore through me, a caged animal thrashing in my chest as I fought for air, for life.

Each breath became a war.

Every second stretched into an eternity of terror.

And in that moment—gasping, choking, collapsing—I finally understood.

The fragility of life.

Of defiance.

Of myself.

Lazarus stood over me, towering and unmoved.

His eyes burned with fury, a storm barely restrained beneath the surface.

He raised his hand—without hesitation, without mercy—and I shattered.

Slammed to the ground by a force I couldn't resist, pain exploded through me. I gasped, mouth open, body convulsing, lungs dragging in ragged bursts of air as pain racked every muscle.

His voice roared above me, every word a hammer blow.

"I know about Alina. I know what Salvatore and Mathias are planning. I know Mathias hunts for the blades. I know my failure to Isabelle and Armand."

His footsteps echoed—approaching.

Closer.

"Do not presume to lecture me. I am painfully aware of what is happening."

He stopped just above me, his shadow swallowing mine, a figure cloaked in power—death itself.

"You dare speak to me like that again, Amir—and I will personally kill you."

His voice was steel, lethal and cold.

"Your death will be unlike anything you have ever felt before."

A groan ripped from me—raw, broken, soaked in agony.

"You don't understand... the pain... the torture I endure..."

"Ah, but I do." Lazarus' voice shifted—no longer steel but shadow and sorrow. A haunted look darkened his face, his gaze drifting—not at me, but through me, to memories that still bled. "I sacrificed everything—my family, my life—for Solaris." His eyes, once cold, now shimmered with grief. Not weakness—but a torment I knew too well. "I know exactly how you feel."

He exhaled, shoulders sagging beneath a weight no one else could see. "Everything I do... is to get us back. To Solaris." His voice dropped to a whisper—raw, aching. "I loved Amara. Still do. My love for her... it consumes me. Just like your love for Elizabeth."

He looked away, jaw tightening, a muscle twitching beneath his cheekbone. "My wife hates me. For choosing Solaris over our family." He paused and then added, "I had to separate my sons. John and Jack. Twins—placed in different timelines. For the mission. To bring Solaris back."

His eyes darkened, pain flickering through the mask he wore. "Do you know what it's like to stand in the shadows of their lives—watching them grow, laugh, suffer—and they don't know you're protecting them?" His fists clenched, knuckles white, breath ragged. "To be a ghost in their world. Invisible. Forgotten. Because that's the only way to save them."

His eyes locked onto mine, fierce and piercing. "Trust me, Amir. Every sacrifice you've made—I've made it, too. And just like I told my beautiful Amara... One day, we will be victorious. But first—we must sacrifice the things we love the most."

He stepped closer, shadows gathering around him like a mantle. His face hardened into stone. "That is the price of

Solaris. That is the burden we bear." His finger pointed at me, firm, unrelenting. "You will let Elizabeth go. Salvatore hunts for the Noctyss flower—and she knows where it blooms. That knowledge alone makes her a target. If he finds her, Amir—he will kill her."

His words struck like a hammer, shattering the last remnants of hope inside me. I felt it in my bones—an undeniable truth. I was no sanctuary for her. I was the danger, the storm that would tear her apart. Salvatore's shadow loomed over us, a specter that would not rest until we were undone.

Lazarus' gaze didn't waver. "When she was here, I took her blood. I cloaked her with it—she's invisible to Salvatore as if she's dead. That's the only reason he can't find her. But if you go to her, the cloak will fail. Your love is too strong. It will draw him straight to her."

His words cut deeper than any blade, a truth I didn't want to hear. Pain surged in my chest, all-consuming. "If I don't protect her," I croaked, "who will? I can't stand by."

"You must," Lazarus said.

His decree fell like a gavel, sentencing me to a fate worse than death. To live while she slipped away into the horizon, untouched by me, unreachable. To breathe when each breath tasted of her absence. That was a torment I hadn't prepared for. But as my soul screamed in rebellion, I knew—this was the only way. Elizabeth's life was not mine to risk. Not for love. Not for anything.

"So be it," I whispered, the words tearing from me like barbed wire. The vow was bitter, a surrender forced by love's cruelty. If I truly loved her, I would become her shadow— always near, never seen. Watching. Guarding. Alone.

Lazarus' gaze turned colder than the grave. "Remember, Amir. You are the shield in the shadows. From there, you will protect her. She's already en route to the Americas, seeking refuge. Pray she stays hidden. Pray you have the strength to let her go."

His voice lingered like a curse, and as I stood in the fading light, I realized that my war had only begun.

"Very well," I murmured, more to myself than to Lazarus, the words bitter on my tongue. "For her, I will become a ghost… forever watching, never touching. But you can't stop me from taking steps to ensure her safety."

If I could not hold her, I would shield her.

I would guard it in silence if I could not speak her name.

I would be her shadow—her silent protector—even if it meant sacrificing the love I could never claim.

Let Salvatore hunt.

She would live.

Even if I had to disappear to make it so.

The temporal winds howled around me as I landed with a muted thud on the soft forest floor of the Americas. The year was 1762. The air hung heavy with pine and earth—a stark contrast to the cold stone and shadowed halls of Anatolia I had left behind. Each breath I took filled my lungs with wildness, with life. It felt foreign after so long in darkness.

With every step, leaves rustled beneath my boots, guiding me toward a clearing where the fire light danced in a hypnotic rhythm. Shadows wrapped across the trees like spirits watching from afar, but I knew who waited for me.

Dancing Fire was true to his name, his movements fluid and untamed. He spun among the rising embers, his sinewy form slashing through the night like a blade of wind and flame. His feet barely seemed to touch the ground, as if the earth itself yielded to him. At that moment, watching him twirl beneath the stars, a pang twisted in my chest. What would it be like to live unburdened by duty? To be free, like the flames he embraced?

"Ah, you're here!" Dancing Fire's voice boomed through the quiet. He halted mid-step, his keen eyes locking onto mine.

I drew a breath, steadying the plea clawing at my throat. "Hello, dear friend." I stepped into the clearing, and we clasped each other in a brief, firm embrace—one forged from battles fought and trust earned.

When he pulled back, his hands gripped my upper arms. "You wouldn't come unless danger followed. Speak."

He knew me too well—read me like a story etched on stone. I didn't waste words. "I need your help," I said, my voice low but urgent. "There's a woman. She's in peril. I need you to protect her."

His brows arched in surprise, but a grin curled his lips, mischief sparking in his eyes. "A woman?" he teased. "Have you finally found love? None of us ever thought we'd see the day."

I rolled my eyes, huffing a laugh that didn't quite reach my chest. "Very funny," I muttered, trying to brush off his jibe.

But he didn't let it go. His grin faded as he studied me, the firelight catching the shift in his gaze—curiosity giving way to something deeper. "You care about her," he said quietly, no longer teasing. "Don't you?"

I swallowed hard. The words came slow, edged with a pain I couldn't hide. "I love her," I admitted, my voice cracking. "But Salvatore is hunting her. And I... I can't protect her. My duty comes first—but my love for her consumes me." My eyes locked onto his, desperate. "You have to promise me. Her name is Elizabeth Alexander, and she is traveling with her maid from England. Keep her safe."

Dancing Fire didn't hesitate. He laid a hand over his heart, solemn and resolute. "Amir," he said, "I pledge to protect her. At all costs."

The flames danced in his eyes, mirroring the gravity of his vow. He stood tall, ready to defend her with every breath.

I nodded slowly, words failing me. "Thank you, my friend."

As I turned away, a hollow ache tore through my chest—the finality of entrusting Elizabeth's fate to another felt like tearing my soul in two. I could not bear to look back, not at the man who now bore the responsibility for my heart, not at the fire that seared behind me, tethering me to all I had been forced to let go.

I slipped into the forest's shadows, each footstep a silent echo of the future I could never claim. The trees closed around me, solemn witnesses to a love sacrificed on the altar of duty. In leaving her under Dancing Fire's protection, I clung to a single truth—that I had freed her from the chains of misery her father had forged.

But fate, as I well knew, was rarely so kind. And its plans were never mine to command.

ELIZABETH

Fortune had smiled upon us at the docks—though whether it was fortune or fate, I could not say.

When Mary and I approached the towering ship, worry clung to us like the mist rolling off the Thames. The impossibility pressed against my chest, heavy as the fear we carried. We had no money, no connections— only the urgency to escape.

The captain's eyes narrowed when he heard my name.

His gaze flicked between us as I explained—haltingly, voice trembling—that I was fleeing Lord Alexander's wrath. He knew the rumors, the fall of my father's society, and the destruction left in the wake of a nameless alchemist. Perhaps that was why he took pity. His voice, gruff and worn with the sea, held no emotion when he said, "The sins of fathers should not chain their daughters." Then he turned away, shouting orders to ready the ship.

∞

As the vessel rocked beneath me, I still heard his words echo in my mind. I couldn't tell if they were a mercy or a warning, but they'd been enough to grant us passage—and carry us into the unknown.

The ship groaned and shuddered as if protesting every wave and gust of wind that battered its hull. I curled on the narrow cot, knees against my chest, willing the nausea to pass. It didn't. The stench of salt, sweat, and unwashed bodies clung to the air like fog, pushing against my lungs with every shallow breath.

Each breath was a battle. Each hour, a reckoning.

And still—the sea carried us forward.

Mary had gone above deck to fetch water, leaving me alone in the cramped quarters we shared with two other women—a widow with a barbed tongue and a silent girl whose eyes darted like a frightened bird. The widow snored in the corner, her bulk blotting out most of the weak light that filtered through the porthole, casting the cabin in a dull, sickly gray.

The ship rolled hard. A wave slammed against the hull with a thunderous roar. My stomach twisted violently—not just from the pitch and yaw of the sea but from the persistent nausea of pregnancy. I gripped the cot's edge, knuckles white, bracing myself against the lurch. This voyage was a torment. How long had it been now? Four weeks? Six? Time had blurred into an endless rhythm of cold, sleepless nights and days spent clinging to the fragile hope that we might one day see land again.

The door creaked open.

Mary stepped inside, her face pale and drawn, carrying a tin cup of water. She handed it to me, her fingers brushing mine. "It's rough today," she said softly, lowering herself beside me.

"Rough would be a kindness," I muttered, taking a tentative sip. The water was tepid and metallic, but it soothed the desert in my throat.

Mary offered a faint smile, her eyes drifting to the porthole. "A sailor told me we've made good progress. If the winds hold, we could reach the colonies in another fortnight."

Another fortnight.

I didn't know if I could endure it.

My body was worn thin, my spirit frayed by the constant motion and the ceaseless noise of the sea. Every creak of wood, every crash of a wave, was a reminder that I was suspended between one life left behind and another not yet begun. But there was no choice now—no return to England, no option to remain adrift forever. Only forward.

I set the cup down, forcing myself upright. "We'll make it," I said, though I wasn't sure if the words were meant to reassure Mary… or myself.

Her eyes softened. She reached out, tucking a strand of hair behind my ear like a sister might. "Of course we will, my lady. You're stronger than you think."

I swallowed hard and nodded, though tears pricked at the corners of my eyes.

Strength wasn't a choice anymore. It was survival.

And I would survive—for Mary, myself, the new beginning waiting across the ocean… and the child growing in my belly.

The ever-mercurial widow often left Mary and me flinching with her biting tongue. But her provisions—oh, how they saved us. For weeks, we'd relied on her stores, each mouthful a gift, no matter how bitter the barbs she laced them with.

One evening, as the ship groaned and heaved, assaulted by another storm, Mary and I huddled near the communal firepit on the lower deck. The mingled scents of brine, sweat, and the acrid bite of smoke filled the air. The dim, flickering light painted every face in shades of desperation and fatigue.

The widow loomed above us, slicing a wedge from a wheel of hard cheese with her ever-present knife—the blade catching the firelight, gleaming like a threat.

"Mind you, don't burn it," she barked, handing the cheese to Mary and a hunk of salted pork wrapped in linen. Her eyes flicked to me, keen and appraising. "And don't waste it either. No matter how long this cursed voyage drags on, my stores are not bottomless."

Mary forced a polite "Thank you," though her cheeks reddened with restrained fury. I offered a tight smile, swallowing the retort that rose bitter in my throat. We needed her more than she needed us—and we both knew it.

Mary took charge of the fire, her fingers deftly balancing the iron pan over the flames. I watched as she worked, melting the cheese until it bubbled and crisped at the edges. The pungent aroma curling in the air made my stomach twist with hunger. She added slivers of pork, letting the fat sizzle and spit before tossing in a handful of dried onions—the last of the widow's generosity from the day before.

Despite the cold and the rolling waves that made every movement a challenge, this small ritual grounded us—a fleeting comfort in a world adrift.

The resulting mixture wasn't much, but after weeks of chewing on hardtack until my jaw ached, it tasted like a feast. I tore off a piece of the stale biscuit, using it to scoop up the savory mess. The salt and fat burst across my tongue, intense and overwhelming, and I closed my eyes briefly, letting the moment linger.

"Better than last week's gruel," I murmured, breaking the heavy silence.

Mary snorted softly, though her gaze stayed on the fire. "Anything's better than gruel."

The widow let out a derisive sniff from her perch on an overturned barrel. "You'll miss gruel soon enough if this wind keeps fighting us."

Her words struck like cold water, dousing the brief warmth of our meager meal. The storm-weary ship groaned around us, its constant creaks and wails a grim soundtrack to the days that bled together in gray monotony. The rolling gait of the vessel had become as natural as breathing, but it offered no comfort— only exhaustion.

Each evening was much the same. Scavenging scraps, coaxing them into something edible, then eating in near silence, save for the occasional groan of timber or the widow's cantankerous grumbling. Her barbed remarks pierced the quiet like a splinter, but we'd long since learned not to bite back. We needed her food more than we needed her kindness.

Morning brought cold hardtack and lukewarm water, just enough to keep us alive. The evening brought this—the smallest solace of Mary's cooking and the flicker of flame against worn faces.

One night, as Mary scraped the last cheese from the pan, I caught her eye and whispered, "Do you think she'll ever smile?"

Mary smirked, her weariness momentarily giving way to humor. "If she does, my dear, it'll be the first sign of land."

The laugh that bubbled out of me was brief but genuine. The cold, creaking ship faded momentarily, and a flicker of hope stirred in its place—however faint. Whatever lay ahead, at least we had each other—and, for now, the widow's provisions.

My legs wobbled as we finally debarked, clutching what little we possessed. The dock beneath our feet felt foreign and shaky like the world had shifted while we'd been lost at sea.

We scurried behind Widow York, who had begrudgingly offered us passage to her brother's home in Minnesota. Her thin-lipped scowl hadn't softened since our first encounter, and I didn't expect it to now.

Her brother, Jules, was as gruff as she was quick-witted—a man whittled from stone and solitude. A trapper by trade with weathered hands and a face lined like tree bark, he met us at the docks in New Orleans with all the warmth of a late frost.

"This the lot you dragged from England, Eleanor?" he asked, barely sparing us a glance as he jerked his chin in our direction —like we were bundles of pelts rather than people.

Widow York sniffed, not bothering to hide her disdain. "They're my burden. Best you let them aboard before I change my mind."

Her daughter peeked out from behind her skirts—pale, hollow-eyed, and silent. The girl clutched a worn doll so tightly I feared it might break, her small fingers gripping it like it was the last thread holding her to this world. I tried to catch her gaze and offer some measure of comfort, but she darted away like a frightened bird.

Jules grunted, then motioned to his flatboat—a rough-hewn craft with bundles of pelts and barrels lashed down with fraying rope. It smelled of fur, sweat, and river water—a far cry from the perfumed halls of my childhood.

"Get in," he said. "We're pushing off before nightfall. If I take you north with me, you'll earn your place. I need help prepping furs for trade. That's the deal."

No ceremony. No welcome. Just survival. Again.

Mary glanced at me, her expression unreadable—but we both knew we had no choice. Not now. Not with the past chasing us like wolves on our heels.

We climbed aboard.

The Mississippi stretched wide and brown before us, its current swift and harsh, churning like it could swallow us whole. This was our path north—through wild, uncharted lands to a future none of us could yet see.

The first days on the river passed in a grim silence, broken only by the splash of oars and the occasional bark from Jules as he snapped orders. Mary and I huddled near the bow, trying to stay out of the way, the spray from the water soaking through our threadbare cloaks. Eleanor sat near the stern, her daughter curled beside her, quietly feeding the child scraps of bread and slivers of dried fruit from her dwindling pouch.

"She's kind to her daughter," I murmured to Mary, watching the widow tuck a stray curl behind the girl's ear.

Mary gave a soft snort. "Only when it suits her."

Even so, I found my gaze returning to them again and again. The widow's biting tongue and harder eyes seemed to soften when she held her child close, wrapping her shawl tight against the wind. It was a side of her I hadn't expected—one I wasn't sure how to feel about.

As Jules guided us through a particularly treacherous stretch one afternoon, the boat lurched hard, nearly throwing us into the river. Mary and I hit the deck with a thud while the widow's daughter shrieked, clutching at her mother's skirts. Eleanor yanked her close, shielding her as the boat rocked violently.

"Hold tight!" Jules barked, his voice rising above the chaos. His oar dug into the water, muscles straining as he fought the current. A half-submerged log loomed ahead, slick with moss and threatening to splinter us apart. With a final, heaving pull, he steered us clear.

We steadied. Barely.

Breathless, I gripped the edge of the boat, my knuckles white. My heart thundered in my chest. "Is it always like this?"

Jules shot me a glance, and for the first time, his lips curved into a grin—crooked, knowing. "This?" he said, eyes gleaming. "This is nothing. Wait till the river gets angry."

Evenings were calmer, though the tension never fully dissipated. We camped along the riverbank beneath a canopy of blackened trees, the stars hidden by clouds that rarely seemed to part. Jules would build a fire while Eleanor prepared our meager food. One night, she handed me a piece of salted pork and a chunk of hardtack so tough it could've been stone.

"Make yourself useful," she said, her voice flat, nodding toward the fire.

My pride bristled, but I took the food without complaint. Mary joined me, and together, we knelt by the flames, warming the pork until it sizzled, the fat spitting in sudden bursts that caught in the firelight. The greasy and acrid smell made my stomach churn—but it was food. And that was enough.

As we ate, Jules spoke—his words like rough-cut timber, shaping a vision of the world ahead. He told us of the northern wilderness, endless forests swallowing the horizon, winters so cold your breath froze in the air, and the tribes that moved silently through the trees, masters of the land in a way no outsider could ever be.

"It's no place for women," he said, his gaze fixing on me.

I sat straighter, forcing the weariness from my voice. "Perhaps not. But we'll make do."

His low chuckle rumbled in the silence, harsh and unamused. "We'll see."

Weeks passed. The river became both ally and enemy— carrying us forward yet threatening to take us under at every bend. Rain fell often, soaking us to the bone, while the sun, when it appeared, burned our skin raw. The widow's child grew quieter, her doll now nothing more than a ragged scrap, its stuffing leaking, its eyes faded. She clung to it as if it could ward off the ghosts that clung to all of us.

Mary and I fell into a rhythm—the rhythm of survival. The ache of constant hunger, the chill that never quite left our bones, the journey heavier each day—we endured.

Strangers bound by circumstance, we moved forward—not as family or friends, but as survivors.

Hope was fragile—fraying with every mile—but we clung to it all the same. We wished that when the river finally released us, we'd find something more than another kind of hardship waiting at the end.

Yet as the waters stretched on—endless, and cold—I couldn't help but wonder if we'd merely traded one prison for another.

The river lapped gently at the sides of the flatboat, its rhythm both a comfort and a reminder of how far I'd drifted from the life I once knew. Each soft splash against the wood was a beat in the slow march away from the ruins of my past—and toward an unknown future, I dared not dream of. I sat at the boat's edge, the rough-hewn plank against my legs, hands folded over the swell of my belly. A tangible weight. A silent promise. A tether to the memories I longed to leave behind... and yet couldn't.

Widow York sat beside her daughter, murmuring to her in a low tone that carried across the quiet water. Jules, his watchful eyes ever scanning the horizon, steered us northward–toward the uncertain life awaiting us. We were a ragged band of survivors, bound by necessity, not trust.

Amid their gruff exchanges and the creak of rope and timber, my thoughts never strayed far from two figures—my father— who, despite his hatred, had shielded me from Salvatore's wrath —and Amir, whose absence gnawed at me like a phantom pain. A void no number of miles could fill.

"Elizabeth, could you pass me that sack of potatoes?" Mary's voice called from the riverbank, where she crouched near a modest fire, coaxing a meal from our dwindling supplies.

"Of course," I replied, mustering a faint smile as I reached for the sack. The simple task, once effortless, now strained muscles already taxed by fatigue. I felt every movement in my back, legs, and deep within—new life growing heavier by the day.

We sat together, slicing and dicing, the rhythmic thud of our knives mingling with the hiss of the river. The fire crackled, casting flickering light across Mary's face, illuminating lines of worry and determination etched deep by hardship. Beside us, Jules' voice rumbled in low conversation with Widow York, their silhouettes outlined against the encroaching dusk—worn, weathered figures in a land that asked everything and gave nothing freely.

Every evening felt the same—survival was woven into each breath, each bite, each silence. But in that shared labor, in the scent of woodsmoke and the rhythmic motion of blade through the potato, there was a sliver of something else.

Not comfort. Not yet. But perhaps… the beginning of it.

"Your belly is too big for someone who's only four months along," Mary observed, her voice soft with wonder, a fragile lightness amid the wilderness around us. "It's marvelous."

I placed a hand over the curve of my abdomen, feeling the stirrings of life within—swift, undeniable, growing stronger by the day. "It's so huge," I murmured, half in awe, half in disbelief.

"Maybe it's a big baby," Mary mused, dropping diced potatoes into the bubbling pot. "Or… perhaps twins."

"Twins?" My voice caught, a thread of unease winding around the word. "No, I don't have twins in my family."

Mary shrugged, smiling as if to defy the world. "You never know with these things. Life surprises us."

Life. Surprises. Some beautiful. Others cruel.

I watched the sun dip low, casting molten gold across the restless river and thought of Amir—stoic, untouchable Amir. His absence was a burden I carried with every step, every breath. He was gone, yet he lingered in every memory, every hope I dared to cradle.

But now, there was nothing to do but press forward—one stroke, one breath at a time—and pray that when dawn broke, it would bring more than silence, more than guilt. Maybe peace. Or maybe it was just another day to survive.

The fire had dwindled to embers when the night erupted into chaos.

It began with a single, piercing cry—a guttural sound that shattered the stillness—a warning, a promise of blood.

I scrambled to my feet, my heart slamming against my ribs, and my breath caught somewhere between a gasp and a scream. Too many shadows spilled across the riverbank too fast. Dark figures materialized from the trees, their movements swift and merciless.

The air split with a terrifying sound—a tomahawk whistling past us, embedding itself with a sickening thud into the tree behind Mary.

We were under attack.

CHAPTER 24

ELIZABETH

"Indians!" Jules' voice was a guttural bark, ripping through the night like a shot. Fear and urgency bled into every syllable as he lunged for his rifle, propped carelessly against a nearby tree.

But he was too late.

A swift and silent warrior exploded from the darkness—a specter of death cloaked in moonlight. The silver glint of his tomahawk flashed once before it connected with Jules' skull in a sickening crack.

He crumpled like a rag doll, no sound escaping his lips. Blood gushed beneath his head, staining the earth, while his rifle slipped from lifeless fingers into the hands of the attacker.

Mary's scream tore through the chaos, high and shrill. My heart pounded, erratic and painful, threatening to rip from my chest. Fear seized me—but the world offered no time for weakness—only flight.

"Run for the woods!" Widow York's voice rang out like a gunshot, her figure darting past in a blur, her daughter clutched tightly to her side. They vanished into the black mouth of the forest, swallowed whole by the shadows.

Mary and I stood frozen, rooted in horror, as warriors surged from the trees. Their faces were painted in streaks of red and white, their expressions unreadable and terrifying in the flickering firelight. Guttural cries filled the air as they swarmed the flatboat, tearing through our supplies, smashing crates, ripping fabric, and splintering wood.

They were everywhere.

"Elizabeth!" Mary's voice was high, panicked. She gripped my sleeve, tugging fiercely. "We have to go—now!"

I stumbled, disoriented, my legs leaden with fear. Together, Mary and I staggered backward—away from the violence, away from the wreckage of everything we had fought so hard to reach.

Away from the life that had, only moments ago, felt within reach—now smoldering, breaking, and lost to the river.

The warriors moved with terrifying ease, their cries loud and triumphant as they hurled our supplies onto the muddy shore. Jules' hard-earned furs—his prized beaver pelts—were tossed into the water like scraps, floating away into the darkness, mocking the ruin left behind.

"Come on!" Mary's voice broke through my daze. She tugged at my arm, dragging me from the horror. I turned my back on the flatboat, on Jules' lifeless body, on the firelit massacre—and fled into the forest's cold embrace.

Branches tore at our skin as we crashed through the underbrush, every step a desperate bid for survival. My heart slammed against my ribs like a war drum, echoing in my ears louder than our footfalls, louder than the cries of our pursuers.

These savages will kill me! The thought raced through my mind, panic blinding me, images of painted faces and raised tomahawks haunting every step.

"Elizabeth!" Mary's voice sliced through the dark, ragged with terror. "LOOK OUT!"

I barely turned before pain ripped through my scalp—a warrior had lunged from the shadows, his hand twisted in my hair. I screamed, stumbling backward, his grip yanking me off my feet. The stench of sweat and smoke clung to him as his face loomed close, eyes wild with fury.

He spat, the hot saliva striking my cheek like a brand of humiliation.

I froze, shock and terror locking my limbs, my voice strangled in my throat. Helpless.

The forest spun around me—night, branches, firelight, his hand like iron. I thought of Mary. Of the child growing inside me. Of Amir.

And I refused to die here.

Time fractured, stretching thin, every heartbeat a thunderclap in my ears. Then—whistle, thud—an arrow sliced through the air, burying itself in the warrior's throat with a sickening crack. His eyes widened, blood spurting in a dark arc across my dress, warm and jarring.

His grip loosened. He crumpled to the earth.

I collapsed beside him, hands clawing at dirt, gasping, retching, scrambling. Terror filled my veins like fire.

Screams—my screams—ripped from my throat, wild and raw. Around us, arrows hissed through the air, finding their marks. Warriors fell. Chaos erupted anew.

Another tribe had come.

No cries, no warnings—only the snap of bowstrings and the heavy thud of bodies hitting the earth.

"Elizabeth! We must go! NOW!" Mary's voice was a lifeline, her hands seizing mine, dragging me up. We ran, stumbling over roots and rocks, ducking beneath branches, zigzagging through the trees like hunted animals.

Where was the widow? Alive? Dead? There was no time—only escape.

Then—movement. A warrior surged from the dark ahead; muscles coiled to strike. Mary screamed—but her cry was cut off as he tackled her to the ground.

I spun toward them, heart in my throat. "MARY!"

Another figure darted from the shadows—silent, swift, deadly. Long hair trailed behind him as he closed the distance in an instant. His blade flashed—once—and buried itself in the attacker's back.

A gasp. A gurgle. The warrior collapsed like a felled tree.

Mary crawled backward, eyes wide, face as pale as bone,

trembling. The stranger turned to me, his gaze keen and assessing.

Not an enemy.

But… who?

"Shh, don't be scared," the long-haired warrior said, his voice low and strangely soothing in this setting. He knelt before us, extending a hand—not as a threat, but an offer. His eyes, dark as onyx, were gentle and warm. "I'm here to protect you. Don't worry—you're safe."

His words pierced the chaos. English. My breath caught, confusion rising through the fear like a wave.

Did they speak English? My mind reeled. These were Indians—savages, my father would have called them—yet this man's speech, though accented, was clear and comprehensible. They weren't what I had been led to believe. They weren't mindless warriors or wild men. This man's voice carried understanding, and something that unnerved me more—intelligence.

Mary and I clung to each other, tears streaking through the dirt on our cheeks, as this enigmatic figure stood guard—a solitary flame in a night gone mad.

The world spun—a blur of shadow, firelight, and the clash of hidden combatants. My breath came in ragged gasps, my heart pounding like it could break free. Mary's grip on my hand was iron; the terror in her eyes mirrored in mine.

"Stay close," I whispered, my voice barely audible, fragile and frayed. She nodded, her eyes locked on the man who had appeared like a specter—and saved us.

The warrior stepped closer, his long, dark hair catching the firelight. "No need to fear me," he said again. His English wasn't perfect—rough-hewn and shaped by a different tongue—but I understood him clearly.

"I am Dancing Fire," he continued, touching his chest. "This is my cousin, Sky Raven." Another man stepped from the trees, silent and intense, eyes scanning the darkness.

I could hardly speak. I had expected grunts, foreign words, not this—this man speaking with clarity and purpose. My world, already overturned, tilted again. Everything I had been taught about Native tribes was crumbling under the truth.

Dancing Fire crouched in front of us, his gaze locked on mine. "What are your names?"

Paralyzing terror gripped me, my heart pounding against my ribcage like a trapped animal's desperate struggle. Mary and I stood at the forest's edge, its towering trees cloaked in a dense, unsettling fog. I locked eyes with her—her pupils blown wide with fear, her breath coming in shallow gasps. Her terror matched my own, palpable and suffocating.

"We are from the mighty Sioux tribe." Dancing Fire stepped forward, commanding but not threatening. "Those bastards— Kiowa—are our mortal enemies. Treacherous, violent men."

His gaze flicked between us, unwavering and sincere.

"Do not be afraid. We came to protect you. If we hadn't arrived when we did…" He paused, his jaw tightening. "They would have defiled you, scalped you, then left your bodies to rot. Our people value peace above all else. We must defend those who cannot defend themselves. Please—do not fear us."

His voice, fierce and reverent, filled the silence, and with it, the moment shifted.

I gasped, my breath shuddering as relief mingled with disbelief. These men—these warriors—had saved us. My voice trembled as I stepped forward, forcing the words from lips still numb with fear.

"My name is Elizabeth Alexander," I managed, the syllables feeling foreign and fragile in this vast, unfamiliar wilderness. "And this is my dear friend Mary. We hail from England."

The words hung between us, as fragile as spun glass, a thread of trust extended to strangers in a world turned upside down.

Dancing Fire's expression softened into a smile—warm, genuine, and so unexpected that it eased the iron grip of fear on my chest.

"It is an honor to meet you both," he said kindly. "Please, come with us. I must bring you before our great chief and council." His invitation was free of command, steeped instead in respect—and something else I couldn't yet name.

Still stunned, we followed them, the only anchor in a night where everything familiar had been torn away. The riverbank unfolded before us, silvered in starlight, lined with birchbark canoes that looked otherworldly against the mist curling off the water. The world was a dreamscape of shadow and motion, and yet, Dancing Fire and Sky Raven moved with a certainty that defied the darkness—as if the forest and river belonged to them alone.

Dancing Fire extended a hand, guiding me to one of the slender vessels. "Careful," he murmured, steadying my arm as I stepped inside. His touch was light and respectful—a balm after the brutal violence of the Kiowa. I offered him a faint nod, unable to find words for the gratitude stirring in my chest.

Under Sky Raven's watchful gaze, Mary found her seat in another canoe. Our eyes met—haunted, weary, but alive. That, for now, was enough.

With barely a word, the warriors took up their paddles. The canoes glided across the river, as smooth as silk, propelled by an almost reverent rhythm. The water mirrored the stars above, a dark glass reflecting the night sky, broken only by the gentle dip and pull of the paddles.

There was none of Jules' gruff shouting, no harsh splashes of our flatboat—only the whispers of the river, the hushed song of the wilderness, and the slow, inevitable passage into the unknown.

I clutched the side of the canoe, my gaze fixed on the dark water ahead. Whatever awaited us beyond the bend, I could only pray it would not ask more than we had left to give.

The canoe's hull scraped the pebbled shore with a muted grind. I jolted, but Dancing Fire's firm grip steadied me as he helped me disembark. My legs trembled beneath me, weak from fear and fatigue, and I staggered on the uneven riverbank. He offered silent support, never releasing my arm until I had found my balance.

Beside us, Sky Raven extended his hand to Mary, who gripped it like a lifeline. Her face was drawn and pale in the moonlight, but her eyes were wide with lingering terror. I reached for her hand as soon as she was upright, and together, we clung to each other—our last thread of familiarity in this strange land.

"Where are you taking us?" The words burst out before I could temper them, edged with anxiety and exhaustion. My voice rang out too harshly in the quiet, shattering the solemn hush of the woods.

Dancing Fire turned toward me, his gaze unwavering, his expression unreadable but clear. "Like I said... to our chief. To the village." He spoke slowly in his halting English, each syllable carrying more than its sound. "Both of you are safe here."

Despite the uncertainty surrounding us, something about his voice—low, certain—cooled the fire of panic that had begun to flare in my chest. His assurance was not just spoken; it radiated from him, as solid and immovable as the earth beneath our feet.

Mary and I walked close, our shoulders brushing, taking comfort in that slender connection thread. As we followed Dancing Fire through the forest's hush, my mind spiraled back through everything we had endured since the flatboat—Widow York's biting commands, Jules' rough kindness, the bloodshed, the loss, the chaos, and Amir.

His name was a wound—raw and silent. His absence was a gaping void I dared not dwell on, not here, not now.

Through the trees, the village appeared like a dream, the silhouettes of cone-shaped dwellings glowing softly with the light of fires and torches. Shadows danced across the stretched leather surfaces, flickering like spirits as we passed. The air was filled with a strange quiet—not silence, but a peace borne of ritual and purpose, of people living by the rhythm of the land.

We wove between the dwellings, the earth solid beneath our feet, anchoring us in a world that felt foreign and strangely grounding at once. For the first time in weeks, I didn't feel like I was falling.

At the village's heart stood a larger structure, its timber beams adorned with feathers, bones, and beads, each a testament to a history I did not yet understand. Firelight spilled from the entrance, casting golden ripples across the ground. Smoke rose gently into the night sky, carrying prayers or warnings to the stars above.

I knew this was where our fate would be decided without being told.

Dancing Fire stepped ahead and motioned us forward. "This is Chief Red Feather," he said with a reverence that made me straighten instinctively. The man before us stood tall, his face lined with age but resolute with strength. His gaze met mine, heavy with a wisdom that seemed to weigh and measure me in a single breath.

They spoke in their own tongue—fluid and melodic, like a song born of earth and sky. The cadence was unfamiliar but oddly soothing like waves lulling you into peace even as they hide the depths beneath. Every so often, the chief's eyes flicked toward Mary and me, assessing, questioning, and deciding.

Dancing Fire turned to me, his expression gentle yet serious. "Elizabeth," he began, and just the sound of my name felt like a lifeline. "My father wishes you to know that the Kiowa are dangerous. If we had not intervened, they would have… harmed you greatly. We are grateful you and your maid live." His voice dropped lower, almost intimate. "He asks that you stay here. As our guest. Among our people. You will be protected."

Protected. The word echoed in my mind, both a relief and a shackle. My chest tightened.

"No, no. We can't stay," I whispered, though the conviction in my voice was thin, cracked at the edges. The baby. Amir's child. I couldn't give birth here, not in a strange place, not surrounded by people I didn't know. We needed to keep moving, didn't we?

Mary's hand gripped my arm, her fingers digging in—not from panic, but from urgency, strength. She turned to me, eyes fierce and clear.

"Elizabeth," Mary said, her voice low, desperation threading through every syllable. "We have no place else. No money. No protection. You can barely stand from fatigue, and that child inside you grows stronger every day. We need rest.

We need safety." She turned to Dancing Fire, her tone softening like worn cloth. "Let us stay. Just until the birth. Please."

Her words struck like an arrow, piercing the fragile shield of denial I had wrapped around myself. I looked around, absorbing the firelight's warmth, the stillness of the chief, the quiet certainty in Dancing Fire's eyes. This wasn't captivity. It wasn't a weakness. This was a refuge—a rare chance at survival. At that moment, with the promise of sanctuary offered by a man as silent and controlled as the moon above, I felt a sliver of hope break through the dense fog of despair.

Chief Red Feather's gaze held mine, unwavering and unblinking. His brow furrowed with thought, his lips moving in quiet words only his son could understand. Dancing Fire nodded solemnly as he listened, absorbing each word with gravity and making my stomach clench.

When he turned back to me, there was something in his eyes —not fear, not pity—but reverence.

"Elizabeth," he said, my name falling from his lips like a sacred secret. I couldn't say why it sent a chill down my spine. "The Chief has asked me to tell you something of great importance. You are... special. The life you carry—twins—was foretold."

I froze, the air stolen from my lungs.

Twins?

The word echoed in my mind—impossible and inevitable all at once.

"There is a chance, a rare and powerful chance," Dancing Fire continued, his voice firm, like stone worn smooth by time. "That your children will be born on the day of the solar eclipse; if that happens, they will not be ordinary. They will be Timebornes—blessed with the ability to travel through time."

I gasped, my heart stumbling over itself in terror. The word Timeborne lanced through me—piercing, unwelcome, unrelenting.

Memories I had tried to bury surged like a tide, clawing at the fragile dam I had built inside me—whispers in dark corridors, stories of those marked by time, cursed with destinies they could never escape.

No.

No, this was not the life I envisioned.

All I craved was peace, not prophecies or power. Not fate. Not time.

"Twins? And time travel?" My voice cracked, shaking with fear. "No—no! I just want peace! I don't want anything to do with Timebornes, Timebounds, Time—"

The words dissolved into sobs. Tears spilled down my cheeks unchecked, and my body trembled as I tried to breathe past the storm inside me. I shook my head, desperate to reject it, to deny it, and pretend I hadn't heard.

Destiny could be changed. It had to be.

"Timebornes. Timebounds. Timehunters," Dancing Fire echoed softly, his brow furrowing, confusion etched into every line of his face. "How do you know these words?"

"My father was a Timehunter," I whispered, broken and breathless. "I ran from that life. I ran from the bloodshed, the death, the evil they carried in their hearts." My eyes locked with his, pleading, desperate. "That's why I left England, why I crossed an ocean. Why I hid. And now your chief tells me I carry twins—twins who might become what I fear most."

The truth poured from me, jagged and raw. "I can't do it again. I can't live like that. I just want to be free of it."

Chief Red Feather stepped forward, his expression unreadable but his aura grounding, like a great oak standing amidst the storm. He spoke, his English broken, but each word was pointed, heavy, and final.

"Elizabeth… you have nothing to fear. You are safe."

The Chief's words moved like wind through leaves—soft, ancient. "My predictions… they may not be true. The future is not always clear. Do not stress. Do not fear. You are tired. Hungry. Let my people care for you."

His gaze, aged and wise, held mine. I wanted to believe him, to drink in the peace he offered. But fear had rooted itself too deeply.

"Dancing Fire will look after you. Sky Raven will guard Mary." His voice lowered. "You are not alone now."

His eyes—weathered by time, shaped by hardship—softened, and with a final word, he dismissed the storm inside me with quiet authority.

"Rest."

Before I could protest and ask the thousand questions forming in my mind, he gestured for Dancing Fire to lead me away. I turned, my steps unsteady, and let myself be guided from the council fire's warmth into the night's cool embrace.

But with each step, dread coiled tighter around my heart.

Twins. Timebornes.

The things I had fled now clung to me like shadows at dusk, impossible to outrun. Fear gnawed at my soul.

I had left a trail of destruction behind me. Two powerful Timehunter societies lay in ruins—because of me. Because of the poison I created. The secrets I carried. The war I started.

Timehunters showed no mercy. They never did. They sought Timebornes and Timebounds like wolves stalking prey—cold, and cruel.

And now, Salvatore hunted me. His name alone sent a shiver through me. He wanted the truth—about the Noctyss flower, the poison, the future growing inside me.

My heart twisted. Amir.

Dead and Gone. Because of me.

His death was a wound that never closed, a punishment I could never escape.

And now, I was to bring Timebornes into this world—a world soaked in blood, ruled by power, haunted by death. What life could they possibly have, shaped by the chaos I'd created, carrying the burden of the path I chose?

Desperation clawed at my ribs, choking me. All I yearned for was escape.

From the nightmare. From the prophecy. From myself.

But deep down, I knew.

My sins would not let me go.

They waited in the dark, patient and silent—

Ready to strike.

CHAPTER 25

ELIZABETH

The leather felt foreign against my skin—a stark contrast to the silks and laces that once graced my wardrobe. Weeks had passed since I found myself living among the Sioux on their tribal land in 1762, yet each sunrise greeted me with novelties that felt neither less strange nor less barbaric than the last.

The garments I now wore, crafted from soft deerskin, clung to my body. Intricate beadwork adorned every surface, tiny stones and shells woven into patterns that told stories I couldn't begin deciphering. I ran my fingers along the fringes that lined the seams—tactile threads binding me to a world not my own—a world of earth and wind, of voices spoken in unfamiliar tongues, of customs as ancient as the stars above.

Dancing Fire had gifted me these clothes—his sister's garments, once worn with pride, now passed to me with reverence. Along with them, he had offered me a place in his teepee. An act of kindness. Of acceptance. Yet, even draped in the trappings of his people, I was still an outsider—caught in a quiet limbo between belonging and exile. I spoke their words in halting fragments and learned their ways through observation and gentle correction, but I could not cross the chasm between who I had been and what I was becoming.

As twilight bled into the sky, the horizon painted in hues of dying fire, I sought solitude in the only place that brought me peace—the forest. Among the towering pines and shifting shadows, I surrendered to the ache that gripped my chest like a vice.

Amir.

His name was a whisper in the wind, a ghost among the leaves. I closed my eyes, breathing in the scent of moss and bark, but all I could feel was him—the warmth of his skin, the deep bronze of his Mediterranean complexion, the soothing power in his dark eyes. I remembered how his arms felt around me, the quiet strength of being near him, and the heartbeat I used to rest my head against.

I wandered deeper into the forest's embrace, chasing his echo. Every rustle of leaves, every shadow between the trees, became a phantom. Each time I hurried forward, desperate and hopeful, it was never him. There was only silence. There was only grief.

My heart splintered anew with every step, pierced by memories like arrows—each feathered with moments we shared—his laughter, his touch, and his whispered promises.

A love that still watched me. Still reached for me.

It was always just beyond my grasp.

Night after night, I was haunted by dreams of him—Amir—reaching for me, his hands outstretched, his eyes filled with longing, only to dissolve into mist the moment our fingers met. Each time, I woke with a cry lodged in my throat, my cheeks damp with tears that became my only companions. They slipped silently down my face, soaking into the earth beneath me as though nourishing the grief that had rooted itself deep in my soul.

"Amir," I whispered into the darkness, his name a prayer—a plea—to release him, yet to never forget. The silence answered, vast and consuming, save for the gentle rustle of the wind in the trees and the quiet assurance that sorrow, like a river, would carve its path through me—slow and unrelenting.

The night air wrapped around me as I returned toward the teepee, my limbs heavy, my heart heavier. Something about the stillness of the forest, the way the world always seemed to hush in reverence, had made his absence feel like he was here. His spirit lingered, unseen yet tangible, wrapped around me like a phantom embrace.

I paused at the threshold of the teepee, drawing in a breath to collect myself, to wear my sorrow as quietly as possible. Inside, the firelight danced softly along the leather walls, casting flickering shadows that felt almost like home.

"Elizabeth," came the gentle voice of Dancing Fire. His words, spoken low and kind, soothed the raw edges of my grief. "I see your pain. You carry it like a stone in your chest."

I met his soulful gaze, his eyes dark pools of empathy and understanding.

"You are strong," he said. "But strength can become a burden if you never lay it down. Let us help you heal. Give us a chance… You might find joy here. Among us."

His words pierced the fog of my mourning, clear and true. My breath caught, the truth of it searing. "You're right," I whispered, my voice breaking around the edges. "I have to let go of the father of my children. Let his memory rest… and move forward with life."

Dancing Fire leaned in, resting his hands on his knees, his expression soft but filled with curiosity. "I am curious about the father of your children," he said, his voice tender. "Who was he?"

My hand drifted to the curve of my growing belly, and for a moment, I just breathed—feeling the quiet flutter of life within, the echo of a love lost but never forgotten. "His name was Amir," I began, my voice barely a murmur, laced with pain and love in equal measure. "He was a darkness—a warrior feared by many, but to me… he was my salvation. He saved me from my father's wrath. In the darkest moments of my life, when everything I knew fell apart, I found him."

I smiled faintly, bittersweet. "Our love wasn't easy. It burned like a storm. We were never meant to be… and yet, our hearts chose each other when the odds were impossible. Even when the world turned against us."

My voice trembled, but I didn't stop. "He gave me everything—and now he's gone. But his children… they are his legacy. I will raise them with love, with strength. For him. For us."

Dancing Fire nodded slowly, his expression unreadable yet filled with quiet respect. "Then Amir's spirit lives on. Through them. Through you."

My hand clenched the soft deerskin of my dress as my voice faltered. "Though he's gone, every day without him feels like a wound that refuses to heal. But I know I must let go. I owe it to these babies—to give them the life they deserve. It's time to move forward, find strength in their future… and maybe I'm ready to try."

"Then let us begin anew," Dancing Fire said, a flicker of excitement lighting his eyes. "Let me teach you how to hunt. To track animals. To use a bow."

The idea was daunting, and yet it stirred something inside me —a flicker of curiosity, a desire not just to survive but to truly live, to master something in this unfamiliar world, to make a place within it. I nodded, more to myself than to him. It was time to embrace this life—to stop surviving in the shadows and begin weaving new threads into the tapestry of my story.

In the days that followed, Dancing Fire became my teacher. Patient and skilled, he guided my hands as I learned to hold the bow, nock an arrow, and draw the string with balanced pressure and focus. The tension of the bow mirrored the tension within me—coiled, ready, waiting for release.

"Focus on your target," he said, standing close beside me as I squinted toward a makeshift bullseye pinned to a tree. "Breathe with the wind. Move with the earth."

I let the arrow fly. It arced through the air and struck the trunk with a satisfying thud, just inches from the center. A thrill surged through me, unbidden and pure. I turned toward Dancing Fire, my face breaking into a rare smile—and saw his answering grin, full of shared triumph.

"Good," he praised, nodding with approval. "Now, tracking. Tracking is about seeing what nature hides in plain sight."

We moved through the forest together, his steps quiet and

intentional, as if he were part of the earth. He gestured toward subtle impressions in the soil—hoofprints imprinted into the soft ground, a trail of matted grass, a snapped twig dangling from a low branch. Faint traces of scat dotting the path like bread-crumbs left by creatures. Each mark was a clue, a story written in the language of the wild, and with every detail he showed me, I felt something shift deep within.

I didn't just exist anymore.

I was becoming.

"Here," he said, crouching by the flattened grass. "Deer passed this way." I followed the line he pointed to, my eyes tracing the gentle curve of the trail. A sense of connection unfurled inside me—not just to the deer, but to the world itself. The grief that had once filled me to the brim began to ebb, replaced by a quiet reverence for the living, breathing wilderness that now surrounded me.

"Feel the ground beneath your feet," Dancing Fire said, his voice a soft murmur in the breeze. "Listen to the whispers of the trees."

We moved silently, two shadows among many, the forest alive with sound and silence in equal measure. With each passing day, I began to understand—not just the hunt but myself. I unearthed resilience, adaptability, and a strength I had never dared to believe I possessed. Each step and lesson stripped away the fragments of the broken woman I had been, revealing someone new beneath.

One morning, between hunts, I knelt by a patch of wild lavender, my fingers gently brushing the delicate purple blooms. Their scent—earthy, clean, and bright—rose into the crisp air, mingling with memories I thought I'd lost. Carefully, I plucked several stems, adding them to the woven basket at my side, and as I worked, my mother's voice echoed in my heart, naming each plant and its purpose.

"Elizabeth," Dancing Fire called gently from nearby, his eyes curious as he watched me gather. "Do you understand these herbal mysteries?"

I stood, the leather of my garments rustling—a sound both

foreign and familiar, strange yet comforting. Turning toward him, I met his gaze with a quiet pride that surprised me.

"I practice healing alchemy," I said softly, the words strange on my tongue—strange, yet powerful. Once an identity I had tried to outrun, now it felt like a lifeline. Not a curse, but a calling.

"Ah." He nodded slowly and thoughtfully, his eyes holding a flicker of respect that warmed me more than the rising sun. "Our healer has walked on to the next life. Many here carry old wounds—aches, lingering pains. Could you... fill that void?"

My hands hovered over the plants in my basket, their scents rich and grounding. "I would love to try," I whispered, not because I was fearless—but because I needed to believe that healing others could heal something in me, too.

As days melted into weeks, I stepped fully into the role of the tribe's healer. Women came to me with their children, their eyes shadowed by worry I eased with poultices and warm teas. Warriors sought me out—prideful yet worn by past battles. I stitched their wounds, rubbed salves into scarred skin, and spoke calmly into the hush of night. Every grateful smile, every sigh of relief, chipped away at the wall I had built around my grief, brick by agonizing brick.

But as my knowledge of healing deepened, so too did my belly swell. With every flutter, every kick, the twins within reminded me that life moved forward. Alone beneath the blanket of stars, I often lay a hand to my womb, wondering if the blood that flowed through my children would doom them to the same tangled destiny that had ensnared me. Would they be Time-bornes? Would they be hunted for powers they never asked for?

My past felt like a fading dream—a tapestry woven with loss, sorrow, and love that still haunted me in the quiet hours before dawn. And yet... despite the uncertainty and fear, I found peace in the present. In the laughter of the children I healed, in the strong hands of the warriors I mended, in the clasp of Dancing Fire's hand over mine—a silent promise that I was no longer just Elizabeth Alexander, cast adrift in the storm.

I was something more now—a healer, a mother, a thread

woven into the fabric of this people. And for the first time in a long while, I believed that perhaps… I belonged.

Dawn had barely begun to paint the sky in soft hues of rose and gold when Dancing Fire appeared at the entrance of the teepee, his silhouette stark against the pale light. "We hunt today," he said—no question, no invitation—just a truth, spoken with quiet certainty.

I nodded, swallowing the nerves fluttering in my stomach. I gathered my quiver, the worn leather familiar beneath my fingers, and slung it over my shoulder. Once foreign and unwieldy, my bow now felt like an extension of my hand.

The forest was alive around us—birds warbling their morning songs, leaves whispering secrets in the wind. The air was crisp and clean, filling my lungs with each step as I moved beside him, moccasins silent against the earth. At that moment, the land felt less like wilderness and more like a living, breathing entity—one I was slowly learning to trust.

We reached a stream, its waters glistening like glass over stone. I knelt, letting my fingers drift through the current, searching for herbs. Yarrow grew in clusters along the bank— good for wounds. Willow bark curled beneath the water's edge —nature's relief for pain.

Then, the light shifted.

A shadow passed over me, sudden and immense, eclipsing the sun's warmth in an instant.

Bear.

My breath caught, the world narrowing to the massive form, stepping into the stream just feet from where I crouched. Its dark eyes locked on mine—curious, calculating. I stumbled back, my heart slamming against my ribs, terror seizing my limbs. Every instinct screamed to flee, to run into the trees, and never stop.

"Elizabeth, don't run!" Dancing Fire's voice cut through the panic, as sharp as an arrow's edge. "Stand still!"

But the bear had seen me. There was no escape.

Its gaze bore into mine—ancient, merciless.

I stood frozen, carved from fear, as Dancing Fire notched an arrow. The string twanged. The arrow flew true, burying itself in the bear's shoulder. A deafening roar ripped through the forest.

The beast turned, fury in its eyes, and charged him.

They collided—force against force, a storm meeting stone. The bear's paw lashed out brutally, striking Dancing Fire across his side. Blood sprayed, as vivid as rubies, against his tanned skin. He staggered but did not fall.

"Find something, Elizabeth! Fight!" His voice was raw, desperate—a lifeline thrown into the chaos.

His words shattered my paralysis. My eyes darted, searching —a rock, jagged and heavy beneath my hand. I hurled it with everything I had.

The stone struck the bear's side with a dull thud. It turned, snorting, rage rekindled. Its eyes locked on mine. Time slowed, and my breath snagged in my throat, caught behind ribs that felt like they might crack.

"Elizabeth, move!" Dancing Fire's voice tore through the haze, but I couldn't. My legs were stone, rooted in fear.

Then—a blur. A flash of steel.

Dancing Fire, bleeding and battered, had seized his hunting knife. With a warrior's cry, he hurled it. The blade spun through the air, catching the sun—a silver streak of vengeance—and struck deep.

The bear howled in agony, rearing high on its hind legs. Then, one final, thunderous swipe brought its fury down on him.

Dancing Fire crumpled. Blood poured from a ragged gash across his chest. He hit the earth with a sickening thud, a sound that stole the breath from my lungs and ripped the world out from under me.

Everything narrowed—to his still form, to the blood beneath him, staining the earth in crimson sorrow.

The bear, wounded and seething, turned from us. A low growl rumbled in its throat like distant thunder threatening to return. Its eyes, dark and vengeful, locked on mine—a promise of retribution. Then it vanished into the forest, leaving behind nothing but torn earth and the memory of blood trailing into the snow-melted waters of the stream.

I fell to my knees beside Dancing Fire, my hands already stained with his lifeblood. His breaths came in ragged gasps, his eyes fluttering open to meet mine—pain and gratitude swirling in their depths.

"Stay with me," I begged, my voice a broken whisper. "Please, don't leave me."

His chest rose and fell, each breath a fragile battle, life clinging to him by a thread thinner than spider silk.

This was the moment—the test. I could not falter.

My hands shook as I tore at the leather of my garment, stripping it into rough bandages. Holding them against his wounds, I fought to staunch the bleeding, to keep him anchored to this world. His blood soaked my hands, but I would not stop.

Night fell cold and cruel, wrapping around us with icy fingers. But the fear in my chest was colder still.

I built a fire, coaxing flame from tinder with trembling hands. As Dancing Fire drifted in and out of consciousness, slipping toward a darkness I could not see, I whispered prayers into the flickering light—pleas to any power that might hear me to spare his life, to give him back.

Memory became my guide. Yarrow to staunch the bleeding. Plantain to ease the inflammation. I worked silently, a sentinel holding the line between life and death, refusing to surrender him to the void.

And as dawn broke, painting the sky in hues of hope, I felt the fever break beneath my palms. His brow cooled, and a true breath—slipped from his lips, as soft as the first light of morning.

He would live.

At that moment, beneath the newborn sun, I dared to believe that healing was possible—not just for him but for both of us. In this wild, unforgiving land, far from where my story began... something new could rise. Something strong. Something whole.

My stomach growled a plaintive cry that matched the whimpers of my heart. By the third day, hunger clawed at me with desperation nearly as vicious as the bear that had mauled Dancing Fire. The forest teemed with life, and I knew I must become part of it—not just an observer, but a survivor. With hands that had once only known the softness of silk and lace, I fashioned a crude snare from the sinews of my tattered leather garments.

"Please," I whispered into the wind, "let this work."

Luck—or perhaps fate—guided a rabbit into my trap. Its soft brown eyes met mine for a brief, agonizing moment before I did what was necessary. I remembered Dancing Fire's patient voice as he taught me how to honor the life taken—to use every part of the animal and waste nothing.

I cooked the rabbit over the fire I had tended, its warmth a small bastion against the encroaching chill of the wilderness. The scent of roasting meat filled the air, and I watched as Dancing Fire stirred, drawn back from the brink by the promise of sustenance.

"Thank you," he rasped as I helped him sit upright. His eyes met mine, wide and searching, filled with something I could not quite name. Gratitude, perhaps. Or awe.

"You're here," he said, his voice steadier now. "You saved me."

"I couldn't let you die," I murmured, those words anchoring deep within my chest. "I had to help you. Besides, you were the one who saved me first."

Shock flickered across his face, quickly replaced by something quieter—respect, deep and unspoken.

"You're stronger than you know, Elizabeth," he said, his voice like the crackling fire between us. "I'm grateful to have met you."

As the days passed and his wounds began to heal, I reflected on the bond that had grown between us. Dancing Fire had become more than the man who offered me shelter. He was my best friend, my connection to a world that was no longer foreign but no less wild. He had rescued me from a life that might have ended or been twisted into something unrecognizable, bent by another's will.

When he could finally stand, we decided it was time to return to the tribe. Our journey back was quiet, the silence between us no longer born of fear or pain but of something else —something steadier. A silent understanding forged not with words but with firelight, survival, and what we had endured together.

As the sky darkened and stars bloomed above us that evening, we sat beside the fire again. Sparks rose into the night, vanishing into the endless dark like fleeting wishes. Dancing Fire turned to me, his face illuminated by the gentle flicker of flame.

"Elizabeth," he said, his voice low and sure, "you've brought much to my people. Your heart and your hands—they've given healing, peace, hope—more than you know."

His words wrapped around me, gentle and unexpected, like the warmth of the fire between us. I looked at him, truly looked, and saw a depth in his eyes that had nothing to do with the pain of the past few days. Something else lingered there—respect, perhaps—or something deeper.

"You've given me something, too," I murmured, fingers tightening around the edges of my deerskin shawl. "A place to belong. I never had that before. Not with my father. Not in England." I paused, the truth pressing hard on my tongue. "Not until here."

There was a stillness after that as if the wind had stopped to listen. In Dancing Fire, I found safety, respect, and friendship. I admired his unwavering strength, quiet kindness, and the way he saw me not as broken but as whole.

And yet… as the flames crackled between us, I felt the ache that never faded. Amir's memory burned as brightly as this fire, etched into my soul like ink that could never be washed away. His love had marked me and shaped me. It was something no distance, no time, could unravel.

"I will always belong to Amir," I whispered, voice nearly lost in the night, a confession meant only for the stars and the shadows—a vow, still binding, still true.

But when I glanced at Dancing Fire, something flickered in his gaze. Something unreadable. His eyes didn't waver, didn't pull away. They held mine, intense, filled with something I hadn't dared to consider. Had I been wrong about what lived between us? Had I been blind to something more?

My heart stumbled, uncertain. I looked away; the fire suddenly felt too warm, and the air hung unnaturally still. Whatever had begun to take root in the silence between us, I wasn't ready to name it.

Not when part of me still lived with a man I could never forget.

CHAPTER 26

AMIR

The air was full of dust and sweat as I lunged forward, my blade cleaving through the dim haze of the training room buried deep within the underground palace. Each clash of steel rang out like thunder in the darkness, echoing off ancient stone walls that seemed to close in tighter with every passing day. This place was no sanctuary—it was a tomb where I buried my grief, one strike at a time.

Pain tore through my arm as my opponent landed a punishing blow, but I ignored it. I welcomed it. The pain was better than the numbness. With a guttural snarl, I pivoted and drove him back, my sword a blur of rage and discipline. Sweat stung my eyes, and my muscles screamed, but I didn't stop. I couldn't stop.

Because if I stopped, I'd remember her.

The one thing I couldn't bury, even in the darkest parts of myself.

She wandered into the forest like she was chasing something she couldn't name.

But it was me. I kept my distance, barely glimpsing her. But I was there.

She didn't know it—couldn't know it.

She thought I was dead.

And still… she felt me.

Drawn to the silence between the trees, to my aura reaching through the branches like a ghost.

She lingered there, standing too long in the shadows, turning as if she might catch a hint of something not meant to be seen.

It wrecked me.

To be so close—to see the way her breath hitched, her arms wrapped tighter around herself like she sensed me there.

And I couldn't go to her.

Couldn't speak.

Couldn't reach for her.

Not even when her eyes filled with tears and she looked straight through the place where I stood.

She didn't know she was breaking me.

But gods…

She did.

Just by feeling me.

And I almost stepped out. Almost gave in.

Almost let the truth shatter everything.

But I didn't.

I stayed in the dark.

And she walked away believing she was alone.

Elizabeth.

Her name was a blade in my mind, sharper than any steel. I saw her in the flicker of torchlight, heard her in the rhythm of my breath, and felt her in the silence that always followed the fight. The memory of her laughter—soft and bright—cut deeper than any wound. And the loss? A chasm devoured me, a darkness I couldn't escape.

"Amir, you need rest," one of my men ventured, his voice hesitant, foolishly brave.

I turned, fixing him with a stare that chilled the room. He faltered, wisely stepping back. There were no words now. No explanations. My silence was a fortress—impenetrable, merciless. I had become the shadow I once feared.

I relived our final moments every night—the way her fingers slipped from mine, the way I let her go. And I hated myself for it.

The rage I harbored toward Lazarus coiled tighter within me, venomous and hot, burning just beneath the surface like molten steel. He had ordered it—decreed that I sever the only connection that had ever brought light into my darkness. And I had obeyed. Like a coward. Like a man with no will of his own.

Steel clashed again. Sparks flared. But I didn't feel it.

I didn't feel anything anymore.

I shook my head, trying to dispel her face from my mind's eye. But it clung to me like a ghost. I gripped my sword tightly, the leather biting into my palms. "I'm going to visit her. One more time," I whispered to the shadows, a vow spoken only to myself—a lie I allowed myself to believe.

Just once more. Just to see her.

But I knew the truth—I could never let her go. Not completely.

The humid air of the American continent clung to my skin as I stood hidden amidst the tall grasses of a vast, sunlit field. Summer had drenched the land in vivid greens, the heat of 1762's cruel sun bearing down like a punishment. In the distance, I heard laughter—light and carefree—voices of the Sioux, their joy carried on the wind.

But my gaze was fixed on her.

Elizabeth.

She moved with a grace that stole the breath from my lungs as if the sweltering heat dared not touch her. Her wheat-blond hair shimmered like spun gold in the sunlight, falling loosely down her back. A dress of soft doeskin hugged her slender form, and by her side, Dancing Fire—my friend, my brother in arms— worked the earth beside her with a tenderness that twisted like a dagger in my chest.

I watched as he reached out, gently wiping sweat from her brow with a touch so careful and intimate that it made my hands ache to do the same.

But it wasn't the touch that shattered me.

It was her belly—round and full of new life.

A child.

Was it mine?

How had I not noticed before?

The thought was a storm, thrilling and tormenting all at once. My heart pounded, torn between the hope that I had not lost everything… and the terror that I had.

With every smile Dancing Fire gave her, every wordless moment of affection, jealousy seared through me, hotter than the sun that blazed overhead. My fists clenched, nails biting into flesh, as the urge to stride into that field and take my place at her side warred with every oath I had sworn.

"Amir," I whispered, voice like gravel. "You have no claim here. You begged him to protect her." I forced the words out like poison. "You'll alert Salvatore if he senses your presence. You'll doom her."

Still, my fists tightened. My heart raced.

And in the silence between the wind and my breath, I stood on the edge of breaking, longing to tear apart their peaceful world… to feel her hand in mine again.

I could bear no more.

The rules of time were cruel. I had to wait for the next full moon to travel again. Until then, I was trapped—neither part of her world, nor able to escape it.

So, I stayed.

Hidden in the forest's edge.

Watching her.

Day after day. Night after night.

It was torture, standing so close and yet so far from the woman I loved desperately.

When the night of the full moon finally came, I turned away from the sight of Elizabeth in Dancing Fire's care and reached for the blade beneath my cloak—the ancient dagger etched with markings older than any kingdom I'd ever crossed.

As its tip kissed my palm, time bent to my will.

I let the veil of time close around me, and in an instant, the moonlit field vanished.

The sudden sting of cold replaced the humid air.

I returned to the shadows of Anatolia's underground palace —its walls damp, its silence suffocating. The transition left me reeling. The contrast between her warmth and this stone tomb only deepened the abyss inside me.

I stormed through the labyrinth of corridors, my footsteps thundering with each stride. Fury boiled beneath my skin, no longer contained or hidden behind the mask I had worn for far too long. My dark eyes scorched with a fire I hadn't felt in months, and I could no longer restrain the storm rising within me.

I burst into Lazarus' study, the door slamming against the wall with a deafening crack. He looked up from his ancient tomes, unbothered, serene as if he'd expected me.

"How long?" I snarled, every word laced with venom. "How long were you going to keep it from me that Elizabeth is pregnant with my child?"

My voice echoed through the stone chamber like the roar of a beast, raw and unrelenting. The air crackled with tension, with betrayal.

Lazarus' gaze didn't waver. He met my rage with maddening calm, his expression unreadable—like stone worn smooth by centuries of storms.

"I assumed you'd figure it out," he said, his voice devoid of regret as if this were a minor inconvenience, as if he hadn't stolen everything from me. "You went to see her. I warned you of the dangers."

The fury in me snapped its chains.

My fist slammed down onto the heavy oak desk, shaking the room. The sound was thunder, the force enough to splinter the inlay of ivory along the edges. Books tumbled to the floor. The flames in the hearth danced wildly in response.

"You knew!" I bellowed, voice hoarse with anguish. "You knew she was carrying my child and said nothing!"

I took a staggering breath, trying to tame the chaos threatening to consume me, but it was useless. "I saw her," I choked out, each word a blade. "For a moment. Just one moment. Her belly was full of life. My child. Ours. And he—Dancing Fire—was at her side. Tending to her. Protecting her."

My hands clenched into tight fists, my knuckles turning white as I struggled to contain the surge of anguish that threatened to consume me.

"Well, consider your reaction," Lazarus said, his voice taut.

"Are you mad? She's bearing my child. My child!" The words escaped through gritted teeth, each syllable heavy with disbelief and raw emotion.

"Children." Lazarus quirked an eyebrow, his expression unreadable, as if regarding a stubborn pupil. "When I took her blood to cloak her, I heard the heartbeats. There are two of them."

"Twins?" The word left me in a whisper, disbelief, and wonder battling in my chest. A surge of protectiveness rose like a storm tide as I pictured Elizabeth carrying not one but two lives—a double miracle… or a double curse?

"Yes." Lazarus' voice deepened as if the shadows leaned in to hear him speak. "When I saved you both from that masquerade… when I began to heal her…" His eyes darkened with memory. "That's when I heard them—the heartbeats. Two of them. And in that moment, I knew. It was my chance. My only chance to perform the ritual of soul rebirth."

My heart lurched. "Lazarus, you've told me before that using such powerful rituals weakens you. Why do this to yourself… to Elizabeth?"

His face tightened, pain flickering in his eyes before it was swallowed by iron resolve. "Amir, we must bring Armand back. Salvatore is gaining ground with Alina and Mathias at his side. He's forging alliances that will crush us if we do not strike first. This was my moment to act… and I did."

He took a breath, his choice settling on his shoulders like a mantle of stone. "Though the ritual drained me—though the pain was unbearable—it was worth it. I needed to bring back Armand first… before Salvatore could destroy everything we've fought for."

His voice dropped, low and resolute, haunted by the burden of what he'd done. "Elizabeth won't understand. But she will. One day, she'll see why this sacrifice was necessary. And why it had to be her."

A storm churned inside me—rage, sorrow, longing—all of it clashing in a maelstrom that threatened to tear me apart. The desire to be with her like a wildfire, but I was shackled, bound by duty and vengeance, a prisoner within these ancient walls. I was a caged beast, yearning for freedom, but knowing release meant destruction.

Lazarus rose slowly, his movements deliberate, the passage of centuries etched into his very posture. "I understand your pain," he said quietly, a flicker of empathy in his eyes before the Shadow Lord mask slipped back into place. "But if you try to connect with her again… she will be destroyed."

"Destroyed…" The word echoed through me, lancing my soul deeper than any blade could. Elizabeth—her gentle spirit, fierce will, the life growing inside her—how could I survive being the cause of her undoing?

"How do you endure this?" I rasped, my voice cracking beneath unspent grief. "You don't understand. You can't. You have no idea the pain I carry."

"Amir." His voice softened, almost faltered. For a fleeting breath, he was no longer the indomitable Shadow Lord, but a man haunted by the same ghosts. "The sacrifices we make… they shape us. They are the price of the power we carry. Do not let your love become her ruin."

Tension rippled through me, my hands curling into fists at my sides, mirroring the coiled tendrils of the luminescent vines twisting along the cavern walls—ethereal and untouchable, like the stars hidden far above. My chest tightened, my breath shallow, rage simmering just beneath my skin at the cruel twist of fate keeping me from her side.

"Then what am I to do?" The words tore from me in a growl,

raw and ragged, a demand hurled into the void, seeking anything to soothe the searing wound of my soul.

"Wait," Lazarus said. The word hung between us like a blade —inevitable, inescapable.

"And prepare. There is a greater battle ahead."

"Waiting is not action," I snapped, the words laced with fire, my impatience clawing at my insides like a beast caged too long.

"Sometimes," Lazarus replied, his gaze hard and unwavering, "it is the only action that can save us all."

"Gods help me… I cannot simply wait," I hissed, eyes squeezed shut as if darkness could silence the storm within me.

Without a word, he crossed the room with practiced ease, his hands steady as he reached for a glass jar. Inside, a bloom as dark as midnight shimmered—its petals absorbing the surrounding light as if the flower were born from shadow. Beside it, a leather-bound book rested, its cover etched with timeworn symbols that seemed to whisper with ancient power.

The Sacred Alchemy of Solaris: Secrets of the Celestial Forge.

My breath caught, shock lancing through me like a snapped wire. "How do you have these?" The words slipped out in a low growl, part accusation, part disbelief—laced with the bitter sting of betrayal.

Lazarus didn't flinch. His gaze locked with mine, resolute, carrying the battles fought and secrets kept. "After I healed Elizabeth," he said evenly, "I gathered everything from her alchemist's cottage." His tone was factual, but beneath it simmered a quiet gravity—an unspoken acknowledgment of what these relics meant.

Drawn by dread and fascination, I lifted the glass jar. Inside, the Noctyss flower pulsed with a dark, unnatural beauty. "Why does Salvatore want this so badly?" I asked, the name like poison on my tongue—a reminder of the darkness poised to consume us all.

The air thickened, the shadows in the chamber seeming to pulse with tension as Lazarus' expression turned grim. "The Noctyss flower is more than rare—it's dangerous to our kind in a way few things are. In Solaris, it was one of the only substances capable of neutralizing a Shadow Lord's power. It can't kill us—but it can strip us of everything that makes us what we are."

My grip tightened around the jar, the chill of the glass biting against my skin. "You mean… it can take your power away?"

Lazarus nodded. "Completely. Our connection to the shadows, the strength we wield, our very essence—it erases all of it. Salvatore and I kept its existence a secret for centuries. We knew if it ever fell into the wrong hands, we could be undone without a single blade drawn."

I stared at the flower, its petals shifting slightly within the jar as though it breathed with a life of its own. "That's why he wants it," I murmured. "To use it against us—or destroy it before anyone else can."

"Exactly," Lazarus said, his voice low. "In the right hands, it's the one thing that could stop him."

The brevity of his words sank into my bones like stone. The Noctyss was no mere relic, no simple poison. It was a weapon—silent and insidious—that could shift the balance of power, not through death but by unraveling what makes us who we are. I turned the jar slowly, watching the flower sway in its prison of air and glass, absorbing the light and casting long, haunting shadows across the tomes and artifacts around us.

"How did it leave Solaris?" I asked, disbelief tightening my voice.

"Ah," Lazarus began, pacing slowly, his robe whispering against the cold stone floor. "When Isabelle separated the blades, she did more than sever metal. She tore reality. Pieces of Solaris bled into this world, like blood from a wound. The flower is one of them."

He paused, turning toward me. "The Timebornes were once bound to Solaris, tethered to our realm. But now… they can be born here. In this world."

With care, I placed the jar back on the table, the cool surface lingering against my fingertips. "Elizabeth told me…" I began, my voice tight with realization, "she found the flower in the

Carpathian Mountains. She never said more, but I'm certain that's where it came from."

Lazarus' eyes narrowed, his attention snapping to mine.

"We have to go there," I continued, urgency rising in my chest like a storm. "If she found it there once, there could be more—or worse, Salvatore may already suspect it. We need to reach it before he does."

"Indeed," Lazarus murmured, a rare flicker of agreement passing over his features.

"Zara can hold the stronghold in our absence," I continued. "If there's an opening to Solaris anywhere, it will be there."

"We'll find something," Lazarus interrupted, gathering a few ancient scrolls and tucking them into his satchel. His eyes caught mine, reflecting a glint of something I couldn't quite name. Hope. Fear. Or maybe it was just grim determination. "Whether it's salvation… or destruction—that remains to be seen."

"Then let's not waste time." There was no room for hesitation—not with so much at stake. Not with Elizabeth carrying a future I had yet to understand.

With a nod that sealed our shared purpose, we stepped out of the palace's shadowed confines. Our path lay ahead, leading toward the Carpathian Mountains and the unknown secrets they guarded like sentinels of fate.

We moved silently, our strides devouring the miles as the mountains rose on the horizon, jagged silhouettes against a darkening sky. The pain of my thoughts was a constant companion, heavy and unrelenting. Elizabeth's image followed me with every step, woven into my mind like a thread I couldn't sever.

Lazarus moved beside me, a figure of ancient power cloaked in mystery. He walked with ease that came not from youth, but from mastery, from centuries of carrying burdens no mortal should bear.

At last, I broke the silence, the words falling from me carefully as we climbed a steep incline, loose rocks grinding beneath our boots. "Lazarus," I said, breath ragged in the thinning air, "I've known you a long time. I've seen what you can do—what you know. You are… extraordinary. If I may ask—how does one become a sorcerer like you? Were you born with this power… or did you learn it?"

The air shifted. Cold. Sudden. As if my question had summoned a frost storm from within him.

Lazarus stopped abruptly, whirling on me with a force that stole the breath from my lungs. His eyes blazed with an ethereal fire—otherworldly, ancient. The air around us seemed to sizzle, the temperature plummeting as the mountain recoiled.

He was no longer just Lazarus for a heartbeat—he was something else. Something vast. Something infinite.

And I knew, in that moment, I had touched a scar that had never fully healed.

"Never call me a sorcerer again," he erupted, his voice cracking like thunder across the barren pass. "I am a Shadow Lord."

The title echoed in the mountain air, heavy and unforgiving. It wasn't just a name. It was a legacy, a curse, a mark seared into the soul.

I felt it then—the bitter sting of curiosity laced with unease. "How does one become a Shadow Lord?"

His fury ebbed, replaced by a cold stillness that seemed to freeze the wind around us. We resumed our march, but now, every step felt like a descent—deeper into shadow, deeper into the truth.

"During my time in prison," Lazarus began, his voice hollow, "thousands of us clung to one dream—freedom. But freedom came at a cost—the Shadow Lord Trials. They promised liberation… but they delivered torment."

His tone was stripped bare of emotion, as though detachment was the only way to survive the memories.

"The trials were created by Morgrath Severen—ancient, merciless. Designed not to test strength but to shatter it. To tear us down to bone and blood and rebuild us into something else." His eyes darkened. "Most failed. Broken. Unmade. The dungeons ran red with the blood of those who begged for death."

A chill swept through me at the cold finality of his words, as though I could hear the echoes of screams carried on the mountain wind.

"And you... survived."

"Only Salvatore and I," Lazarus said quietly. "We endured. We were reforged in pain, remade in darkness. Not by choice—but by necessity. And when it was over, we emerged not as men... but as Shadow Lords. The price of survival was losing everything that made us human."

A silence stretched between us.

"How did you end up in prison, Lazarus?" I asked, the words careful and cautious. A part of me already regretted the question.

Lazarus' gaze drifted, distant and veiled, as though staring into a chasm no light could reach. "That," he said, voice low and resolute, "is a secret I shall never speak of."

The air around us felt heavier, charged with unsaid truths. I didn't press him. Some wounds were too deep, too old to reopen.

We continued, the mountains looming like ancient gods, silently witnessing our passage. The wind howled through the peaks, whispering fragments of forgotten stories, indifferent to the burdens we carried.

But I couldn't shake the thought of the trials—the blood-soaked path that led to power. The darkness clung to Lazarus like a second skin woven into his very being. Whatever he had endured or become was not simply a title. It was a transformation etched into every breath he took.

We trod upon a mosaic of stone and earth, our boots scuffing the remnants of a path long claimed by time. The air was thinner here, scented with pine and something older—something eternal and watching. The Carpathian wilderness whispered around us, promising secrets only the brave or the foolish dared to seek.

"Salvatore's name," I said at last, unable to contain the growing curiosity, "it falls from your lips with history. You speak as if you were bound by more than rivalry."

Lazarus halted, his eyes distant, lost in memories that had long since turned to ghosts. "We were close," he admitted, and the words seemed to cost him, pulled from a place long buried. "Brothers, in all but blood. But power..." His jaw clenched.

"Power overcame him. Twisted what we were into something unrecognizable."

His voice was hollow, as though speaking it aloud made it real again—reopened a wound long buried beneath layers of time and silence. I felt the pull to ask more, to peel back the layers of that darkness, but before I could form the words, Lazarus raised a hand—a silent barrier, firm and final.

"No," he said, his voice a blade. "I will not answer more questions. Some truths are too perilous to unearth."

The silence that followed wasn't empty—it was alive with what remained unsaid. And I knew then that whatever had passed between Lazarus and Salvatore left more than scars. It had caused a chasm no words could bridge.

Resigned, I let the silence settle over us once more.

We pressed onward, the mountainside begrudgingly yielding beneath our steps as though the earth resented our intrusion. Then the land began to speak—not through sound, but through signs. A trail of withered flowers stretched before us, their once-vibrant petals shriveled and gray, crumbling beneath unseen decay. We were touched by something unnatural, something wrong. Like breadcrumbs from a forgotten fable, they led us forward—not to guide, but to warn.

Our journey culminated at an imposing stone wall—but this was no ordinary barrier. Shaped into the mountain's face stood an ancient door, weathered yet immovable, the final guardian of realms long forgotten. The structure was monumental, flanked by towering columns worn by time and wrapped in creeping ivy. Moss clung to every crevice, while intricate carvings—symbols of a lost age—etched their way up the stone facade like veins of memory.

At its center, the door loomed, forged of greenish-blue stone streaked with veins of age, its surface marred by the slow erosion of centuries. Twisting wrought-iron designs formed an ornate gate before it, delicate yet impenetrable, like vines frozen in mid-growth. Above the archway, a stone relief crowned the structure, engraved with runes half-worn by time and over-growth. The doorway seemed to pulse with dormant power as if the mountain had been cleaved open to protect the world beyond.

"This is it," Lazarus declared, his voice slicing through the hush of the wilds. He placed a hand upon the cold, rough surface of the door; reverence creasing every line of his face. "Beyond this stone lies our realm—Solaris in its veiled glory. Whatever awaits us there," he turned, locking his dark gaze with mine, "will change everything."

A shiver crawled down my spine—not from the mountain's chill but from the meaning of his words. This was no mere crossing.

It was a reckoning.

We stood together, two men haunted by shared and solitary pasts, poised on the precipice of an uncertain future. Bound by fate, secrets, and the world that waited beyond the stone.

CHAPTER 27

DANCING FIRE

I stepped softly through the underbrush, the bow in my hands grounding me. The forest wrapped around me in its quiet embrace—whispering leaves, the scent of pine and damp earth, the faint rustle of prey in the distance. This place was my refuge. Here, time moved differently, and for a fleeting moment, the heavy mantle of being a Timeborne could be set aside.

My eyes traced the green canopy above as shafts of sunlight pierced the dense foliage, casting shifting patterns across the forest floor—light dancing with the breeze. The hum of life surrounded me—birdsong, the chirp of insects, the distant murmur of a stream. When one carried burdens from other worlds, this world's heartbeat remained unbothered.

The hunt had always been a meditation—a way to find stillness amidst chaos. Every step careful, every breath purposeful. But today, the tranquility was broken, fractured by thoughts of Elizabeth. Her eyes, the color of a storm-washed sky, wide and watchful, mirrored the vastness of her spirit. Soft but certain, her voice held a strength that resonated beyond words. Thoughts of her wove around my heart like vines, binding me to her in ways I still struggled to understand.

She was the source of the disquiet that shadowed my every move. I had saved her once—pulled her from the edge of danger, not because the spirits demanded it, but because something within me recognized her.

Not her face, not her voice, but the flame behind her eyes.

It was familiar.

As if she carried echoes of another time—of a promise made long ago, before either of us had names. A thread woven through the stars that tugged at my spirit with quiet insistence.

Since then, she had become part of our tribe. She was a balm over wounds I thought had long since scarred. But they hadn't. Not truly. And now, with each passing day, I could feel her becoming more than just a guest.

Yet she belonged to another—Amir, my closest friend. Amir's dark eyes missed nothing, and his sense of honor was as steadfast as the ancient stones that anchored our land. When he came to me, his request had been simple and solemn—watch over Elizabeth and protect her. I had freely given that oath, an extension of the brotherhood that bound us.

But oaths, no matter how sacred, could not silence the heart's longing for what it must not possess. Elizabeth brought something new into my life—a light that reached the darkest corners, a warmth I could neither ignore nor embrace. How could I reconcile these growing feelings with the loyalty I owed Amir? He spoke few words, yet every one he spoke with purpose. Beneath his clipped commands lay the quiet weight of a homeland lost and a love for Elizabeth so deep it defied expression.

I paused beneath the towering oak, leaning against its rough bark, grounding myself in its solidity. I closed my eyes, letting the forest speak—wind in the leaves, the distant cry of birds, the pulse of life untouched by conflict. I needed this hunt, this momentary escape, to still the turmoil rising within me.

As the leaves rustled overhead, I reminded myself that my path was clear. I was her guardian, sworn to keep her safe. The longing that threatened to consume me had to be crushed before it could take root.

There would be no betrayal of Amir. No yielding to desires that could only lead to ruin. I was Dancing Fire, a warrior shaped by tradition and time itself. My path was one of sacrifice —that was all I could see for now.

The forest embraced me, its ancient trees standing sentinel as I moved silently among them. My bow rested in my hands, an arrow nocked and ready. I was a shadow over the earth, a whisper in the wind. Yet the most practiced hunter could not silence the soft crunch of leaves beneath his feet—a sound that now betrayed the approach of another.

"Ah, Lazarus," I greeted without turning, recognizing the deliberate tread. "I am honored by your presence."

"I'm glad," came the low rumble of his voice—deep, commanding, yet not unkind. "I've come to ask how Elizabeth fares."

I hesitated, her face rising in my mind like a flame in the darkness—sky-blue eyes reflecting quiet purpose, her existence a strength within our community. "She's adapted to our ways," I replied, masking my tangled emotions beneath a warrior's stoicism. "She is preparing to have her twins."

"Twins…" Lazarus murmured, almost to himself, before his gaze met mine. "Does your father believe they will be Timebornes?"

"Father sees great potential in them," I answered, pride flickering despite the storm within. "He believes they will be powerful warriors."

"Your father is correct," Lazarus said, his tone weighted. "But I did not come merely to speak of prophecy."

He stepped closer, and the forest seemed to still around us, holding its breath. When he spoke again, his voice was like stone breaking.

"When Elizabeth gives birth… you will give her only one son."

His words struck me—not a blow of flesh, but of prophecy, cutting and sudden, threatening the fragile balance I had fought so hard to maintain. The forest, once a sanctuary, now felt suffocating. The trees loomed like prison bars, binding me to a fate I could neither accept nor escape.

My legs gave way, the words reverberating like thunder.

"No!" Raw and unrestrained, the denial tore from my throat. "I can't do that!"

Lazarus stood unflinching, a monolith amid the storm of my anguish. "You will," he said, voice as immutable as the turning of seasons. "This is a command."

He stepped into the shattered silence between us, his gaze cold and unwavering. "One of the twins will carry darkness— like his father. The other… is the reincarnation of Armand. That child shall remain with her."

The world spun. Greens and browns blurred into chaos, the forest twisting into something unfamiliar. My bow slipped from my fingers, the arrow thudding silently into the loam. I could feel it then—the crushing power of destiny, heavier than any burden I had borne.

"Please, Lazarus…" The plea escaped me like a breath stolen by the wind, barely audible. "I can't betray her like this." Her image filled my mind—Elizabeth, strong yet delicate, like a prairie bloom resilient against the storm. Her soft voice, her healing touch… she had become part of me, woven into the fabric of my soul.

But Lazarus was relentless. His hard and unflinching eyes pierced through my despair. "You must see the larger picture," he said, his voice like iron. "One will stay with her. The other will be mine."

He paused, letting his words settle into my bones like stone.

"That is not a request. It is an order."

An order. The word opened like a chasm at my feet, threatening to swallow me whole. To defy him was to risk everything —our people, mission, and chance to reclaim what was lost. Yet in the deepest part of me, where the fire of my name still burned, I knew this command would scorch her world to ash.

The forest spun around me, the familiar trunks of oak and birch blurring into a haze as Lazarus' voice echoed like a curse in my ears. "I can't do this," I gasped, reaching out to balance myself, fingers digging into the rough bark of a nearby tree.

Lazarus stepped closer, his authority both an anchor and a burden. "I know you care for her, Dancing Fire," he said, the timbre of his voice firm. "But we are fighting for the greater good. To restore Solaris, to reclaim what is rightfully ours—this is the path we must walk."

His words were meant to fortify me, to harden my resolve—but they only twisted the knife deeper. I closed my eyes, seeking refuge in the memories of her—the way her laughter drifted like music across the prairie, the strength in her gaze that outshone the evening star.

I remembered the day I found her—wounded and alone—how I had gathered her into my arms, her fragile strength trembling against my chest. Her spirit had reached into mine, igniting a flame I could neither deny nor extinguish.

And now, that fire threatened to consume me.

And the bear… that monstrous beast, towering above us, death gleaming in its claws. I could still feel the searing rush of blood from the gashes in my side, the terror that gripped my throat like a vice. But her hands had saved me. With her healer's touch and unshakable tenacity, Elizabeth had faced fear and defied it. In those moments, under the shadow of death, I began to fall—not from weakness, but into a love I could never speak aloud.

"Her life is entwined with yours," Lazarus' voice said, pulling me from the tide of memory and grounding me in grim reality. "But the path ahead requires sacrifice."

Sacrifice. The word settled in my stomach like a stone. How could I cause such pain to someone who had given me nothing but healing? Elizabeth—whose touch had closed my wounds and opened my heart.

"Please, Lazarus," I whispered, each word a struggle against the storm swelling inside me. "There must be another way."

But deep down, I knew there wasn't. Not if we were to save our world. The fate of Solaris demanded a price, and I was being asked to pay it—not with blood, but with betrayal.

With a heavy sigh, I turned toward the path home, my steps leaden with the burden I carried. Elizabeth's image in my mind —a beacon calling me back, and now, a reminder of the storm I would bring to her doorstep.

As I emerged from the dense thicket, the village unfolded before me—a living tapestry of warmth and life. The scent of roasting venison filled the air, mingling with the crackle of the central fire and the rhythmic chants of the evening gathering. Children's laughter echoed through the trees, the sky above gold with the last light of day.

And then I saw her.

Elizabeth sat among the women, her blond hair cascading over her shoulders like strands of sunlight, catching the firelight and turning it to gold. She laughed softly, radiant in the flickering glow—unaware of the sorrow I carried, unaware that I might be the one to break her heart.

Her hands moved with effortless grace, kneading away the weariness from a woman's shoulders with a gentleness that seemed to seep into the soul. Children danced around her, their giggles rising above the hum of conversation, drawn to her as moths to flame. They spun and leaped, small feet kicking up dust, until, as if sensing I watched, they paused—bright eyes turning toward me.

"Dancing Fire! Dancing Fire!" they called, their voices a chorus of joy and affection.

But I could not share in their delight. A knot tightened in my chest, each chant of my name a reminder of the betrayal clinging to my shadow.

I lingered at the firelight's edge, trapped between duty and devotion, my oath pressing against my chest like armor. To hurt Elizabeth would be to sever the last thread of humanity that bound me. Her spirit had become part of our tribe's soul, her touch mending more than wounds—restoring hope where none should remain. She was a healer not only of bodies but of hearts. She taught us to believe again, when belief felt like a forgotten dream.

The thought of betraying her trust was unthinkable. My hands—once steady in battle, unwavering as I drew my bow— now trembled at the thought of delivering pain to the one who had saved me from death's cold grasp.

"Dancing Fire, come sit!" Elizabeth's soft yet strong voice

rose above the din, through the noise to find me. Her blue eyes met mine across the firelight, reflecting not just its warmth but the unspoken bond between us—a bond I was being commanded to break.

I took a breath, steeling myself. Each step I took toward her was a silent vow—I would be her shield, even if the storms I stood against were ones I had been ordered to summon. This I swore—not as a Timeborne, but as a man whose heart had been touched by an angel in mortal form.

She smiled as I neared, welcoming, radiant, unaware of the tempest hiding behind my heart.

"Join us," she said, patting the ground beside her.

And though my place was at her side, my mind was leagues away—trapped in the war between the love that gave me strength and the destiny that demanded I sacrifice.

CHAPTER 28

ELIZABETH

The scent of sagebrush and sweetgrass mingled in the air as I crushed herbs between my fingers—a ritual that now felt as natural as breathing. Six moons had waxed and waned since my feet first touched the sacred earth of the tribal grounds, the land of those I came to know as the Sioux. Each step I took here forged a new path vastly different from the life I once knew.

"Like this, Elizabeth?" a soft voice asked beside me.

I saw Little Dove carefully mimicking my movements, her nimble hands working with the same reverence for the healing plants we nurtured.

"Exactly like that," I said, offering her a smile. My voice still held the faint lilt of another world—a place I had all but left behind. We were preparing poultices for the winter months, yet every task was a lesson in resilience, survival, and the quiet strength of the community. The women here had become more than companions; they were my sisters in every way that mattered—the sinew to my bones, the peace to my once-unsettled spirit.

And yet, amid this newfound harmony, thoughts of Amir Hassan rose like endless tides in the quiet sea of my heart. Stoic. Resolute. He lingered within me, etched into memory with a clarity time could not blur. It was a silent longing, one I tucked beneath the rhythm of daily life, hidden like a note between the pages of a well-worn book.

"Elizabeth?" Mary's voice pulled me from my reverie, her hand brushing lightly against mine.

"Apologies, I was…" I trailed off, shaking free from the web of memory.

Sky Raven stood beside her—a quiet strength, a testament to their growing bond. Their connection was as tangible as the crisp breath of fall that stirred the golden leaves at our feet, whispering promises of change.

"Are you ready for the eclipse?" Mary asked, her eyes alight with the same anticipation that seemed to ripple through the tribe. In the distance, the rhythmic beat of drums began to echo, a primal heartbeat growing louder as the celebration neared.

"Of course," I lied, offering a smile that didn't quite reach my eyes.

In truth, a deep-seated terror coiled in my chest. While others awaited the eclipse with wonder, I sensed only dread—a shadow poised to swallow the light. Where they saw beauty, I saw a harbinger—a darkness looming on the horizon.

But preparations continued, undeterred. Children's laughter rang out as they wove strands of black and gold into their hair, mimicking the celestial dance of the sun and moon. Men erected viewing structures, determined to greet the skies with reverence. Elders gathered in circles, their voices weaving stories of eclipses past—tales steeped in mystery, awe, and ancient wisdom.

"Look at them," Mary said, gesturing toward the bustling crowd. "They've been planning this for weeks. It's going to be a beautiful ceremony."

"Beautiful indeed," I murmured, watching young braves paint their faces with ochre and charcoal, transforming into celestial spirits beneath the open sky. My hands drifted to rest on my belly, where life stirred—a secret dance all its own, known only to me.

"Are you alright?" Mary's concern softened her tone.

"Merely the season's chill settling in my bones," I replied, though we both knew it wasn't the autumn wind that had unsettled me. It was the eclipse—the timing. The fear gripped me like frost in my veins.

As the tribe rejoiced in the promise of the celestial union, I clung to the warmth of the fire, willing it to push back the cold creeping into my bones. And I prayed—not for myself, but for the light I had found in this place, among these people, for the life I now carried. I prayed the darkness would pass us by and that I would not be forced to bring my children into a world shrouded in shadow.

Before long, the sky began to dim as though the heavens were drawing a curtain across the sun. I stepped from my teepee, clutching the doorway, as a sudden, searing pain lanced through me. My breath hitched. The contractions came swiftly, each crashing wave stronger than the last.

"Mary!" I called out, my voice barely more than a whisper against the wind's rising murmur.

But there was no answer. She was gone, her attention fixed on the approaching eclipse like everyone else's. The tribal grounds, once filled with laughter and companionship, felt foreign now—isolated. Every soul was entranced by the sky, moving with a singular purpose, blind to everything but the celestial dance above.

I stumbled forward, searching for the grounding authority of Dancing Fire, the one I trusted most. But he, too, was absent, lost to duties I could not grasp.

"Please," I gasped, reaching out to those who passed me by. No one stopped. Their eyes were fixed on the heavens, faces alight with awe. Desperation clawed at my throat as the realization struck hard and cruelly—in this moment, I was alone.

Then—movement. An older woman, her face etched by years and seasons, noticed my struggle and hurried toward me. Her grip was firm as she took my arm, steadying me and guiding me back into the sanctuary of my teepee. Inside, the fire blazed defiantly against the encroaching darkness outside, its crackle loud in the silence, as though it, too, sought to ward off what lurked beyond.

"Mary… Dancing Fire…" I choked out, each word a blade twisting through me, laced with agony. "Please… find them."

The woman nodded, her eyes relaxed in a way I desperately wished to feel. She vanished beyond the tent flap with a silent promise, leaving me alone with the searing flames and the constant tide of contractions.

I collapsed, the cool earth grounding me as I focused on the fire's rhythmic dance. Its flickering became my anchor—the warmth, the light, the life it represented. I surrendered to the force within me, raw and unstoppable, driving my children into the world. Each wave of pain tore through me, but with it came a strength I hadn't known was mine.

Outside, the world waited to witness a cosmic wonder, yet within my teepee, under the fire's glow, I braced to meet the souls who would eclipse everything I had ever known.

The tent flap rustled. The woman returned, breathless, her face shadowed with worry. "They are nowhere to be found," she said. "They must have gone to the high point to see the eclipse with the others."

"Yes," I gasped, teeth clenched against the storm inside me.

The high point was a serene hill draped in emerald over-looking the lake, its towering pines swayed gently in the breeze, sunlight dappled the earth through needled branches. It was a place of peace and awe. But for me, there was no serenity—only chaos.

While others turned their eyes skyward, breathless before the cosmic wonder, I was in the dirt, trapped in a war of pain and fury. My body was no longer mine—it was a vessel of agony. Every breath I took was a ragged cry. Every contraction felt like it would tear me apart. This wasn't transcendence—it was survival. It was blood and fire and the ancient, terrifying force of life demanding to be born.

Time lost all meaning. It blurred, tracked only by the spasms that racked my body, each one a fresh wave of torment. Pain consumed me, stripped me bare. I wasn't Elizabeth anymore—I was raw flesh, trembling on the edge.

"Help is coming," the old woman murmured, her hands

hovering helplessly over my clenched fists, useless against the storm ripping through me.

At last, as the sky darkened into an eerie twilight, the tent flap shifted, and another figure stepped inside. Her arrival hit me like relief, and a command all at once—solid, grounded, unshakable. Her hands were rough with years of labor, her face a map of every birth she had guided. She knelt between my legs, all business.

"Push now, Elizabeth," she instructed.

I didn't want to push. I wanted to scream, to run, to escape this torment. But there was no choice. My body took over, instinct driving me. I pushed because I had to. Because life was demanding it of me.

Outside, the eclipse reached its totality. Day bled into night, and the world fell silent as if the sky held its breath, waiting.

And then—amidst the darkness, a sound. A wail. Piercing, fierce, alive.

I gasped, sobbed, and broke apart as the midwife laid my baby on my chest, slippery and warm and real. "You have a son," she whispered.

A son. My son.

Tears blurred everything as I clutched him to me, his tiny chest rising and falling against mine. "I love you so much," I breathed, kissing his damp forehead. "Your father gave me something beautiful."

At that moment, the eclipse vanished. The world vanished. There was no tribe, no fire, no Mary or Dancing Fire. Only him. Roman. My son. And the wild, ferocious love that tore through me like the sun reborn, scorching everything else into ash.

But then the pain returned.

"There's another," the midwife said, urgency lacing her voice. "Push, Elizabeth."

No time to breathe. No time to grieve or revel. Only the fight. Again.

With everything I had left—every shred of strength, every piece of me that hadn't already shattered—I pushed, crying out as the second child slipped from my body into the hands of fate.

I held Roman close, clinging to his warmth, his cries anchoring me.

And then—silence.

A sudden, heavy silence.

The cries stopped. Cold fear gripped me, wrapping its fingers around my throat. My heart thundered, trying to drown it out. I clutched Roman tighter, my only light in the growing darkness, unwilling to let fear claim this moment, unwilling to let death creep in.

But something was wrong.

My arms ached with the weight of my son—and yet, they felt unbearably empty. My soul split in two, searching for what was missing.

"The other one," I whispered, my voice cracked and fragile. "Give him to me."

The elder woman looked at me, and in her eyes, I saw sorrow, deep and ancient, like the shadowed sun outside. She knelt beside me, and her words destroyed me.

"Your other baby… he didn't make it."

Her voice was gentle, but it hit me like a scream. Like the sky itself had broken open.

"No." The word ripped from my throat. "Give him to me!" My voice a plea, a command, a mother's cry born from the marrow of my bones. "Please, I need to hold him."

She shook her head slowly, her face lined with the burden of many such moments, but this was mine. Mine to carry. Mine to grieve.

"No," she whispered. "The child is dead. We can't."

The world collapsed.

A guttural cry ripped from the depths of my soul, as if grief itself had found a voice through me. My body convulsed around the sound, and in that moment, I ceased to exist as anything but pain.

The entrance of the teepee darkened. A silhouette filled the space—broad, strong, yet burdened. Dancing Fire stepped inside, and in his arms lay something impossibly small, impossibly still.

My breath caught.

He was holding my child—my lifeless baby—and the sight cleaved through me, a blade of agony so vicious I thought it might kill me where I lay.

"Marcellious…" The name was a whisper of despair, a fragile prayer to a god who had not answered. I stared at that tiny face—peaceful, untouched by breath or laughter—a little warrior who had never drawn his first breath yet had stolen every part of me.

Dancing Fire's eyes, always fierce, were dim now, dulled by sorrow. He held my baby close, his arms trembling.

"Give him to me, now!" I gasped, my voice hoarse, torn raw by anguish.

"Elizabeth…" His voice cracked, and he turned slightly, shielding the baby from my sight as though he could spare me. As though he could stop the bleeding of my soul.

"Give him to me!" I screamed, the words shredding my throat, a mother's plea.

His face twisted in pain as he relented, stepping forward. With shaking hands, he placed my stillborn child into my arms.

Tears poured from me—silent, ceaseless—as I held him, my fingers tracing his perfect, lifeless face. I kissed his forehead, my lips trembling.

"My sweet boy," I choked out. "Your father would have wanted you to be strong." I held him close as if I could will life into him. "I love you so much, my little Marcellious. I love you so much."

Against my chest, Roman stirred, his small body close to mine as he suckled hungrily, alive and warm. One child in my arms, clinging to life—one lost to death's quiet claim.

The contrast was unbearable. Roman's heat, his breath, the rhythm of his heartbeat—against his brother's cool, unmoving form. My arms were full, yet I had never felt so hollow.

Tears ran like rivers down my face, and I clung to them both—one of flesh and fire, the other now a memory etched in sorrow. Death had come for my son, but it could not take my love. Not ever.

Sobs racked my body, violent and unrelenting, each one a dirge, a farewell to dreams never lived, to whispered promises now lost in the void. I clung to Marcellious, desperate to hold onto the fading warmth in his fragile body, as the shadows of the eclipse seemed to pull him from my arms, from this world.

Dancing Fire knelt beside me, and with a tenderness that defied the hardened calluses of his warrior's hands, he reached for Marcellious. I resisted, tightening my hold, unwilling to surrender even in death—but the cold had already claimed him. With shaking hands, I let go.

He took Marcellious, reverent, silent. Then, with a murmured word, he passed him to a waiting woman, who disappeared into the fading light beyond the tent flap. I watched every motion, every step, my eyes pleading, my heart hollowing. It felt like a piece of my soul was being carried away with my silent babe. Gone.

I couldn't bear another loss. Not now. Not ever again.

"Roman!" The name burst from me like a cry of war. I clutched my living son, holding him so tightly he whimpered in protest. I pulled him against me, skin to skin, my body curled around him like a fierce, trembling shield.

"You can't have this one!" I sobbed, hysteria rising like floodwaters in my throat. "You can't take Roman. I won't let you take him!"

Dancing Fire didn't move. He stood before me, still, grounded, his eyes full of sorrow—and something more. A knowing that chilled me more than the loss.

"I won't take him," he said softly. "He is yours to raise."

My breath hitched, raw and uneven, as I looked up at him, barely able to comprehend.

"Elizabeth," he said, voice composed, despite the tremor of grief between us, "Roman is a Timeborne. Like me."

Through the veil of my tears, I met his gaze, desperate to find a lie, a crack, some sliver of doubt—but all I saw was solemn truth, ancient and immutable.

"How do you know?" I rasped, my voice hoarse from crying, from screaming, from surviving. My heart pounded, a frantic rhythm against Roman's tiny chest, his fragile life held close. Alive. Safe. Mine.

Dancing Fire said nothing. Instead, he reached into the folds of his garments and drew forth two daggers. At first glance, they seemed ordinary—but then I saw it. A faint glow pulsed from the intricate carvings on the hilts and blades, a soft, rhythmic light that shimmered perfectly with Roman's heartbeat. It was not a coincidence. It was a connection. Proof.

I stared at the blades, my breath catching, the blood in my veins turning ice-cold. The memories came rushing back— memories of my father, of bloodshed, of Timebornes hunted like animals—my father's cruelty, his thirst for control, painted in crimson across history.

"No." My voice was hard, edged like flint. "Take it. Hide it. Bury it where no one will ever find it. He will never know about this. Never."

Dancing Fire's eyes didn't waver. "Elizabeth, you can't decide his destiny," he said, and in his voice was the knowledge of centuries of lives lived and lost under the burden of prophecy. "This is who he is."

Anger surged, blinding, fierce. It eclipsed my grief, burning through my veins like fire. "I can, and I will!" I snapped, my voice cracking under its force. My hands curled into fists, nails biting into my palms. "My father was a Timehunter. He slaughtered Timebornes—your people. If they find out Roman is one of you, they'll hunt him too. He'll die because of what he is."

I pulled Roman tighter, closer, as if I could shield him with my body, as if I could force him back into the womb where nothing could touch him. My whole being trembled with the need to protect him—no matter the cost.

Dancing Fire knelt setting the daggers aside, his hand hovering over them but never touching to honor my defiance and grant me this small illusion of control.

"Elizabeth," he said softly, his eyes shadowed by something deeper than sorrow. "Not even the shadows of time can hide what fate ordains."

But I had already made my decision.

Clutching the tiny, fragile beacon of hope that was Roman, I whispered, fierce and resolute, "I will never let him fall into the clutches of people like my father." The vow etched itself into my soul, a binding promise written in blood and grief.

Dancing Fire's words lingered in the air, heavy with a truth I didn't want to face. "You can't run from this forever," he said, his gaze unwavering, dark, a mirror reflecting inevitability.

I pulled Roman closer, feeling his chest's gentle rise and fall against my skin, each breath a fragile miracle. Sadness flooded me until tears blurred my vision. "I've already endured too much heartache," I said, my voice breaking. "First Amir… and now Marcellious. He's gone. I can't stay here, Dancing Fire. I won't. Roman and I—we're going back to England. We'll start over, far from all this sorrow and this cursed land."

My voice trembled with mourning too vast to name—yet beneath it, a steel edge of determination.

"Elizabeth," he began softly as if he could reach into my despair and pull me free, but the gentleness in his voice couldn't dull the edge of the warning that followed. "You're making a mistake. Stay. I will protect you. I care for you… more than you know."

I lifted my defiant gaze as my heart cracked. "Then what do you suggest?" I demanded, the question biting with desperation. "What would make this right?"

"Marry me."

The words fell from his lips, simple and shattering.

"No." My answer came too fast and harsh, recoiling like a torn open wound. "You and I—we come from different worlds. You're a savage. A barbarian. And I…" My voice faltered. "I am a lady."

The hurt in his eyes pierced me—quick and deep, sharper than any dagger could ever be. He stood abruptly, the shift in his body language a storm barely contained.

"You call yourself a lady," he said, voice low and raw, "and yet you opened your legs to a man who wasn't your husband. And you call me a savage?" His words struck like thunder, bitter, edged with betrayal. "A man who would die for you?"

I flinched as if he had struck me, but the wound wasn't on my skin—it was deeper, tangled in my heart. His words should have broken me. Instead, they freed something buried, something unbreakable.

"Yes, I did," I said, voice firm now, no longer shaking. "I gave myself to him. And now, I will give my life to be the best mother I can be to this child. That's all that matters."

Without another word, Dancing Fire turned and stormed out of the teepee, leaving me alone—again—with the fragments of my shattered world.

Tears streamed down my cheeks, hot and endless, as I cradled Roman to my chest. Everything fell apart, piece by piece, slipping through my fingers like sand. All I had—all I was—rested in the child's fragile body in my arms.

"Roman," I whispered, my lips brushing his soft, warm forehead. "I will protect you, no matter the cost. I will be the best mother I can be. I promise."

A silent oath, sealed in grief and love, binding my heart to his. But deep within me, an uneasy truth stirred—words spoken in the glow of new motherhood could crumble like dust when faced with the man he would one day become.

CHAPTER 29

AMIR

The clanging of steel echoed through the desolate chambers, each strike of my blade a cry into the void. I drove the weapon again and again into the practice dummies, their straw-stuffed forms bearing the brunt of my fury—futile stand-ins for the anguish tearing me apart. Every swing was a desperate attempt to silence the cacophony of loss that resounded in my skull, to drown out the unbearable silence left behind by Elizabeth's voice—the one I'd never hear again.

Days had bled into weeks into an endless blur of sweat, blood, and exhaustion. I had made these cold, stone walls of the underground palace my prison, exiling myself from rest and reason. Sleep had long abandoned me; food was an afterthought, and pain... pain was the only thing that still reminded me I was alive.

My knuckles were torn open, raw, and bleeding, skin peeling back like my sanity. Still, I persisted. A hollow shell of the man I once was, filled only with rage, haunted by a grief that would not loosen its grip.

My men had tried. Their words—pleas to stop, rest, heal—were whispers lost on a storm wind. I didn't hear them. I couldn't.

"Amir."

My name cut through the haze of exertion like a knife, but I didn't stop.

"Amir!" This time, the edge in Lazarus' voice snapped something inside me, and the blade stilled in my hand.

Chest heaving, I staggered back, the weight of my limbs suddenly unbearable. I slumped to the cold floor, my back hitting the stone wall with a dull thud. Once so vast and filled with weapons, the room now seemed to close in around me, pressing against the hollow of my chest.

I lifted my head, my gaze locking with Lazarus'. His face was unreadable, but I knew that look—it was the calm before a storm. My voice ripped from my throat, hoarse and worn from disuse.

"What?" I snapped.

Lazarus didn't flinch. "It's time," he said. "We're going to the New World. Your children—" he paused, letting the words fall like stones in a still pond, "—they're about to be born."

The world tilted beneath me. The blade slipped from my hand, clattering to the floor, useless and forgotten.

But through the haze of shock, suspicion clawed at the corners of my mind. My brow furrowed, and I fixed him with a piercing, wary stare. "Why would you let me see Elizabeth now," I demanded, voice low, edged, "when you forbade me from getting close to her before?"

The question hung between us, heavy with accusation and the remnants of hope I couldn't quite smother.

Lazarus' eyes remained unreadable, his next words cold and precise, each syllable a dagger. "I have ordered Dancing Fire to inform Elizabeth that one of the children did not survive. I must raise one of the twins."

His declaration punched the air from my lungs. I staggered, my chest tightening around a grief that was not yet real but already unbearable.

"You what?" The words scraped from my throat, disbelieving, guttural. My body screamed in protest as I forced myself to my feet, trembling with rage. "Out of the question!" I stepped toward him, every fiber of my being bristling. "You think I'll allow this? That I'll let you take my child like some—some pawn?"

But the image of Elizabeth—her hearing those words, believing one of her babies was dead—ripped through me more viciously than any blade. The pain of her grief, of her being deceived, gutted me. I could see her face crumple. I could feel her sorrow.

Anger and desperation clashed in violent waves, our voices ricocheting off stone walls like war drums. Fury scorched in my veins, but Lazarus stood firm, unmoved by the fire in my eyes.

And then came his final blow, his ultimatum slicing through my rage with ruthless precision.

"Do you want to see your newborn babies, or don't you?"

Silence fell. My breath hitched, broken. My heart beat against the walls of my chest like a caged beast.

"Will I get to see Elizabeth?" Her name cracked from my lips—part plea, part curse, part prayer. Just her name. That was all I had left.

Lazarus' face hardened, his voice a hammer driving nails into the coffin of my hope.

"That is out of the question."

The journey passed in a blur—time and space folding around us, warped by the shadows that carried Lazarus through the in-between. Reality bent and twisted, packed with anticipation and dread. Then, suddenly, we were there.

The plains stretched before us—vast, wild, and breathtaking. A land so foreign, so achingly beautiful, it felt like stepping into a dream painted in colors I'd never seen before.

Here, where the sky bowed low to kiss mirrored lakes, where earth and water met in harmony, Elizabeth brought our children into existence.

And yet, despite the beauty that stretched endlessly before me, torment gnawed at my insides. My heart beat not with joy but with aching because I was not by her side. I was denied that moment, exiled from the most sacred threshold of life.

Lazarus' hand gripped my shoulder firmly, steering me away from the tribal village where my soul strained to go. His touch was a shackle, and I resented him for it with every breath I took.

We veered toward the edge of the forest, where a modest cabin stood nestled among towering pines. It rose from the earth as if it belonged there—logs weathered smooth by time, unassuming yet grounded, rooted in silence and solitude.

A creek wound nearby, its gentle chuckle threading through the night air, mocking the staccato beat of my troubled heart. Its soft melody clashed against the storm inside me—a calm I could not reach.

Beyond it stretched a lake, its surface silvered by moonlight and endlessly still. Dancing Fire's tribe revered this place, weaving their stories into its waters for generations. The lake's gentle lapping whispered a song of peace through the darkness, a lullaby for the earth.

But there was no peace in me.

Smoke drifted from the chimney, curling into the star-kissed sky, betraying the life within that solitary home—Dancing Fire's sanctuary, where he retreated to when even his tribe's company could not soothe him.

The air was filled with pine, damp earth, and something else —the ache of what could never be. Nature tried to soothe, to console the soul, but it couldn't reach me—not when the woman I loved was just beyond the trees, bringing our children into the world… without me.

As Lazarus and I neared the cabin, Dancing Fire emerged, like a storm breaking over waters. His face was carved with rage and something deeper—betrayal. In his arms, he cradled a bundle wrapped in soft cloth, from which a tiny fist emerged, punching the air in silent, newborn protest.

My heart constricted, each beat like a knife, echoing the pain I knew Elizabeth must be enduring. I ached for her. For them. For the life I was being kept from.

"Step inside," he ordered, his voice low, taut with barely contained fury.

We obeyed, silent and hollow, like sheep herded to slaughter.

The cabin was cloaked in dim candlelight, flickering shadows across the rough-hewn walls. The scent of pine and woodsmoke clung to the air, grounding. A fire crackled in the hearth, offering warmth that could not thaw the cold in my chest.

The space was humble—a simple bed, a sturdy table, and chairs worn smoothly. But what caught my eye were the dream catchers delicately strung across the windows, each a masterpiece of thread, bead, feather, and bone. They danced in the sunlight filtering through the trees, casting colored prisms against the walls, beauty born from pain.

On the table, his tools lay scattered—feathers, beads, leather strips, the remnants of his craft. The air was rich with the scent of freshly cut wood, oil, and smoke—a sacred harmony of the old ways he cherished.

Dancing Fire was not just a man of the Sioux. He was a Timeborne—born beneath the eclipse, chosen to walk through centuries. But he carried time not like a weapon, as others did, but like a story passed from elder to child. Each journey was a thread, each moment a prayer.

He was a bridge between worlds—past and future, spirit and flesh.

Then Dancing Fire spoke, and every word was a flint strike against a stone.

"I've done what you asked," he spat, his voice honed like a weapon. His eyes locked on Lazarus, intense. "I played the Grim Reaper to Elizabeth. I convinced her that one of her twins had gone to the afterlife." His voice cracked. "And then—then I placed the lifeless child of another in her arms."

His jaw clenched, pain etched deep into every line of his face. "Two souls departed that night—mother and child—but the deepest wound… was the lie. The deceit I laid upon Elizabeth's beaten heart."

A shadow passed over Dancing Fire's face, the fury in his eyes dimming into something far more dangerous—sorrow. "It's unfathomable," he muttered, voice trembling with restrained rage. "The pain we've inflicted… for what? I wash my hands of you and your agenda." His gaze pierced Lazarus, blazing with the sheer defiance of a man who had been pushed beyond the breaking point—a firestorm contained within the flesh.

Lazarus didn't flinch. His expression remained a mask—stoic, unmoved, shaped from stone. "You may be done with me," he replied, "but the deed needed doing." No regret, no hesitation. It was just a cold calculation. "The boys, separated, stand a chance. Together, Salvatore's reach would ensnare them both."

A feral growl rumbled in my chest, shaking loose from deep within, rattling my ribs like a beast waking from slumber. My gaze dropped to the infant still nestled in Dancing Fire's arms, so small, so helpless—already born into war. He had been given no chance to breathe peace. Not even for a day.

My teeth clenched, a silent vow etched behind them. No one —no god, no demon, no man—would harm him.

Lazarus, as if carrying his sin, stepped forward. Carefully—too carefully—he reached for the squirming bundle, cradling him for a breath before thrusting him toward me.

"Meet Marcellious. Your son," he said, his voice heavy with forced solemnity, crushed my chest.

Time stopped.

The world narrowed to the small, perfect face peering up at me—my son. Our son. Blood of my blood. The war I had fought and the losses I had endured all led to this fragile moment.

Emotion surged in me, wild and consuming, a storm that tore through everything I thought I understood. My hands—hands that had wielded swords, shattered shields, and taken lives—trembled as they reached out.

And then he was there, against my chest, his warmth bleeding into my bones like sunlight after endless winter. His breath fluttered like a whisper, his heart beating against mine—a rhythm that ignited a different war within me.

A fight not of blades and blood—but of love. Of protection. Of insolence against a world of shadows that would seek to swallow him whole.

At that moment, I became something more than a warrior.

I became his father.

And I would incinerate the world to keep him safe.

Cradling Marcellious to my chest, I felt the dam—the barrier that had held back oceans of dread, guilt, and sorrow—shatter. Tears slipped down my face. I didn't wipe them away. I let them fall, let them trace the jagged edges of the man I had become.

His tiny fingers curled around one of mine, gripping with pure instinct, a silent trust that tore through every hardened layer of me. That grip wasn't just survival—it was faith in me.

"Marcellious," I breathed the name of a wound and a balm in the same breath. Saying it out loud felt like bleeding and healing at once. Elizabeth… she remembered. Across the chasm of lies and forced separation, she had honored my wish. She had given our son the name I had dreamt of, spoken to her long before the world fell apart.

That choice… was her whisper of love, carried to me across time, distance, and grief.

My heart surged with a love so fierce it threatened to break me. And beneath it, a new pain. The agony of holding our son while knowing she was gone, knowing that the gulf between us might never close.

And then Dancing Fire's voice, rough with bitterness, broke through the fragile stillness.

"She will return to England," he said, his gaze distant, fixed on something far beyond the cabin's walls. "She won't stay here. She refuses to be a party to this madness any longer."

The words didn't register at first. They floated in the air, senseless, foreign.

"What?" I muttered, breath catching like a snare in my throat.

"That's what she told me," Dancing Fire said, arms crossed, his stance as solid as stone. "She's stubborn. I begged her to stay. But she refused."

Lazarus—ever the immovable force—merely nodded as if none mattered. "Let her go," he said. "England will serve as a sufficient veil over the truth." His words held no emotion, no mercy. "The twins must grow under different skies, unaware of each other's existence."

My grip tightened around Marcellious, his warmth against my skin, the only living tether to Elizabeth I had left. The chill that radiated from Lazarus' words felt like death creeping under my skin.

"Have you no heart?" I grated, the question tearing from me, raw and bitter. "Elizabeth bears wounds deeper than flesh. You've torn her child from her arms, cast her into grief. Shouldn't she at least know why? Shouldn't she have the chance to kiss the brow of the son she'll never see again?"

Dancing Fire's voice joined mine, laced with steel. "A final goodbye—that's not too much to ask. Do you want to shatter her world but deny her even at that moment? Cruelty doesn't begin to name it."

"No!" Lazarus' voice cracked through the room like thunder, silencing us all.

His gaze locked on me, on the baby cradled in my arms—the child I would die to protect. His eyes held no remorse, only resolve. "The boy comes with me. He shall be under my tutelage. He must be prepared for what lies ahead. Some truths are too dangerous, too heavy to bear. This is the path we must walk —for their sakes, for the world's."

I stepped back, the instinct to shield Marcellious rising like a tidal wave in my chest. No. Not him. Not now.

But then Dancing Fire stepped forward, rebellion burning in every line of his face. "No. Give me the child," he demanded, hands outstretched, eyes locked on the infant in my arms. "I am here. I can raise Marcellious, train him, and guide him. Let me shape him rightly for the road ahead."

His voice cracked, grief threading through the fire. "Elizabeth will never allow him to fulfill his destiny. She told me herself. She wants to shield Roman from his Timeborne gift— she would do the same for Marcellious. She would smother the power in him... out of love."

The tension between the two men was tangible, ready to ignite. But I said nothing. I couldn't. I only held Marcellious tighter, his small body against my chest as if I could somehow will him to stay mine.

Their words weighted with bitter truth. Yet the thought of being severed from my son was a torment too deep to name—a blade slowly carving me open from the inside.

"Please," I heard myself whisper, my voice thin, raw, a man stripped bare. "Let me stay. Let me raise my son alongside you, Dancing Fire."

The plea hung between us, a fragile thread of hope against a storm of inevitability.

Lazarus shook his head, finality etched in the motion, cold and merciless. "I cannot allow it, Amir. But I will grant you this —you may visit them here." His gaze locked onto mine, cold and calculating. "But understand this—whatever permission you once had, it ends now. You are never to see Roman or Elizabeth again. That chapter is closed. In time, Roman will find his destiny. And we must be ready when that time comes."

His decree settled over me like a burial shroud. I understood the reasoning—the cruel strategy. The war ahead demanded separation, anonymity, and sacrifice. But knowing this didn't stop my heart from rebelling, raging, against the loss.

Marcellious stirred in my arms, soft and unaware, untouched by the chaos that had shaped his birth. He deserved more. More than a father hidden in shadows, more than a love kept at arm's length by prophecy and war.

With every breath, I vowed—to him and to the woman who still held my soul across oceans and lies—

I will guard you both and Roman. Unseen. Unwavering. Until the end of my days.

"Just… let me stay," I croaked, my voice raw with everything I couldn't bring myself to say. "Give me until the next full moon."

Lazarus paused, his silhouette a clean slash against the dying light beyond the doorway. A breath passed—one heartbeat of silence—before he spoke.

"Very well."

He didn't turn to face me.

"But don't forget your purpose, Amir." His voice was steel now, cold and honed. "You are a warrior first and foremost."

A warrior.

And yet, as I looked down at my son's face—peaceful in sleep, untouched by the world's chaos—I knew that was only half of who I was.

Now, I was a father. And I would never forget.

"I will protect them," I vowed into the silence of Lazarus' departure. "With everything I have."

The heavy wooden door closed behind him with a deep, echoing thud, sealing us in the small, cloistered cabin. That sound wasn't just the end of a conversation—it was a seal on my soul, binding my promise deeper than any oath I'd ever sworn on the battlefield.

I turned to Dancing Fire, standing like a sentinel in the fading light. Betrayal hung between us, heavy, unspoken—but too real to ignore. I met his gaze, his eyes shadowed with sorrow and spoke through the knot in my throat.

"I'm sorry," I said softly, struggling to keep my voice from cracking. "Sorry for what you had to do… for betraying her trust like that."

His expression shifted—the anger in his brow easing, replaced by a deep, aching sadness.

"You have nothing to apologize for, Amir," he replied quietly. "It is I who owe you both… everything. She saved my life once. Tended to my wounds not as a duty but with a kindness I didn't deserve."

His eyes drifted toward the forest beyond the cabin's rough-hewn walls as if searching for something—or someone—already lost.

"She's leaving now," he murmured, his voice catching. "Taking with her the light and warmth she brought into my life. I'll feel her absence every day."

In my arms, Marcellious stirred, blissfully unaware of the war, the grief, and the shattered bonds that welcomed him into this world. He was innocence incarnate, the embodiment of all we had lost and all we had left.

Dancing Fire stepped forward, his hand settling gently on the baby's soft head, a gesture filled with quiet reverence.

"This child is yours, and I will raise him with all my honor and strength. For you. For her. That's the least I can do."

"Thank you," I whispered, my voice filled with the sting of tears I refused to shed.

Between us was a bond that needed no words—not forged by blood but by fire. Brotherhood born from adversity, sealed by choice, and now, by this child.

Marcellious would be raised with love, even in my absence.

As silence settled around us, broken only by the gentle gurgling of the nearby creek, I felt the last vestiges of resistance crumble within me. We were fated to walk this path—not one of choice, but of necessity—each of us bearing our own burden of sacrifice. The future loomed uncertain, cloaked in shadow, but one truth remained immovable—

I would guard them all. From the shadows, if I must. Until fate deemed otherwise.

Marcellious' cry pierced the stillness, a plaintive sound that melted the numbness in my chest. I shifted him gently in my arms, soothing him with murmurs. He was a comfort and a searing reminder of what I had lost... and what I was about to lose.

"Amir," Dancing Fire said, drawing my gaze to his solemn face, filled with the same sorrow I felt. "Your duty is clear. If you cannot stand beside her, you must still protect her. Elizabeth must never want protection—even if it comes from the shadows."

I nodded, the muscles in my jaw tightening as I swallowed the anguish rising in my throat. "I will watch over them," I said, the words grinding like gravel. "As if I were a ghost... haunting the periphery of their lives. A silent guardian, warding off invisible threats."

A pang twisted inside me—a jealous, aching thing—as I looked at the man who would raise my son in my stead. "You will raise him," I murmured, unable to hide the bitterness in my voice. "Teach him to fight. To stand strong against the storms that await him."

"I will," Dancing Fire replied, his voice unwavering. "And I will honor your name in doing so."

I stared at him, knowing my trust in him had to be absolute. There was no other choice. "Do well by him," I said, my voice steady despite the ache threatening to splinter my chest. "Marcellious will grow to be a warrior under your guidance. And one day… one day, the brothers will stand united."

"Until then," Dancing Fire agreed, his gaze fierce with conviction, "we keep them apart. For their safety. For the future."

"Until then," I echoed, the words like a stone in my mouth. I looked down at my son, his innocent eyes wide and unburdened, untouched by sorrow or our choices. His tiny fingers curled around my thumb, gripping with quiet strength.

And my heart shattered anew.

"Until the full moon. I will watch over him. After, I will protect him… even if it's only from the shadows."

Dancing Fire nodded, his eyes softening. "I know it's hard, Amir. Be with him while you can. But when the moon is full, you must let him go. For his safety… and the future we fight for."

I said nothing. There were no words for this—only the fierce, aching need to hold on. I cradled my son closer, memorizing him—the softness of his cheek, the rise and fall of his breath, the warmth of his body against mine. I would stay for as long as the moon allowed.

As long as I draw breath, you, your brother, and your mother will know peace, I vowed in silence.

And until the moon demanded our parting, I would remain— watching, waiting, protecting.

CHAPTER 30

ELIZABETH

The chill of early morning bit at my cheeks as I cradled the tiny bundle of warmth against my chest. Roman. My son. His soft breaths rose and fell in sync with mine, grounding me in a world that had begun to feel foreign.

It had been several weeks since his birth, and with each passing day, my heart grew heavier. This land—once a refuge—now felt distant, unfamiliar. The open skies and endless plains could not soothe the anxiety inside me.

England was calling me home.

I stood still, watching the Sioux tribe move through their morning routines. The scent of burning wood and damp earth filled the air, mingling with the rhythmic hum of life around me. Despite their warmth and acceptance, I remained an outsider, tethered to a place—and people—that no longer existed in the way I'd known them.

My gaze drifted to Mary, her laughter lifting on the breeze as she bantered playfully with a group of children. She was light incarnate, a contrast to the storm I carried within.

"Mary," I called softly, stepping forward, my voice brittle with unspoken ache.

She turned, her smile open and easy, as vast as the prairie sky. "Elizabeth! What brings you this way with little Roman?"

Her eyes shone affectionately as they fell on the baby in my arms.

"I wanted to ask…" I hesitated, clutching Roman closer, seeking courage in his gaze. "Are you coming with me? To England?"

Mary's smile faltered, shifting to gentle empathy. "England?" she echoed, her voice softening with understanding. "No, Elizabeth. I'm staying. There's a man here… someone who's brought joy back into my life."

I swallowed the lump rising in my throat, managing a faint smile. "You deserve that happiness. Truly."

Her hand reached out, squeezing mine, grounding me for one last moment.

"Promise me you'll stay in touch?" I asked, my voice quivering despite every effort to keep it composed.

Mary's eyes brimmed with unshed tears, but she nodded. "Always."

Her promise hung in the air, fragile and uncertain. It was a thread of hope we both clung to, even knowing the world could fray it beyond repair. Still, it was a comfort—a sliver of light in the gathering storm.

Turning away, I hugged Roman tighter, his tiny form a lifeline anchoring me against the waves of grief and fear rising within. The journey ahead was unknown, but I would walk it—for him.

Cradling Roman in the crook of my arm, I moved through the camp, each step heavy with memories. The crisp morning air filled my lungs but did little to ease the pressure in my chest—the unrelenting ache of everything I was leaving behind.

And still, there was one wound I could not bear to leave untended.

The rift between Dancing Fire and I had widened with each passing day, our once-strong bond scorched by harsh words, silent stares, and unspoken grief. I could no longer bear the distance—not now.

I found him where I always did—in the quiet dawn light, seated by his tent, grinding his tools with methodical strokes.

The rhythmic sound was jarring against the uneven beat of my heart, a stark reminder of the man who had stood beside me through darkness and loss.

Swallowing the knot of hesitation, I stepped forward.

"Dancing Fire," I began, my voice barely more than a whisper, "I came to apologize. I was cruel… during our argument."

His hand stilled. Slowly, he looked up, eyes as deep and still as the night sky. His gaze held no anger, only sorrow.

"Elizabeth," he said quietly, setting aside the blade and cloth. "I also owe you an apology. I should not have spoken to you that way."

His sincerity bridged the chasm between us, and the tension that had lingered like a wound was now beginning to close.

I stepped closer, my free hand reaching out to him, uncertain but needing connection. He opened his arms without hesitation, and I stepped into them, holding Roman between us. Warmth. Forgiveness. The first I had felt in days.

"Thank you… for all you've done," I murmured into the fabric of his shirt, breathing in the familiar scent of woodsmoke and earth. It grounded me, steadying me in a world that felt like it was unraveling.

His arms tightened around us—not possessive, but protective —a shelter against the storm, a silent acknowledgment of all we had endured. Whatever roads now lay ahead, we had weathered this storm together.

Dancing Fire gently took my hand, his calloused fingers intertwining with mine, rough and sure. His eyes met mine, open, earnest, unwavering.

"Please stay," he said, voice low but resolute. "Marry me. I will protect you and Roman."

The words struck me—soft in delivery but cutting all the same. His offer stirred something inside me—duty, honor, comfort—but another image rose, fierce and consuming—Amir.

His face. His touch. His absence.

I could not forget.

"I can't," I whispered, the words tearing from my throat like splinters. "My heart belongs to Amir."

His name was a sacred incantation, etched in sorrow and devotion. It was pain and release—a vow I could not break.

Dancing Fire's gaze didn't falter, though grief pooled in his eyes. He nodded slowly, understanding settling over him like ash.

"The love of darkness is strong," he said, his voice tinged with something ancient, mystical. "Potent. It will always pull you toward it. I hope it brings you peace."

His eyes flicked to the worn tools at his side as if they could save him from his churning emotions. He hesitated, then drew in a deep breath.

"I can't thank you enough… for all you've done," he said, his voice cracking beneath unspoken gratitude.

Then, carefully, he reached for Roman, and I let him go for a moment. Dancing Fire cradled him in strong arms, the contrast of infant innocence against a warrior's burden almost too much to bear. His gaze softened, reverent.

"One day we will meet again, little one," he murmured, his voice low, prophetic—the kind of truth that clung to your soul, no matter how hard you tried to shake it off.

But I shook my head abruptly, desperately, as if I could cast off his words with that single, defiant motion.

"No. You will never see him again," I said, each word forged in steel, my voice hard with finality—even as my heart screamed in protest, tearing itself apart. "I won't allow it."

His eyes flickered with pain, with something more—but I didn't waver.

I couldn't.

I wouldn't let Roman be dragged back into this world—a world of war, prophecy, and burdens carried across lifetimes. I wouldn't let the legacy of time-traveling bloodlines and dark destinies shackle him. He was innocent. Pure. And he would stay that way.

His gift… his fate… I would bury it all.

He would grow up free, untouched by the shadows that had shaped my life. And if it took ruthlessness to keep him safe, I would become whatever I needed to be.

A mother. A shield. A storm.

Dancing Fire met my gaze—steadfast, unflinching, a warrior to the end. "I hid the dagger," he said, quiet but laced with meaning. "As you asked. It's gone from sight—but not from the world."

That dagger—the mark of Roman's Timeborne blood—a weapon I could not bear to hold yet could never truly destroy. A reminder that his power still lingered, silent, waiting.

"But remember this, Elizabeth—you can't stop destiny."

His words hung between us like a fog rolling over the plains —dense, cold, foreboding. A promise. A warning.

I said nothing. What could I say?

With a silent nod, I took Roman back into my arms, his small form curling against me as if he, too, felt the finality in the air.

And I turned away—from the man who had shown me kindness, from the land that had given me both life and death, from the world I no longer belonged to.

I didn't look back.

I couldn't.

The wind howled through the harbor, tugging at my shawl as I clutched it tightly around my shoulders. My fingers trembled— not from the cold, but from the desperation coiled in my chest like a serpent. Before me, the ship loomed, massive and imposing, its sails creaking against taut ropes, the timbers groaning like a beast at rest.

At the gangplank stood the captain, a weathered man with a salt-and-pepper beard and eyes like flint, barking orders in a voice that cut through the chaos. He moved with purpose, authority clinging to him like a second skin.

I stepped onto the slick wooden dock, Roman shifting against my chest, nestled securely in the satchel bound tight to my body. My deerskin moccasins sank slightly into the damp boards, but I kept my footing, his presence grounding me, propelling me forward.

The town's eyes followed me—curious and wary. I was dressed in traditional Native attire, a suede dress adorned with intricate beadwork and fringe, the wind tugging at the hem as I walked. Their stares cut, but I had no time for them. I only hoped it wouldn't deter the crew from giving me a chance.

My heart thundered as I neared the ship, the rehearsed plea tumbling through my mind one last time. Then, drawing in a breath that tasted of salt and fear, I stepped forward.

"Captain." My voice rang out, firm despite the knot twisting my stomach.

He turned, eyes narrowing as they swept over me—calculating, indifferent. It was the kind of look a man gave when he'd seen desperation a hundred times before and learned to ignore it.

"State your business, miss," he snapped. "I've no time for idle chatter."

I lifted my chin, willing my voice not to waver. "I seek passage to England. I have no money, but I offer my skills in return."

His brow arched, skepticism etched deep into his face. "Skills? And what might those be? I do not need fancy needlework or songs to entertain my crew."

I squared my shoulders, clutching Roman protectively. "I'm a healer, Captain. I've treated fevers, stitched wounds, and eased pain with herbs and remedies. Surely, aboard a ship full of men, you'll need someone to keep them alive and fit for the journey."

The wind howled through the harbor, cold and unrelenting, tugging at my shawl as I clutched it tightly around my shoulders. His head tilted, arms folding across his chest as he regarded me with measured doubt. "A healer, you say?" His gaze flicked to the bundle at my chest, then back to me. "And how do I know you're not all talk?"

Without hesitation, I reached into my satchel and pulled out a small jar, unscrewing the lid to release the familiar scent of comfrey and honey, bittersweet and strong. "This mends wounds faster than any surgeon's stitches," I said with confidence. "Let me show you."

Before he could reply, a shout rang out from behind him—a sailor staggered forward, his face pale, blood dripping from a gash in his forearm. He clutched at it, trying to stem the flow, pain etched across his features.

The captain's eyes narrowed, flicking from the injured man back to me. "Very well," he said. "We'll talk—if you can fix that without him keeling over."

I knelt beside the sailor, my hands steady. There was no room for fear now. As I cleaned the wound with seawater and applied the salve, I murmured to the man, wrapping the injury with a clean cloth. His pain eased as the salve worked its way into the gash, his breathing evening out.

When I stood, wiping my hands on my apron, the captain's eyes had shifted—calculating, impressed.

"You've earned your place," he said with a curt nod. "But mark my words, miss—if you can't keep up, I'll leave you at the next port."

"I won't disappoint you, Captain," I replied, my voice unwavering as Roman stirred against me.

I wasn't just leaving for safety—I was returning to fulfill a promise. My mother's work—the Noctyss flower alchemy—awaited me in England, a legacy I was determined to perfect.

The creaking of the hull became my constant companion as we crossed the Atlantic. Life aboard was harsh—a rhythm of cold, hunger, and salt, broken only by the shouts of sailors and the roar of the waves.

But in the chaos, Roman was my anchor.

His tiny fingers curled around mine when seasickness tore at me. His rare, precious gurgles soothed my frayed soul. In his scent and warmth, I found the strength to face another day aboard that floating prison of wood and sail.

I would reach England.

For him. For my mother. For the legacy that still burned in my blood—the alchemy of the Noctyss flower, a gift I had vowed to perfect, just as she had once dreamed. Her promise was my compass, even when the world felt hopeless.

And I would not fail.

My skills as a healer were tested more times than I could count. Splintered bones from brutal falls, deep cuts from careless blades, bruises from drunken brawls—night after night, by the flickering glow of a lantern, I stitched and wrapped wounds. My hands remained unwavering as my body begged for rest, weariness clinging to me like a second skin.

Yet amidst the chaos, there was solace. The women aboard—hardened by the sea yet tender in spirit—became a lifeline. They cooed over Roman, their eyes softening as they rocked him to sleep, singing lullabies drowned beneath the ship's endless groan. When duty called me away, I entrusted him to them—temporary guardian angels in the cramped quarters of our drifting world.

As the ship forged onward, carving white foam trails through dark waters, I clung to the image of England's shores—a dream I could barely grasp, its edges frayed by fear. What waited there, I did not know.

After eight long weeks, the dock's wooden planks groaned underfoot as I stepped off the ship, Roman cradled against my chest. The tang of salt and fish filled my nostrils, grounding me in a reality far colder than memory. This was England, yet it felt distant, unfamiliar, like the ghost of a home I no longer belonged to.

I had nothing. No coin. No plan. Only regret coiled tightly around my shoulders.

"Why did I come here?" I whispered, the words snatched away by the wind—a ghost of a question, unheard and unanswered.

I wandered through the streets, Roman nestled close, each step more aimless than the last. The buildings loomed overhead, their windows dark eyes, watching with indifferent curiosity. My feet carried me to the entrance of a tavern, its weathered sign swinging in the wind. The stench of stale ale and sweat seeped from within, a warning.

I thought of renting a room—just one night, a chance to rest.

Before I could open the door, a man sidled beside me. His breath reeked of drink, his gaze sliding over me and lingering too long on the blanket swaddling Roman.

"You look like you could use some money," he slurred, a lewd grin on his lips. "Maybe we can… make an arrangement."

His insinuation sliced through my exhaustion, igniting a rage that snapped me awake.

Without a word, I turned and fled, quickening my pace, my heart pounding as I ducked down narrow streets until I was sure we were alone.

In the silence of a deserted alley, I collapsed against the cold stone, my body trembling.

I sobbed, the tears falling freely, mingling with Roman's soft whimpers—a mother and child, both lost, both yearning for comfort that would not come.

"I shouldn't have left," I choked out. The confession fell against the bricks, hollow and broken, swallowed by the silence of the alleyway.

The night pressed in around us, cold and relentless but even in the dark, I clutched Roman tighter, drawing what little strength I had from the warmth of his small, fragile body.

I had to survive.

For him. For the promise.

For the legacy that refused to die in me.

When the sobs finally ebbed, a fragile resolve rose in their place, like the first flicker of dawn against a storm-wrecked sky. Despite the regrets that clung to me like burrs, I forced myself to breathe, to move.

"Let's go back to my childhood home," I whispered to Roman, trying to infuse my voice with hope. "Maybe… maybe it's still standing."

The journey there was one of ghosts. Every step echoed with memories—my mother's laughter, the gentle hum of her voice as she spoke of the Noctyss flower, of the alchemy we were meant to perfect together. Those halls had once been filled with light and purpose. Now, I walked toward them as a stranger.

But the house that greeted me was not the sanctuary of my youth.

Another family's laughter rang from within, soft and foreign, replacing the silence that once belonged to us. The walls were intact, the garden overgrown, but nothing remained of what was once mine.

I knocked, hesitant, each rap of my knuckles a plea for something I could never reclaim.

A maid answered, her eyes scanning me—disheveled, worn, clad in strange attire with a babe in my arms. Her gaze had no recognition, no flicker of understanding—just polite confusion.

"I'm sorry, miss," she said gently. "But you can't stay here."

The door closed.

And with it, the last tangible piece of my past.

I stood motionless momentarily, the loss pressing down like a stone. Then I turned, staggering through the dimly lit streets, Roman's cries slicing through the night air. Each wail was a lash against my soul—a reminder of the ruin I had brought upon us.

My father's world was gone.

His once-vibrant society—now dust and echoes.

Because of me.

Because of Salvatore. His betrayal, the murder of my father, stained my soul like ink spilled across a page, a mark that could never be washed away.

"Shh, my sweet boy," I whispered, cradling Roman close, my words trembling and feeble. I rocked him gently, my shoulders shaking with exhaustion and fear. "What will we do?"

The question lingered in the night air, unanswered, suspended like a fragile thread in a world that no longer made sense. We wandered beneath the streetlamps, their glow illuminating a city that had once been my home—and now held nothing but shadows.

My feet, driven by instinct and the ache of memory, carried me down a familiar path. The cobblestones led me to the remnants of a life that now felt like it belonged to someone else.

Amir's townhouse loomed ahead—silent, a ghost of what it

had once been. I remembered it alive with warmth, with laughter that spilled into the night air, and with love that wrapped around me like a cloak. Now, the windows were dark, the light inside long gone, and I stood outside a place I could no longer enter.

The iron gate groaned beneath my touch as I pushed it open. I climbed the stone steps, my body trembling beneath my son, of my grief, of the shattered pieces of my heart.

There, I sat—clutching Roman tightly to my chest, his small body the only light left in the darkness.

"I promised you the world," I whispered, tears cascading freely, each one a testament to broken dreams. "But I've failed you. No money. No family. No home. What kind of mother am I?"

Roman clung to me, his tiny hands gripping my dress, his whimpers echoing the sorrow that consumed me.

The night deepened, the wind biting as it swept through the empty streets. I shivered, putting my face into Roman's hair, mourning all we had lost.

Then, something stirred. Wisps of black smoke curled through the air, twisting around us and coalescing into a familiar form. My breath caught in my throat, and my heart stalled.

Strong arms enveloped me. The scent of cedar and leather filled my senses, wrapping around me like a dream I never dared to believe in again.

I gasped, my heart slamming against my ribs. Slowly, I lifted my head.

Amir.

His eyes met mine, filled with pain, love, and a thousand unspoken regrets.

"Amir..." It was all I could manage—his name a whisper of disbelief, of wild, reckless hope.

A sob broke free as I clung to him, collapsing into the only arms I had ever truly belonged to.

"I'm so sorry, my love," he murmured into my hair, his voice breaking with every word. "I should never have listened to Lazarus. I should have fought to be with you."

Tears blurred my vision as I raised trembling hands to his face, needing to feel him, to prove he was real—solid, warm, alive. My fingertips brushed his skin, and a sob escaped me.

"You're alive," I breathed, a fragile mix of wonder and grief. The impossible had happened. He was here.

Amir nodded, eyes locked onto mine with fierce, unwavering purpose as if anchoring me back to the world we once shared.

He surrounded me, impossible and undeniable, a sanctuary against the storm of despair I had lived in for too long. His warmth seeped into the frozen corners of my soul, thawing the despair that had wrapped around me like a second skin. His touch was spectral—gentle yet brimming with the strength I had always known in him—a warrior's hands, a protector's heart.

"Watching you alone has been torture," he said, his voice low, raw with anguish that mirrored my own. "I never stopped watching over you. I never stopped loving you."

Tears streamed down my cheeks as he gathered us into his arms—Roman and me—with a tenderness born not just of love but of loss and longing too vast to name.

He lifted us effortlessly, holding us close as if we were the most precious things he had ever touched. As we crossed the threshold of the townhouse, the door swung open without protest, as though the house itself recognized our return— welcoming us back into the embrace of shadows and memories.

Inside, the floorboards creaked underfoot, familiar, mournful sounds echoing through the stillness. The air smelled faintly of cedar and old paper of time long passed. The remnants of our love still lingered here.

For the first time in months, a glimmer of happiness pierced the sorrow. It was fragile, flickering like candlelight, but it was there, fiery in the darkness.

But I knew happiness never came without a price, not for us.

Never for us.

What would the cost be this time?

I didn't know.

But with Amir's arms around me, Roman safe against my chest, I would face it—whatever it was.

Because love like this didn't die. It endured.
Even through darkness.
Even through time.

CHAPTER 31

ELIZABETH

Perched on the edge of Amir's bed, my hands trembled, unable to still the storm within me. The room was quiet —too quiet—and its opulence was a stark contrast to the chaos that had become my life. The crisp lines, the polished wood, the heavy curtains... it all felt unreal, like a place I no longer belonged to.

Tear tracks cooled on my cheeks, but fresh ones welled up unbidden, hot against my skin.

Across the room, Amir moved with reverence, tenderly laying our sleeping baby, Roman, on a bundle of blankets nestled in the corner. The sight of him—this warrior, this ghost made flesh again—handling our son with such care and awe was enough to cleave my heart in two.

Amir straightened, the dim light from the window casting shadows across his face and illuminating the chiseled lines of his Mediterranean features. His eyes—dark, fathomless orbs—landed on Roman with quiet wonder, as though seeing him was a miracle he scarcely dared to believe in.

He stepped toward me, the rigid stoicism he once wore like armor now stripped away, leaving only the man beneath.

"Our child is so beautiful," he whispered, his voice cracking with unshed tears.

"Yes," I managed, the word catching in my throat. "He is... a comfort. A gift." My gaze followed his, drawn to the peaceful rise and fall of Roman's breath. My heart swelled with love so fierce, so profound, it ached.

I reached out as if to steady myself on the world, slipping back into color and life. "Amir..." The name trembled from my lips, a prayer, a plea, a thousand questions wrapped in a single breath.

"I thought I lost you forever," I said, the words spilling out, broken and desperate. Relief, joy, fear, yearning—I was drowning in them all. My eyes searched his face, for answers, for truth. "How are you here? I thought... I thought you were dead."

Amir didn't speak at first. He knelt before me, a man once forged by war, now humbled by fate. He took my hands into his, grounding me.

"I never stopped watching you," he murmured. His voice— usually clipped, commanding—was now a velvet rasp, raw and vulnerable. "Even when I couldn't touch you. Even when it broke me."

He lowered his head, bringing my hands to his lips as though reassuring himself in my reality. "I've been in the shadows. Watching. Protecting. Always."

"All this time... you've been watching over me?" I breathed, the truth crashing like a tidal wave—months of longing and loneliness suddenly reframed in the staggering light of his return.

"Yes." His gaze met mine with an intensity that stilled every- thing inside me. "I was forbidden to get any closer, but I vowed to keep you safe."

I sat there, reeling, my world unraveling and stitching itself back together. The time apart, the pain, the fear—it had never been mine alone. Amir had carried it, too, in silence.

He moved beside me on the bed, a grounding force. His hands encased mine, roughened by war and time but tender as they trembled in my grasp.

"Elizabeth," he said, his voice low, the storm still flickering behind his eyes. "There are things you must know."

He paused, inhaling deeply, bracing himself—not for his sake, but for mine.

"After the masquerade, Lazarus saved my life."

My breath caught, his name a blade slicing through memory. Lazarus—the enigma, the legend, the man who had stolen so much and returned Amir to me.

"I was nearly dead," Amir continued, his voice dipping into the shadows of memory. "For hours, many snakes injected me with their venom to counteract the poison coursing through me. I lay in the serpents' den, not knowing if I were alive or already gone. Their venom… scorched through my veins. They fought death for me, and I couldn't even scream."

The image struck like thunder—Amir, strong and fearless, now a man torn between life and death, writhing in the cold embrace of serpents, saviors of a kind no one would ever expect.

A sob rose in my throat. "Oh, Amir… that must have been awful." My voice tremored as the horror of his ordeal sank into my bones. I reached for his face, cupping it gently, my thumbs brushing over the strong lines etched by pain and time. "You suffered so much…"

His eyes fluttered closed as he leaned into my touch, seeking absolution, anchoring himself in the present—in me.

"Enduring that pain," he said, locking his gaze with mine, his voice a low, raw confession, "was better than the thought of never seeing your beautiful face again."

The intensity behind his words ignited something in my heart —a surge of love so fierce it left me breathless. Embers I feared had long since cooled roared back to life, filling the room with warmth and ache.

For a moment, we breathed—two souls reunited, fragile yet whole.

But then, his expression shifted—urgency shadowing his features. "Lazarus saved your life, too, Elizabeth."

I frowned, confusion knotting in my chest. The fog of memory closed in, heavy and elusive. "Lazarus saved me? But I thought—Mary—she was the one who took care of me."

Amir shook his head, tension etching deep lines into his

brow. "No—Lazarus saved you from the damage Salvatore inflicted. Mary couldn't have healed that. Not even with all her skill. And the poison from the masquerade didn't affect you because of your Timehealer bloodline. That resilience—it's in your blood."

His words hung in the air, peeling away the truths I'd clung to. I stared at him, stunned, my breath caught.

"After the masquerade," Amir continued, his voice low, "Lazarus took us to his underground palace in Anatolia. He healed you there."

Anatolia.

The word echoed like a tolling bell through my mind, stirring something ancient and buried. Images flickered at the edges of my vision—stone walls, cold air, the scent of herbs. My hands trembled.

"I remember…" I whispered, the memories clawing their way to the surface. "I thought I saw an old man… I thought it was a dream."

But it wasn't a dream.

Images crashed over me—vivid, fragmented, real.

Lazarus hovered over me in a darkened chamber, his hands moving with a ritual. A sudden sting, the warmth of blood trickling down my skin. Red, faintly glowing symbols etched onto my flesh, then fading into nothingness, like whispers lost to the wind.

"There were symbols…" My voice broke, the memory crawling from the shadows. "He marked me—with blood. On my arms… my chest. And then it was gone."

"Blood runes," Amir said quietly, as if naming them carried weight. "A rare healing rite. Ancient. Forbidden. Lazarus used them to save you—at a great cost."

I put a hand to my chest, fingers trembling as if I could still feel the symbols beneath my skin, branded into my soul.

"Mary said I never left home…" I whispered. "She swore it."

"Magic distorts memory," Amir murmured, his grip on my hand tightening, returning me to the truth I had never known I needed. "He altered what you saw. How he put you back… made you believe you were there the entire time."

The pieces of my past shifted like sand, slipping through the fingers of a woman who didn't recognize the life she'd lived. Each memory fractured, realigned, leaving a tapestry I couldn't decipher.

The revelation hung heavy in the room, each word tethered me to a reality I scarcely understood.

Amir's eyes locked with mine, obsidian reflecting a sorrow older than time. "It was all Lazarus' doing. He made you forget to protect you."

"Protect me from what?" The question slipped from my lips, born of fear and the ache of confusion.

Amir's gaze darkened. "From Salvatore."

The name fell like a stone, echoing in the silence. A blanket of dread wrapped around me, and I shivered, a cold finger tracing the length of my spine. A memory flashed—Salvatore in my father's study, his malevolent gaze locked with Father's, both men ensnared in a dance of power and deceit. The room. The tension. The promise of danger.

My hand flew to my mouth, stifling the gasp that clawed its way up. "Oh gods."

Amir's expression hardened, the protector awakening in him like fire stoked from embers. The lines of his face, carved by war and loss, now bore the fury of love's vow.

"You're safe, my love," he said, his voice firm, a fortress built in sound. "Salvatore is hunting the person who crafted the Noctyss poison."

He paused long enough for the truth to settle like ice in my veins.

"But he doesn't know it's you."

His declaration sliced through the silence, ferocity forged into every syllable. It wasn't just a truth—a shield, a ward against the darkness that still hunted us. It was as if by naming it aloud, Amir could make it permanent, forever locking the threat away.

"Lazarus cloaked your blood," he continued, his voice low

and unwavering. "To Salvatore, you are dead. It's like you don't exist."

His words painted a stark image—me, a ghost in the eyes of a predator. Unseen. Untouched. Unreachable.

"You wouldn't be seen as that person—the one who crafted the poison." He searched my eyes, his dark gaze filled with something I couldn't name—hope, fear, perhaps guilt. Maybe he was asking forgiveness for the life he was begging me to live—a life in hiding, wrapped in shadows, stripped of everything I had once been.

"But still… you must be careful." His voice was a bell tolling in the night, its warning clear. "Danger is never far, Elizabeth. It prowls at the edges, watching. Waiting."

I nodded, the truth of his words sinking deep into the marrow of my bones. Safety was a fragile illusion, a breath held in silence. And I was the fulcrum, balanced precariously between peace and peril.

A shiver coursed through me, Amir's revelations a heavy cloak draped over my shoulders.

"What must I do?" My voice cracked, barely audible over the drumbeat of my heart.

Amir's hands clasped mine—strong, sure, yet heartbreakingly gentle. His touch was both a tether and a plea.

"Elizabeth," he said, his voice solid with resolve, "you must stay away from alchemy. Live a normal life. Become a seamstress. Keep your head down. Avoid herbs, healing, and anything that draws attention."

His words were a requiem—a burial hymn for the life I'd lived and the purpose I had breathed. Each one cut deeper, slicing into the core of who I was.

Tears welled up, spilling over like a dam breached by sorrow.

"I can't," I whispered, my voice breaking. "I can't give it up. It's part of who I am."

The words shook from me—raw, anguished. Alchemy wasn't just a practice—it was the rhythm of my soul, woven into the fabric of my being, how I touched the world, and how I understood it.

"I made a promise to my mother, Amir." My voice cracked, but I continued, needing him to understand. "She devoted her entire life to alchemy. Before she died, she made me promise to carry on her work. I can't turn away from that now. I won't."

I drew in a shuddering breath, tears streaking my cheeks, that vow etching into my soul. "If I walk away now, I betray her. I betray myself."

Amir's gaze locked onto mine, intense and pleading, his fingers tightening gently around mine as if to tether me to him.

"You must, Elizabeth." His voice was soft, but beneath it lay an urgency. "You can never practice it again. You must have an ordinary job. Something simple. Safe."

The cold truth of his words seeped into me, slow and unforgiving. A life stripped of alchemy felt like a sentence, not salvation—as if he'd asked me to sever a part of myself and still learn to breathe.

"There's more, my love." His hand brushed away a tear from my cheek, the gesture tender, even as the world beneath me shifted.

"While in the Americas, you met a man named Dancing Fire. He is my best friend. I asked him to watch over you, to protect you. Always."

His confession wrapped around me, startling and strange, yet it settled the chaos of my thoughts—a protection I hadn't known I'd been given.

"Even as I served Lazarus," Amir continued, his voice teeming with emotion, "I ensured you were never alone. You were cared for. You were watched over."

The depth of his loyalty and the sacrifices made in silence struck me. Amid the storm of fear and uncertainty, his devotion filled me with gratitude.

As I met Amir's gaze, the reality of my new, fragile existence hung heavy between us—a tapestry of protection he had woven, thread by thread, leaving me sheltered... but shackled.

My heart thundered against my ribs, each beat a drum of shock, the revelation crashing through me, fierce and unrelenting. Dancing Fire—Amir's closest confidant? The man who had stood at my side through loss, through birth, through betrayal—a protector cloaked in secrecy?

The pieces clicked together, sudden and jarring. He had been my guardian angel in disguise, an invisible thread woven through my life, pulled tight by Amir's unseen hand.

And I—I had never known I was bound.

"Amir," I whispered, the name catching on my breath. "I... I cannot fathom…"

He sat beside me, the stoic mask he always wore softened by moonlight, casting silver across the sculpted angles of his face. "The last thing I ever wanted was to leave you, Elizabeth," he said, his voice low and threaded with sorrow that mirrored the ache in my soul. "I did not choose to part ways with you, nor did I do so out of desire."

A single tear traced down his chiseled cheek—silent, unbidden, and devastating. It glistened in the dim light, a testament to the war he fought within himself.

"Your safety is paramount. My presence alone endangers you. But tonight, when I saw you wandering the streets, alone, lost…" His voice broke. "Something inside me stuttered. I could no longer remain hidden."

"Can you stay?" The plea escaped me, raw and desperate, a choked whisper of longing. "Please, Amir… I cannot bear this solitude."

He cupped my face in his hands, the warmth of his touch grounding me, as fear coiled tight in my chest. His thumb brushed away a tear, but the dread remained unmoving.

"Elizabeth," he murmured, "my heart is tethered to yours. But our fates... they are cruel. Twisted with dangers greater than either of us can imagine." His eyes—dark, bottomless wells of pain and resolve—held mine, refusing to let go. "Salvatore's shadow looms. And he is ruthless. He hunts without rest."

"Because of the flower?" The words escaped me, haunted by

memory—the Noctyss flower, its beauty a lie, hiding the lethal power that flowed through its veins.

"Yes, my love," Amir confirmed, his jaw tightening. "That flower holds the key—the only known force that can neutralize a Shadow Lord's power. Salvatore seeks it. Seeks you. Though he knows not yet who you are."

A chill lanced down my spine.

I had held the flower.

I had wielded its alchemy.

And now… I was the key to Salvatore's downfall.

"Then what are we to do?" I breathed, desperation lacing every word, fear gnawing at the frayed edges of my composure.

"Live quietly. Blend into the tapestry of this city," Amir said, each syllable resolute. "And should I find a way, I will come to you. But without a pattern. Without expectation. Our encounters must remain cloaked in secrecy—for both our sakes."

"Amir…" I reached for him, my fingers trembling as they brushed against the coarse fabric of his sleeve, trying to anchor myself in him. Could I truly accept this life? A life of fleeting shadows and stolen moments?

"Promise me you will endure, Elizabeth," he whispered, drawing me close, placing a kiss on my forehead—a benediction, a plea, a goodbye all at once. "For us. For our child. For the future, we dare to dream."

He rose, leaving a chill in his absence. His footsteps echoed in the chamber, back and forth, a metronome counting down the seconds we had left.

Our son lay curled in sleep in the corner, peaceful and unaware. His breaths were soft and even, a fragile rhythm of life in a world that teetered on the edge of war.

Then Amir stilled. When it came, his voice was heavy—each word crushed the air around us.

"Elizabeth… our son must never know about me."

The room spun.

I stood, stunned as if the ground had been yanked from beneath me. "What? No!" I stepped forward, my voice breaking, refusing to accept the sentence he had just laid before me.

"Our son must never know about me," Amir repeated, quieter this time but with a finality that pierced my heart. "Make up a story about our affair. Let him believe I abandoned you. Let him hate me. If you must."

My breath hitched, the protest clawing up my throat. "Amir, I can't… I can't do that." To deny Roman his father—to bury this love, this truth—it was a betrayal I couldn't fathom.

"You must." Amir's eyes locked on mine, filled with sorrow and torment—yet unwavering. "He must despise me. It will prepare him for his destiny."

"I can't do this!" I shot back, my voice breaking under anguish. "I'm proud of what we created." The thought of tainting our love with lies—turning it into something shameful, something forsaken—was more painful than any wound.

"I'm sorry," Amir whispered, the words like glass underfoot, his voice full of pain. "But it must be this way."

My gaze faltered, unable to hold his any longer. The room seemed to shrink, the walls compressing, whispering secrets of heartache and sacrifice, of all that was being lost.

"Amir… I love you. So much." My voice trembled, a fragile thread in the silence. "Knowing you're watching over me—it takes away the pain. But how—how can I do this to our son?"

His expression upset me—his pain a mirror to my own, as though we were both torn apart by the same cruel hand.

"You must tell him a story," Amir urged, his voice fierce with desperation. "Say I used you. Betrayed you. Let him hate me." He swallowed hard. "I will always be with you—but in the shadows."

His words crushed me, a burden too great, yet I could not cast it off.

"Lazarus will punish me if he knows I'm here," Amir continued, his voice darkening with urgency. "And Salvatore must never find you. I cannot risk your life, Elizabeth—not for anything. I love you too much. And that means… forcing a chasm between me and my son."

Tears blurred my vision, burning hot as reality cemented itself into me, leaving no room for denial. Amir's love—a fortress, immovable and fierce—now stood as a wall between us, protecting and shielding me but never allowing me close.

"Promise me, Elizabeth." He stepped forward, his hand rising to cup my cheek, his touch a flicker of warmth in the cold desolation of this moment. His thumb brushed away a tear, his eyes seeking mine. "Promise me you'll do this. For him. For us."

In his touch, I found the strength I thought I'd lost. I nodded —a small, quivering motion—yet it sealed a pact that would alter the course of our lives forever.

"Promise me," Amir repeated, his voice heavy with deep sorrow; it seemed to hollow the air between us. "You will embrace the ordinary, the mundane. I will provide for you from the shadows. Steal moments when I can. But Roman… he must never know."

The world I had just begun to rebuild crumbled again, each jagged shard a cruel reminder of the impossible path before us. My heart fractured, the pain unfathomable—yet within it, my resolve hardened like steel forged in fire.

"I will do whatever it takes," I whispered, my voice brittle with unshed tears. "But this… this will break me."

Amir's gaze held mine, unwavering, fierce, a lifeline in the storm of my despair. "No, Elizabeth. You are the strongest woman I know."

His faith wrapped around me, a shield against the crushing weight of sacrifice.

Before I could speak, before I could drown in the ache, Amir closed the distance between us. His arms enveloped me, drawing me into the eye of the storm, where only we existed. "Gods, how I have wanted to do this for so long," he breathed against my hair, his lips brushing my temple, igniting a fire in my soul.

To be in his arms was serenity, a fleeting sanctuary from the war outside and within.

When his lips met mine, time ceased to exist. The kiss was everything—a promise, a plea, a branding of love and desperation. Passion, raw and consuming, melded us together, two broken pieces finding wholeness in each other.

His eyes burned into me as he pulled away—fierce, unwavering, the same fire I felt blazing in my chest.

"I want to marry you," Amir confessed, his voice a fervent whisper, hoarse with need and truth. "But it must be in secret. Know this, Elizabeth—I love you. I will always be devoted to you. Always."

Shock tore through the grief, scattering the darkness with a wild, untamed hope. Lord Winston's cold, leering face flitted through my mind—a prison I had once been chained to. And this —this was its antithesis. Not duty, not arrangement—this was love, sacred and defiant.

My answer came from the deepest part of me, pure and unshakable.

"Yes. Yes. Yes. I'll marry you," I vowed, my heart surging, my voice unshaken. "My heart belongs to you. You're not just Roman's father, Amir. You're my everything."

His eyes locked onto mine in the room's dimness, igniting a fire that devoured me from the inside out. There was no fear, no hesitation—only need. Need for him. For us. For this.

His hands were rough, hungry, as they found the frayed edges of my doeskin dress. The fabric barely held together, and he tore it open with a growl, letting it slip to the floor, exposing me inch by inch to the heat of his gaze. His eyes devoured me, dark and molten, and then his mouth was on me—every kiss a scorch mark, his tongue drawing shivers as it traced the sensitive hollow of my throat, the peaks of my breasts, the dip of my stomach.

I gasped, arching into him, my skin alive, tingling, desperate. Every nerve on fire with anticipation. His lips latched onto a nipple, sucking hard, then softer, then biting just enough to make me cry out—a cry he swallowed with a fierce, claiming kiss.

Exhaustion was gone—obliterated. There was only this hunger, and I was drowning in it, gladly. He pushed me back against the wall, his thigh forcing mine apart, and I moaned as his fingers slid down, unerringly finding the slick heat between my legs.

"Gods, Elizabeth, you're soaking," he groaned against my

neck, his fingers teasing my entrance, spreading me, tormenting me. "I need to be inside you—now."

"Then take me," I panted, writhing, aching, every part of me begging. "No more waiting. Take me. Hard."

His growl was feral as he lifted me effortlessly, pushing me against the wall. I wrapped my legs around him, needy, greedy, and with a rough thrust, he buried himself inside me—deep, thick, filling me to the hilt.

I cried out, my nails digging into his back, his name a breathless chant on my lips as he pounded into me, every stroke a brutal, beautiful claim.

"Mine," he snarled, driving deeper, faster, until the room dissolved, and all that remained was this—his cock inside me, our bodies slamming together, sweat and moans, and pure, wild ecstasy.

"Yours, always yours," I gasped, clutching him closer, begging, unraveling.

We collapsed onto the bed, panting, flushed, limbs tangled. I straddled him, taking control, his cock still hard and ready beneath me. His eyes blazed up at me, dark and savage, and I guided him back inside, slowly, this time—teasing us both with every inch I took.

"Elizabeth, fuck—" he groaned, thrusting up, but I pushed my hands to his chest, holding him down.

I rode him slowly at first, savoring the feel of him beneath me—the way his hands guided my hips, his dark eyes locked on mine with that familiar mix of desire and reverence. Our rhythm was built with each movement, every stroke drawing a soft gasp from my lips, and every shift deepened our bond.

His chest rose and fell, muscles taut and slick with sweat, and beneath my palms, I could feel the power he held— restrained but simmering.

"Elizabeth..." Amir's voice was a low groan, barely controlled. His grip tightened, grounding me in the moment. "You feel perfect."

I leaned forward, brushing my lips along his jaw, letting the swell of my breasts press to his chest. His hands roamed my back, tracing the curve of my spine, anchoring me as I moved—slow, deliberate, dragging out every sensation.

I saw the tension building in his body, the wild need beneath the surface, and when he suddenly stilled me, I knew.

His hands gripped my hips—firm, commanding—and in one fluid motion, he withdrew. The sudden emptiness punched the breath from my lungs, a whimper tangled in my throat. But then —a gasp. He turned me, guiding me onto all fours with a possessive ease that left no space for question, only surrender.

The air kissed my flushed skin, but then he was there—behind me, against me, his chest warm against my back, the heat of him overwhelming.

One hand slid along my waist, the other between my shoulder blades, holding me still, anchoring me as his body aligned with mine. His breath was hot against my ear, and his voice was low, rough silk when he spoke.

"Like this, Elizabeth. Let me have you. Let me feel you—all of you."

I pushed back into him instinctively, my body yearning, open, ready. A soft cry left my lips as he entered me again, slowly, deeply, filling me until I was breathless, his groan a sound of raw satisfaction.

We moved together, the pace unhurried but intense, every stroke deep, designed to make me feel every inch of him. His hands roamed over me—my hips, my back, one sliding beneath to tease my breast, the pad of his thumb brushing my nipple until I moaned his name, shivering.

"You're mine," he whispered, his lips brushing my neck, his voice a mix of tenderness and command. "Like this. Always."

My hands fisted the blanket beneath us as I matched his rhythm, meeting every thrust with a grind of my hips, our bodies locked, our breath coming in gasps and sighs. The heat built slowly, sweetly, each moment pulling me deeper into him, into the intensity of our connection, until there was nothing but him —his touch, his voice, his love.

"Don't stop," I gasped, my voice shaking with need.

"Never," he growled softly, pressing a kiss to my shoulder,

moving harder, deeper, his pace tightening, tension coiling between us like a storm ready to break.

His rhythm shifted—deeper, harder, more urgent—his hands anchoring me with a possessive grip, guiding every thrust. Each stroke undid me, pulling me closer to the edge until my body trembled, desperate for release.

"Amir… please—don't stop—" My voice was breathless, cracked with need, my body arching into his, surrendering to the fire between us.

"I've got you, love. Just feel me. Let go." His words, low and urgent, wrapped around me like silk, a command and a promise in one.

His hand slid beneath me, finding that bundle of nerves slick and throbbing, his fingers circling, coaxing. The sensation hit me hard—pleasure sparking like wildfire, my breath catching, my limbs shaking.

And then I shattered.

A cry tore from my throat, his name on my lips as my climax ripped through me, blinding and hot, my body tightening around him, clenching, pulsing, lost in the storm of sensation.

Amir groaned—a deep, raw sound of surrender—his pace faltering, hands gripping my hips hard enough to bruise as he thrust deep one final time, holding there as his release overtook him. I felt it—the tremble of his body, the tension breaking, the heat of him spilling inside me as he held his chest to my back, breath ragged against my skin.

We stayed there, bodies entwined, our breaths loud and uneven, filling the space like music.

Slowly, tenderly, Amir eased out of me, drawing a soft gasp from my lips as the last tremors of pleasure rippled through me. The air between us felt packed with heat, our skin damp, breath ragged. He didn't let me go—instead, he pulled me down onto the blankets, guiding me into the warmth of his embrace, our bodies still flushed, tangled, utterly sated.

I melted against him, my back to his chest, every inch of me against his skin. His arm was tight around my waist, fingers splayed low over my stomach, possessive and protective. His heart beat against my spine, the rhythm grounding me, as a different kind of heat curled low in my belly—not urgent but smoldering, alive.

His soft and slow lips brushed my neck, tasting the salt of my skin. He didn't speak at first. His hand wandered lazily, fingertips tracing the curve of my hip, the waist dip, sliding over my thigh in a sensual path that made my breath catch.

"You are like no other woman," he whispered, his voice husky, grazing my ear. "There is more fire in you than in all of Persia."

A shiver rolled through me, and I turned in his arms to face him, our legs entwined, my hand sliding up to rest on his chest, feeling the rise and fall of his breath beneath my palm.

"I could say the same about you," I murmured, my lips brushing his jaw, my fingers gliding over the hard lines of his torso, lingering on the scars that marked him, each one a story. "You make me feel alive… like I'm burning."

He kissed me—slow, sensual, a kiss meant to savor, not devour. His tongue teased mine, coaxing, tasting as if he needed to memorize me. And when he pulled back, his gaze was molten, filled with a need that never seemed to fade.

"I wish we could stay like this forever," he murmured against my lips. His fingers slipped lower, caressing my thigh. His touch was lazy and tender but laced with the promise of more.

I let out a breath, content and aching, pressing my forehead to his. We both knew forever wasn't ours to have, but in this moment, with his hands on me and his scent surrounding me, the world faded to nothing.

His hand slid to the small of my back, drawing idle circles, his touch sparking little flickers of heat as his voice rumbled low, right against my throat.

"I love you," he said, not a whisper but a claim, a vow, every syllable sinking into my skin.

The words wrapped around me, a warmth deeper than his embrace, binding us.

"This is our secret," he continued, his hand drifting to cup my breast gently, his thumb teasing over the sensitive peak, drawing a sudden, shuddering breath from me. "We will keep it, protect it. Protect you... Roman... us."

His plea was a fortress built around our fragile space, a sanctuary from the chaos of the world outside.

I pulled back, needing to see him, read the truth in his eyes, and settle myself in the depth of what we shared. My hand rested on his chest, feeling the beat of his heart beneath my fingers.

"Promise me you'll always come to see me," I whispered, trembling, laced with hope and dread.

He didn't flinch, didn't look away. But it wasn't enough.

I swallowed hard, leaning closer, my lips brushing his. "Promise me... there will be no other women. Just me. Just us. My love, I can't bear to be yours secretly and wonder if I'm alone."

The words tore out of me—raw, vulnerable, a need I couldn't hide.

Amir's hand rose to cradle my cheek, his touch reverent and grounding, and his eyes dark and unwavering.

"There is only you, Elizabeth," he said, his voice low, firm, full of truth. "I could never touch another. You are my beginning and my end. You have all of me. Always."

He kissed me then, slow and deep, not with urgency—but devotion, sealing his vow in the heat of that touch. In the way he held me. The way he trembled slightly, as though the thought of losing me could undo him.

His lips lingered on mine, and the earnestness in his gaze bore into me, a promise etched not only in words but also in the essence of his being.

"I will never betray you," he vowed again, sealing it with another kiss that spoke every silent word we could not say aloud.

As his lips left mine, a hush fell between us, heavy with our promises and the reality waiting beyond this fragile peace.

I clung to him, willing time to stop—because somewhere in my bones, I knew it wouldn't be long before this world tilted again.

Because love like ours?

It was never meant to survive.

And far beyond the city, in the depths of shadow and fire, a man moved across the chessboard of our lives—a hunter with no mercy and a name that hunted my blood.

Salvatore was coming.

And this time, he would not leave without blood.

CHAPTER 32

ELIZABETH

The needle dipped and rose steadily, the thread weaving through delicate fabric with practiced ease. Each stitch was a small defiance—a quiet survival. In the stillness of Amir's townhouse, where the bustle of London was reduced to a distant murmur, I found a semblance of peace—false, fragile, but mine.

My fingers moved nimbly, attaching an intricate lace trim to the hem of Lady Harrington's dress, a commission that filled my days and allowed me to pretend life was as ordinary as it seemed that I was simply a seamstress. That I was not Elizabeth Hassan, wife of a man the world believed a ghost.

But within these borrowed walls, every corner whispered of his absence.

Eighteen years had passed since I became his, Amir put a ring into my hand, kissed me beneath a silvered moon, and vowed that no matter the years or distance, I would always be his. And yet, each moment without him gnawed at me, leaving a hunger unsated.

The ache was constant—a wound that never quite healed— an emptiness that should have been filled by his arms, his voice, him. My husband, my love, bound by duty, secrets, and a world that had never allowed us to be anything but stolen moments and whispered vows.

I paused, lifting the gown to the light, inspecting the neatness of the hem—but my mind was not on stitches or patterns. It was elsewhere, tangled in memory—fleeting touches and stolen kisses, the way his breath would hitch when I touched his jaw, the way his eyes darkened with need, then softened with love. His laughter—rare, precious—was always cut short by the call of duty.

Always gone before dawn.

Only the lingering scent of sandalwood, the faintest echo of his warmth on my skin, was left behind to haunt me.

A soft sigh slipped from my lips. I set the dress down and reached for the bundle of letters hidden in the drawer of my worktable, fingers trembling despite the familiarity of the ritual. Their edges were worn, smoothed by countless readings. Each word was traced by his hand, written in the brief hours he could steal from the darkness.

They were all I had of him.

Letters were sent with no pattern and no warning. Letters that came like lightning at night illuminating everything, only to vanish again.

I held the letters to my chest, eyes closing. The ache flared—not just for his touch, but for the life we were never allowed to live. A life not stitched in secrecy, not experienced in stolen nights and shadowed dawns.

As I unfolded the topmost letter, a question rose like smoke in my mind— impossible to ignore—

How much longer could love survive in the shadows... before it withered in the light?

"Dearest Elizabeth," I read aloud, my voice barely a breath. The ink was slightly smudged, his hasty script etched deep into the parchment. I traced the curve of his letters with my fingertip, imagining his touch on my skin, the calloused pad of his thumb trailing the same path. The paper crackled softly beneath my touch, worn and fragile from how often I unfolded it—a ritual of longing, of reaching across miles and months to find him.

His words, though reassuring, could never still the storm that lived within me. The longing was my constant companion, an ache that never eased, not even in dreams. Our life was a mosaic of fragments, scattered moments snatched from time's cruel hand—a look, a kiss, a whisper of his name against my lips. And though they were fleeting, they were everything—my treasure, my torment.

A tear slipped free before I could stop it, trailing down my cheek. I brushed it away, chastising myself for the indulgence. Tears would not bring him closer, nor would they hasten the next letter, the next reunion, the next reminder that I still existed in his world.

With a shuddering breath, I folded the letter and returned it to its place. Then, with numb fingers, I reached for my needle again. The fabric tugged beneath my hands, the rhythmic pull of thread through cloth anchoring me to the present, to the illusion of normalcy, I wore like a second skin.

But as I stitched the hem of Lady Harrington's gown, my thoughts remained tethered to Amir, like a thread tied around my soul. Each loop and knot were a silent prayer, a message sent out into the void—a hope that somewhere, he felt my fierce and undiminished love.

Somehow, he knew—no matter the distance or silence—our love endured.

Ceaseless as the turn of the earth.

Boundless as the sky.

Roman entered the room then, shifting the air, commanding attention as Amir once had. He moved with a certainty that belied his youth, his stride solid, purposeful, each step a quiet echo across the wooden floor.

He stopped behind me, gaze flicking over my shoulder, his eyes locked on the lace trim I was stitching.

"Your stitches are impeccable, Mother," Roman said, his voice rich, warm—a timbre so like Amir's it struck something deep within me. Bittersweet nostalgia bloomed in my chest, sudden and aching, like a wound reopened.

"Thank you, my dear." I smiled at him, my eyes lingering on the familiar lines of his face. In his features, Amir lived again— the strong jaw, the proud nose, the intensity that radiated from him in waves. Only his eyes, vivid and storm-blue like mine, marked him as distinctly my own.

"How are you?" I asked, needing to tether us to something safe. "Have you finished your studies? Have you been well?" Yet as I spoke, I knew. His mind was elsewhere, reaching far beyond the confines of this townhouse, beyond the life I had carefully crafted to keep him safe—and ignorant.

"Quite," he replied, but his eyes held a storm, his thoughts dark and distant, unspoken and simmering.

Roman had grown. Not just into a man—but into a force. One who carried his father's blood and, unknowingly, his father's destiny.

"Your father would be proud," I murmured, my fingers pausing mid-stitch. The words slipped out before I could catch them, and my heart swelled with a fierce, painful pride.

His eyes snapped to mine. A flicker of something dangerous ignited in his gaze.

"Would he?" Roman's voice was low, coiled tight. "Is that why he abandoned you? Abandoned me?" The words dripped with disdain. "Is that how he shows his regard for his son?"

His sneer was a lash, and I flinched—not from surprise, but from the familiar sting of Amir's long-ago command, echoing in my mind like a curse I could never outrun.

He must despise me.

Promise me, Elizabeth.

Make him hate me.

Prepare him for what's to come.

And I had.

Gods help me, I had.

"Undoubtedly," I said, masking the tremor in my voice as I returned to my stitching, each loop of thread a lifeline I could no longer grasp. "You have his determination, his strength. And like him, you carry a sense of destiny that cannot be denied."

He scoffed, harsh and hollow, but I saw the flicker of something haunted in his eyes. And for a fleeting heartbeat, Amir stood before me, not Roman. A ghost of love and loss, shadowing the man my son was becoming.

"Destiny..." Roman echoed, his voice a murmur, his gaze turning inward. That word held weight—a future just beyond the horizon, both promise and peril wound together. It was the same look Amir wore when duty called him away, the same steel in his spine, the same fire in his blood—a resonance that defied time, defied absence.

"Indeed," I whispered, placing the final stitch, my hands numb. I tied off the thread, but there was no sense of completion —only the sense of something slipping away.

"Mother." Roman's voice cut through the hush. He stood before me, Amir's reflection in the flesh, save for those sapphire eyes—mine, and mine alone.

"What is it?" I asked, though dread coiled tight in my belly.

His jaw set, the line hard and familiar. His voice was calm, certain, and unshakable.

"I've decided. I'm going to fight in the American War of Independence."

The world tilted. My heart seized.

"No!" The word escaped me like a wound torn open.

"You can't go. I forbid you."

Desperation, raw and primal, surged to the surface—an attempt to hold back the tide, to assert the only power I had left —the power to protect him.

"Mother! I must!" Roman's eyes flashed, his voice, a mirror of Amir's battle cry. "It's my duty."

My heart twisted, and the ache that had long since nestled there clawed its way up my throat. Amir's words reverberated in my mind, melding with Lee's—voices of destiny, of paths one must walk alone.

"Roman," I began, my voice softer now, laced with fear. "Please, understand that..."

But I saw it in his eyes—the same unyielding fire that lived in Amir, a flame no plea could extinguish. This was destiny, pulling at the threads of our lives, weaving a tapestry I could neither predict nor prevent.

He was stepping onto a path that would change everything, a journey that might alter our family forever. And as I looked at him—like the man whose absence hollowed our world—I knew I could no more restrain him than stop the earth from turning.

"Your duty..." I whispered, resignation settling over me. "Just like your father."

"I am nothing like my father," he hissed. "I won't abandon my duties or ignore those I love."

I saw it then—not just Amir's likeness in him but his legacy, too—a legacy of honor bound by something greater than us all.

I let out a broken breath, wishing my deceit hadn't worked so well.

Roman loathed his father.

His hand, firm yet gentle, closed around mine, stilling the tremble that had begun as I worked the needle through the fine fabric.

"Mother," he said, his voice filled with conviction, echoing from some deep, immovable place within him. "I know you're scared. You're afraid you'll lose me. But I have to fight—for something bigger than myself."

His words struck like cold water, jolting me back to a reality I wanted to deny. My eyes, blurred by tears, met his—so familiar, yet resolutely his own.

"I have lost so much already," I choked, the pain of years past overwhelming me. "Your twin brother... I lost him. I've lost family. Roman, I can't—" My voice broke. "I can't bear the thought of losing you too."

Silence. Then—

"Wait, what?"

His confusion was palpable.

"Twin brother?"

I froze. The memories I had buried beneath years of silence broke free, rising like ghosts between us. The secret I had guarded with my life now hovered in the space between us, a truth I could never take back.

"Never mind," I murmured, the words brittle, meaningless.

But it was too late.

Roman didn't let it go.

"No, Mother—wait. What is this about a twin?" His gentle

but unrelenting voice pressed for an answer I had never meant to give.

I swallowed hard, my heart pounding as though it could beat the truth back down. "Long ago, in a world that feels lifetimes away and as close as yesterday, I went to the New World. I had a baby—a boy, your brother. There were two of you." The words tore from me, raw and bleeding. "He didn't make it, Roman. He never took a breath in this world."

The revelation hung heavy, a specter of loss filling the quiet room, mingling with the morning light and the faint scent of beeswax polish. As Roman stood there, grappling with the ghost of a brother he never knew, I realized no amount of stitching could mend the tear in our family that destiny had wrought.

Roman's face froze—disbelief etched in every line, hurt creeping in like frost.

"And you didn't think that was important to tell me?" His voice cracked at this new reality. "Why now? Is it to keep me from leaving?"

"Gods, no, Roman." The words rushed out, frantic, my hands reaching for him, desperate to pull him back from the edge. "I just can't bear to lose you too. Don't go."

In my panic, the secrets I'd buried began to surface.

"There's so much you don't understand. About time travel, about Dancing Fire—"

"Time travel?" He stared at me, incredulous, an eyebrow arched in disbelief. His look said it all—he thought I had lost my mind.

"Listen to me," I begged, my voice breaking. "You were born during the solar eclipse. And with your birth... a dagger appeared. A sign of your heritage. Roman—you are a time traveler."

"Mother—" The word landed like a wound reopened, and the skepticism in his eyes cut deeper than any secret I had ever buried.

"Roman, please." My voice shook, but I kept going. "If you go to the New World, you will find your destiny. I've only tried to protect you—from dangers and truths that would burden your soul too soon."

My plea hung heavily between us—a mother's last desperate attempt to shield her son from a world far too eager to claim him.

He stared at me, those piercing blue eyes—his father's gaze, softened by dawn light. Disbelief still clung to him, but something shifted—a subtle loosening of his jaw, a flicker of something that might've been understanding… or pity.

"Mother," he said, softer now, his tone laced with the kindness of a man who believed he was humoring someone fragile. "You've been alone too long."

Roman stepped forward, closing the distance I hadn't realized had stretched between us. His hands rested on my shoulders, warm and reassuring. "These ideas… they're preposterous. Time travel? Daggers?" He shook his head gently, like one comforting a child.

Before I could speak, he bent down and kissed my forehead—a benediction or perhaps… a farewell.

And then he turned away, leaving silence in his wake—vast, unspoken, and final.

I stood frozen, bereft, watching the back of the man who was both my son and the living legacy of a love that burned eternally… yet always out of reach.

"Where are you going?" My voice broke the stillness, and I trembled with desperation as I watched him gather his meager belongings.

He didn't look up.

"I must prepare for my journey," Roman said, steadfast. "The ship leaves in two days."

The finality in his voice hit me like a door slamming shut. My time to protect him was running out.

"Two days?" The words tumbled from my lips, with disbelief and a dawning horror. "You've already secured passage?" My heart sank. The room seemed to darken around me as if the light knew to retreat in the face of such sorrow.

"Please… don't go." The plea slipped out as a whisper, barely audible, trembling between us.

Roman straightened and turned to face me. His eyes—so achingly like Amir's—held the fire of untested courage. "Mother," he said gently but firmly, "I am a man. I have to fight for something. I must go."

Tears welled in my eyes and spilled freely. I saw not the man he had become but the child I had once cradled against my breast—the one I had sworn to protect. "What if I lose you?" I choked out, my voice thick with anguish. "I've buried my entire family, Roman. I can't bear to lose you, too."

He stepped closer, taking my trembling hands in his. His touch was warm and steady—too steady for someone I still saw as my boy. "You're stronger than you know," he said softly. "And I will come back. I won't be on the front lines, not at first. I'll be cleaning weapons and running errands. I probably won't see battle."

His reassurances fell hollow against the pounding dread in my chest.

"Nothing will stop me," he added, his tone hardening. "Daggers and time travel… they're stories. Fantasies. They don't exist. Please, let me go. I promise I will return."

But as he spoke, I knew—some promises were made in love, not in certainty. And some were broken by fate.

Two days later, I stood at the threshold of Amir's townhouse, watching Roman's figure grow smaller as he strode down the cobblestone street—toward destiny, toward danger, away from me.

My heart shattered into fragments, each jagged piece a testament to love lost, a life altered, and a future teetering on the edge of the unknown. He had left—just as Dancing Fire foretold, just as Amir had warned. *Our son will leave… and find his destiny.*

The pain was searing, a hollow ache that pulsed with every

heartbeat. I clutched the doorframe as if it could somehow tether me to the life I once had. How I needed Amir now—his strength, his touch—but he was gone. The letters had stopped. His visits —those precious moments I clung to like breath—had vanished into the ether.

Silence constricted like a closing fist. As the final glimpse of Roman disappeared around the corner, I turned back inside. The door shut behind me with a heavy finality, an echo of farewell that seemed to stretch across the years, sealing away the last flickers of hope I still harbored in my weary soul.

Months drifted like autumn leaves spiraling to the ground— colorful, dying, forgotten. Each day bled into the next beneath a veil of solitude, the townhouse filled with the absence of laughter, life, and love. Roman's voice, once a constant, now echoed only in memory.

I lost myself in the delicate threads of my work, the needle a metronome for the grief I couldn't speak aloud. Lady Harrington's emerald masterpiece gown shimmered in the candlelight— vibrant, alive—everything I no longer felt. I stitched as if the fabric could hold me together when everything else was gone.

Where was my son?

Where was Amir?

The questions haunted the silence. And still, no answers came. Only the rhythmic pull of thread through cloth—and the suffocating pain of love left unanswered.

Then—a sudden knock at the door.

I jolted upright, my breath catching, my heart slamming against my ribs. Hope flared, sudden and reckless, an ember igniting in the cold ashes of solitude. I cast aside the gown, the needle slipping from my grasp and vanishing into the folds of fabric at my feet.

"Please be him," I whispered, already moving, nearly stumbling in my haste as I reached for the door.

My fingers fumbled with the latch, and I threw it open with a force born of desperation.

Not Amir.

A young post boy stood there, cap askew, cheeks flushed

from the chill air. He grinned, oblivious to the storm behind my eyes, and thrust an envelope into my hands.

"Miss! A letter for you!" he chirped, his voice far too bright for the shadows clinging to my home.

"Thank you," I managed, voice hoarse, fingers trembling as I accepted the worn envelope. The edges were smudged, the paper soft from many hands, but the name scrawled across it was unmistakably mine.

I turned it over, holding my breath. The script wasn't Amir's.

A knot tightened in my stomach. Confusion prickled along my skin, and the spark of hope guttered. Still, I tore the seal open, parchment crinkling like dry leaves in my hands.

The scent of ink and faint smoke rose from the page.

I froze. That scent—I knew it.

Dancing Fire.

My heart plummeted.

"Dear Elizabeth," it began.

I couldn't read further—not yet. My hands clutched the letter as dread laced my veins. The room tilted, narrowing to the parchment in my hands and the storm of memories rising.

I closed my eyes.

"Please," I whispered—to no one, the heavens or the gods I no longer trusted. "Let this be good news."

But as my eyes fluttered open and the inked words took shape, I felt that dark and inevitable tremor creeping in to claim me again.

"Mary has died."

The world buckled beneath me.

I couldn't breathe.

Mary—gone? The woman who held my secrets, who knew every shadow of my past, every fracture in my heart. She had been my refuge, my constant in the void Amir's silence had left behind. Our letters—once a lifeline—were now relics of a bond severed far too soon.

We had written endlessly, confiding in each other as though stitching together a tapestry of sisterhood I believed even time could not unravel. But now... her thread was cut. Too young. Too cruel.

A sob bubbled up my throat, and I sank to the floor, the letter crumpling in my fist as I folded in on myself, drowning in grief. The walls closed in, the dim light casting shadows that danced like ghosts—echoes of all I'd lost.

"Amir..." My voice was a broken plea, barely more than a breath. "Where are you?"

No answer.

No arms to gather me close.

No voice, no kiss against my temple to make the pain ebb away.

Only silence—a beast devouring the last scraps of my strength.

Mary's death snuffed out the final ember of hope within me, leaving only ashes.

Leaving me in darkness. Alone.

And in that silence, one truth became clearer than ever— everyone I loved was either dead... or had vanished into shadows.

And I feared—no, I knew—

I was next.

CHAPTER 33

AMIR

The rhythmic scratching of my quill halted as a faint knock echoed through the chamber door of my underground study. "Enter," I commanded, setting the black feather aside.

The door creaked open, revealing my servant, head bowed low. In his outstretched hand lay an envelope, its edges frayed as if it had crossed continents and centuries to find me. "This just arrived for you, Pasha," he murmured.

I rose and took the letter with a nod. "You may go."

The door closed behind him softly, leaving me alone in the dim, flickering light. My fingers traced the rough parchment, and my breath stilled as I recognized the unmistakable scrawl clawing across the seal—the mark of Dancing Fire.

With a practiced flick, I broke the wax and unfolded the missive, the parchment trembling between my fingers. The words inside bled sorrow onto the page, each line steeped in grief, raw, unflinching, and heavy with heartbreak.

He wrote of Marcellious—my son—and how the boy's departure to Rome had cleaved through his heart like a blade. He spoke of the silence that filled his home now, the ghostly echoes of laughter that once danced through the halls, and the unbearable weight of a son who no longer called him father.

Each sentence was a wound drawn deep across my chest. I

felt his pain as if it were my own—because it was my own. Reflected, refracted, returned to me in cruel, haunting clarity. I had entrusted Marcellious to him not only out of duty but out of necessity—a choice born of love, forged in the hope that it would protect them both.

And now, that fragile bond was severed.

Then came Roman.

He stepped into Dancing Fire's life, and, for a time, light and hope returned. Together, they began to heal. But that peace was short-lived.

Roman was never meant to stay.

It was time to reunite him with his brother. And now Roman was gone too—both of your sons, lost to me. Roman has traveled to Rome. I've lost them both. And the pain is unbearable. But I let them go—because the future depends on the strength they will forge in the fires of the past. I have followed Lazarus' instructions… and sent them back to Ancient Rome. Both of your sons are now in the past, shaping themselves into the warriors they were born to be—for the war that waits.

The letter shook in my grip, the ink smudging beneath my thumb as I clenched it.

Elizabeth.

Her name struck like lightning across the storm of my mind. It had been too long since I had touched her skin, tasted her breath, and buried myself in her love. Too long since I'd felt her fingers threading through my hair, her whispered promises curling around my soul like smoke. The ache surged like a tide—relentless, savage—tearing open wounds I had long since forced into silence.

Memories of her flooded me, vivid and merciless. Each

recollection was a blade, each fleeting moment we'd shared over the years a spark stoking the inferno of longing that consumed me. I had tried to bury it—by gods, I had tried—but love this profound defied suppression. It dragged me toward the edge of madness, dismantling my resolve piece by piece, whispering her name into every breath I drew.

I refolded Dancing Fire's letter with care, laying it atop the sprawl of maps and manuscripts that charted the path of our grand design. This was no time for hesitation. My brother-in-arms needed me. Though the wheels of destiny turned, grinding ever forward, they would not crush the bond we had forged in blood and fire.

I would go to him.

Dancing Fire—stoic, steadfast—now stood on the precipice of loss, his heart shattered by Marcellious' and Roman's departures. I would offer comfort, as only one who had walked beside him through war and ruin could. In a world teetering on the brink of upheaval, such simple acts of loyalty were rare... and sacred.

The air in my study seemed to pulse, alive with anticipation. The time had come.

Marcellious and Roman were in Rome, unaware. They were two sons, born of the same blood, carrying the same legacy, and walking blindly toward each other's fate.

I stood slowly, my hand trailing across the ancient scrolls and yellowed parchments scattered across my desk. They whispered of secrets long kept, of power waiting to be claimed. I let my fingers rest atop the map of Rome, its veins etched in ink, its heart beating with destiny.

"Rome," I murmured.

The time had come.

Every piece on the board had shifted.

The twins had stepped into the lion's den.

And the game was about to begin.

Lazarus, Amara, and their daughter, Theodora, had already begun their journey into Rome, where destiny and danger intertwined with every breath. When news came that Marcellious had time traveled, there was no hesitation.

They followed.

A family forged in sacrifice, bound by love, and tempered by loss, they stepped willingly into the flow of time, traversing centuries, crossing the boundary between worlds, all to protect the most precious asset we had left—Roman.

They went to shield him and ensure that the brothers would become what they were born to be.

Warriors.

Legends.

As I paced the perimeter of my underground sanctum, destiny settled over me like an old cloak—familiar, heavy, inescapable. Lazarus and Amara had tasted the bittersweetness of reunion only because of Roman's birth—a child conceived in turmoil, destined to shake the very foundations of empires.

"May the gods watch over them," I muttered, a rare invocation slipping past my lips. They were more than protectors—they were sentinels of fate, guardians of a legacy too dangerous to fall into the wrong hands. The twins, torn apart by the cruel hand of destiny, would now come full circle. Their bloodline was the key—the spark to ignite the future we had all bled for.

It was in Rome that they would be forged. They would rise among swords, fire, and sand under the Colosseum's roar. I could see it in my mind—Roman, every movement honed by purpose, every clash of steel drawing him closer to the brother he had never known. And above them, Lazarus—ever watchful, ever vigilant—standing guard, a silent sentinel over their fate.

I strode to my desk, planting my hands upon the cold stone surface as maps and ancient texts rustled beneath my fingertips. The silence throbbed with anticipation.

Our pawns were in place.

The board was set.

And now... the war for the future would begin.

∞

The full moon cast a silver sheen over the wilds of the New World as I stepped through the veil of time, leaving behind the ancient stones of Anatolia. The night air hit—crisp, untamed, carrying the scent of pine, river, and distant fire—a savage contrast to the cold opulence of my underground palace.

I found Dancing Fire's cabin nestled in seclusion, its flickering light a beacon against the darkness. The door yielded to my hand without resistance, and inside, I saw him, hunched over his desk, shoulders shrugged with silent torment.

"Forgive the intrusion, my friend," I said, my voice even despite the knot twisting in my gut. "But we both knew this day would come."

The floor creaked under my boots as I stepped closer. He did not turn at first. But when he lifted his head, his eyes—red-rimmed and shadowed—met mine with a depth of sorrow I had not seen in years.

"I know," he rasped, voice as rough as gravel. "It's just... hard. I raised Marcellious as my own. And Roman—I've worked beside him these past three years. Guided him. I fought with him. Both of them are my sons in every way that matters."

His words struck me like a blow. The man before me had done what I could not—stood in the light, loved them without restriction, and touched their lives openly. My chest tightened with regret, but duty did not weep.

"It's because you love them that you must now step into the fire," I said, resting a firm hand on his shoulder, preparing him to the gravity of what must come. "It's time for you to play for the other side."

His brow furrowed, confusion flashing behind his eyes as he turned to face me. "The other side?" Suspicion and exhaustion tangled in his voice. "You mean... the side of evil?"

"Yes," I confirmed. "That serpent bitch Alina has betrayed Balthazar. She's hunting the blades now. Lazarus has already set pieces in motion. A man named John James will guide her to you. She's vicious. Ruthless. Born of shadows."

A flicker—no, a roar—of flame ignited in Dancing Fire's gaze, the battle-hardened warrior rising beneath the sorrowed surface. "I can handle her," he said, his voice edged with steel, his pain receding behind armor forged in duty and rage.

"I know," I replied, the words laced with warning and faith. "But this is a game we must play carefully. She won't see you coming."

Our shared history pressed upon us—two soldiers standing on the precipice of chaos, fates tangled in deception and blood.

I pulled him into a firm embrace, the clasp of warriors, of brothers. "Now," I murmured, stepping back and locking eyes with him, "it's all about playing this game. And playing it to win."

I stayed with him until the next full moon, letting the days blur into the rhythm of old camaraderie—hunting, riding, fishing. The forest welcomed us with its scents of pine and loam, the air alive with the trill of birdsong and the rustling of leaves. We rode side by side, hooves pounding the forest floor, like the beating of war drums to come.

At night, under a quilt of stars, we shared stories around the fire, kindling flame, and memory.

On the eve of my departure, I spoke the words heavy with reminiscence. "Remember when we were in France, to destroy the French Timehunter society?"

Dancing Fire arched a brow, cautious but intrigued. "Of course," he said, the corner of his mouth quirking into a faint smirk. "It proved perilous for both of us."

I nodded, but the smirk vanished from his face when I spoke.

"Elizabeth was the one who crafted the poison," I said, my voice unwavering despite the storm I knew these words would bring. "She was the alchemist. She and her mother discovered the Noctyss flower—a rare bloom that only grows on Solaris. But when Isabelle separated the blades, the barrier between realms tore open... and the flower bled through. It grew here, too."

His eyes narrowed, the flicker of intrigue in them instantly smothered by something darker—suspicion. And beneath that, I saw it—hurt.

His brow furrowed, lips a hard, thin line. "Why are you

telling me this now? After all these years?" His voice was tight, laced with frustration and undeniable pain beneath that. "When I was finally starting to heal from the loss of Elizabeth... and her two boys."

Elizabeth's and my two boys, I corrected silently. But jealousy had no place here. Not now. Not with everything we stood to lose.

I inhaled slowly, grounding myself in the bond we'd forged —not just through friendship but through war, blood, betrayal, and brotherhood—a bond that had survived lifetimes.

"Because," I said, meeting his gaze without flinching, "you and I have been more than allies—we've been brothers. And true brothers don't keep secrets... not ones like this." I paused, letting my words settle. "That's why, all those years ago, I asked you to watch over Elizabeth for me. Because I knew she was in danger. Salvatore was hunting her, and I trusted you to protect what mattered most."

Dancing Fire nodded, his gaze distant. "She was never mine to love. Just as Marcellious and Roman were never mine. We are but shadows cast upon this stage, bound to play the roles fate has chosen for us."

A bitter smile tugged at my lips as I looked away, his words settling heavily on my chest. "Yes," I whispered, sorrowful. "I know... But that doesn't make it any easier, Dancing Fire. Can you begin to imagine my pain? My heart breaks every time I see them, my flesh and blood, my sons... and they don't know me. I never got to teach them to hunt, fight, and stand tall as men. I was a ghost, watching from the shadows while you stood in my place, guiding them, shaping them."

My voice wavered, raw emotion pouring out as the truth sliced through me. "It shattered me... every day. But I bore it because it was necessary. Because this is the part I was meant to play. Just a player... just a shadow. No more, no less."

Dancing Fire's eyes softened, his shoulders heavy with understanding. Silence stretched between us, bursting with unspoken words and years of sacrifice.

On the day of my departure, I stood before him, my heart

burdened with unspoken words, my soul worn from destiny. My voice was barely a whisper, fragile and fleeting like a dying breath. "It's time for me to go."

He did not look at me, his gaze fixed on the strip of leather clutched between his calloused fingers. His jaw was set in concentration. The sun danced on the blade of his knife as he sliced through the supple material, each strip a necessary fragment for the delicate dreamcatcher taking shape in his hands. His brow furrowed, lost in the rhythm of his craft as if avoiding the finality of my words.

For a long moment, the only sound between us was the whisper of leather and the faint rustle of wind. Then, without lifting his eyes, he spoke, "The moon is full tonight. I knew this day would come. Where will you go?"

"To Elizabeth," I murmured the name, a plea that clawed at my chest. "To the love of my life." My voice trembled, rough with the ache of longing, a desire that grew fiercer each day.

Dancing Fire's hands paused, his fingers brushing the half-formed dreamcatcher. A shadow crossed his face, the ghost of a longing he could never voice. His shoulders sagged just slightly before he nodded. "Then you must go. You're fortunate to have someone waiting for you."

"I know," I replied, forcing the words past the lump in my throat. I wanted to say more, to promise that one day he would find a love to heal his wounds. But the words tasted hollow, false. I had no right to offer hope when my heart was heavy with doubt. "One day... you'll find someone to cure your pain."

He set the knife down, his fingers brushing the leather with a tenderness that broke my heart. His eyes met mine then, weary and ancient, carrying the burden of a thousand unspoken truths. "I cannot live in a future I cannot see. I can only survive in the now."

Silence hung between us, heavy and final. I nodded, swallowing the promise I could never keep. There were no more words to say, no more comfort to offer. We were shadows in this cruel game, bound by fate and divided by destiny.

We pored over every intricate thread of the grand tapestry we were about to weave for hours. The air between us crackled with intensity as we mapped out each possible move, each potential betrayal, and I gave him everything—every scrap of knowledge I had gathered on Alina's schemes and shadows.

She was a serpent in human skin—slippery, deceptive, and dangerous. Her web of lies had ensnared many, her tongue silver with deceit, her steps always just beyond reach. But together, Dancing Fire and I had evaded worse. With his fierce resolve and my tireless pursuit of our endgame, I had no doubt—we would outwit her and claim what was rightfully ours.

Solaris.

As the sun dipped below the horizon, casting the world in a wash of indigo and gold, we stood silently at the edge of the lake. The moon crested the sky, full and bright, its silver light dancing on the still waters like celestial fire. The sacred lake mirrored the heavens, a quiet witness to our parting.

Dancing Fire turned to me. He was clear-eyed, filled with all the wisdom of a man who had lived too long, lost too much, and still stood unbroken.

"The winds whisper of trials ahead," he said, his voice low and resolute. "But remember this—your heart burns brighter than any storm. Walk with purpose, Amir. Let the spirits guide your steps. If we meet again..." He paused, emotion flickering behind his stoicism. "Let it be with stories of triumph."

A lump rose in my throat—rare, unwelcome, but undeniable. "And may your path be lit with wisdom, my brother. Even in darkness, your strength is a beacon. Whatever comes..." I reached out, gripping his arm tight, warrior to warrior. "I will carry the memory of your courage with me."

Our eyes locked—a silent pact forged in fire and brotherhood.

Then I turned and walked into the dark, leaving behind the only man who truly understood what was coming.

And knowing—no matter how the winds raged, no matter what blood was spilled—this war would remember our names.

CHAPTER 34
AMIR

Time split me open.

The vortex yanked me from the nothingness between seconds, ripping through flesh and thought, until reality slammed back with a sickening jolt.

I landed in the front room of my English home and stepped straight into a nightmare.

Fabric lay across the floor like discarded skin, torn and twisted, as though the house had tried to tear itself apart. A cracked vase spilled petals like blood. The curtains sagged from their rods, limp and heavy, like nooses after the fall.

And the silence…

The silence was unnatural. Not peaceful. Not still. But bloated—swollen with grief, too full to breathe.

Then the scream tore it open.

"Roman is dead! My son is dead!"

It pierced the room like shrapnel, raw and unfiltered, a sound born from the marrow of suffering.

Elizabeth stood in the center of the wreckage, a ghost made flesh.

Her skin was pale, her eyes wide with a horror no soul should ever carry. Tears carved down her cheeks, but she didn't seem to feel them. She was locked in place, frozen in the moment her world died.

In her trembling hand, a letter flailed—fragile, broken, desperate, it seemed, to escape the truth written within.

I moved toward her, each step heavy with the truths I could no longer withhold, secrets I had kept for a grander purpose, for the love that bound me to her in ways words could never capture.

Roman wasn't dead. But he was far beyond her reach, lost in the sands of Rome.

Gently, I took her by the shoulders, feeling the shivers that coursed through her body. She was unraveling before me, breaking under a lie she believed was truth. I guided her to a chair, my touch firm yet tender, grounding her in the here and now. "Sit, my love," I urged, my voice low, every piece of the shattered room fading from my mind as her pain became my sole focus. "It's time you knew everything."

Her breath hitched, and she looked up at me, her gaze lost and desperate. "Amir… the Commander of the Army in the New World wrote to me…" Her voice wavered, breaking on the sob that ripped from her chest. "He said Roman is dead."

The agony in her words tore through me, raw and visceral, leaving wounds I could never allow her to see. She searched my face, eyes brimming with confusion, searching for a hint of deception, a glimmer of hope.

I took her hands in mine, grounding us both in the moment. "Roman… is alive," I said, each word a fragile lifeline cast into the depths of her despair. "He's not dead. He has traveled through time… to find his twin brother."

Her eyes widened, her mouth falling open as disbelief warred with hope. "Alive?" she echoed, the word a whisper, trembling on her lips. "But… the commander said… he's dead. And his twin… his twin brother died at birth!"

Her words hung between us, heavy with grief and confusion.

"No, my love." My voice was a low, unwavering rumble against the storm of her grief. "Dancing Fire raised our other son, Marcellious. He has been alive… all along."

A strangled cry tore from her lips as she lunged at me, her fists small yet fierce, striking my chest with a fury born of heartbreak. Blow after blow rained down, each carrying the strength of her sorrow, betrayal, and disbelief.

I sat unmoving, the stoic Pasha Hassan, weathering the tempest of her anguish, letting her pain batter against me like waves against a stone. I would take it all—her fury, her heartbreak. I deserved no less.

And when her strength gave out, when her hands fell against me, I caught her, gathered her into the safety of my arms, cradling her like something sacred, something I had failed to protect.

"Elizabeth…" Her name was a murmur against her hair, my voice breaking where hers had cracked. "You're right to be angry. But we did it to protect them both. And to protect you."

She wrenched away, eyes wild, grief-stricken, demanding answers I didn't know how to give. Rising from my lap, she stood before me like a storm contained in human form. "I don't understand!" she cried, her voice splintering with agony. "How does protecting me end with breaking my heart?" Her breath hitched, shoulders trembling. "What will he think of me when he finds out? That I let him go? He was alive all along, raised by another… and you knew?"

Her words stabbed deep, clean, merciless. I stepped forward, gently cupping her face in my hands, holding her like she was the only truth in a world of lies.

"Shhh." I hushed her, my thumbs brushing her tear-streaked cheeks. "We made choices—harrowing choices. But they were made with love. With fear. With the weight of the world on our backs. One day… You will understand. Trust in that, even if you can't trust me right now."

Silence stretched between us, overflowing with the ghosts of what we had lost.

A sudden, searing pain bloomed in my chest, like a dagger twisting beneath my ribs. I had done this to her. I had kept the truth buried, thinking it would save her. And now, I watched disbelief carve into her soul, the shock hardening her expression, turning love into something jagged.

Without a word, I reached for her, gently guiding her to the worn sofa—the very place where I had sat for countless nights, haunted by this moment's inevitability. The cushions sighed beneath her weight, echoing the heaviness now stifling the room.

"Sit," I murmured, far more gently than I felt inside. These were the same hands that had led armies, wielded blades, and drawn blood—and now they trembled.

"I don't believe you!" Her voice cracked like thunder, raw and breaking. The softness in her tone was gone, scorched by betrayal. "Our sons are dead." The words were a curse, a desperate defiance hurled into the void—as if saying them could will the truth into falsehood.

I sat beside her, but our closeness did nothing to bridge the vast chasm. The air between us felt like an ocean—too deep, cold, and impossible to cross.

My jaw clenched, and I could feel the dark, seething fire of frustration and desperation smoldering beneath the surface. "I don't keep things from you without cause," I growled, the words laced with the fury of a man who'd sacrificed everything to protect the woman who now doubted him. "Everything I've done was to shield you from dangers you can't begin to fathom."

Abruptly, I stood, unable to sit still, the restless energy inside me threatening to consume me whole. My hand clenched at my side, aching to reach for her—and yet knowing that my touch might harm rather than soothe.

She looked up at me, her sky-blue eyes awash with tears, her entire being trembling. "Are you leaving again?" The question was a cry, a plea, a blade twisting in my chest. "I can't bear to be alone again."

"Gods, Elizabeth. No!" I spun to face her, my chest heaving as the words tore from me, raw and unfiltered. "This time... I'm staying." The declaration hung heavy in the air, a promise from the depths of my soul, an oath that bound me to her irrevocably. I had sworn to Lazarus that I would stay away and protect her from Salvatore's wrath by keeping my distance. But I couldn't do it anymore—I couldn't keep pretending to live without her.

Twenty years had passed since she crafted the Noctyss poison.

Twenty years of exile, watching from the shadows as she raised our son alone. Surely Salvatore had long forgotten about the poison… forgotten about her. There was no more reason to hide or deny the truth that had always been inside me. Nothing and no one could destroy our love. Nothing would take her away from me again.

I closed the distance between us, my heart thundering in my chest, every fiber of my being drawn to her. I wanted to comfort her, to worship her, to give her the life we had been robbed of. All those years apart, I had been nothing but a ghost, slipping in and out of her life just long enough to ensure she was safe, always leaving before Roman could see me. I watched her from the shadows as she bore single motherhood and gave him the love and guidance I could only dream of sharing. She did it all alone, and it broke me. I wanted to be there with her, share the joys and struggles of parenthood, and be the father Roman deserved.

Elizabeth's shoulders trembled, her face crumbling as tears spilled down her cheeks, each drop a testament to the pain we had both endured. My resolve shattered. I sank to my knees before her, my heart aching with every sob that tore from her. Gently, I took her hands in mine, feeling the cool softness of her skin against my own. Her touch was a balm to the storm raging inside me, grounding me, healing me.

"My darling Elizabeth…" I whispered, my voice fracturing beneath everything I'd never said. "When we crashed into each other that day all those years ago, you walked into my world of darkness—and you changed it. You changed me." My thumb traced slow circles over her knuckles, savoring the feel of her, the woman who had anchored me when I was lost.

Her tears slowed, her gaze falling to where my hands cradled hers as if she couldn't believe I was real. I held on tighter, a surge of desperation flaring in my chest. I would never let her go again.

A memory surfaced, raw and vivid, one that had haunted me since the night it was born. I breathed, the words tumbling out before I could stop them. "Do you remember… the night we conceived our sons?" My voice was low, rough, heavy with emotion. "You asked me… what my daughter would be like."

Elizabeth's breath hitched, her eyes widening in surprise, her lips parting as the memory washed over her. Her fingers tightened around mine, her body trembling as she whispered, "I remember." A soft, broken laugh escaped her, mingling with a fresh tear that slipped down her cheek.

I smiled, my heart swelling as I remembered that night, the hope and love we had shared, the dreams we had dared to weave. "I never stopped thinking about it," I confessed, my voice cracking as our daughter's vision filled my mind. "I've dreamed of her… of us. I want her to have your gentleness… your quiet strength. I want her to be brave enough to defy the world if it means finding the truth. I want her to carry your light, to walk in this world unburdened by the shadows that haunted us."

Elizabeth's face crumpled, a sob breaking free as she clung to me, her fingers twisting in my shirt as if letting go would end her. Her forehead rested against mine, her breath warm and shaky, her tears falling like rain between us. "Oh, Amir… I dreamed of her too," she whispered, her voice fractured with years of longing. "I dreamed of you… of us… of the life we were never allowed to have."

My heart ached at the pain in her words, the shadows that clung to her even now. Gently, I cupped her face, my thumbs brushing away her tears, lingering on her soft skin, memorizing the feel of her. "Then let's make that life," I vowed, my voice fierce with determination. "Let's make another baby. Let's defy fate… together."

Her breath caught, her eyes wide and shimmering with tears that she was no longer trying to hold back. Hope danced in her gaze, fragile and beautiful, a flicker of light breaking through the darkness. Her lips parted, the question tumbling out as if she were terrified to say it aloud, as if it might shatter the delicate hope between us. "Do you… Do you mean it?"

I pulled her closer, my hands trembling as I cradled her face, touching my forehead to hers. "More than anything," I breathed, my voice raw, vulnerable. "Yes, Elizabeth… I mean it. I want to give you that life… the life we were robbed of. And no one—no one—will raise our daughter except you and me."

Her tears fell freely, her body trembling as she choked on a sob. I took her hand, raising it to my lips, placing a tender kiss against her palm, feeling the rapid beat of her pulse beneath my touch. "Forgive me… for all the secrets, all the lies," I whispered, my voice breaking. "Everything I did… every decision, every concealment… was to protect you. Even when it broke me to leave you."

Her fingers tightened around mine, her eyes locked on me, her face searching mine for the truth behind my words. "You… you stayed away to protect me?" she choked, her voice quivering, a mixture of pain and understanding flooding her gaze.

I swallowed the lump in my throat, my heart raw and exposed. "I thought I was doing the right thing… keeping you safe from Salvatore's wrath. I thought… if I stayed away, you could live in peace. But I was wrong. I was a coward… too afraid to fight for us. Too afraid to lose you."

Her lips trembled, her tears flowing in rivers, but her eyes were soft and forgiving as she cupped my face, her thumbs brushing away the tears I didn't realize I was shedding. "Amir… you never lost me. Not then… not now… not ever."

The relief that crashed over me was overwhelming, a tidal wave that left me gasping, my heart thundering in my chest. I pulled her into my arms, holding her close, feeling her warmth, heartbeat, and love. "I love you, Elizabeth," I whispered, my voice shaking. "I love you more than time, fate, or any force in this world. I love you… And I'm *never* letting you go again."

A sob broke free, her shoulders shaking as she buried her face in my chest, her arms wrapping around me as if she were afraid I would vanish. "I love you too… I always have," she whispered, her words muffled against my shirt. "Even when you were gone… even when I thought you'd never come back… I loved you."

I kissed her hair, temple, and cheeks, tasting her tears and feeling her smile against my lips. "Then let's write our story…

our own ending. Let's bring our daughter into this world… let's give her the love we've carried for so long."

I kissed her then, pouring everything into that moment—love, pain, hope, and promise. And in that kiss, I sealed my vow. I was staying… for good. No more shadows, no more lies. Only truth, only us.

When we finally broke apart, our foreheads resting together, our breaths mingling, I brushed a strand of hair from her face and smiled. "I have something to show you."

Her eyes widened, curiosity flickering beneath the shimmering tears. "Show me?" she echoed, a laugh breaking through her raw emotion, the sound light and soft.

I could feel the power of my blade humming within me, the energy of centuries coursing through my veins, ready to bridge the expanse of time. "Time travel," I revealed, the words slipping from my lips with wonder. A chuckle escaped me, mingling with the crackling fire in the hearth. "I want to show you time itself."

Elizabeth's face softened, but doubt crept into her eyes, and her shoulders tensed. "I can't possibly time travel, Amir," she whispered, a tremor of worry lacing her voice. "That's your gift…not mine."

I took her hands, cradling them gently between mine, my thumbs stroking the delicate skin as if grounding us both.

"Yes, love… You have time traveled before," I said softly. "But you don't remember."

Her eyes widened, confusion furrowing her brow, her lips parting in silent question. I held her gaze, supporting and tender.

"After the masquerade… when you went against Salvatore—reckless, fearless—and almost dying in my arms..." My voice broke, but I forced myself to go on. "I was desperate. Broken. And Lazarus... he saved you. He saved us."

I exhaled slowly, the memory as damaging as broken glass.

"He took us both… and healed us. But in doing so, we traveled through time to Anatolia."

Her mouth fell open, her breath catching, disbelief warring with intrigue. "Time travel… to Anatolia?" Her voice pitched high, a mixture of astonishment and fear shadowing her ice-blue eyes. "Truly?"

"Truly, my darling," I vowed, my heart aching at the uncertainty in her gaze. "You were unconscious then, on the brink of death. You never saw the ancient city, walked the streets, or breathed the air."

She swallowed, her hands trembling in mine. "You want to take me… through time? How is that possible?" she whispered. "I'm not a darkness… or a Timeborne. Or a Timebound."

"You're right," I said softly. "You're none of those things. But I am a darkness. And a shadow can take one person with them—just one—when they travel through time."

I watched her eyes widen, watched the pieces start to fit together behind her silence.

"I want to take you to Ancient Rome… to see our sons." Her lips parted, her eyes widening as she stared at me, stunned and breathless. "I want you to see the men they've become… to see the legacy of our love."

Tears brimmed in her eyes, her fingers tightening around mine as she rose. Her body trembled, history and destiny converging at that moment, our intertwined fates poised to unfurl across the tapestry of time. "Take me."

The full moon cast a silver glow over the garden, illuminating Elizabeth's pale face as I clutched her hand. Her pulse raced beneath my fingertips—a staccato rhythm of fear. Her skin was ice-cold, her breath shallow—terror had wrapped its claws around her heart.

"Amir…" she whispered, her voice as fragile as glass, barely rising above the rustling leaves stirred by a restless wind. "I'm frightened."

I turned to her, gently lifting her chin and anchoring her gaze to mine. "Look at me, Elizabeth." Her wide and uncertain eyes locked onto mine, shimmering with dread and trust.

"You've braved horrors that would break the strongest of men—and you endured. This..." I said, brushing my thumb across her cheek, "This is just another step. And I will take it with you."

She nodded, a flicker of courage lighting her features, and I took a breath, preparing for what came next.

Elizabeth had crafted the garments herself—woven with care, and a fierce love I didn't deserve. Elizabeth—my Elizabeth—looked as if she had stepped straight from the heart of Rome itself. Regal. Timeless. Draped in a flowing stola, the fabric clung to her like water, cinched at the waist and falling gracefully over her shoulders. Her dark cloak billowed behind her like shadowed silk, her face partially veiled by the hood.

At her side, I wore the toga she'd made for me—dyed deep crimson, trimmed in gold, cut in the old ways to honor the time we were entering.

I reached for my dagger—the one that had tasted time and blood—and sliced my palm with ease. Blood welled instantly, warm and bright. With my other hand, I gripped Elizabeth's tightly, crushing our palms together as crimson mingled between us.

"Hold on to me," I murmured.

Then I began the incantation—ancient words spilling from my lips like a forgotten song, the language of time wrapping around us like a spell-woven shroud. The wind rose, sudden and biting, carrying with it the grit of time itself, stirring the garden's leaves into a frenzy.

As the first tremors of the shift began, Elizabeth's grip tightened, her nails digging into my skin—a desperate tether to the world we were leaving behind.

The garden, our sanctuary, blurred and dissolved around us—as if a painter had swept his brush across a vibrant canvas, wiping it clean. Color, sound, and sensation all vanished into the void.

"Amir!" Elizabeth cried out, her voice echoing into the darkness, striking against the silence like a hammer against a stone.

"I'm here," I said, my voice an anchor in the sea of nothingness. "Stay with me, my love. Trust me… as you always have."

And then, in a breath, the blackness shattered.

Blinding light exploded around us.

And we were gone.

The roar of a crowd surged in our ears, the heat of the Roman sun scorched our skin, and the scent—olive oil, sweat, dust, roasting meat—assaulted us with brutal intensity. We stumbled forward, disoriented, onto marble streets lined with towering stone buildings and flanked by a tide of humanity.

"By the gods…" Elizabeth gasped, her fear melting into wonder. Her eyes swept over the grandeur—ancient Rome's ruthless beauty. Merchants shouted, coins clinked, and oxen bellowed. Life pulsed all around us in vivid, chaotic detail.

She clung close to me.

"Come," I said, taking her hand and guiding her into the city's beating heart.

Ahead, the Colosseum loomed, a titan of stone and blood. Inside, the air pulsed with the breath of thousands, the roar of anticipation electric. Beneath our feet, the ground trembled—not from fear, but from the promise of violence.

The scent of sweat, blood, and oiled leather permeated the air, clinging to our skin as I led Elizabeth through the stone arteries of the Colosseum. The crowd's roar—deafening, primal—swelled around us, masking the sound of our footsteps as we slipped through the chaos, my grip unrelenting on her wrist.

A rowdy knot of equestrians jostled past, laughing, coins clinking in their palms as they argued over wagers. I used the distraction, slipping through a narrow gap between two towering columns framing a row of privileged seats—seats paid for with influence, blood, or both.

I guided Elizabeth down onto the stone bench; my body angled as a shield while she adjusted the folds of her stola, the fabric trembling with her unease. No one spared us a glance. In their eyes, we were just another noble couple here to feast on violence.

But from our vantage point, we saw everything.

The sun blazed overhead, turning the sand into a golden sea. Iron gates creaked open, their sound lost in the roar of anticipation. And there, our sons stepped into the arena, blades drawn, eyes locked, unaware of the blood that bound them.

Elizabeth's gaze followed to the sand-strewn arena below, her breath catching in her throat. Roman and Marcellious moved with lethal focus, blades flashing under the sun as they clashed in a dance of war and destiny.

Her hand flew to her lips, her voice barely a whisper, loaded with disbelief and dawning horror. "Are those…?"

I nodded, never looking away. "Our sons. Yes."

Roman and Marcellious—my sons, our sons—circled each other like twin storms, gladius slicing through the air with lethal grace. Their movements were fluid, almost balletic, yet nothing about their combat was tender. Every strike was calculated, every parry precise. Their bodies had been forged by years of brutal training, their instincts honed by blood, legacy, and duty.

I leaned close, my voice a whisper, a command. "Now we watch."

"They're going to kill each other!" Elizabeth's voice broke as she clutched my arm, her nails digging into my flesh. Her whole body coiled, as if she might leap from the stands and tear them apart with her bare hands.

"No," I said, gripping her hand tightly, anchoring her to me. "We brought them here to forge their strength—to prepare them for what's coming. They fight not for death… but for life. For something far greater than this arena can contain."

Her eyes remained locked on the scene below, wide with fear and awe. The clash of steel rang through the air, mingling with the crowd's roar, yet she heard only the beat of her heart.

"They're so… handsome," she murmured, voice trembling with pride and pain. "Marcellious… he looks just like you."

"Like father, like son," I replied, the words tightening in my throat. Bittersweet pride surged through me, as sharp as any blade. Marcellious was the image of me—a reflection of my youth, my fire. Roman was her—relentless, unstoppable. Both were ours. Both were the future.

The arena floor was littered with bloodstains, the echoes of past violence etched into the earth. This was a grim reminder that every fight was more than a spectacle—it was survival.

And this was no mere duel.

Roman and Marcellious moved with lethal grace, their clash a symphony of steel and fury. It was a dance of war, choreographed by fate, secrets, and a history neither of them knew.

Roman struck like a panther—fast, agile, precise. Every movement was calculated as a pursuit of victory. His sword sliced the air purposefully; each strike a silent scream for dominance and understanding.

Marcellious met him like a bull—indomitable, powerful, a force of raw might. His attacks were bold and reckless but carried the weight of a man who had survived battles far worse than this. He didn't flinch or falter—he fought like a man with nothing to lose.

Amid their brutal battle, sparks burst like shooting stars, igniting in the fading light as their blades collided with feral intensity. The air crackled with the scent of blood, sweat, and iron, the Colosseum's glow painting them in hues of gold and crimson. Injuries marred their bodies—slashes and bruises that would've broken lesser men—yet still, they fought, unrelenting, driven by a destiny neither could escape nor comprehend.

A cruel twist of fate had turned brothers into enemies, siblings into strangers locked in a war of survival.

Beside me, Elizabeth trembled, her slender frame quaking with every thunderous blow that echoed across the arena floor. Once calm and serene, her sky-blue eyes were now storm-tossed pools of anguish, tears threatening to spill as her gaze never wavered from the scene below. Her hands gripped together so tightly her knuckles had turned white, as though she could hold their pain inside herself, shielding them by sheer will alone.

The sun dipped low, casting long shadows across the bloodstained sand, draping the arena in an eerie, golden hush. Both men—our sons—staggered, their movements slower, labored. Roman's grip faltered, his sword slipping from bloodied fingers. Marcellious dropped to his knees, then collapsed under the crushing weight of pain and exhaustion, his armor torn, his body bruised and battered.

A collective silence descended upon the Colosseum, and the crowd was stunned. The spectacle was fading, replaced by a solemn reverence for the battle's grim toll.

"I suggest we depart," I said. The urge to protect her, to shield her from this torment, threatened to fracture the composure I clung to. But I would not fall apart—not now, not for her sake.

"No!" Elizabeth's voice broke, ragged with desperation. Her body slumped against mine, and I caught her instantly, holding her as if the world itself might shatter beneath us.

Two litters appeared, carried by a swarm of guards, who descended into the arena and lifted the broken bodies of Roman and Marcellious. They were rushed away, vanishing into the labyrinth of corridors beneath the Colosseum.

Elizabeth clutched my tunic, her breath hot against my ear as she whispered—a mother's plea that pierced the crowd's roar and lodged itself in my soul.

"I must see them. Take me to them at once," she demanded, her voice trembling but resolute. "I did not come here to witness the demise of my two sons."

Elizabeth's desperate pleas tore at me, but I held her arm tightly, my voice low and urgent. "My love, please—understand. It's too dangerous. Lazarus doesn't know I'm here. If he sees us together—" I locked eyes, willing her to see reason. "It could ruin everything."

She wrenched free, her strength belying her petite frame. "Take me to them, Amir!" Her voice cracked like a whip, slicing through the heavy air. Without waiting for a response, she pushed through the crowd, her stola trailing behind her like a banner of rebellion.

"Elizabeth!" I called, striding after her as the fading light of dusk bathed the streets in gold. Her usual grace was gone, replaced by a mother's frantic urgency.

"Amir, please," she begged, eyes burning with fear and love. "They are my sons. I must help them. I must heal them."

I knew then—there was no stopping her. No words would turn her from this path. My breath left me in a rush, heavy with dread and devotion, as I surrendered to fate.

Drawing her into my arms, I summoned the shadow veil. Darkness enveloped us, swallowing sound and light—and in the next heartbeat, we stood in the stone-walled chamber where pain and healing merged.

The air was crowded with the scent of blood and crushed herbs—pungent, cloying, and impossible to ignore. Before us, Marcellious lay broken—his body a tapestry of bruises, gashes, and swelling, his breaths shallow, each inhale a battle he was barely winning.

Amara knelt at his side, her hands steady despite the chaos in the room. She uncorked a small glass vial, its contents a deep-amber hue that caught the dim light. Without hesitation, she poured the tonic between his lips, cradling his head with care as he struggled to swallow.

Her other hand worked quickly, putting a salve of her own making into the torn skin across his chest—her touch gentle yet filled with urgency born of fear.

At the sound of our arrival, her head snapped up. For a moment, shock flickered in her eyes, quickly replaced by concern. Rising swiftly, she crossed the room with urgency, her gaze darting between us.

"Amir," she hissed, her voice taut and low, barely contained. "You shouldn't be here. If Lazarus finds out—" Her eyes shot to the door, then to Elizabeth, filled with unspoken questions and rising dread.

"I'm sorry, I..." I started, but the words faltered on my tongue, crashing into me.

"Please," Elizabeth interrupted, her voice trembling but unwavering as she stepped forward, drawing all eyes to her. "That man—lying there—is my son. The same child they told me was dead the moment he was born. I never saw him... not once. Not until today." Her breath hitched, but she continued. "I am also a healer. I have skills. Let me help him."

Her plea settled heavily in the chamber. The flickering

torches seemed to still, their crackling subdued by her words. For a long moment, no one moved.

Amara's gaze softened, compassion flickering in her eyes. Wordlessly, she stepped aside, granting Elizabeth passage.

Elizabeth moved to Marcellous with a fragile, yet graceful, step, each one intentional and reverent. She knelt beside him, her hands hovering just above his bruised, bloodied form. His chest rose shallowly, each breath a struggle—his body a testament to the violence he'd endured.

"I'm so sorry, my son…" Her voice cracked like glass underfoot, tender and broken. "I didn't leave you by choice. They tricked me—lied to me. Not a day passed that I didn't imagine you, what you'd be like and become. And now… now I see I was deceived. You are alive… but barely." She reached for his hand, her touch feather-light. "This will not be the first and last time I see you. I swear it."

A tear slid down her cheek, and I moved beside her, wrapping my arm around her shoulders, trying to ease her sorrow, though I felt it, too, as a blade buried deep in my soul—a pain shared, a past that refused to rest.

She stared at Marcellious, her eyes wide with dread and desperate love. "Can he survive this?" she whispered, her words barely audible, a fragile plea lost in the stillness.

Amara met her gaze, her expression gentle but resolute. "Elizabeth… I am a Timehealer, as you are. And I swear to you —I will do everything I can to save him. To protect him." She paused, then added with quiet conviction, "And to tend to Roman as well."

Elizabeth's hand slipped beneath her stola and retrieved a small glass vial at that moment. The movement was fluid, almost instinctual, but it hit me like a punch to the gut.

Disbelief surged through me, a storm of shock tightening in my chest.

What was that?

Panic laced my thoughts, twisting into fury as realization clawed forward. Alchemy. She had been practicing, defying everything I'd warned her about. The very thing I'd pleaded with her to forsake for her safety, she had kept it alive in secret.

Rage, sudden and slicing, surged inside me—not anger at her, but at the unbearable fear that gripped me. If Salvatore sensed her alchemical presence—if her work had drawn his attention—she could be in grave danger. Every precaution I had taken, every shadow I had lived in to keep her safe, now hovered at the edge of ruin.

"I concocted this remedy," Elizabeth said. She held the vial like an offering, unaware of the war breaking inside me. "It will accelerate bone healing. It's potent, but safe. It will help him."

The vial glinted in the torchlight, casting faint green and gold reflections across her fingers—like hope, distilled. But to me, it was something else—proof of her defiance. Of the risk she had embraced without telling me.

I stared at her, torn between fury and helpless admiration.

No. I had to trust her. I swallowed the bitter knot rising in my throat. Perhaps it was an old tincture she had crafted before she swore to abandon alchemy. Perhaps it had simply survived the years, like our love.

Amara stepped forward, accepting the vial with care. Her wise and knowing eyes flickered with understanding as she nodded. "These young men mean the world to me. I'll give them the care they deserve—as if they were my own sons." She cast a nervous glance at the door, tension bristling in her posture. "Now, quickly, my dear. You must leave. The emperor has eyes and ears in every shadow."

Elizabeth embraced her tightly, the contact fierce and grateful—a silent promise between women bound by their love for the same boys. As they parted, I felt a swell of conflicting emotions rise within me—pride, fear, anger, and love battling beneath the surface.

She trembled as I led her through the winding stone corridors, the echo of her quiet sobs trailing behind us like a mournful hymn. The ancient and unfeeling walls absorbed the sound but offered no comfort. Each step carried the pain of parting, each breath a struggle between duty and despair.

Just as we neared the exit, her soft and broken voice halted me in my tracks.

"Amir… wait."

Her eyes locked on an open narrow cell to our left. There, lying motionless on a stone slab, was Roman. His chest rose and fell with labored breath, his body bruised, battered, yet alive.

I said nothing as she moved toward him as if drawn by an invisible thread that had tethered her to him since the moment of his birth. She knelt beside him, her fingers trembling as they gently brushed the damp curls from his forehead.

"My son," she whispered, the words spilling from her lips like a sacred prayer. "I love you more than words could ever capture." Her voice, heavy with love and longing, seemed to fill the small cell. "I pray the stars will guide us together again one day."

A single tear slipped from her eye, tracing a glistening path down her cheek before falling onto his still hand. She leaned in, placing a tender kiss on his brow, her lips lingering there as if to imprint her soul onto his skin. Roman stirred not, his eyes closed, but his breath remained shallow, fragile, but steady.

Her gaze turned to me, and I felt my composure fracture under her anguish. The sight of her there, fragile yet fierce, seared into my memory.

"We must go," I murmured, stepping forward, my voice low with urgency. "Amara will care for him. She vowed to treat them as her own—she would not fail them."

Reluctantly, I helped Elizabeth to her feet, the torchlight casting flickering shadows over her tear-streaked face. She nodded, her sorrow etched into every line of her expression, but her steps were firm as we left the chamber behind.

As we entered the night, I wrapped my arm around her shoulders, drawing her close. Her body against mine, seeking warmth in a world suddenly colder.

"There are dangerous eyes everywhere," I murmured, my lips near her temple. "For now, only their ignorance keeps our sons safe. But fate is not yet finished with them. One day, Roman's wife will reunite them."

"His wife?" Elizabeth's voice was barely a whisper, taut with confusion.

"She hasn't yet met him," I murmured, my gaze fixed on the moonlit streets ahead, though all I could see was the anguish etched into her face.

Her breath caught—fractured, ragged—a sound that pierced straight through my chest. "I don't want to leave," she confessed with unshed tears. "I want to watch over them, even if only from afar. Can we stay in Rome for a little bit?"

The raw ache in her plea struck something deep within me. I understood all too well—the agony of parting from one's blood, of walking away when every instinct screamed to protect. I turned to her, cradling her face in my hands, my thumbs brushing away the tears threatening to fall.

"Yes," I said, my voice low and certain. "We will stay. Until the next full moon, we will remain here. Together."

She exhaled a breath she hadn't known she was holding, her body leaning into mine, seeking solace in the only place left to her—my embrace. Her sorrow clung to her like mist, but beneath it, I felt her resilience awakening, steady and fierce—the same resilience that had drawn me to her all those years ago.

In the shadow of the Colosseum, with the city of emperors slumbering around us and the past bleeding into the present, we would stand vigil over the two sons fate had stolen from us once —and now returned.

Until the moon called us home, we would not leave them again.

The full moon had waned; with it, the mystical tether that bound us to ancient Rome released its hold. The familiar mustiness of our English parlor wrapped around us like a well-worn cloak, the scent of aged wood and hearth smoke a stark contrast to the blood and sand we had left behind.

Elizabeth's breath came in excited bursts as she spun through the room, her skirts sweeping around her ankles. The weight that had clung to her shoulders in Rome now lifted, vanishing like mist beneath the dawn. Her bright, unburdened laughter rang out, and it was the sweetest sound I had heard in years.

"I'm going to make you the best dinner," she declared, her eyes dancing with light, a spark of the girl I once met flickering anew in her gaze.

"Go then," I murmured, a rare smile tugging at the corner of my mouth. Her grace was an elixir that soothed the quiet storm forever brewing within me.

She disappeared into the kitchen, her laughter trailing like the last notes of a song. I stood in the quiet that followed, savoring the illusion of peace—until I saw it.

A parchment lay on the table, a blemish on the polished wood. My fingers, calloused from battle, curled around it with growing dread. The seal was already broken. The moment I unfolded it, I knew.

You think you can protect her forever, Amir? But the shadows are my domain, and I am always watching. One day, your plans with Lazarus will crumble beneath my power, and Solaris will fall to me. But more importantly... You will lose her. Mark my words—when that day comes, nothing will save her from the fate I have planned.

The blood drained from my face.

My pulse thundered in my ears.

The scrawl was unmistakable—elegant yet cruel, every line dripping with mockery and menace.

Salvatore.

Only he could lace ink with such venom.

Only he could turn parchment into a weapon.

A declaration of war.

A harbinger of the shadows to come.

A cold dread settled deep in my gut, creeping through my veins like poison. He hadn't shown his face, but his intent was etched into every stroke of the letter—he would unravel everything. Everything I had built to keep her safe.

I crumpled the parchment in my fist. The brittle paper crackled like bones under pressure.

This wasn't just a threat.

It was a promise.

"Amir? Is everything alright?"

Elizabeth's voice floated in from the kitchen, warm and gentle, unaware of the chill that now clung to the room like a curse.

"Everything is fine, my love," I called back, masking the storm gathering in my chest.

My gaze drifted to the window, where twilight devoured the last light of day.

And in that deepening dark, I made a vow—quiet but unshakable.

Whatever hunted us, whatever shadows crept from the corners of our lives—

I would be her shield.

Her sword.

Her sentinel.

And if fate dared to take her from me…

I would burn the world down.

CHAPTER 35

ELIZABETH

1798

Tucked deep beneath our cottage, hidden behind layers of stone and sealed by an old oak door Amir never questioned, was my sanctuary—and my sin. A forgotten cellar, once used for storing food and wine, now transformed into something darker, where I came to remember, create, and indulge in the alchemy I once vowed to abandon.

It had been fifteen years since I last saw my sons fight beneath the sun of Rome.

Fifteen years since darkness haunted our every step.

Fifteen years of peace. Of love. Of family.

Amir and I had lived every one of those days together, without separation, without fear, free from the shadow of Salvatore's name. We had built a life we once thought impossible—a life where laughter echoed through our home, not screams—a life where we were no longer survivors but a family... whole.

Reyna was born that same year, conceived beneath the golden skies of Rome when I visited Roman and Marcellious. It was a moment of love, unity, and hope, and she became our light, our joy, the bond that made Amir and me believe—if only for a while—that we had outrun the shadows.

But shadows had long memories.

And I had long-kept secrets.

The air in the cellar was damp, tinged with earth and mildew, but tonight, it reeked of something harsher. Smoke curled thick and black, wrapping around me like the guilt I had carried all these years. It clung to my skin, clothes, and soul—an old companion I learned to bear, hidden beneath practiced smiles and soft words.

The cauldron hissed and spat, the black liquid within swirling like ink in water—dangerous, volatile, forged not from weeks but years of secrets. Of forbidden work I swore to leave behind... but never truly did.

The scent of Noctyss petals, crushed bone, and sulfur hung heavy in the air, charring my lungs with every breath. It should have driven me away. It should have reminded me of the promises I made.

But I didn't care.

I was so close to finishing what I started.

This wasn't the poison crafted to end Salvatore—no. That was already hidden, waiting for its moment. This... this was something else—a failsafe. A final weapon only I understood. A creation meant to bend darkness back on itself—if it worked.

I knew the risk. I knew the cost.

And still... I couldn't stop.

Then—

A strangled gasp behind me.

I froze.

The ladle slipped from my fingers, clattering against the iron rim. My heart slammed against my ribs as I turned, dread crawling up my spine like ice.

Amir stood in the doorway.

And everything shattered.

"Elizabeth."

His voice cleaved through the air, cutting straight to the bone. My blood turned to ice.

The flickering firelight from the cauldron danced across his face. His shadow stretched long across the floor, and in his eyes —shock, fury... betrayal.

He wasn't supposed to be here.

He was supposed to be training with Reyna. I timed everything perfectly—except this.

"You claimed you needed air," he said, stepping closer, his gaze a blade. "But this reeks of secrets—not fresh air."

He stepped forward, and I instinctively stepped back, clutching the ladle tightly as if it could shield me.

"You weren't supposed to see this," I whispered. "You were with Reyna... Amir, please—"

"How long?" he cut in, his voice like steel, eyes locked on the cauldron. "How long have you been doing this?"

His gaze swept across the mess of alchemical tools—powdered minerals, aged vials, bloodstained cloth. I couldn't lie anymore.

Amir's fists clenched, trembling with fury. "I forbade this," he snarled. "All those years ago, I told you never to practice alchemy, that it would alert Salvatore, that he would sense it. That he would come for you."

His voice dropped, low and deadly. "And you defied me."

"I had no choice!" The words tore from my throat, my eyes stinging with tears. "I couldn't stop without fulfilling my mother's wish."

Amir's face twisted in confusion, in pain. "Your mother's wish?"

"You didn't see her," I said, voice cracking. "You didn't see what he did to her, Amir. Salvatore used her. Drained her. Every breath she took was soaked in agony, in torment. Her last words —her dying wish—were that I finish what she started. That I destroy him."

Silence.

Amir stared at me, stunned. "Elizabeth... what are you saying?" His voice was softer now, raw. "Your mother knew Salvatore personally?"

My throat tightened. My body trembled. The truth clawed at my chest.

"Amir..." My voice broke again, hoarse with shame. "I've been keeping secrets from you. Since the day we met."

His eyes darkened, a storm gathering just behind them. "Secrets."

"Yes," I whispered, my voice trembling like a fraying thread. "Do you remember the night we conceived our sons? The night you told me your story—how you came from Solaris, how your realm was destroyed when Isabelle separated the blades?"

He nodded once, warily, his expression guarded.

"And I told you about my mother... Isolde Ravencroft."

His eyes flickered, the name igniting a spark of recognition, a shadow of memory that hadn't meant much to him—until now.

"You said you didn't know her," I whispered, the words barely forming as my throat tightened. "That she was just a Timehealer."

Amir's gaze didn't waver. His voice was low, cautious. "Yes. I remember that night."

I felt the weight of it then—the chasm between us, whittled by years of half-truths and omissions. My breath came shallow, and still, I pushed forward.

"Well... that night, when you opened up, when you told me about Solaris... about the Shadow Lords, Salvatore, and Lazarus, and how Isabelle shattered the realm by separating the blades..." I paused, my chest constricting. "I already knew who they were. I already knew everything. Because my mother and I—" My voice broke. "We spent years trying to perfect the Noctyss flower. Years... trying to neutralize their power."

His jaw tightened, the fury in his eyes rising like a tide. "Tell me, Elizabeth," he growled. "How is your mother connected to Salvatore?"

A piercing ache bloomed in my chest. There was no easy way to say it—only the truth.

"Long before I was born," I said slowly, "before she lost herself in this world... my mother belonged to Salvatore."

His expression twisted in disbelief. "Belonged to him?"

I forced the words out, every syllable tasting like blood. "She was his sex slave, Amir. In Solaris."

His eyes ignited, blazing fury crackling through him like lightning. "What?"

"He used her," I whispered, my hands shaking. "Her body, her mind, her soul. He fed on her suffering—drained her of everything she was to fuel his power. She was his, Amir. Until Isabelle found her... saved her. Brought her back to safety."

I saw it then—the battle in his eyes, the collision of past and present. He knew the realm I spoke of. He had lived there.

"You had to know," I said, voice cracking. "You lived in that realm—you must have heard something."

Amir shook his head slowly, rage simmering beneath the surface. "Elizabeth, during the chaos... the battles... the days leading up to the blades being separated, everything collapsed. My job was to train the army of darkness, to keep Solaris from crumbling. I didn't have the luxury to... indulge in what was happening beyond the war front."

I swallowed hard, blinking back tears.

Amir's voice was tight, laced with disbelief and barely restrained fury. "Tell me, Elizabeth... if everyone's memories were wiped, if no one remembers what happened, then how the hell did your mother know? How did she remember?"

"She didn't have her memories," I said, stepping closer. "Not until she found the note. In the alchemy book, you discovered... my mother had written herself a message, a desperate attempt to piece the fragments together. A message to herself to remember. To finish what she started."

I could see his heart breaking in his eyes. But I couldn't stop.

"When Isabelle saved her, they tried to find a way to destroy him. But Salvatore was impossible to kill—is impossible to kill. There's no way to destroy a Shadow Lord. So, they searched for another way to weaken and sever his power."

I took a trembling breath. "That's when Morgrath Severen came to them. He told them of a rare flower. The Noctyss flower. It could neutralize a Shadow Lord's power, strip them of what made them invincible."

Amir didn't speak. He didn't move. He was stone.

"My mother and I traveled to the Carpathian Mountains. We found the book. We found the flower. And we began to craft the poison together. We worked side by side for months—until the day it killed her."

A tear slipped down my cheek. I didn't wipe it away.

"She was going to test it on my father's Timehunter Society," I whispered, my voice hollow with the memory. "But it failed."

Amir's face fell—grief and fury tearing through him. His breath caught, ragged. "And you continued?"

I nodded, my throat tightening. "I had to." My voice cracked. "Her last breath—her final plea—was for me to finish what we started. To destroy him. I couldn't stop, Amir. Not when I had the chance to give her peace. Not when her whole life was stolen, ravaged by Salvatore."

He stepped back as if the truth had struck him like a blow, his hand briefly gripping the doorframe to support himself. His eyes, once filled with love, now flickered with betrayal.

"I know I promised you," I whispered. "I swore I would stop practicing alchemy and let it go. But I couldn't. Not with her dying wish bearing down on me—constant, stifling, like a breath I couldn't release."

Amir's face twisted into a storm of rage and disbelief. "You lied." His voice cracked like thunder—pained. "You lied for years. While I loved and trusted you, you were crafting a weapon behind my back."

Tears welled in my eyes, but I didn't look away. "I did it for her," I said, my voice barely a breath. "For the part of her that Salvatore stole. For the revenge she never lived to see."

He shook his head as if trying to make sense of a nightmare. "You think this poison—this obsession—will bring you peace? You think your mother would want you to die chasing revenge?"

I stepped forward, the firelight dancing across the tears on my cheeks.

"I think," I said, steel beneath the sorrow, "she would want me to finish it. And I have, Amir. The poison is ready."

I paused, the memory lancing through me, cold and unrelenting.

"Do you remember that masquerade night? When I tried to strike Salvatore, when I threw the poison, and it failed?"

My voice faltered, just for a breath.

"I thought it was enough. I thought it would end him. But I was wrong."

My eyes locked with his, fierce and unflinching.

"This time... I made sure it's perfect. When Roman returns to Solaris and his wife rises to face Salvatore and Lazarus, this poison will have fermented long enough to strip them of their power and make it a fair battle."

Amir's voice cut through the firelit silence, low and tight. "Where did you get the Noctyss flower? The Alchemy Book of Solaris? Lazarus took everything from your cottage."

I met his gaze, unwavering.

"When Roman left for the war... I was alone. I went back to the Carpathian Mountains myself. I found a withered Noctyss flower, clinging to life in the shadows—and I brought it back. Slowly. Patiently. I nurtured it and breathed life into it. And I hid it away... where no one could find it."

"And the book?" he asked, suspicion and wonder woven through his voice.

I gave a faint, bitter smile. "I didn't need it. I memorized every word. Every instruction. They're etched into me now—I became the book."

His expression darkened. "And the blood of darkness? You needed it to complete the poison."

I stepped closer, my hand brushing his.

"I took your blood, Amir. You didn't know, but I had enough. Just enough to make it strong... and potent."

His breath caught, eyes searching mine.

I didn't flinch.

"I did what I had to—for her. For us. To end this."

He stared at me, breathless, shaking his head in disbelief.

His voice cracked then, softer, breaking under the enormity of it all. "Elizabeth... my love... you should have told me this sooner."

My heart ached, every beat a dagger. "I couldn't, Amir," I said, stepping closer and reaching for him. "If I had told you, you would've stopped me forever. And I needed to finish this

—I had to keep it from you. I'm sorry... I'm so sorry, my love."

I reached for him—hesitant, trembling, desperate to feel his warmth. My fingers brushed his hand, and for a breathless moment, he didn't move. I just stood there, caught between everything we'd built... and everything I had broken.

"Please, Amir..." My voice broke on his name. "Forgive me."

He stared at me, his jaw tight, his breath uneven. For a heartbeat, I thought I'd lost him—that my betrayal had driven him beyond reach.

But then... his hand closed around mine.

Not in anger.

In love.

His arms pulled me against him with a fierce urgency, holding me as if letting go would break us both. I collapsed into him, the sob rising from my chest before I could stop it. The tears I had held back for so long finally spilled, soaking into his shoulder as he held me tighter, grounding me, anchoring me to him.

"I'm sorry," I whispered repeatedly, my voice raw, breaking. "I'm so sorry."

He buried his face in my hair, his voice low and rough. "I forgive you... I forgive you, Elizabeth."

I clung to him, my body trembling with release, with grief, with the crushing relief of not having lost him. His hands slid over my back, reassuring and warm, holding the pieces of me together.

For the first time in years, I let myself fall apart. And he held me through it all.

But then—

A chill swept through the air like a curse.

The flame beneath the cauldron sputtered violently. The shadows in the room seemed to recoil, then twist unnaturally, crawling along the walls like serpents. Amir stiffened in my arms, his breath catching—shallow and strained. Slowly, he turned his head.

I followed his gaze, and my blood ran cold.

A figure stood in the doorway, tall and cloaked in darkness that seemed to breathe—alive, pulsing with power. His face was pale, vicious, and cruel, with a smile that cut like a wound freshly opened. And his eyes—cold, bottomless, ancient—locked onto mine, and I knew… he was here for me.

Salvatore.

He was the same man I saw all those years ago when he murdered my father in his wheelchair.

His voice coiled through the air, smooth and poisonous. "Now this... this is touching. I do love a good reunion."

My heart plummeted.

The air choking as the light in the room dimmed beneath his presence. The shadows obeyed him, curling toward him as they worshipped him.

Amir stepped in front of me instantly, his body shielding mine. Tension radiated from him like fire.

But I couldn't move.

I couldn't breathe.

He had felt the alchemy...

He had followed the trail...

And now, he was here.

The nightmare we had fought so hard to avoid had come to our doorstep.

And it had Salvatore's face.

Salvatore consumed the room like a storm swallowing light, devouring the air. Shadows crawled to him, wrapped around his form like living things—servants to their master.

Amir's hand gripped mine tightly, his other still poised on his blade, but I could feel the shift in him—the tension, the fury, the protective desperation. His body was a shield, but I saw the flicker of something else in his eyes—recognition. Fear.

"We have to go," Amir muttered, his voice low and urgent. He grabbed me by the waist, pulling me toward him. "Hold on to me."

Black mist erupted around us—Amir's power surging, dark, and swirling, cloaking us in shadow. The cottage walls blurred, vanishing into the abyss of his darkness as he tried to pull us away, to escape.

But before we could vanish, Salvatore raised a single hand, his fingers curling in the air as if clutching something unseen.

And Amir screamed.

The mist dissipated around us as Amir buckled, his cry ripping through the space, filled with such agony that it pierced my soul.

"Amir!" I caught him as he fell, his body writhing in pain. His hands clutched his chest, fingers digging in like he was being torn apart from within.

Salvatore's cruel and cold smile widened. "Did you forget, Amir?" His voice slithered through the air, bursting with venom. "I am the Father of Darkness. You were born from my power—you cannot outrun me."

Amir gasped, convulsing, veins darkening beneath his skin. "No—" he choked out. "I'm not yours."

Salvatore's eyes burned with malevolent delight. "You were always mine. Every shadow you command... bends to me. Your heart was forged in my darkness. And now, it answers me."

I dropped to my knees beside Amir, my hands on his chest, trying to steady, save, and do anything. "Amir, please—stay with me. Just breathe. Stay with me."

His eyes met mine, wild with pain. "Run... Elizabeth... go—"

"No!" I cried, pressing my hand to his heart, feeling it falter beneath my palm. "I'm not leaving you—I won't—"

Salvatore stepped closer, the shadows recoiling and then surging at his feet like waves. His voice dropped, cold and commanding.

"Tell me where it is."

I looked up, my hands still trembling over Amir's body, tears streaking my face. "What...?"

"The Noctyss flower," Salvatore said, his eyes gleaming. "Tell me where it is, Elizabeth, or I will tear his heart from his chest and make you watch."

My blood turned to ice. Amir groaned beneath me, his body seizing again.

"Don't..." he gasped. "Don't tell him..."

Salvatore stepped closer, towering, merciless. "Your choice, Elizabeth. His life... or the flower."

"I don't know what you're talking about."

Salvatore's hand shot out like a viper, his fingers clamping around my chin, bruising the skin. His grip was ice-cold, but his eyes were fiery with rage.

"Lies," he hissed, his voice dripping venom inches from my face. "Lies will only make this more painful. Where does it grow? Where did you find the Noctyss flower?"

I met his gaze, my heart pounding, but my voice was clean and cold. "I will never tell you. It's hidden far beyond your reach."

His eyes darkened, and the air around him became heavy with power. Shadows surged, coiling at his feet like serpents. His anger bled into the space, choking it.

"I made the poison strong enough to annihilate your power," I said, my voice laced with cold fire. "I crafted it to bring you to your knees."

A snarl tore from his lips, his shadows crackling like a storm. "You think you can destroy me?" he spat, his voice rising with fury. "Foolish girl. No poison, no flower, no one can stop me. My power is eternal."

I curled my lips into a bitter smile, eyes blazing with defiance. "There was one man who could. One man who held the power to rival yours. And he was the one who told my mother about the Noctyss flower."

His expression flickered, suspicion honing the lines of his face.

"There's only one other who would know of that flower..." Salvatore murmured, voice low and wary. Then, realization struck. His eyes narrowed into slits. "Lazarus. It had to be him— he gave it to her—"

"No," I cut in, my voice a dagger. "It wasn't Lazarus. It was a man named Morgrath Severn."

At the sound of that name, Salvatore exploded.

His roar shook the walls, shadows ripping through the air

like claws, splintering wood, and shattering glass. Darkness surged in a cyclone of fury, spiraling out of control.

"Severn is dead!" he bellowed, his voice a monstrous echo. "Lazarus and I destroyed him! His whispers—his shadows— they haunt me no more!"

My laugh tore through his rage, cold and mocking. "You destroyed his body, Salvatore... but his legacy lives on. His whispers still echo in the dark. His shadow still moves through this world, and he guided my mother, alongside Isabelle, to craft this poison. To destroy you."

"No!" Salvatore's voice fractured with rage and fear. "I ended him! Tell me where he is hiding! Tell me where you found the Noctyss flower—and who the fuck is your mother?!"

I met his fury head-on, my voice boiling with hatred.

"My mother was Isolde Ravencroft—your sex slave in Solaris."

His face twisted into pure malice.

"She endured you. Survived you. And now, I carry her vengeance. I will never tell you where the realm opens... or how Severn and Isabelle have set your doom in motion."

His eyes blazed, shadows converging violently, thickening the air like smoke, suffocating, lethal. His power slammed into me, slithering around my body, coiling tighter, crushing my lungs.

"You dare defy me?" he snarled, voice a low, dangerous growl.

A smile curved on my lips—bloodied, fearless. "Do your worst, Salvatore. Your reckoning is coming... and nothing you do can stop it."

His roar was inhuman, a sound of rage, fear, and unraveling control. The shadows descended, wrapping around my throat, crushing. My body convulsed, my vision flickering—but the fire in my eyes didn't fade.

Amir's scream echoed through the darkness, raw and broken. "No! Elizabeth!"

He tried to reach me, crawling through the shadows, his face contorted with horror and helplessness.

"Let her go!" he begged, his voice ripping through the storm.

But Salvatore only smiled.

And tightened his hold.

The shadows around my throat constricted like a noose, crushing my windpipe and stealing the air from my lungs. My vision blurred, black spots dancing at the edges. Every breath was agony. Every heartbeat felt like it could be the last—thudding in my ears, slowing, slipping.

My limbs turned cold and numb.

My body... was giving out.

My soul was slipping.

"Amir..." My voice was barely a breath, a fragile thread on trembling lips.

He was there—fighting through the storm of shadows, clawing toward me, his face twisted with desperation and terror.

"No—stay with me, Elizabeth! Please!" His hands reached mine, brushing my fingers, powerless against Salvatore's crushing grip.

I could barely see him now, but I felt him—his love, the weight of everything we were... and everything we would never get to be.

"I love you..." I choked, blood lacing my lips. "I love you... so much."

Tears streaked down Amir's face as he caught me and cradled me, his hands trembling as if he could somehow hold me together. Stop time, save me. But it was too late. I could feel myself fading, slipping from his grasp.

"No, no, no... please," he whispered, voice breaking. "Stay. Just stay... don't leave me..."

I rested my head against his chest, my body shaking violently, growing weaker. "One day... we'll see each other again," I breathed. "I know it... in another life... another world... I'll find you."

His arms tightened around me, rocking me, desperate. "Don't leave me... I can't do this without you... Elizabeth... please."

"You can," I whispered, my voice barely audible now, more spirit than sound. "You have to... for them... for our children."

I clutched at his hand, my grip weak but determined. "Promise me... promise me Roman and Marcellious will fulfill their destiny. You'll guide and protect them, even if it kills you. They must finish this. They must end him."

Tears slipped from his eyes onto my skin, his voice shattering. "I promise... I swear it... I'll protect them. I'll protect Reyna, Roman... Marcellious. I won't let him touch them."

"Don't let Salvatore take them too..." I murmured, breath hitching.

My fingers brushed his cheek, my final touch, my final breath.

"You're the love of my life, Amir... always..."

Amir's voice broke, raw with pain. He touched his forehead to mine, his arms trembling around me. "And you're mine... forever. I love you, Elizabeth... I love you."

And then everything...

Went dark.

Silence.

Stillness.

Salvatore's laughter echoed through the air, cold, triumphant, a dagger twisting in the heart of the world.

Amir's scream tore through the night—a sound of pure anguish, rage, and heartbreak. A sound that fractured the sky... and shattered the soul.

And I was gone.

But the war...

The war had only just begun.

The Journey Continues....
Blade of Shadows Origin Novel: Rise of the Shadow Lords

Lost Legacy of Time
Blade of Shadows Book 7 the Final Saga
Coming Soon

THANK YOU

TikTok
Instagram
Facebook
BookBub

APPRECIATION

Throughout the *Blade of Shadows* series, you've known that Roman and Marcellious held deep resentment toward their father. They despised him because they never knew the full truth. All they saw was the silence, the distance, the man who was never there. They didn't know the pain he carried, the sacrifices he made, or the love he was forced to bury. But in *Sweet Venom of Time*, you stepped into the past. And for the first time, you saw the truth for yourself.

You heard Amir's voice, aching and raw, and with it came the love story that had always been hidden beneath the shadows. A love story that belonged to him and Elizabeth. One forged in devotion, heartbreak, and impossible choices. We'd heard hints of their past before—names, secrets, whispers between chapters —but it wasn't until *Timehunters* that the truth began to surface. That's when the layers started to peel back. And now, in *Sweet Venom of Time*, the full picture finally comes into view.

Elizabeth always knew more than she let on. And Amir... Amir sacrificed everything to protect the people he loved.

Writing their story was one of the greatest honors of this series, and I'm endlessly grateful I was able to bring it to life. I hope you felt it too—and I hope it stays with you the way it stayed with me.

After reading this book, I strongly recommend re-reading

Timehunters. I promise—it will hit differently now. You'll see things you missed the first time, feel moments with a deeper weight, and understand just how far Amir was willing to go.

I hope you felt their story. I know the ending is bittersweet, but this isn't goodbye. We'll see them again in *Solaris*, the final book.

And now… I hope you're ready for what comes next.

In *Sweet Venom of Time*, you caught glimpses—brief, burning moments—of Salvatore and Lazarus. But their story? Their *truth*? It's just beginning. The next book will unravel everything through their eyes, and let me tell you… the journey is far from over. It's darker, deeper, and far more devastating than you can imagine.

Thank you for reading. For continuing. For walking this long, twisted road with me. It means more than you know.

Charity… what would I do without you? You've been with me through every step of this author journey, and I honestly wouldn't be where I am without you. You've helped me grow not only as a writer but as a person, and I'm endlessly grateful for everything you've done—for the editing, the proofing, the encouragement, the lessons in patience, and most of all, for always having my back. You mean the world to me. Thank you for being such an incredible part of my life. I'm so lucky to have you.

Briana… I don't even know where to begin. Thank you for everything you do—for the endless support, the quiet strength, and the laughter you bring into my life. You're so much more than my assistant—you're my best friend, my anchor, and the heart I lean on when things get overwhelming. I'm beyond grateful for every moment we've shared on this journey, and I honestly can't imagine doing any of this without you. Thank you for being by my side through the chaos, the joy, and everything in between. I'm so lucky to have you.

A big shout-out to Krafigs Design for making my book cover a true work of art. Your creativity turned my ideas into a beautiful reality that speaks to anyone who sees it. I am forever grateful for your brilliant contribution.

Finally, a huge thank you to my amazing beta readers, ARC, and street team. Your enthusiasm and dedication to spreading the word have been incredible. Every post, reel, comment, and video has helped build an incredible buzz, and I am so appreciative of your efforts. You are the best supporters an author could ask for. Your support means the world to me.

ABOUT THE AUTHOR

SARA SAMUELS is the author of the Blade of Shadow series. When Sara isn't daydreaming about her stories and time travel, she spends her day reading romance, cooking and baking, spending time with family, and enjoying life. Sara loves to connect with readers on Instagram, TikTok or by email, so feel free to email her, or message her on social media because she will reply back! Follow her on Instagram or TikTok @story-tellersarasamuels to get related updates and posts. Email her at sara@sarasamuels.com

Visit her website at https://www.authorsarasamuels.com/ and sign up for the mailing list to stay informed about new releases, contests and more!